SHADOW DANCERS

By the Author

Moon Shadow

Shadows of Steel

Shadow Dancers

Shadow Dancers

by

Suzie Clarke

2022

SHADOW DANCERS

ISBN 13: 978-1-63555-829-6

THIS TRADE PAPERBACK ORIGINAL IS PUBLISHED BY
BOLD STROKES BOOKS, INC.
P.O. BOX 249
VALLEY FALLS, NY 12185

FIRST EDITION: JANUARY 2022

CREDITS
EDITORS: VICTORIA VILLASEÑOR AND SHELLEY THRASHER
PRODUCTION DESIGN: STACIA SEAMAN
COVER DESIGN BY TAMMY SEIDICK

Acknowledgments

No author can complete a novel without many helping hands along the way. Thank you to my family and friends for their continued support. A grateful acknowledgement to my beta readers for their valuable insights. And to my editors at Bold Strokes Books, your expertise, guidance, and encouragement made all the difference.

To my readers—thank you for taking this journey with Rachel and Claire. I hope you enjoy their final adventure.

To Megan,
My reflection in the mirror. My light in the shadows.
Oh, how we soar when we spread our wings!

CHAPTER ONE

The Cleveland hotel room was pitch-dark. An unnatural chill hung in the air. Rachel Portola reached for Claire but found only cold sheets and an empty bed. She threw the covers off and swung her feet over the side of the mattress, vaguely remembering the lamp hitting the floor, its porcelain base shattering into hundreds of small, triangular shards.

She scanned the murky blackness. Straining. Listening.

A sliver of light crossed the floor.

A flashlight losing power?

Captured in the weak beam, her grandfather's pearl-handled hunting knife lay among the broken pieces of shattered lamp. Blood coated its sharp edge.

Claire's dead!

The realization wrapped around her like a thick, heavy shroud— smothering her, choking her. She flailed against it, gasping, but her chest constricted with each breath, forcing the air from her lungs. She swallowed hard, her tongue like sandpaper against the back of her throat.

More light pierced the darkness, as if beckoning her to look.

Claire would be there on the floor, amid the shattered pieces of lamp, her dull, lifeless eyes staring back, her wheat-colored hair soaked with blood.

Something moved behind her on the bed. She stiffened, shifting her gaze to check the floor. The knife was gone. Danger was there, right there, about to grab her.

She tried to lunge forward. Something—someone—gripped her, held her tight. She writhed to free herself. She screamed but heard

SUZIE CLARKE

no sound. Only pain. Deep, cutting pain in her side as Eshee Yumiko stabbed her and thrust the knife upward.

"Rachel. Rachel, wake up."

Claire's familiar, melodic voice grew stronger. It drifted in and out, as if echoing off a canyon wall. Rachel fought to open her eyes. "Rachel, wake up."

Something brushed her shoulder. She bolted upright.

Claire lay next to her in the faint light of early dawn. With warm, delicate fingers, she caressed the curve of Rachel's jawline. "You look like you've seen a ghost. Did you have a nightmare?"

Rachel wrapped her arms around her, forcing out the lingering images, holding Claire tighter, unable to get close enough.

Claire slipped her arms around her. "Your heart's beating a mile a minute."

Rachel buried her face in Claire's neck. Warmth and love reached back to greet her, comfort her.

"Do you want to talk about it?"

Rachel cleared her throat. "No. It's nothing."

"You don't look like it's *nothing*. Talk to me."

The anxiety and apprehension of the possibility that Yumiko might harm her or Claire were vivid and intrusive, creeping into her dreams. It was unrealistic to be so anxious. Yumiko was locked away in prison and couldn't harm either of them, yet the anxiety persisted. She couldn't explain why, only that it did, lingering like a wolf after the kill. As hard as she tried, she couldn't shake the feeling that somewhere, somehow, she'd have to face Yumiko again, that Yumiko would go after Claire this time, and she wouldn't be able to protect her. She wanted to forget Eshee Yumiko and everything that had happened. Oh, how she wanted to forget!

"It's just the same old concern. It makes it worse if I talk about it. You have your memory back now, and we're here together. That's all that matters." She kissed Claire's neck, then brushed her cheek against her soft skin. "It was nothing but a nightmare."

She pushed the thoughts out, forcing them back into the darkness. They began to fade, receding like a stop sign in the rearview mirror. She knew what would help fill the dark space, what always helped. Claire was here now. "I need you."

Claire rolled Rachel to her back and slid over her, covering her with her body. Rachel embraced her, almost in desperation, and held on.

Claire whispered in her ear. "Baby, you're trembling. Talk to me. Was it her?"

Rachel pressed her cheek against the side of Claire's face and nodded.

"Was it bad?"

"Just the part about you."

"Let's take your mind off it. I'll help you forget." Claire kissed the side of Rachel's neck and moved to her mouth, pressing her lips against hers. She pushed herself up on her hands, hovering over her, looking into her eyes.

Rachel reached behind Claire's ear and gently traced the rigid scar. Claire had most of her memories back now, and she was safe. Derrick was dead and couldn't hurt her anymore. But Yumiko...what about her?

Claire smiled and lay back down beside her, leaning on her elbow. "Let it go." She glided her hand down Rachel's waist to her stomach and then to her breasts, touching gently, kissing her with lips full of warmth and promise.

The wanting began in Rachel's breasts, radiating into her core. Nipples hardened. Muscles relaxed. Pressure and heat began to build, mingling and fusing with desire and need. She ran her hands through Claire's silky hair and down her firm back. "What you do to me."

The flecks of gold in Claire's sea-green eyes caught the reflection from the first rays of the sun shining through the hotel window. "Does that mean I get to do whatever I want?"

Rachel smiled as Claire's love flowed into her, forcing out all the darkness and foreboding.

CHAPTER TWO

A gust of bone-chilling Cleveland winter wind caught Eshee Yumiko off guard, making her shudder and whipping her long hair into her face. She dropped the cell phone into her purse and slid into the taxi. The pungent odor of rancid deodorizer and body sweat hit her the minute she closed the car door. She breathed through her mouth and spoke quickly. "Evie J's nightclub, West Sixth."

The burly cab driver nodded and drove away from the curb, his pale-white stubby fingers sticking out of his frayed half-gloves as he gripped the steering wheel.

The Cleveland skyline loomed over her, bulging with steel and glass. The buildings seemed cold and harsh, as if protesting the brutal winter. The sharp crunch of snow beneath the tires reminded her of how much she missed the warmth and comfort of her home in the Philippines.

"What part of Asia are you from," the cabdriver asked.

She didn't answer.

His broad shoulders lifted. "Whatever."

She was glad she wouldn't be staying in Cleveland and was going back to Los Angeles, and then on to her home island. It was the height of the best weather of the year.

Her cell phone rang. The picture of her stepbrother, Alon Ocampo, appeared.

"The FBI has Jamison at their facility in Arizona. Ralston handed him over to them in Cleveland." He didn't bother with small talk or niceties. It wasn't his style, or hers. "Do you think he talked?"

Yumiko lowered her voice and turned away from the driver. "Of course, he talked. I'm sure he told Ralston everything he knew before he turned him over to the FBI."

"What do you want me to do?"

She grabbed the door handle as the taxi driver swerved to miss a pedestrian. "It's just a matter of time before Jamison talks to the FBI and makes a deal, but he doesn't know as much as he thinks he does. Get someone to take care of him as soon as they move him out of Arizona and into wherever prison they put him in. Make sure he knows the message is from me. He's already done the damage. Increase security at the compound in Los Angeles. That's the last place Jamison knew where I was. If I know Ralston, he's already on his way there."

"When Ralston took Jamison, I'm sure he contacted Brice Chambers at MI6. It would be wise for you to get back here to the Philippines as quickly as possible. When can you leave?"

She didn't have a firm answer yet, and it irritated her. She hated uncertainty. "Soon. I need to take care of something here in Cleveland first. Then I'll go back to the compound in Los Angeles, and then home."

Alon began to speak Tagalog, and she smiled as she listened. She missed home. She'd been away too long.

She handed the money to the cab driver through the opening of the scratched, smeared Plexiglas. When she opened the door, the harsh winter air raked her lungs as she took in a deep breath.

She slipped on her skin-tight, black leather gloves and stepped to the entrance of Evie J's. The piercing cold gnawed her fingers as she gripped the frozen metal handle and pulled. The heavy wooden door shut behind her with a loud *thud*, immediately blocking the sunlight. She walked forward, squinting. The dim light from the neon red, yellow, and blue signs seeped down the dark-bricked walls, trickling onto the round tables crammed together so tightly she was forced to walk sideways between them or put one foot directly in front of the other, like a tightrope walker.

As soon as her eyes adjusted, she quickly scanned the room, spotting her prey. Tilly Evans was on the stage, papers in her hand, talking to a man holding a bright neon-blue electric guitar.

Yumiko pulled her gloves off as she maneuvered to one of the tables in the darkest area at the back of the room. She unbuttoned her pleated mohair overcoat and removed the gray-and-green silk scarf from around her neck. She sat, slipped her arms out of the coat, and wrapped it tightly around her shoulders, never taking her eyes off Evans. The stench of stale beer and fried foods assaulted her senses as she ordered a White Russian from the waiter. *American pigs.*

She eyed Evans like a buzzard circling roadkill. She wasn't as tall as she thought she'd be. She'd spent hours looking at pictures of her and Sarah Reynolds, close friends of Rachel Portola, deciding which one would be the easier target. Reynolds was a registered nurse and worked at one of the difficult-to-access Cleveland hospitals. But Evans sang in nightclubs, had later hours, parked in mostly open lots, and traveled between Cleveland, Chicago, and Las Vegas. Yumiko could have her people take Evans whenever it suited her. She'd do nicely. She was trim and looked like she worked out but could be overpowered easily. In the end, it wasn't about Evans. It was about Rachel Portola.

Yumiko's thoughts slipped back to when she'd taken Portola to the Philippines and what she'd done to her because Portola had put the trigger into her computer program and destroyed the system. She'd beaten Portola into submission, and after she'd fixed the program, Yumiko ordered her killed. Unfortunately, Portola had been taken from her before her men could do it. She tightened her hand into a fist. Jack Ralston and his security team had shown up and disrupted her plan. Now, once again, he and Portola had interfered in her life. She would deal with Portola when it suited her, but Ralston would have to be taken care of if he showed up at the compound in Los Angeles.

Evans brushed her mid-length blond hair out of her face and set a bottle of water on the wooden stool beside her on the stage. A short, bald, red-faced man adjusted her microphone for the second time. Obviously a rehearsal day. The crowd noise from the fifty or so people milling around the room faded in and out as the band tuned.

Yumiko readjusted in her chair, watching, unimpressed.

Evans put her hand up above her eyes, as if to block the lights, and peered out toward the audience. "If any of you in the back can't hear us, you should have bought better tickets."

The people laughed, but Yumiko didn't react. She slowly rolled the bottom edge of the half-empty glass of alcohol on the table, periodically watching Evans and the band, imagining a variety of ways to hurt Rachel Portola, an activity she'd richly enjoyed in recent weeks.

She had bargained her freedom with MI6 in exchange for giving up her stepfather, which in the end had worked out well for all parties, except maybe her stepfather. That didn't really matter, though. He was dying of liver cancer anyway. She hadn't felt anything six weeks later when she'd gotten the call that he'd died. As a matter of fact, she was relieved. She remembered his foul breath and his sweaty body as he humped her when she was twelve. She'd tried to fight him off, but the more she struggled, the more excited he got. She'd learned how to manipulate him to get what she wanted.

Once she gave him up to MI6, she took over the family's illegal operations in the Philippines and reestablished her connections in the US. She gripped the glass tighter. MI6 and Portola had gotten into her operation in the Philippines and exposed it, and then Portola and Ralston's people managed to interfere in her US operation as well. But they hadn't exposed everything, and now she'd get even. Time to put an end to Rachel Portola once and for all. She had disrupted too much of her life. Cost her too much money in lost revenue. She was a thorn in her side, and it was time to remove it.

She drank more of the alcohol, which burned, smooth and pleasant, as it went down.

Portola and Ralston were in the security business, and she was right in front of them, watching Portola's friend, and no one realized it. She knew Portola's location, what she was doing, who she was with, and she could do whatever she wanted to her, like she'd done before. She breathed deeply, satisfied with herself. She could take Portola any time.

All the details weren't worked out yet, but one thing was certain— she was going to kill her. And she intended to enjoy tormenting her as much as possible before she destroyed her life. If it meant going after Portola's wife and her friends, so be it. Thinking about it brought a satisfaction she hadn't experienced in a long time. Portola would feel the pain and know loss. She cursed her under her breath, then sipped the alcohol, the taste washing away the bitterness of having failed to kill her the first time.

It wasn't hard to obtain information about Portola, her wife Claire Davenport, or their close friends. Yumiko had enough cash to buy any kind of information she wanted. Money wasn't important to her, not anymore. What was important was what it got her. And she'd get Portola—at any cost.

The security team Portola worked for had taken Jamison, her main advisor in the US. He was weak, like most Americans. She knew he would talk, so she threw him away. She was steps ahead of them and had enough time to deal with whatever information he might provide them.

She drained the glass, then signaled the waiter and tossed the cash onto the table, not taking her eyes off Evans as she put on her heavy coat, scarf, and gloves. The possibilities of what she could do to unsettle Portola were deliciously limitless. She'd go back to Los Angeles and then on to the Philippines to regroup and formulate her plan. Revenge, however long it took. She had no reason to hurry. She smiled as she left the club.

Chapter Three

Yumiko glanced out the kitchen window at the Los Angeles sunset, glad to be out of Cleveland and the miserable weather. She added the creamer to the cup of coffee and tossed the spoon into the stainless-steel sink. She picked up her cell phone once again off the kitchen counter.

Alon spoke louder, as if it would help her understand his concern. She understood perfectly. She just didn't care. He was the one who couldn't understand, not about this.

"Don't let your obsession about these people distract you. This is serious. Ralston isn't someone to mess around with. If he's on his way to Los Angeles, you should not be there."

"Do not forget your place, Alon. I am the head of the family. Not you."

"That's exactly my point. You need to be here, leading this family, not there, planning some kind of sick vendetta."

"I'll be home when I get home." She abruptly ended the call. He constantly pushed her, and she didn't like it. She'd been away too long. Alon had taken liberties. He'd gained too much influence on the family. But she couldn't leave, not yet.

"Remember, don't do anything," she told the armed guard beside her. "I want them to get into the house."

"You *want* them to get in?"

She sipped her coffee. "Yes. Pull all the guards except two. Don't make it easy for them, or they'll sense a trap. I want Ralston and whoever comes with him alive. I doubt Portola will be with him, but if she is, I don't want her hurt. Do you understand?"

The man nodded and went outside.

It was just a matter of time before Ralston showed. She would stay and enjoy the pleasure of seeing him get what was coming to him. She remembered his expression when his team held her at gunpoint. Now it was his turn.

She went into the surveillance room and sat beside Akira.

He leaned back in the chair and stretched his arms. "I shut off the alarms but left all the monitoring systems on."

Yumiko scanned the monitors. "They're coming. Either tonight or tomorrow night."

He checked his watch. "It's after two. Just a few more hours until daylight."

"Relax. It will be soon if he chooses tonight. Make sure the cameras down the street are on."

Akira rechecked the control panel and adjusted two of the cameras. "What makes you so sure he'll try this?"

"Because he thinks he's superior and has the skills to do it." Yumiko tapped the desk. "Keep a close watch on the cameras, especially on the street. If we have any weak spots in the perimeter, Ralston will find them. I don't want any surprises."

She left and climbed the spiral staircase to the master bedroom. She lay on her back, spread-eagled on the bed. Should she leave or stay? What if Ralston did manage to get some type of advantage once he was in the house? No. She would make sure he didn't. She would go home to the Philippines, but not before he arrived, and she saw how it would play out.

Something touched her shoulder, and she jerked awake.

Akira stood over her. "They're here. Two. They just passed the street and are working their way toward the compound."

Yumiko bolted off the bed. "I want everyone ready. No mistakes."

She went to the surveillance room and watched but spotted nothing on the monitors. "You sure?"

"Yes. They're here. Our weakest point is the garage. They'll most likely come through there and through the door to the kitchen," Akira said.

Yumiko put on a protective vest and met three of her men at the kitchen door. Her heart pounded. Sweat dripped under her arms. Just a few more minutes.

Ralston was first through the door, his semiautomatic aimed and ready to fire.

They were taken down quickly and carried into the back room. She sat in a cushioned armchair, waiting, staring at them, unconscious on the floor, as she ruminated on how to use them to get what she wanted. Ralston finally woke, his hands secured behind his back. He watched her as he struggled to free his hands. The other man next to him on the floor was moaning.

Yumiko stood between two of her men, one hand on her hip, glowering at him. "Welcome." She nodded. A rifle butt went down on Ralston's cheek.

She waited a few minutes until his eyes fluttered open again and then kicked him in the side. "You Americans think you can do whatever you want."

He squinted, as if trying to focus. "That would be you, honey. You're the one who tried to scam our hospitals and help yourself to the insurance dollars. That didn't work out too well for you, did it?"

Immediately Akira kicked him in the stomach. Ralston grunted. The other man moved his legs.

Yumiko flicked her hand. "Stand them up."

Akira and a guard grabbed Ralston and forced him up, while two more guards dragged the other man to his feet.

Ralston weaved.

Yumiko eyed the other man. "I know you. You were with him in the Philippines."

"Yes."

"What's your name?"

He straightened his shoulders but didn't answer.

She grabbed the gun from the guard next to her and aimed it at the man's head. "I won't ask you again."

"Go ahead and answer. There aren't any more secrets," Ralston said.

"Frank Hawkins."

Yumiko grinned. "Ah. Two for one."

Akira wiped Ralston's blood off his hand onto the front of Ralston's protective vest.

Hawkins spit on Akira's boot. "Ass-wipe. You kick like my eighty-year-old grandma."

A guard beside Yumiko immediately stepped forward and drew down his weapon toward Hawkins's head. Hawkins moved to his left and blocked, ramming his shoulder into the guard's chest, then kneed him in the groin.

The guard doubled over.

Hawkins took a step back and kicked the guard in the face with his boot. Blood splattered onto the guard's pants as he fell backward onto the floor, unconscious.

Another guard hit Hawkins in the head with a rifle butt, sending him to the floor.

The guard stepped in front of Ralston, lifting his rifle butt smeared with blood. "You want some?"

Ralston stood quietly, not saying a word.

"Search them and strip them, and make sure they're tied together, not separate." Yumiko stabbed her finger in front of Ralston's face. "If he dies," she said, tilting her head toward Hawkins, "I want *him* right next to him."

They were stripped to their underwear and T-shirts. The knives in their boots and the built-in Plexiglas cutters in their pants were discovered and taken. Everything they could use was taken.

"I want the light on in their room. Make sure there are no obstructions on the bedroom window." She planned to use them as bait.

The rest of Ralston's team would be along to fetch them. If she stayed, Ralston's people might arrive in force, and Portola might not be with them. She had men with her if they came, but the guard on the floor was useless, and now seven remained. As hard as it was to admit, she would be safer if she left. Should she risk staying?

CHAPTER FOUR

The Glock 17 balanced perfectly in Kathrine Henderson's hand. She moved it to her left eye and sighted down the cold steel of the barrel, a wisp of her own warm breath gliding over her knuckles as she breathed slowly, deliberately. She released the magazine, grabbing it as it dropped out of the handle, then placed it on the office desk, turned the gun downward, pulled the slide back, and caught the round as it ejected from the chamber. She set the gun down and inserted six more nine-millimeter rounds into the magazine from the box of ammunition near her open laptop. She palmed the fully loaded clip into the handle, hearing the distinctive *click* as it locked into place. She thumbed the catch, instantly snapping the slide back into position, launching the first round into the chamber. The precision and craftsmanship of the weapon fascinated her.

She'd been shooting since she was twelve years old. She was an expert marksman and had a silver medal from the London Summer Olympics to prove it. She reset the safety and placed the Glock back into her shoulder holster, reattaching the leather catch around the gun. She loaded seventeen more rounds into a second magazine and slipped it into the side pocket of her charcoal-colored, tailored jacket.

She nodded as she passed Caroline, one of the support staff at the main communication desk. Caroline gave a half salute and smiled as she continued to talk, her earbuds readily noticeable against her vibrant red hair pushed back behind her ears.

The echo of Kathrine's footsteps bounced off the cream-colored block walls as she made her way through the hallway to the rear exit. When she entered the security code and opened the heavy gray metal door, David Hampton, her partner for the interview, stood just outside, hands in his pockets, a brown leather carry bag slung over his shoulder.

Strands of Kathrine's hair, tied tightly into a ponytail, broke loose and whipped against her face in the turbulence from the waiting helicopter. As they maneuvered closer, she tried to corral the runaway strands, but she quickly gave up and leaned toward David's athletic frame, forcing her voice to be heard over the increasing, deafening whine of the helicopter's engine. The vibration from the whirling blades rattled around under her tongue. Each word she shouted bounced back into her face. "Do you really think this Jamison guy knows where Jack and Frank are?"

David quickened his pace and shouted back as they stooped and continued toward the helicopter. "I hope so. Otherwise, we may not get to them in time."

When they stepped into the helicopter, she bumped against his broad shoulder as she adjusted her harness. She leaned back into the padded seat and slipped on the headgear, repositioning the microphone, still hearing the faint whirr of the rotor blades.

The female pilot's voice came through her headset. "We should be at FBI Prescott in about an hour and twenty minutes."

"Roger that."

She looked down at the Nevada desert, the cars moving like multicolored Hot Wheels along I15, the Las Vegas strip growing smaller as the helicopter turned and gained altitude. She could still faintly see the tinge of red from the roof of Jack Ralston's security agency, which they all affectionately called *the shed.* You wouldn't know what the building was used for if you drove by it. It was designed that way. It was located on a back access road, nestled at the far end of similar-looking commercial buildings but without loading docks and semi trucks, and names on the buildings like *Interstate Transport, Huntington Roadway,* and *Southwest Express.* Jack's building was nondescript, a light tan with a black-and-white sign above the front entrance simply announcing *Ralston Enterprises, LLC.* From the front, no one could see the side entrance for vehicles to pull into the building. No one would know about the back soundproof room called *the chat room,* or the rooms full of weapons, state-of-the-art communication equipment, and tactical gear, or the conference room with one side enclosed in glass that faded to opaque to hide the identity of its occupants.

The inside of the building was anything but nondescript or simple. It was the headquarters for some of the most skilled security professionals in the southwestern United States, including Steve, Frank, David, Beth, José, and Rachel.

Kathrine had gone to work for Jack right after her tour in the military. Not by accident, but by design. She had planned it, like Jack had planned his building.

She settled into her seat and watched the desert terrain expand as the helicopter gained altitude, the landscape now a panoramic vista of beige to reddish-brown mountain ranges against the clear, deep blue of the sky.

Cassie would have enjoyed this view.

Sharp Kodachrome images of the billowing black smoke and the orange-and-red fireball flashed into her mind. She immediately blocked them. After over six years, the pain and vivid memories of the boat explosion that had killed her twin sister were still etched deep in her psyche, reappearing with the slightest trigger.

She grabbed the thick metal handle above the side door when the helicopter began its descent. The queasiness in her stomach rushed into her throat. She swallowed, forcing it down. No matter how many times she flew in a helicopter, she couldn't get used to the landings.

She and David stepped through the FBI main entrance, showed their authorization papers and IDs to the armed guard at the desk, and surrendered their weapons and armament. At least all of the obvious ones that the scanner would detect. They were led to an interrogation room.

Lionel James Jamison sat stiffly in the metal chair, his hands cuffed in front of him to a steel ring on the scratched wooden table. One knee bounced. His gaze darted from the exit to David.

Kathrine sat across from him. His evident apprehension was a good thing. It would make it easier to get what they needed from him.

David stood beside her and nodded to the security guard, who left the room, the heavy metal door slamming shut behind him. David folded his arms across his chest and stared at Jamison.

Kathrine sat intentionally stoic.

David leaned close to Jamison's face. "We have fifteen minutes, and in those fifteen minutes you're going to tell us everything we need to know." He focused his glare on him.

Jamison smirked and shrugged.

Kathrine immediately grabbed a handful of his thick, dark-brown hair and slammed his face into his hands. Blood gushed from his nose.

She let go when he raised his head. His eyes were wide, his face full of anger. He clenched his fists so tightly the muscles in his forearms flexed.

"Oh. I'm sorry. You thought *he* was going to be the tough guy in this interview." She pointed to David.

David raised his voice. "What did you tell Jack Ralston when he made me leave the room just before we turned you over to the FBI in Cleveland?"

Jamison eyed David, then slowly surveyed the room, blood running down his chin. "I don't remember."

Kathrine leaned toward him. "There aren't any cameras in here, if that's what you're looking for." She reached into the left vest pocket of her jacket and pulled out a small pair of black plastic pliers. "Your nose looks bad. Let me help you." With lightning speed, she grabbed his left nostril with the pliers and clamped down.

Jamison screamed.

"Focus, asshole. He's going to ask you one more time, and you're going to give him the answers he wants, or the next thing you'll feel is me clamping down on your nuts." She looked at the large, round, black-rimmed clock on the wall. "Thirteen minutes."

Jamison lifted his hands as far as he could, the metal cuffs rattling against the steel ring. "Okay, okay."

She opened the pliers and let go of his nostril, then wiped them with a tissue, ignoring him.

"He told me he would personally kill me if I said the name of who was behind the operation before he said it was okay."

David pressed his hands onto the table, the color blanching on the tops of his fingers as he leaned forward. "Did you tell anyone?"

Kathrine offered the used tissue.

Jamison snatched it and glared at her.

She glared back, hoping he would say it, hoping he would tell her what a bitch she was so she could slap that look off his face.

He lowered his head and wiped the blood from his nose and chin. "Hell, no. I didn't say anything." He dabbed at his nose again.

David moved slightly toward him and raised his voice. "What's the name?"

"I can't. If he doesn't kill me, they will."

Kathrine held out the pliers.

"I swear to God, they'll kill me. Somehow they'll kill me."

She stood.

Jamison tried to protect his nose and then raised his hands as far as he could, as if pleading. "You've got to understand. I'm a dead man if I tell you."

"Then we're looking at a dead man because you will tell us," Kathrine said.

He shook his head.

Kathrine grabbed him again by his hair.

He hesitated, then swallowed hard. "Please. She'll kill me."

"She who?" David demanded.

Kathrine let go of his hair.

Jamison shook his head. "I'm dead."

David slammed his hand on the table. "Who?"

Jamison's gaze darted from Kathrine to David. "Eshee Yumiko."

"Oh, shit," Kathrine said, slumping into the chair.

David stiffened.

She immediately flashed back to Manila. The team had gone into the building to rescue Rachel Portola. Yumiko and her men had beaten her half to death to get her to fix the computer program she had sabotaged. When the team had Rachel and Yumiko on board the helicopter, Yumiko had wrestled the semiautomatic from Kathrine's hand and managed to get her finger on the trigger, shooting David in the upper arm before Kathrine punched her in the face and she fell backward out of the helicopter. MI6 agents shot Yumiko with a dummy shot. If it had been Kathrine's decision, she would have killed her, and it would have ended it, but MI6 took her, probably to make a trade.

Kathrine hated the politics and games, and because of all of it, they were dealing with Yumiko again. Jack Ralston and Frank Hawkins were missing. And because Eshee Yumiko was clearly involved, their chances of getting them back alive had just dropped dramatically.

David slammed his fist onto the table again. "Where?"

Jamison startled, then lowered his head. "Los Angeles. That's all I know. Los Angeles. I swear to God that's all I know. She wouldn't let me in on much. I think she knew I was going to get caught. That bitch probably set me up."

Kathrine stood and leaned toward Jamison, swiping her fist gently on his chin. "I hope you enjoyed the music. Now you can dance with the devil." She and David turned to leave. She took a few steps and looked back, pointing at his face. "I bet that hurts. Some ice will help."

She heard him swear but didn't look back. She'd been called that lots of times.

The trip back to Las Vegas didn't seem to take as long.

She watched as Steve Hathaway, second in charge at the shed, paced and winced, gripping his coffee mug.

In the years Kathrine had worked for Jack at the security firm, she'd never seen Steve this concerned. Whatever Jack and Frank had gotten themselves into, it was bad. She flicked her tongue against the back of her teeth and gently bit her lower lip. She could guess what they'd done. Jack had found out from Jamison that Yumiko was involved, and then after the team wrapped up the case in Cleveland, he and Frank took off after her. Kathrine suspected Jack did it to protect Rachel. She still couldn't believe MI6 had let Yumiko go. She must have had one hell of a bargaining chip.

Now Jack and Frank were missing.

Steve set his coffee mug on the table and continued to pace. "No one but Rachel can get deep enough into the programs to find out the information we need. Both Jack and Frank's trackers are off-line. They probably used the scanner before they left the office to purposely take themselves off-line so they couldn't be tracked."

"At least we know they're most likely in Los Angeles. Unless Jamison lied, which I don't think he did," David said.

"We're going to have to get Rachel back here right away. She's the only one who can get deep enough into the program to override the system and offset what they did to their trackers. Kathrine, I want you to call her and convince her to come back."

Kathrine slowly swirled her partial mug of coffee. "It's not going to be easy. She and Claire are at the hotel, and they haven't been there that long. Are you sure we need her?"

Steve nodded. "Without her help, we'll wander all over Los Angeles looking for Jack and Frank, and waste valuable time. It could cost them their lives."

"We can't call Rachel or Claire," she said.

Steve's facial muscles tightened. "Why not?"

She rubbed her forehead and ran her fingers through her hair. "Tilly said they shut their phones off. I tried to contact them a little bit ago. Both of their cell phones went directly to voice mail."

"Call the hotel and send someone to their room."

"That won't work. Claire won't allow it. She won't understand the importance of this, and if I ask Tilly to go over there, Claire will throw her out of the room."

She didn't want to interrupt them, not after what they'd been through. It'd been a year since Claire had been shot in the head. It'd been only a few days since she'd finally gotten her memory back about her marriage to Rachel. They deserved to be together without anyone around. "Steve, they just got there. You know what it's been like for them."

"Yes, I do know, but we have to have her with us. You fly there and drag her back here if you have to. Our charter jet can be ready in an hour."

She put her hand up to her face and scrubbed it gently. This couldn't be happening at a worse time for Rachel and Claire, but finding Jack and Frank was more critical right now.

"You have to do it," Steve said again.

She wanted to say no, but what choice did she have?

CHAPTER FIVE

Claire watched the muted light from the full moon shine into the hotel window. It seemed to caress Rachel, bathing her in its luminous rays, highlighting her beautiful skin, her oval classic face, thick arched brows, delicate nose, and defined chin.

Claire slid her leg over Rachel's long, slender thigh, moving her hand slowly over the sensuous curve of her hip and then cupping one of her ample breasts, the nipple hardening between her fingertips. She pressed into her, her own nipples swelling against the warmth and feel of Rachel's toned body.

Rachel moaned.

Claire moved closer, taking her earlobe into her mouth, then licking and sliding her tongue down the nape of Rachel's neck, kissing soft, warm skin, fingers eager to touch. "Wake up. I don't want you to leave me."

Rachel turned toward her and slipped her hand between Claire's thighs, gently touching, entering ever so slightly. Claire immediately pressed herself against Rachel, straining, desire starting to ignite. It had been only a few hours, but she ached for her touch again, and she knew Rachel wanted more.

Claire glanced at the nightstand clock. She'd gotten the hotel room Christmas Day and waited for Rachel to arrive so she could tell her she'd regained her memory of their marriage. After the shooting, it'd been a year of not knowing if the memories would ever return. They'd been married a little more than a year, and she was just now remembering. She could have been doing this for an entire year.

She smiled, nestling her face in the warm, soft, pulsating skin of Rachel's neck, thinking about Rachel's reaction when she'd told her, her joy and relief, and her desire. Not all the memories had returned, but she didn't care right now. She didn't want to work at remembering. All she wanted to do was be with her wife. *My wife!*

Rachel slid gracefully down and turned her over onto her back. She kissed Claire's stomach, then licked her navel as she moved upward, the heat and wetness of her mouth sending chills deep into Claire. Rachel covered her breasts, moving from one hard, erect nipple to the other, entering her more deeply with her fingers.

Claire pulled her to her, her nipples aching for more when Rachel's mouth released. She wanted to reach down and slide her breast back into her mouth, but she also wanted to kiss her, deep and long. She throbbed all over with each small movement and anticipation of Rachel's touch.

"It feels so wonderful to love you again." Rachel's rich, sensuous voice surrounded her, encasing her in a chrysalis of ardor that almost took her breath away.

She searched Rachel's eyes, seeing the deep-brown, sparkling embers. She tried to close her thighs on her hand when Rachel started to withdraw.

Rachel took her diamond wedding ring off and set it carefully on the nightstand. She rolled Claire over with her, repositioning her on top, then guided her hips, kissing the inside of her thighs as she spread her. Claire maneuvered closer, feeling Rachel's hot breath on her thighs. She reached down and cradled Rachel's head in her hands, lowering herself, heart pounding, breath catching in labored anticipation, aching, knowing Rachel knew what she wanted—what she needed.

She pulled Rachel more firmly to her, feeling Rachel's warm, wet mouth and tongue surround her, her fingers sliding in, sending bolts of radiating pleasure through her. She moved her hips rhythmically, meeting Rachel's urging with each thrust. Nothing existed now but her rising ecstasy.

"Yes...yeeesss."

Rachel's mouth and tongue massaged in firm, demanding circles, sending rivulets of pulsating, molten heat deep within her.

Claire let out a long, low, deep, throaty moan as the pinnacle of her climax began. Her thighs quivered and her hips thrust, moving in unison with Rachel's touch and caress. The waves of exquisite release washed over her, again and again. "More. I want more." She entangled her fingers in Rachel's hair, moving her hips slowly, lingering, the need for release immediately building again. "Please don't stop."

Rachel continued to caress, sending Claire onto the sexual pinnacle again. She rode it, enjoying every last possible prurient throb of release.

She lifted herself and slid down beside Rachel, pulling her over onto her as she weaved her fingers into her hair. They lay still for a time, entwined in each other, and then Claire reached out and began to touch Rachel, wrapping her legs around her. "I need to love you." Rachel moaned and kissed her. Claire rolled her over and slid down to her breasts, caressing with her hand and mouth. She rose slightly. Rachel's eyes were half-closed, now almost a vivid amber. She slid her fingers into Rachel's hot, wet center, thrusting slowly, feeling her want and need.

She pulled out and pressed against her, rubbing her breasts over her warm, muscled body, moving on to her swollen, triangular mound of thick, dark hair, running her fingers through it, anticipating. Rachel lifted herself slightly. Claire's heart beat faster, wanting, craving again. She moved down and spread Rachel slowly, seeing the tip of her firm, protruding clit. She entered with her tongue, then slowly slipped out, raking upward but not touching her want, watching its raging beauty, knowing Rachel would climax with the slightest stimulation.

Rachel moaned and pleaded. "Please…don't tease me."

Claire lifted onto her elbows to watch her. Rachel was biting her lower lip, clutching the sheets with both hands, moving her legs, her nipples hard and erect. She slid onto her, taking a welcoming hard nipple into her mouth, moaning with pleasure as she sucked, playfully squeezing her other nipple. She licked and kissed, then saw the unleashed fury of sexual heat in Rachel's eyes. She felt the power of knowing Rachel wanted her, that she could completely satisfy her, fulfill her. She didn't want to make her wait any longer. She eagerly slid down, cradling Rachel's hips as she went into her, tasting and devouring.

Rachel moaned and tensed, pushing into her, lifting to meet her, the erotic, sensuous dance of her hips increasing to the rhythmic motions of Claire's mouth.

Claire wanted to stop and watch her, to languish in her pleasure. Every time she saw Rachel do it, it mesmerized her. It took all her concentration to focus. She wanted to talk to Rachel, to whisper in her ear, encourage her, listen to her moans and gasps as she came, feel her heart beat wildly against her own breasts. She repositioned, taking her firm, throbbing sex into her mouth, and began to caress, slipping her fingers into her.

Rachel pushed more firmly against her, calling out for her as her hips lifted higher and she arched, muscles tensing and straining. Claire exaggerated her penetration, pressing into Rachel with her mouth, hungering to satisfy. It was all she could do to hold Rachel down on the bed until she reached satisfaction.

She slid up Rachel's body and lay quiet in her arms, molded to her. Rachel whispered softly to her in her Native American language. "What did you say?"

"I said, *I am complete.*"

Claire ran her fingers through the silky, rich, dark strands of Rachel's long hair. "Have we always been like this?"

Rachel smiled. "Yes. Pretty much. It was always great but not quite like this."

"Am I different in bed now?"

Rachel nodded, a soft laugh flowing out as she kissed her neck.

"How?"

Rachel gave her a thoughtful look and touched her chin. "You're more relaxed, open somehow."

"Oh, I'm open all right. I feel like a slut."

Rachel frowned. "Hey, you're my wife, and you can have whatever you want, whenever you want it. You told me that once when I questioned my own feelings about wanting you."

Claire tried to remember the times they had made love, but her memory was foggy, and parts were still missing. "Did we have sex before we were married? I think we did."

Rachel slid her arm over her waist. "What do you remember?"

It was frustrating that Rachel never told her, only hinted, but she understood why she made her work to remember. She breathed deeply, quiet for a long time, not wanting to talk but to enjoy their shared silence. The interlude brought peace and comfort. "In my house here in Cleveland, you were there after the plane crash. I'm sure we had sex because I'm sure I couldn't keep my hands off you."

Rachel's eyes danced as she smiled. "We didn't have sex right away, not until after I recovered from my injuries. You left it up to me."

"We never had sex before that, not in college or anything?"

"No. We wanted to but never talked about it because we were both insecure and naive. Then we each got married, and it was no longer an option."

Claire grasped at the memories, as if trying to break through a giant spiderweb. She had divorced her husband Richard before Rachel and her husband Alex moved here to Cleveland for Rachel's job, and then Alex died in a car accident.

"Why did we decide to move to Las Vegas and not stay here in Cleveland?"

"We didn't decide right away. I went on an assignment to London with Brice Chambers from MI6. You ended up at Tilly's in Vegas and stayed with her until I got back from…" Rachel stopped.

"What? What's wrong?"

"Do you remember what happened after that?"

Claire closed her eyes to concentrate. They were at Tilly's with security guards because of Eshee Yumiko. She remembered Rachel's long months of recovery after Jack and the team brought her back from the Philippines. She smiled and put her hand to Rachel's face and stroked it. "We decided to marry after your recovery." She watched the smile slowly appear on Rachel's face. "We pledged ourselves on the reservation and honeymooned in our teepee." She basked in the memory. "It was a wonderful honeymoon."

Rachel took her hand in hers and kissed her diamond wedding ring. "Yes, it was wonderful, and then we married at the courthouse when we got back."

"How did I get so lucky to be married to you?" asked Claire.

Rachel leaned over and kissed her. "We've wanted to be together all of our adult lives, and we've both struggled with it, and we've been through some bad things. I almost lost you."

"How did you stand it all this time being around me and not touching me, waiting for me to get my memory back but not knowing if it would happen? How on earth did you do it?"

Rachel sighed and touched Claire's face. "This past year hasn't been easy. I almost didn't make it."

"Thank you for not giving up and hanging in there with me. If I had remembered and you weren't there, I don't know what I would have done."

"I would have never left you, no matter what happened."

Claire kissed her, lingering. Sometimes, when the memories flooded in, she had a difficult time processing it all. What would her life be like without Rachel? Empty? Unfulfilled? She couldn't imagine. The thought of not being with Rachel sent a stabbing ache into her heart. Her life would be nothing without Rachel in it.

CHAPTER SIX

Rachel watched Claire yawn and stretch. She rolled over onto Rachel and wrapped her arms around her.

"Rachel, let's order breakfast in. I'm not sharing you with anyone, not even a waiter in a restaurant. We have this suite for another night."

Rachel smiled and studied her face. The inch-long scar on her temple was barely visible now, just a hint of skin pucker near her hairline. She caressed it with her fingertip, like touching a flower petal. "It's a little early for room service, but whatever you want."

Claire ordered breakfast, then slid out of bed and put on a turquoise silk negligée.

Rachel breathed deeply. A momentary pulse of sexual heat passed through her as she watched the bouquet of color slip over Claire's defined back and onto the sensuous curves of her hips, past her firm buttocks and thighs. Her heartbeat quickened. She swallowed, then smiled, feeling the joy of Claire's beauty and being near her.

Claire walked to the door and opened it.

"What are you doing?"

"I'm checking to make sure the Do Not Disturb sign is still on the outside door handle. The food won't be here for a while. I'm going to shower." She walked over and kissed Rachel.

Rachel fluffed the pillows and sat up. "Hey. I don't have any clothes except what I wore here—no toothbrush, nothing. Everything's at Sarah's."

"Yes, you do. Tilly and I bought you some things before she went to Sarah's. Your clothes are in the closet, toothbrush is in the bag on top of the dresser, and panties and bras are in the drawer." Claire pointed to the dresser near the closet. "Enjoy. I know I will." She laughed and walked toward the bathroom. "Come take a sauna with me when you're ready."

Rachel left the bed and sorted through the items they had bought her. Lace. Silk. Skinny, button, faded jeans. She chose an outfit to wear, then went in with Claire. Their shower was sensual and relaxing—exactly what she needed. They got out and dressed, and within minutes someone knocked at the door.

The waiter set up their breakfast, poured coffee for Claire and herbal tea for her, then left.

When Rachel finished the last bite of her meal, Claire laughed and took her hand. "You must have been hungry."

"I worked up an appetite."

Claire's eyes twinkled, a blush lit her cheeks, and the sound of her laughter filled the air. Rachel needed to kiss those soft lips again, to feel Claire respond to her touch.

"Do you want to do anything later today? I'm sure I can get us tickets for Playhouse Square or wherever you want to go," Claire asked.

"I'm exhausted. I don't want to do anything but be here with you. The case wore me out, then all my emotions, and the incredible sex." Rachel smiled. "Do you remember anything about our lovemaking before?"

"Bits and pieces. Intense ones." Claire walked over to Rachel and sat on her lap, putting her arms around her neck. "Believe me when I say that I want to be with you. Can this really be happening? I feel like I've been lost, struggling to get back, and now I'm finally home."

Rachel slid her arms around her and brought her close. "You are home." The heat and want were rising again, the need to have her close, to touch her. A feeling of exhilaration swept over her, knowing she could have her whenever she wanted. "My heart ached every day for you. I missed being close to you." She touched one of Claire's firm breasts, feeling her own response and Claire's. "So many times I wanted to hold you, to feel you next to me."

Claire straddled Rachel's lap. "I doubt if I'll ever get enough of you."

Rachel brushed her fingertips over Claire's thighs, then lifted her blouse, sliding her hands behind her, touching bare skin, gliding over her firm back and then moving to her breasts. Claire let out a long breath and moaned as her nipples hardened, and she pressed into her, kissing deep and wet, full of hope and promise.

A loud knock on the door broke their intimacy. A female voice called out, "Claire? Rachel?"

Claire pulled away from Rachel's lips and put her hand up in protest. "Absolutely not. Damn her. What in the hell does she want? I knew I should have taken you out of Cleveland and not told anyone where we were going."

Another loud knock on the door made them both wince.

"Tilly, go away." A look of pure panic transformed Claire's face. Her eyes were pleading, as if she expected Rachel to magically make Tilly disappear.

Rachel took a deep breath and looked into Claire's eyes, feeling a momentary surge of desperation, like they were being torn apart again. She fought the feeling. It wasn't like that anymore. She saw panic on Claire's face because that was what she felt. They were together now. She kissed Claire's neck, enjoying her taste and scent. She didn't want to go to the door. She wanted the world to leave them alone. She wanted Tilly to go away, just like Claire did, but she slowly guided Claire's inviting body from her and stood. Claire's blouse slid back down over her bare stomach, as if in slow motion. Every movement, every fold of the beautiful blouse covered her, shutting out what Rachel wanted, what she craved and needed, what was hers to take.

Claire grabbed her arm. "Don't answer it. She'll go away."

"She won't go away. She never does."

"If you open that door, we'll both regret it."

Rachel tore herself away from her, reluctantly walked to the door, and opened it.

Claire followed, putting her hand out as though to bar the entrance. "Tilly, this better be important."

Tilly and Kathrine walked past them and into the room, both looking determined. Rachel's heart sank.

"Rachel, I'm so sorry for interrupting you two, but we need to talk." Kathrine put her hand on Rachel's arm. "Jack and Frank have disappeared."

Rachel's mind and heart were still at the table where she and Claire had been a moment ago, and it took her a second to focus. "I thought you flew back to Las Vegas. What are you doing here? What do you mean they've *disappeared*?" She saw the worry and concern in Kathrine's face.

"I did fly back, and when I returned to the shed, David told me no one has seen Jack or Frank since they were here in Cleveland, and I mean no one. No one can trace their tracking signals. No one's heard from them, and they can't be reached." Claire put her hands on her hips. "That's ridiculous. Call Steve Hathaway. He'll know where they are." Kathrine shook her head. "I've already met with him. Several times."

Rachel sat at the table again, motioning for Kathrine to sit. Tilly walked past them sheepishly and shrugged when Claire gave her a dirty look.

"It's not my fault," Tilly said, sitting on the bed.

Claire folded her arms tightly across her chest and glared at her. "It's always your fault. I swear to God, if there was one speck of trouble left on the earth, you'd be the one to pick it up."

Rachel touched Claire's arm.

Tilly frowned. "It's not my fault."

Claire continued to glare at her.

"After we all had drinks at the hotel and celebrated the end of the case, Jack and Frank left for the airport, and that was the last time anyone saw or heard from them. David and I flew to Arizona and interrogated the man we picked up here in Cleveland and turned over to the FBI. Do you remember?" asked Kathrine.

How could Rachel forget? Just when she finally thought she'd woken from the nightmare, she was pulled back into it again.

❖

Rachel stood next to the second-floor bedroom window of Sarah's house. She watched as the thick flakes of white, heavy snow continued to accumulate on the already sagging branches of the bare maple trees, painting a picture right out of a Currier and Ives Christmas scene.

Claire threw a cream-colored lace blouse into her suitcase, forced a pair of red patent-leather high heels into a plastic bag, and stuffed them into the side compartment. "I don't see why we have to go to Vegas. Kathrine, Steve, and the rest of the team can take care of this."

Rachel finished zipping her suitcase. "Baby, I told you. I have to go. I know the tracking computer protocols, and I'm the only one right now who can run the security and satellite surveillance programs we need to get deep enough into the program to track them. You don't have to go. Stay here at Sarah's and enjoy the rest of the holiday with her, Ricky, and Tilly."

"Absolutely not. I want to be with you. I don't want us to be separated, especially on New Year's Eve."

Rachel went around to Claire's side of the bed and put her arms around her, feeling her tremble. "I wouldn't go unless I had to."

"We just got our life back. I want to be with you. We need to be together." Her voice was muffled against Rachel's shoulder. "Please don't leave."

"I know how difficult this is for you. I feel exactly the same way. I don't want us to be apart, not after what we've been through, but I have to go."

Claire pushed back from her. "I'm trying so hard not to be selfish, but this is too much to expect. How can you leave me? Not again. Not after what we've been through."

"How can I stay? I wouldn't be doing this unless I thought it was absolutely necessary. Claire, I just spent over a year without you, wanting you and needing you every single day. I don't want us to be separated, but I have to do this. I can track them. How can I turn away? I want to make this as easy as possible for you. Are you sure you don't want to stay here with Sarah and Tilly?"

"How long do you think you'll be needed?"

Rachel shook her head slowly. "It depends on what's going on. I'd rather you be here with Sarah and Tilly than alone at the house while I'm at the shed or gone with the team."

Claire sat on the bed and put her face in her hands.

Rachel knelt in front of her, took Claire's hands, and held them. "Please don't. It breaks my heart to see you this upset. I can't stand it. It's okay if you want to stay. I'd rather you be here, where I know you'll be safe. I think you need Sarah and Tilly right now. I don't want you to be alone."

Claire placed her hand on the side of Rachel's face. "You're the one I need. I don't want us to be separated, but I don't want to sit alone in the house waiting for you to get back. Can't you just work from here on your computer?"

"I wish I could, but I need the programs and laptops at the shed. If there was any other way, I swear I'd do it."

She studied Claire's worried face as the tears welled in her eyes. They'd been through so much. But Jack was in trouble, and she owed him. He'd stood by her, saved her life, been their friend, supported them through all they'd endured. He'd been there when Justin tried to kill her, her kidnapping, their marriage, Claire's injury. She had to help him. He would do the same for her. He *had* done that for her.

She brushed her lips against Claire's. "Stay. I don't want you to be alone, and I don't know how long it will take. Just don't have too much fun without me." She smiled and kissed her again.

Claire lay back on the bed, pulling Rachel on top of her, her eyes brimming with tears. "I can't stand this. When are we going to be able to live our lives without the world crashing down on us?"

Rachel agreed. They deserved to finally be together. They'd earned it after all they'd been through, and no one could deny it. She ached at the thought of leaving her, but not leaving to help find Jack and Frank also ripped through her. She forced the words out of her mouth. "I'll call you later tonight, after we get in and I can meet with Steve and the team."

She made herself get up. She wrapped her fingers around the handle of the suitcase and squeezed as she started to roll it toward the bedroom door. She glanced at Claire and then back at the door. How could she leave her? She could barely move her feet. She stopped midstep and went back and lay on top of her.

"I don't want to go." She kissed her one last time, feeling Claire open her mouth for her and kiss her back, feeling the yearning and want to be near her, to enjoy their love after so long away from each other.

"Rachel, it's not right. We should not have to do this, not after what we've been through."

Claire's gaze seared her, like someone had taken a red-hot poker and stabbed it into Rachel's chest.

Tears slid down the side of Claire's face, her voice quavering. "Be safe, my wife. Hurry back to me. Please hurry back."

"I miss you already." Rachel grabbed her suitcase, forcing herself to leave the bedroom, unable to look back, hearing Claire cry as she shut the door, the scene and pain all too familiar.

Chapter Seven

Claire lay on the bed for a long time, numb, unwilling to move. She turned over and buried her face in the pillow, balling her fists in the sheets. How could Rachel leave her? Why wouldn't everyone just let them alone? Someone knocked softly on her bedroom door. Her heart skipped a beat. She quickly sat and held her breath, watching as the door opened. Rachel?

Sarah entered the room.

Claire exhaled deeply and slid back onto the bed, not trying to hide her disappointment.

Sarah walked over and wrapped her arms around Claire, her warm hug comforting and reassuring. Sarah could always comfort her, from the time she, Tilly, and Sarah were in grade school together. Always their rock. Always the calm one. Rarely lost it. Always quick to reason things out. That's probably why Sarah was such a good nurse.

"Don't stay in here alone. It will just make you more miserable. Come downstairs and visit with us. Tilly wants to know if you want to play cards."

"I hate this, Sarah. It's so unfair." She slid off the bed and wiped her face.

"I know, honey. Come on. You'll feel better if you aren't alone."

Claire started to walk out of the bedroom. Muscles tensed. Anger began to rise. "It's Tilly's fault." They started down the stairs, each step bringing more anger, more pressure, building like someone had turned the burner on high and slammed the lid on the pot. She squeezed her hands into tight fists. *Step...If it wasn't for Tilly coming to the hotel, I'd be with Rachel right now. Step...Tilly likes to cause trouble. Step... She's jealous and can't stand for someone else to be happy.* Each breath caught in her chest. By the time they sat at the game table in the rec room, she'd reached the boiling point.

She grabbed the cards off the table and started to shuffle but then slammed them down and glowered at Tilly. She couldn't hold herself back. The words spewed out like an eruption of Mount St. Helens. "Damn it to hell, Tilly. I hope to God you're happy now."

Sarah's eyes widened, and she stiffened.

Tilly's eyes filled with tears. "I only wanted to help."

Claire pushed the cards away and jumped up. "Help, my ass. You better explain right now, or you're not going to live long enough to sing another note." She moved toward Tilly, hands curled into tight fists, a pounding in her chest, a flush of heat in her cheeks. The anger continued to erupt, and she couldn't control it.

Sarah stood and stopped her, grabbing her arm and sitting her back down at the table with her.

Tilly reached out, as if pleading. "I swear to you, Claire, I just wanted to help. I've known Jack for a long time, and he and I have been good friends. When Kathrine called me from the airport and told me she needed to get to Rachel, I knew she was worried, and I knew Rachel would want to know."

"Tilly, do you have any idea the shit storm you started?" Claire stood again, pushing the chair out with the back of her legs, her voice an octave higher than normal as it bounced off the walls, startling even her. She felt like someone had taken a knife and ripped her open. The feeling was so visceral she held her stomach with both hands.

"I just tried to help." Tilly put her hand to her mouth. "He could be in real trouble."

"He owns a security agency. He's not stupid. They can take care of themselves."

Tilly stood and moved to her, putting her hand on her forearm. "Please don't be mad at me. I didn't want to cause any trouble. I just wanted to help. Please forgive me?"

Claire jerked away. "No. I don't *forgive* you. What you did is horrible. You have no idea what Rachel and I have gone through this last couple of years. You don't know what I've gone through since I got shot. I finally get to be with my wife after a year of hell, and now as soon as someone says they need Rachel's help, you tell them exactly where to find her and destroy any chance of us having time to reconnect. You're an idiot."

Tilly put her hands on her hips and stiffened. "Claire, I think you're overreacting."

"Oh, shut the hell up. You have no idea what I'm thinking or feeling."

Sarah stood. "Don't tell her to shut up, Claire. She just did what she thought was right."

Claire shouted back. "Butt out, Sarah."

"Don't tell Sarah to butt out. She has just as much right as you do to have an opinion here."

"Tilly, if you say one more word, I swear to God I'm going to slap the shit out of you."

Sarah raised her hands. "Both of you calm down."

Tilly and Claire turned to Sarah and told her to shut up at the same time.

Out of the corner of her eye, Claire saw Ricky, Sarah's husband, come through the hallway.

Tilly's face turned red. "Just because you had a head injury doesn't mean I won't slap the shit out of you too, Claire."

Claire made a fist and took a step closer to her. "That'll be a cold day in hell."

Sarah wedged between them and tried to stop her.

Tilly half-shoved Sarah out of the way. "You don't have to protect me, Sarah. I can take care of myself."

Claire let it fly. "Yeah, like you took care of this?" Unable to slap Tilly because Sarah blocked her hand, she grabbed a handful of Tilly's hair and started to pull her toward her.

"Sonofabitch." Tilly grabbed a handful of Claire's hair in return.

Sarah tried to separate them, but they all became entangled in each other.

A loud, shrill whistle broke through the air.

They immediately stopped and looked toward the hallway. Ricky stood with his hands held out, looking at them.

"Enough," he boomed. "What in the hell is going on?"

"Ask the idiot savant," Claire said, nodding toward Tilly. "Why don't you tell him what this is all about?"

"That's it. You're out of control," Tilly said, and slapped Claire's face.

Claire recovered quickly and reached back, delivering a Rachel-by-the-lake slap to the side of Tilly's face, sending her sailing into Sarah.

Tilly grabbed ahold of Sarah's shoulder for balance and then turned to go after Claire again, but Ricky stepped forward, grabbed Tilly around the waist, and strong-armed her toward the couch by the game table.

"I said that's *enough*. Now, all three of you sit down and shut up."

Claire sat near the opposite end of the couch from Tilly, and Sarah chose the chair she'd been sitting in before the fight started.

"Now, what's this all about?"

Claire pointed at Tilly. "Ask her. She's the one who has to be in everyone else's business because she has no life of her own."

Tilly stood and stabbed her finger in the air at her. "You're just a spoiled, overreacting crybaby, and if you'd think about someone else besides yourself for one second, everything would be fine."

Claire stood and stabbed her finger back at Tilly. "Oh yeah? Like you'd know what it's like to care about anyone other than yourself. You self-absorbed twit."

"Crybaby."

"Bitch."

"Go to hell, Claire."

"You first."

Sarah raised her hands vehemently in the air. "Stop it, both of you, right now."

Tilly sat. When Claire saw her sit down, she sat, and the room got quiet.

"What's this about?" Ricky asked again.

Sarah explained to Ricky what Tilly had done and why Rachel and Kathrine had left for Las Vegas.

"I don't see what the problem is," Ricky said. "I know you're upset, Claire, but it sounds to me like Rachel needed to go back to help find Jack. Surely you wouldn't put your time with her over someone else's life. What's really bothering you?"

Claire burst into tears.

Sarah went to her, sitting beside her on the couch and putting her arm around her. Tilly scooted over by her and patted her thigh.

"Rachel's going to get killed doing that damn job." She trembled to her core. She couldn't bear it. Not after what they'd been through. The old anxiety and fear of losing Rachel crept in, vivid and intrusive. Every time Rachel left her to go to that job, she ached, felt sick at heart. She didn't put her time with Rachel over someone else's life, but God help them, when would they be able to live their lives in peace?

Chapter Eight

Kathrine could barely see the gray puffs of clouds below as the sun began to set, its light reflecting off the wing of the jet. On the ground, when the rain clouds covered the sky, you had to get above the clouds to see it. The thought seemed symbolic, but she was too tired to think about it. She leaned back and closed her eyes, memories elbowing their way in. She tried to resist, but they demanded center stage, like some spoiled has-been actress in an off-Broadway play.

She'd walked away from the cabin cruiser and down the dock, on her way to get the groceries for their weekend trip to La Jolla. She hadn't seen Cassie, her twin sister, in over three months, unusual for them, but their lives were busy. Cassie spent what time she had building her clientele for her art dealership, and Kathrine was adjusting to the changes in her life after military service. Cassie stayed behind on the boat, the one Kathrine should have been on. And then it exploded.

The familiar, unsettling shudder began in the pit of her stomach, the memories so powerful they caused a physical reaction. She could smell the fumes from the gasoline and the suffocating stench of the thick, dark smoke. Her hands and forearms began to sting as she recalled the fireball and pieces of the burning boat raining down around her. She had watched in complete disbelief and horror, desperate to get to her but knowing she could do nothing.

Pieces of a detonator had been found in the debris, but the investigation had gone cold. She'd spent six long years tracking down the men who had set the bomb. One by one she found them and made sure they paid. They'd been after Kathrine that day. She'd seen one of the men during a robbery and intended to testify in court as a witness. They'd gone after her but killed Cassie instead.

Jack's security agency ranked among the top three nationwide.

She'd stayed in Las Vegas to work there. She wanted to learn from the best. She needed their training and expertise to locate the men who killed Cassie. And that's exactly what she'd done, while finding friendships in the process. None of her closely knit team had any idea about her extracurricular activity, and they'd never need to know. Still, she couldn't help but feel a little guilty about keeping things from the people she trusted with her life.

The jet touched down smoothly.

"I've never flown into any airport in Vegas other than McCarren. I didn't even know this one was here," Rachel said, following Kathrine down the steps of the plane.

"Actually, there's three here. A lot of the private jet owners use this one in North Las Vegas or Henderson because of the heavy air traffic at McCarren."

"Who's picking us up?" asked Rachel.

"David will meet us at baggage claim."

She rolled her shoulders and waited for Rachel to catch her as they followed other passengers toward the claim area. Her mind raced through the list of possibilities about what might have happened to Jack and Frank. None of them were pleasant. Unfortunately, Eshee Yumiko headed the list of possible suspects. Her stomach churned. Did the team have the skills to get Jack and Frank back alive if it involved Yumiko? Could Rachel face Yumiko again?

❖

Rachel watched David closely when they approached him. His smile seemed forced. He shifted his weight from side to side and glanced from Kathrine and then back to her. He helped them with their luggage, quickly loading it into the back of the black SUV. Did he have bad news about Jack and Frank? Had something happened? Rachel got into the passenger side as Kathrine slipped into the rear seat behind her.

"Any word?" Rachel asked.

He glanced at her and pulled away from the curb. "We couldn't get deep enough into the tracking program without your help."

She grimaced and bit her lower lip, guilt sweeping over her. She'd been in a hotel room making love with her wife when she should have been back at work. Jack and Frank could be dead somewhere. Kathrine unlocked the gun case on the seat and reached for her Glock, checking the gun, her fingers moving swiftly and skillfully. She sighted it, then laid it next to her on the seat and put the shoulder holster on. "I'm going to need a couple more clips."

"Everything's at the shed," David said.

"Any ideas about what they were into before they went missing?" Rachel asked.

"From what we've found out, Steve thinks it had something to do with the last case we all worked in Cleveland and DC," David said.

Rachel's stomach knotted. The case hadn't been typical. Everything about it made her uncomfortable, from Claire's involvement to the clandestine way Jack and Frank had acted when they'd taken the man they'd brought with them into the interrogation room.

"Does she know?" David took a long look at Kathrine in the rearview mirror.

"No. I didn't tell her everything yet."

Rachel turned back toward Kathrine. "Didn't tell me what?" Out of her peripheral vision she saw David grip the steering wheel tighter. What were they both so hesitant to talk about?

"Kathrine and I went to the FBI facility in Arizona and interrogated the guy from Cleveland." He sounded matter-of-fact, as if purposely void of emotion.

"Why would you do that?" She didn't like not knowing what they knew. She didn't like that they held it back. "I knew something happened in Cleveland. Jack and Frank both acted odd, and Jack made me pack my computer equipment and sent Kathrine and me out to the main room to wait, just before you came out. He and Frank seemed a little shaken when they left the interrogation room after the FBI took the guy."

"Did Jack or Frank say anything to you?" asked David.

He completely avoided her question, obviously choosing his words carefully. She shook her head.

Kathrine reached for the Glock, inserted the clip with a swipe of her hand, and slipped the gun into position in the holster under her arm, routinely, like she had done it a thousand times, which she probably had. She looked at Rachel with a stoic expression. "We'll fill you in on the rest when we get to the shed."

"Can't you tell me now?"

"It's better if we wait."

She'd torn herself from Claire. Now the people depending on her were keeping information to a minimum. They traveled back to the shed in an uncomfortable silence.

Once they were there, each time she tried to make eye contact with Kathrine, or David, they looked away. She finally gave up and stared at the lo mein noodles on the paper plate in front of her, stabbing at them halfheartedly with a plastic fork. The silence grew more deafening by the second.

Steve motioned toward her with his chopsticks. "Eat. We don't know when we'll be able to eat again." He took a bite of his egg roll.

She forced some of the noodles into her mouth.

Steve continued to update them as they tried to decide the best way to proceed.

Kathrine laid her chopsticks on her plate. "She needs to know, Steve."

"I want you and David to gather the gear and brief the rest of the office staff. Rachel and I will set up here and be ready when you get back." Steve glanced at his watch. "I want to be on the road by twenty-one hundred hours."

Kathrine nodded, gulped one more bite of her egg roll, and then she and David started to leave. She looked back at Rachel, as if she wanted to tell her something, but kept walking.

Steve cleared his throat. "David and Kathrine made a visit to the FBI facility in Arizona."

"I heard."

He shoved his plate away. "Rachel, the man they interrogated told them Eshee Yumiko was involved in the case all of you were working on."

The air rushed out of her lungs. Her heart skipped a beat. Undulating nausea swept through her stomach. The plastic fork broke in her hand. She watched the pieces drop into the food on her plate, as if in slow motion. The words Eshee Yumiko reverberated in her ears, knocking around inside her head like a baseball landing in the empty seats of a stadium. It took her a few seconds to comprehend what he told her, or at least what she thought he told her. "That…that can't be. She's in prison."

"No. MI6 must have taken her and used her for something. It's not uncommon for agencies like that to trade or bargain for information. No matter what happened, I think when Jack found out about her involvement, he went after her."

She placed her hands in her lap and locked her fingers together, trying to hide the trembling. Her entire body recoiled, as if autonomically responding to what he'd said. It took her a few seconds, but the reality of the situation finally started to sink in.

He's serious. It's not some kind of sick joke.

She felt him watching her, but she avoided his gaze, trying to hide the panic. Yet she couldn't. Her cheeks flushed, and her mouth went dry. She might as well have had a flashing yellow caution sign above her head with the words *woman under extreme duress.* It was embarrassing.

"I know this is a shock."

She squeezed her own hands so hard, her knuckles ached. She needed to relax. Slow her breathing. Not anticipate but focus on what he actually said. She released her grip.

"And I know, given what you went through, this is going to be difficult for you, but we need you. No one can get into our security systems like you can." He continued to watch her. "Are you up to this?"

She took a stuttered breath and looked down as she unlocked her fingers and gently brushed at her pant leg. She knew he saw through the stalling technique, but to his credit he said nothing and sat quietly, giving her the time she needed.

What if, at the last minute, she couldn't do her job because she froze or choked? What if someone got hurt because she hesitated? What if she saw Yumiko? Could she face her?

She put her hand to her mouth and coughed softly. She had to get herself together, and she had to do it right now. She could help put Yumiko away for the rest of her life, so she'd never be able to do to someone else what she'd done to her. She looked into Steve's blue eyes. "Yes. I'm up to it." The self-doubt immediately lashed back. Was she?

He patted her arm, a momentary tense expression on his face. He didn't seem totally convinced, but what choice did they have? Only she could get deep enough into her program and into the network to track Jack and Frank. It was her program. She designed it, and she could modify it. Even if their trackers were off-line, she could find them. Her heart rate slowed. She took deeper breaths. Muscles relaxed. The knot in her stomach started to dissipate.

"As soon as you pack what you need, I want you to take a break. You look exhausted. Go lie down in the back room. David and Kathrine won't be back for a while."

"I will, but I need to make a call first."

"How'd she take you leaving?"

Rachel scooted her chair back and crossed her legs. "We've been through so much. I'm really worried about her. She's with her best friends in Cleveland, so at least she's not alone."

He put his hand on her shoulder as he stood. "Rachel, this job is tough on all of our spouses and significant others, and that's why so many of us are divorced or alone. It takes a strong relationship to make it work under these circumstances. When this is over, you and Claire need to go away for a while. You two never even got to celebrate your first anniversary."

"How do you make it work between you and Lisa?"

His eyes sparkled, and a broad smile flashed across his face. "Lisa and I have been sweethearts since we were sixteen. We've never been with anyone but each other. She's my rock." He winked. "We spend a lot of time in bed, and we never leave the house fighting, or at least without telling each other *I love you* no matter how crappy our day or night is. We don't let anything tear us apart, and believe me, things come at us all the time."

She nodded.

"I guess the real answer is that you still have to do your job, but don't take anything for granted. Now get packed and rest."

He left the room.

She reached for her cell phone and called Claire.

Claire sounded subdued.

"Claire, are you all right?"

"Sarah, Tilly, and I just got back from visiting Tilly's mom."

Rachel laughed. "I bet that was fun. Did Tilly behave herself?"

"I'm still mad at her."

"Why?"

She didn't answer.

"Claire, why?"

"Because she brought Kathrine to our hotel room, and if she hadn't, you wouldn't have left to go back to Las Vegas."

"That's not true. Kathrine would have found me eventually, with or without Tilly's help, and if not her, then Steve would have." Rachel heard her sigh deeply. "You two okay now?"

"Yes. We made up."

"What are you doing tonight?"

"We're playing poker with Ricky. I miss you so much."

"I miss you. Let's not talk about it because it makes it harder to be away from you."

"Rachel, is it bad?"

No way on earth would she tell Claire what she'd just found out. She'd fall apart at the seams. She wasn't ready to hear it, but more than that, Rachel wasn't ready to say it out loud. "I don't want you to worry. We have some good leads, and we're leaving in a few hours for Los Angeles. I'm sorry we aren't together right now."

"What would you do to me if we were together?"

"Stop it." She heard Claire laugh. "You're such a tease."

"But I'm your tease, and I can't wait to get you back in our bed again. I love you. Please be careful."

Claire's concern and anxiety poured out of the phone and into Rachel's heart. It shot through her, leaving a burn and ache deep inside. "It's all right. I'm with the team. You be safe too, and watch Tilly. She likes to bluff when she's losing. She tries to buy the pot. When she bets big out of the gate, bet over her, and she'll back down."

"Good night, wife."

"Good night. Love you."

Rachel ended the call and closed her eyes. This was the job. It had always been the job, but she couldn't help but wonder if the price was worth it. How much more would she or Claire have to pay?

CHAPTER NINE

Kathrine set the monitor carefully in the back of the van, half listening to David say something about the Los Angeles weather forecast for the night. She diverted her thoughts to Tilly, the memory making her smile. She'd seen her perform at the Caprice in Las Vegas several times. Her voice clear and strong, each note she sang rang out into the audience, and into her soul, mesmerizing her.

Claire had introduced them at her and Rachel's wedding party at Lil' Nell's, not far from the shed. She had the opportunity to sit with her for several hours, talking and laughing. That laugh, like an unexpected gift floating in the air, went right into her heart. She was even more beautiful up close. Her blond hair, full lips, cream complexion, lithe figure, and those penetrating eyes, kind of a grayish blue with flecks of gold around the iris, made for a stunning package. She was a few inches shorter than Kathrine. A good thing.

They had an attraction, a connection, and she hoped they would have more nights of laughter and visiting—and other things. She repositioned, feeling the edge of want slowly seeping in. Although they hadn't had any kind of intimate conversation, she sensed Tilly's possible attraction to her. She definitely wanted to find out.

She stuffed the last piece of surveillance equipment into the back of the van. "That's it," she told Steve.

Rachel came out of the side door of the shed and climbed into the back seat with her, and given how pale she looked, she knew who they were up against. David got into the driver's side, and Steve slipped into the passenger seat.

Steve looked back to Rachel and her. "Remember—no hesitation, no regret."

She and Rachel nodded, repeating the phrase with David.

❖

Rachel tried to position her head to get comfortable against the small pillow, but the constant invading freeway lights flashed rhythmically in her eyes. She gave in and sat up, massaging her temples. The vehicle lights flashed in the side passenger mirror, taking her back to the Philippines. She had given in to the torture and beatings. Yumiko broke her, shattered her into a thousand tiny pieces, and she did exactly what she vowed she wouldn't do—she fixed the computer program and gave Yumiko what she wanted.

She touched her right knee and traced the ridge of the long, thick scar through her slacks, visualizing the expression of satisfaction on Yumiko's face when she swung a metal bar onto her kneecap and shattered it. The scars on her back twinged as she remembered the beatings with the brown leather strap and the diluted acid she poured onto the open wounds.

Yumiko took everything from her. Stripped her of her self-esteem, of her existence. The feelings overwhelmed her as they started to rise in the pit of her stomach. She fought to push them away. It wasn't enough that Yumiko had tried to destroy her body…No. She'd tried to destroy her soul. Her heart rate increased, and her chest tightened as the memories flooded in. Sweat formed on the back of her neck. Her knees trembled.

She couldn't bring herself to tell Claire who they were up against. Claire would have demanded she not go, and she couldn't fault her. She didn't know if she could deal with this, if she could face her again.

She jumped when Kathrine touched her shoulder.

Kathrine half laughed, but her eyes were full of concern. "Are you all right?"

Rachel nodded, looking away, watching the stream of traffic. She had a few hours to think, to worry, to stress. She had to get hold of herself and push Yumiko out of her head. She sat back, feeling the familiar yearning for Claire's comfort.

"Rachel, don't let Yumiko get to you."

How did she know? Was it that obvious?

Kathrine had become a good friend—steady, extremely skilled at her job, and self-assured. She and Frank were the senior lead agents at the shed and had taught her the ins and outs of the business. Kathrine grew up in Denver and had come to work for Jack after she got out of the military. She'd asked her once how she knew Jack, but Kathrine said only that she'd served with him, and the subject was dropped. Rachel suspected that whatever Kathrine and Jack did in the military must have had something to do with intelligence, because neither one of them would talk about it. Jack had been in special forces. Had Kathrine also?

Kathrine was a lesbian. She didn't make a big deal about it or talk about it. As a matter of fact, she rarely talked about herself. Rachel had to pry information out of her. She liked that about her.

She saw the way she looked at Tilly when they were at Sarah's. She suspected Kathrine and Tilly liked each other, but she didn't know how much. She had difficulty reading Tilly. She was Claire and Sarah's friend, so she would leave that to Claire to find out. Once Claire got hold of it, she wouldn't let go until she found out every detail. Claire's tenacity made her smile.

Kathrine leaned forward. "Who here wants to kick Yumiko's ass?"

Everyone raised their hands.

Rachel laughed, but inside the nagging doubts continued. The haunting question they were all asking themselves loomed over them, whether they wanted to admit it or not. *Are Jack and Frank still alive?*

She'd chosen this job because she loved what she did and the camaraderie she felt for the people she worked with. Yes, danger played its part, but at what point did it outweigh the benefits? She couldn't make up her mind if the adrenaline coursing through her meant readiness to face what lay ahead or if fear took the driver's seat.

She looked at her laptop, holding it, shifting for a better position. "I've got Jack's signal. It's weak but transmitting." She entered the sequencing, searching for Frank's signal, but had no response.

CHAPTER TEN

R achel watched her computer program and rechecked the signal as the team continued to track Jack's now-clear signal. They were close.

"Stop! That house." She pointed to the barely visible, tan, two-story mansion set back from the street and surrounded by foliage and high security walls.

Steve and Kathrine each grabbed a pair of binoculars and left the van, coming back a short time later.

"It figures. It looks like they're planning for a visit from a military assault team. They've got state-of-the-art surveillance equipment. I even saw military-grade sound detection. How do these people get away with this shit on American soil?" Kathrine asked.

"Probably because they aren't causing any trouble and no one is paying any attention to them," David said.

"They've got trouble now," Steve said. He adjusted the outside antenna on the van at Rachel's request as she entered the coordinates for the information she needed.

The house plans appeared on her computer. She merged the information, placing Jack in the bedroom closest to where they were parked. She switched on the infrared and swung the computer toward Steve and the rest of the team, pointing at the cursor.

"They have three guards on the outside perimeter, and six bodies are in motion inside the house." She pointed to the screen at the two images in a back room. A blue dot shadowed one of the moving figures. "There's Jack for sure. That's his microchip signature. I'm hoping Frank is the one active next to him. His microchip isn't functioning."

"Well, Jack's alive, and hopefully Frank. That's good news. Let's keep them that way, shall we?" Steve said.

Rachel helped David adjust his body cam, then helped Kathrine with the more complex surveillance program. Claire had used it on the job in Cleveland because of her enhanced vision, but tonight it would be Kathrine. David took the miniature earbud out of the small case and handed it to Kathrine. She inserted it and then lubricated the contact with the microchip and inserted it in her eye.

Rachel booted up the program. "Blink three times to initiate the program."

Kathrine blinked, and the images she saw appeared in a box in the upper left corner of Rachel's computer screen.

"Are you good?" Rachel asked.

Kathrine gave a thumbs-up.

"Remember, I can see where you're looking, but you may not be aware of what I see because of the enhanced visual acuity of the camera in the microchip."

"I won't be as good as Claire, but I'll do my best."

"You'll be great."

Steve left the van and came back a little later, night-vision binoculars in his hand. "We've got a problem."

Everyone stopped what they were doing.

"They're waiting for us."

"What did you see?" asked Kathrine.

"Something's not right. I can clearly see Jack through the window, none of the guards are on the south side of the perimeter, and the entire thing smells like a trap."

"What do you want to do?" David asked.

"They want us to see Jack, which means they're using him as bait. Since we have bait, let's go fishing. Wait here." He took the tactical pen and binoculars. "I'm going to see if I can get Jack's attention and transmit some intel through signals or something."

He came back a short time later and gave a thumbs-up. "Frank is alive. He and Jack managed to get free of their restraints. They have a few more minutes until the guard checks on them again. They'll take him down as soon as he comes into the room."

Kathrine and David nodded.

"We don't have time to take out the ground surveillance. Kathrine, you disable the cameras. You and David take the northeast perimeter. I'll take the other end. We'll coordinate the attack as soon as I see Jack and Frank handle the guard. Stay tight, and remember, no unnecessary noise. Rachel, keep us informed," Steve said.

She nodded. She wanted to go in with them, mostly to deal with Yumiko. Throw her to the floor or drag her out by her hair. Maybe beat the crap out of her in the process. Kick her while she was down or take a metal bar to her kneecaps and see how she liked it. What if Yumiko had left? What if she was prepared for their arrival? What if she got the upper hand somehow and captured them all? She'd already seized Frank and Jack. How many times had she outsmarted the best security agencies in the world? Her mind raced with a plenitude of scenarios, each building on the other, filling her with more uncertainty than the next. A momentary shiver of fear passed through her.

Steve put his hand on her shoulder as he waited his turn to step out of the van. "You're where you need to be, Rachel. Don't worry. If she's in there, we'll get her."

She adjusted the images on the computer screens. The team quietly and quickly made their way down the street toward the perimeter wall. Kathrine fired at a camera concealed near a metal power box next to the street.

"Now let's see how they react when they don't know how many of us are coming their way," Steve whispered.

Rachel maintained her visual on the house and the perimeter as she monitored Kathrine and the others moving into position. She listened through the headset as Kathrine and David coordinated with Steve.

Rachel recognized the burst of repeated noise, like someone opening pressurized soda cans. The guards went down quickly.

"All guards down outside," reported Kathrine.

Rachel scanned the satellite images on the main computer. "It looks like one is down and not moving in the room Jack left. Jack and four others are in the room beside the pool." She reviewed the schematics. "They're in a kitchen. Two are stationary, two have slight movement. Jack looks down but is moving. Be careful when you go in."

The team maneuvered quickly, crossing the pool area. Steve went through the doorway first, immediately going to Jack, lying on the floor by the entrance to the living room. Frank had crouched by a dining-room table. Kathrine stopped at the doorway and scanned. Rachel saw one of the men rise on his elbow as Kathrine turned her head.

"Two o'clock," Rachel yelled into the microphone.

Steve turned and fired, but not before the man fired his weapon. Steve collapsed beside Jack. Kathrine quickly shot twice. The man slumped back onto the floor.

Kathrine rushed to Steve and rolled him over, lifting him toward her, holding his head. He was choking and gasping, his eyes wide, his face filled with what appeared to be panic. He grabbed Kathrine's protective vest and pulled at her as she put her hand over the gunshot wound in his neck, trying to stop the arterial bleeding.

"Lisa…" Steve choked and stiffened, then stopped breathing and went limp. Rachel watched on the monitor as the color drained from him, the ghostly expression still etched on his face. Her hands began to tremble, and bile rose in her throat.

Kathrine laid him flat and checked his heartbeat. "No, no, no… Stay with us." She started CPR.

Rachel watched helplessly as Kathrine continued, refusing to quit.

Jack gave the order to contact the local police and paramedics. David made the call.

Rachel locked everything and quickly entered the house. Jack sat on the floor, grimacing, holding his leg with both hands. She avoided looking at Steve's lifeless body as she helped stabilize Jack's leg, the wail of sirens growing louder in the distance.

She went to each of the bodies, looking, hoping, but they were all male. Maybe she'd find her somewhere else in the house. Perhaps the body in the back bedroom.

"She's not here," Jack said from where he sat propped against the wall, blood already seeping from the makeshift bandage on his leg. "She left before it all started."

Rachel avoided his gaze.

The foreboding blackness of the night surrounded them like a tomb. Steve was dead. Yumiko had gotten away—again. Would she come after her or Claire? Would the body count continue? Whose life would that monster ruin next?

CHAPTER ELEVEN

Rachel's eyes burned and stung from the lack of sleep and the reflection of the Las Vegas morning sun beating down on the etched glass in the front door of Steve and Lisa's house. She forced her hands to her sides, almost unable to stop herself from grabbing Jack's hand so he couldn't ring the doorbell. Too late.

He shifted his weight from side to side. His hand trembled where he held on to the cane keeping him upright. The muscles in his jaw were rigid. His blue eyes glistened in the sunshine. Obviously his leg hurt, but more than that, the pain in his face revealed his grief. The entire team felt the loss, but none of them more than Jack. He carried it in the way he moved, even in the way he breathed, as if each inhalation caused a deep ache. Rachel saw the pain in his eyes through the monitor the moment Steve took his last breath.

He could barely walk but insisted he would tell Lisa. He hadn't said more than a few words since they left Los Angeles, and when Jack got quiet, you knew he hurt. She could scarcely endure watching him, let alone see Lisa go through this ordeal.

Lisa threw the door open. Her shaking hand went to her mouth as she staggered and slumped against the doorjamb. She knew why they were here and her husband wasn't. Rachel reached for her, helping her into the living room and on to the couch. Jack sat close on one side of her, Rachel on the other.

Lisa began to weep. Her deep, moaning wails pierced the silence, shattering the heart-wrenching space between agony and all the happiness and goodness in her life.

"I knew it." She gasped, the sound barely making it out of her mouth. "I felt it." She choked out the words, her breath catching in between more tears, more sobs.

They sat together, hearts knit by the cords of Lisa's unspeakable pain. They seemed suspended in time, the constant ticking of the grandfather clock declaring its now-meaningless existence. Rachel left to meet Claire at the airport. Jack said he'd stay to help Lisa with whatever came next, and in truth, Rachel was glad to leave. She needed time alone to process all that had happened, to shed her own tears without feeling guilty about other people's pain being worse than hers.

She took a taxi to the airport and paced at the bottom of the escalators near baggage claim, waiting for Claire's flight to arrive. When she'd called to give her the basic details and to let her know she was safe, Claire had insisted on returning right away. Rachel lunged for her when Claire reached the bottom step.

Claire threw her arms around her, drawing her in, holding her, burying her face in Rachel's neck. "It's so sad. I'm so sorry, Rachel."

Rachel couldn't speak. She wrapped her arms around her more tightly and held on, feeling Claire's immediate comfort and strength. She wouldn't let go of her hand as they took a taxi back to Lisa and Steve's.

Claire immediately went to Lisa and held her as she continued to cry. The anguish on Lisa's face told the story of how much she loved Steve, and how horrendous his death was for her. Rachel watched them as they sat together in the den, seeing the way Claire gave comfort, how it seemed to be so easy for her to reach out and offer a part of herself to Lisa.

Would Claire have to go through this someday? Would she? The idea of losing Claire caused an unbearable ache. She'd almost lost Claire once. She couldn't endure it again. Claire had almost lost her also. How would she endure it?

She wanted to leave, get away from the emotions and thoughts, yet Lisa needed support, especially until her family arrived.

Jack whispered something to Lisa, put his arm around her, and then stood, limping out of the den. Rachel used it as an excuse to follow him from the room.

He turned to her when she closed the door. "I have to go put my leg up. The pain is worse."

Was he leaving because of the pain in his leg, or was it from the pain in his heart? Watching Lisa struggle was almost unbearable. Did he blame himself for Steve's death? They all felt guilt at not seeing the shooter fast enough. They'd left him alive for information, and it had cost them one of their own. But it was a judgment call and part of the job.

She put her hand on his broad shoulder and felt him relax as he inhaled deeply.

"Go home and take care of yourself. We'll stay here until her parents arrive." She saw the anguish in his chiseled face, yet also a trace of gratitude and relief. "Jack, it's all right. We'll take care of this." He didn't speak. He looked back toward the den, hesitating, as if he wanted to say something, then nodded slowly and walked toward the front door.

"Jack, it's not—"

He held up his hand and walked out the door.

When Lisa and Steve's ten-year-old son and twelve-year-old daughter arrived with Patty, one of Lisa's neighbors, Rachel stood close by as Lisa tried to comfort them. They held on to each other, as if grasping for a far-too-distant lifeline while they were drowning. More tears, more pain.

Lisa shook her head slowly. Rachel moved to her and helped her back to the den and closed the door while Patty and Claire stayed with the children. Lisa put her face in her hands and continued to sob, rocking back and forth. Rachel did the only thing she could. She wrapped her arms around her and cried with her.

As if on cue, Claire came in. "Lisa, I thought you should know that Kathrine, Frank, Beth, José, and David are here. They brought some food from the employees and their families at the shed."

Rachel took Claire's hand as they followed Lisa into the living room, watching her greet each one and fighting back her tears as she thanked them for their love and care.

"Please, all of you make yourselves at home." She looked at each one of them as they hugged her, then went back into the den and closed the door, her heart-wrenching sobs echoing out of the room.

Kathrine wiped her eyes.

"She shouldn't be alone," Claire said.

Rachel and Claire went back into the den and sat with her.

"Why Steve, Rachel? Why him? Tell me what happened."

"I didn't go in the house during the operation. I ran the monitoring programs out in the van." She knew exactly what had happened, every excruciating detail. She'd seen it all on the satellite feed and on Kathrine's program, but she couldn't say it out loud. She couldn't speak those unspeakable words to her. "Would you like me to get Kathrine?

She can tell you what happened." She knew it was cowardly, but she couldn't help it.

Lisa nodded and wiped her tears with a tissue, not looking up as Claire put her arm around her.

Rachel left and returned with Kathrine, who sat beside Lisa.

"Would you like to be alone with Kathrine?" Claire asked.

Lisa shook her head, wiping more tears. "I want you and Rachel here with me." She took Claire's hand. "Can you stay until my mom and dad get here? They should be here later tonight."

"Do they need a ride from the airport?" asked Rachel.

"They're driving in from St. George," Claire said.

Rachel nodded.

"Don't worry. We won't leave you alone," Claire said. "We'll stay as long as you need us."

"What are the kids doing?"

"They're with Frank, Beth, and the others. Your next-door neighbor, Patty, is still here," Kathrine said.

"Tell me, please," Lisa said.

Rachel saw Kathrine's strength and the depth of compassion she had for Lisa and for her. She had a quiet inner dignity that showed in the way she spoke, in the way she didn't speak, and in the gentle way she interacted with all of them.

"He just happened to be the first one through the door. Normally he stays behind, and either Frank or I lead, but last night he went first." She told her the details of what happened, slowly, carefully, compassionately.

Lisa sat silent for a long moment after Kathrine finished and then took a shaky breath. "I know what you all do is very important. Steve loved his job. He wouldn't have been the man he was if he hadn't worked with Jack and all of you."

"He was a great man," Kathrine said, tears filling her eyes, her voice quavering. "We were with him when it happened. He spoke your name with his last breath."

Lisa gasped, putting her hand to her mouth, saying nothing for what seemed like an endless amount of time. Finally, she spoke. "Did you know he served a mission for our church in Fiji?" She smiled. "I wanted to get married right out of high school, but he insisted he should go on his mission."

Kathrine smiled. "Yes. He talked about it a lot."

Lisa began to cry again. Rachel's heart pounded. Her wrists and palms began to sweat. Nausea shot through her, and she couldn't catch her breath. She stood, fighting gravity as she walked out of the room, wanting to lean against the walls that seemed to be closing in on her. She had to get away. Pictures of Lisa, Steve, and the kids, and their extended family were hanging on the walls, in frames on the end tables and on the bookcases. She groped for the front door. She fell out into the fresh air and leaned against the porch railing, looking at the cloudless blue sky, the houses, and the lampposts. Children were playing. People were talking to each other on the sidewalks. The world continued to spin on, but Lisa's life was shattered into a million pieces, and it would never be the same. She put her hands on her hips and took deep breaths, almost gasping for air.

Frank came out and stood next to her, putting his arm around her shoulder.

"I keep thinking about Jacob, and now Steve. Jack could have been killed, and for that matter, you and Kathrine could have been also. You came out of it with a broken arm, and Jack was shot in the leg. Lisa said she knows how important our work is and how much Steve loved it, but is it worth it? Is it really worth it? We risk our lives. We're gone all the time from the people we love. The stress. I don't know anymore."

She searched his eyes, desperate for answers.

He withdrew his hand from her shoulder and rubbed his casted arm. "Is it worth it? What we do *is* dangerous, but what we do is worth the risks. Lives are saved, deaths are prevented, and the bad guys don't always get away with it. Are we the only ones who do this kind of work? Certainly not, but we're good at our jobs, better than most, and it's because of Jack, and Steve, and you. You've given us some tools through your computer skills that have saved our lives, and others' as well. Don't question the integrity of what you do because someone we love lost their life. Steve wouldn't want you to do that, or Jacob, and neither does Jack or any of the team. You're doubting yourself because you're mourning and afraid. Time will heal your mourning heart, and there are ways to help you not be afraid anymore."

"What do you mean?"

Frank smiled. "You'll see."

❖

Kathrine watched Lisa with her children. She watched her as she sat with them, comforting, holding them, putting aside her own grief to help them. She had always admired Lisa, but never more than today. She saw Rachel and Frank through the window. Rachel looked pale and vulnerable, as if falling apart before her eyes. She could understand it. How much could one person endure?

She'd gone to see Rachel in the hospital when they had brought her back from the Philippines, and then during the long weeks of recovery at home. They'd all been concerned about her, but none of the team more than Jack. He was in love with Rachel, but to his credit he never crossed the line, and he loved Claire and was a true friend to both of them.

She'd grown to love Rachel's spirit and determination to overcome and rise above the obstacles put in front of her. But she saw her vulnerability. Yumiko had devastated her physically but more so emotionally. Just as the physical beatings had left her scarred, the mental torture had also taken its toll. Yumiko was a monster masquerading as a human being who enjoyed destroying human life and dignity.

She observed Rachel more closely. Yes, she was physically healthy again. Strong-willed? Yes. But pile on what had happened to her, and to Claire, and what they went through, and she could clearly see Rachel's emotional and mental vulnerability put her at risk, whether she realized it or just didn't want to admit it. And that could be dangerous for Rachel and for each member of the team.

In that moment, looking at her through the window, Kathrine committed to be extra vigilant in watching over Rachel and standing by her. Rachel needed her help and her friendship, now more than ever. She would be her watch-guard until she didn't need it anymore, not just because she had earned it as a team member, but because she deserved it. Rachel had put her life at risk to complete the mission with MI6. She'd given all she had to that mission and to the team, and Kathrine would do no less for her. No hesitation. No regret.

CHAPTER TWELVE

Rachel took off her silk blouse and slipped it onto the hanger. Claire came into the bedroom and lay on the bed, looking at the ceiling. Rachel came over half dressed and lay beside her.

"Do you think Lisa is going to be okay?" Claire asked.

Rachel pondered the question. "It'll take time, but yes, I think she will. She seemed to do okay at the funeral today, and she and the kids are going back to St. George to stay with her parents for a while. She has a lot of family support."

Claire continued to look at the ceiling. She took Rachel's hand. "Life is over as she knew it. I know you don't want to talk about it, but what you all do is so dangerous. I know from experience. Don't forget I worked with the team when I used your enhanced program. I worked on that last job, and that last night in DC, when I left and went home, I swore I'd never do it again. I'm scared for you, Rachel."

Rachel could say nothing. She agreed with Claire. Danger came with the job, but she realized after talking with Frank on the porch that day that she wasn't upset about her job. It made her feel good about herself. Her work gave her purpose, meaning, and stability, and she excelled at it and wanted to do it. But she worried that something might happen to Claire. Yumiko lurked in the shadows out there somewhere, hovering, waiting, and she wouldn't go away.

"When we were at Lisa's house, I questioned myself and the work we do. I asked myself if it was worth it. I know it bothers you, but it's important because we help people who have no one else to turn to. I hope you can understand and accept it."

Claire kept staring at the ceiling. "I'm trying to." She sighed heavily again and made a circle with her finger and thumb, peering at the ceiling through it.

"Baby, what is it?"

"I hate this house."

"It's a rental. What would you like to do?"

Claire pushed herself onto her elbows, squinting as she scrutinized the room. "Let's build a new one or get one we really like and remodel it so we can make it our own. We have money. Let's spend some of it and get what we want."

Claire now thought long-term and wanted to build something stable. Her attitude indicated her readiness to move forward. "That's a fantastic idea. Where would you like to live?"

"I'd like you to get the hell out of the security business so we could move to Arizona, but that's not going to happen, so somewhere outside of Las Vegas, with lots of property and room for the horses."

"Horses? We board. Why would you want to keep them at home? They'd stink up the property. Flies would be everywhere, and every time we wanted to ride, other than in circles, we'd have to trailer them. It's more hassle than it's worth."

"We board at your cousin Joseph's on the reservation in Arizona, and that's hours away from here. We can't ride when we want. Don't you miss Ash?"

"Yes. I miss riding him, but I'm busy. I can't ride that often, and he's fine at Joseph's. He gets ridden, and maybe someday I'll release him and let him run wild."

Claire gasped and put her hand on her chest. "You wouldn't?"

Rachel laughed. "Maybe, someday."

"But you love Ash. How can you think of doing that? What would happen to Łichíí if you let Ash go? She'd die of loneliness for him."

"We could turn her loose with him. We could just take their shoes off, kiss them good-bye, and *let the horses run*." Rachel had a picture of Ash galloping wild, his long, dark mane flowing, his buckskin coat gleaming in the sun as he roamed the hills, rearing on a mountaintop, pawing at the fiery evening sky.

"Yeah, and two days later, some asshole would spot them, run them down and take them, or shoot them for sport. Or they'd die of dehydration or starvation because they wouldn't know how to make it on their own."

Rachel's picture turned to Ash lying on the ground with a gunshot in his neck, blood everywhere. "You're a buzz kill. You know that?"

Claire smiled. "I'm a realist. I want you to take some time off so we can go to the reservation. We can stay at our teepee. I need to be with you, and we need to be together, and I want to go riding before you *let the horses run.*"

Rachel laughed. "I'll call Joseph as soon as the weather is warmer and ask him to set up our teepee."

"Really. You'll do it?" Claire turned over and lay on her, hugging her.

"Yes. We need to get away."

"Do you think Ilesh will come visit us?"

"It depends on what he has going on at his gallery in Phoenix. When we're ready to go, call him and see. I'm sure he'll come visit if he can."

Claire kissed her. "Rachel, it will be so fun. Thank you." She kissed her again, lingering. "And maybe while we're there we can do some research and find a home or land we want to build on."

Rachel put her hand over Claire's breast and touched gently. "In Las Vegas, Claire. We already own land next to the reservation in Arizona, but we can't build on it, remember?"

Claire kissed her neck. "I'm sorry. That memory slipped away from me."

Rachel lightly kissed one breast and then the other. "It's all right, baby. I know."

"You wouldn't really let Ash go, would you?"

Rachel laughed. "No, not if it'll upset you, although I do think he deserves someone who spends way more time with him. When does our flight leave for Cleveland?"

"Eight tonight, and don't forget to pack your sweaters and your silver heels. Our evening gowns are already covered and ready to pack."

"What time does Tilly's show start tomorrow night?"

"I think it's nine. Sarah said the tickets will get us into the New Year's Eve party, the show, and the meal."

"Are you going to get drunk?"

She watched as Claire's grin grew into a full-on smile. "I'm going to get so plastered you'll have to carry me out."

Rachel laughed.

Claire didn't drink on the plane or at Sarah's but started with champagne as soon as they were seated at the club.

Rachel watched Ricky scoot Sarah's chair in and bend over and kiss her cheek as they joined them at the table. The waiter immediately came over and poured champagne into their glasses, then refilled Claire's and Kathrine's.

Tilly waved to the crowd after she performed her last song and then came to the table and sat beside Kathrine.

Claire leaned near Rachel's ear and put her hand over her mouth. "I think Tilly and Kathrine are sitting a little too close."

Rachel smiled and put her arm on the back of Claire's chair. "I think if you drink any more champagne, you won't be able to see either of them, let alone know how close they're sitting beside each other."

Claire tossed her head back and laughed. "You're probably right."

Rachel looked down the front of Claire's red sequined dress, which revealed just enough cleavage to keep her gaze and cause her to heat. She leaned closer, the scent of Claire's perfume filling her with thoughts of seduction and sex. "You look so beautiful tonight. Happy New Year."

Claire stroked Rachel's face. "You are gorgeous in that dress. Happy New Year to you." She kissed her, opening her lips slightly, probing with her warm, wet tongue.

The heat of their kiss seeped into Rachel's breasts and permeated downward, but she remembered where they were and stopped Claire, moving slightly away, looking at her and then around at the crowd. Two women and a man were staring at them from two tables over, frowning, with judgmental expressions.

"Easy, tiger," Rachel whispered. She'd been hyperaware of everyone around them, but she'd been trying to appear relaxed. She decided that the people watching were non-threats and turned away.

Claire laughed. "You're mine tonight."

Rachel blushed.

Tilly lifted her glass of champagne. "To a great year, full of laughter, good friends, and," she looked at Kathrine, "new adventures."

Claire lifted her glass and elbowed Rachel.

Rachel's glass of ginger ale splashed out onto the white tablecloth. She shook her head as the others laughed. She scanned the room again, catching sight of the back of a petite woman with long brown hair and light-brown skin. The hairs on the back of Rachel's neck stood up, and her stomach churned. Something about the way the woman walked slowly toward the far door was unsettling yet familiar. She stared at her until she blended into the crowd.

Claire leaned into her. "What's wrong?"

Rachel tensed her jaw. Thoughts of Yumiko surfaced, trying to claw their way out, but she forced them down. "Nothing. Are you ready to go back to the hotel?"

"What? This party's just getting started."

Rachel sighed slightly, holding back the disappointment so Claire wouldn't notice, not that she'd be able to in her condition. Kathrine smiled.

Sarah nudged her. "Is Claire all right?"

"She's fine. She's just had a lot to drink."

"A lot? That woman has put away more booze than she did at the Westfield party," Sarah said.

Tilly started laughing. "Oh yeah, the Westfield party."

Claire looked over at Tilly and then at Sarah. "I'll have you know I am not nearly as intoxicated as the Westfield party."

Tilly and Sarah laughed.

Sarah poked Rachel again. "She was so drunk she got lost coming back from the bathroom and yelled out across the room for me and Tilly."

Tilly slapped the table and roared. "And don't forget about the pâté."

Claire pouted.

Rachel stroked Claire's shoulder. "Be a good sport. I've never heard this story. Why don't I know this story?"

Claire traced her finger over the lip of her champagne flute. "I have to admit, I don't remember very much."

Sarah and Tilly laughed harder.

"Oh my gosh, she outdid herself that night," Tilly said.

Sarah touched Rachel's arm. "It happened over Easter weekend. You two had had a big fight about something."

"Rachel wouldn't go to bed with me." Claire spoke like she'd just ordered from the dinner menu.

Rachel's cheeks became warm. "I was married to Alex, and you were married to Richard."

"A huge mistake," Tilly said.

"Clearly," Claire said.

Sarah laughed. "Anywho, Claire and Richard, Tilly, her mom and dad, me, and Ricky were all at the Westfield party in Pepper Pike, and Claire and Richard got into a big argument. She threw a dish of pâté at him."

"Yeah. She picked up that dish and smacked him right in the kisser. Served the asshole right," Tilly said. "About time she did it." Tilly lifted her glass of champagne to Claire.

Claire smiled and toasted back.

"What did he do?" asked Kathrine.

Tilly laughed louder. "He started to walk toward the bathroom to clean himself, and I tripped him with my foot. He went flying into the next table. The host came over and wanted to know if he could help. Claire straightened herself and, with as much dignity as she could muster, said, 'Why, yes. You can. Please help my asshole husband. I believe he's on his way to a divorce.'"

Everyone started laughing.

Claire raised her glass and slipped her arm around Rachel's waist. "To finally standing up for yourself and getting what you want."

Everyone raised their glasses and drank.

Tilly raised her glass again to Rachel and sipped her champagne.

Rachel hesitantly searched the room. She couldn't get the dark-haired woman out of her mind. Could Yumiko be here? A ridiculous thought. Was paranoia setting in? She rubbed the back of her neck again.

Chapter Thirteen

Weeks had passed with no sign of Yumiko. Since they'd purchased a house and started the remodel, Claire seemed happier. Rachel slept better, and the nightmares weren't as frequent, but those fleeting feelings of foreboding wouldn't leave her.

She and Frank circled like two tigers ready to do battle.

"Don't take your eyes off me. Keep watching," Frank instructed her.

Rachel tried to watch his hands but became fixated on the skin of his recently un-casted scaly, dry arm.

He pointed to his eyes. "Remember. Watch my eyes. Always watch their eyes. They'll give it away at the last second."

She tried to concentrate on his eyes but noticed the way his upper lip formed into an almost snarl when he pronounced each *s*.

He came in with lightning speed, and it was instantly over. She found herself flat on her back, looking up at him as he smiled at her. He reached out and lifted her.

"You're not focusing, Rachel."

"I'm sorry. Let's try it again." She cracked her neck, bent her knees slightly, and raised her hands even with her waist.

"Now you've got it." He moved slowly around her, ready to attack.

He repositioned his hands and feet to distract her, but she managed to keep her focus. He stopped, stood straight, and looked over her shoulder. She turned to see what he was looking at, and he went in for the kill. He flipped her once again, but this time, when she landed, her mouth pressed into the sweaty, rubbery cushion. She spit out the taste and pushed herself up. "That's disgusting."

He swung his arm toward her, but she blocked and stepped back.

"No! Never retreat when you have the advantage. Go into them. Force your body to move them, using their momentum against them. Let it flow from your hips and the brunt of your hands. Never, never relinquish your advantage."

Rachel repositioned and saw the weakness in his stance. She went in with an eagle strike.

He blocked.

She countered with an elbow strike and then threw him.

He sailed into the air and came down hard, his face mashed into the cushioned support.

She bent over him and offered her hand to help him. "You like apples?"

He laughed, his voice muffled as he answered into the mat. "Yes."

"How do you like those apples?"

He laughed again as he stood. "Didn't that feel good?"

She smiled. It did feel good. The workout had been hard, but she was a little better, almost lighthearted.

"That's enough for today. You get any better, and Jack will want you to lead a team in the field."

She hesitated and looked down.

"Claire still has a problem with it?"

She nodded. "She's just scared."

"You need to get her in here and let her train. We'll take the fear out of her and make her wish she could walk down a dark alley so some big, obnoxious, drunken sailor could attack her."

She grimaced. "I don't want her in here. One wrong blow to her head, and she'd be back in the hospital."

"Rachel, she's healed, and that plate in her head is protecting her beyond anything her skull could ever do. She's tougher than you think she is. Don't be such a wife. I promise, you get her in here and let Beth, Kathrine, and me work with her, and she'll surprise you. With her exceptional visual acuity, she could read body movement before someone even realized what they were going to do."

"She's had enough of security work. The last case in DC did her in. You know, the one we found out Yumiko had her hand in? She's content to stick to her pottery doing special orders now. Ilesh offered to show her work at his studio in Phoenix. Now she's got it into her head we should move to Arizona. If I tell her Yumiko is back in the picture, that would be all it would take for her to drag me out of here, new house or not."

"You and Claire paid for this gym setup. It has everything we could ever need or want to work out, build up, and practice. It's state-of-the-art, and she should be in here, taking advantage of it." Frank looked around the room. "This was more than generous of you and Claire. I love coming in here whenever I have time."

Rachel also looked around at the exercise equipment, running track, and ring. "It is nice, but I don't want Claire in the ring." The possibility of a relapse made her skin crawl. She didn't care what Frank or the doctors or anyone else thought. But, with Yumiko out in the world now, maybe Claire having some solid self-defense training would help protect her.

"Do you really think she'd be safe boxing, Frank?"

"Absolutely. It's a great skill to learn. It'll build her up, help her coordination, and I know whoever sparred with her would be careful. I'd be happy to work with her on some self-defense." He rubbed his arm. "The dry skin on my arm from having that cast on so long is disgusting."

"Try some tanning lotion. It works better than oil."

Self-defense? It wouldn't hurt Claire. How could she protect herself if Yumiko did come after her? Would Yumiko come after her? Rachel drew in a deep breath, unable to release the heaviness from her heart. Their meeting again seemed inevitable.

Chapter Fourteen

Yumiko's private jet touched down on the runway of Palawan Island, Philippines. The Gulfstream's door swung open, and the steps unfolded. The sun's reflection bounced off the silver metal of the jet as she stepped out from the hatch. Her cousin Danilo stood by the waiting Jeep, smiling slightly, arms folded in front of him. She walked down the steps.

He hugged her. "You must not look so disturbed, cousin."

"I'll feel better when we open the bottle of tequila I brought from California and discuss why I'm here. Let's go to the beach house."

He nodded as they got into his Jeep. "It has been too long."

Of all her relatives, Yumiko trusted Danilo the most. She had purposely not involved him in her business affairs to keep his perspective as her trusted advisor.

Once she'd dropped off her things, they walked from the house to the edge of the white, pristine beach, the aqua-green water changing to a deeper blue farther offshore. Her family owned two miles of this side of the island. No one dared come close for fear of reprisal. The surf was calm, almost tranquil, as if greeting Yumiko. She stood quietly, looking out at the panoramic view, the surf, the ocean, the rich, green, forested, rugged mountain ranges off to her left. The rhythmic waves of the surf swirled over her bare feet. She dug her toes into the sand and breathed deeply. Her shoulders relaxed. She arched her back, feeling her skin absorb the sun's gift. Nothing could compare to the peace of this island. She'd spent every summer here in her youth—swimming, scuba diving, playing on the beach, climbing the mountains, exploring the jungles. Nothing bad happened to her here—only good.

Danilo stood quietly beside her. She could see her reflection in his sunglasses. He moved his feet in the surf, then bent and cupped water in his hand. He held his hand up and let the water run down his arm. "We sometimes think we can control it, but we can't. Come. Let's drink." They walked back to the beach house. Yumiko pulled the bottle of tequila from her suitcase while Danilo cut the lemons. They took the alcohol, the bowl of lemon wedges, and a salt shaker out to the wooden table beside the house.

She opened the bottle of tequila and poured a small amount onto the ground. "*Alay sa demonyo*," she said solemnly.

"An offering to the spirits. Americans have no idea how to drink. Pigs," Danilo said.

Sitting in one of the wooden chairs, she licked the back of her hand, poured salt onto it, licked the salt, took a swig of the tequila, then bit into a juicy wedge of lemon, her throat still burning. The juice squirted out the corners of her mouth and ran down her chin. She swallowed loudly and passed the bottle to Danilo as she threw the half-eaten wedge of lemon beside the bowl on the table. Danilo repeated the ritual.

Eight lemon wedges later, Yumiko finally spoke. "I have to get rid of Alon. He's never been loyal to me. He questions everything I do, and I think he's vying for control by turning my leadership against me. He has to go."

Danilo looked up into the sky, now filled with small white puffs of clouds. "If you mean to get rid of him, you'll have to clean house."

Yumiko took another large swig of the tequila but didn't bother with the salt or lemon wedge. She passed the bottle back to Danilo. "What do you mean?"

"Too many of your leaders are leftovers from your stepfather. They are a split force and half loyal to you. They stand with one foot in the surf and the other on the shore. They constantly move to keep their position. Most of them have heard you gave your stepfather up to MI6. You'll have to take them all out at once, or you'll lose your power and the element of surprise." He lifted the bottle and took a long drink, then passed it back to her.

"How many?" she asked, following his lead. Her head began to spin, and her vision started to blur. She held the bottle against her thigh.

"Including Alon, six out of the eight leaders. Agapito and Crisanto are totally loyal to you and have been since you were twelve. They know what your stepfather did to you and hated him for it."

She blanched. Six out of eight. Worse than she'd feared. "I don't want it messy. I hate that."

"Then the only option is poison."

"How?"

"In two weeks at your leadership meeting. Take the cobra's antidote and give it to Agapito and Crisanto before the meeting. Make sure it's at least thirty minutes before you offer the toast of alcohol at the meeting. You will have to be confined, but all three of you will live. Your strength will return, and you will be back to normal within a week or so. Then you can replace the leadership with people loyal to you."

She took a drink and passed the bottle to Danilo, signaling she was finished.

He took a final drink.

She would do it. Yes. She would get rid of them. Reset her leadership. Get her life back on course. But what about Portola? How much longer should she wait? She had left the compound in California just in time. At least one of them had been killed, although not Jack Ralston. She should have killed him while she had the opportunity. She dismissed the thought. He didn't matter anymore. What about Brice Chambers from MI6? He mattered. And Portola mattered. But she could wait a little longer. First Alon and her unfaithful leadership, then reorganize and get operations back on track. Then Portola.

She would play and tease first. The titillation of the thought of it surged between her legs. She shifted in her seat. Tilly Evans would be an easy target. Brice Chambers would be more difficult, but not impossible. Planning, timing, and patience were the keys. They would bring her what she wanted. They always did.

CHAPTER FIFTEEN

Claire heard the air conditioner kick on as she reached for the hot mug of freshly brewed coffee Olivia had made her, its rich, delicious scent permeating the dining room, wafting into her nose. Her mouth watered, and her stomach growled in anticipation of the first sip.

She sat engrossed in sipping the brew and inspecting the house plans spread out all over the dining-room table. Their six-thousand-square-foot home, southwest of downtown, was far enough away to get out of the city and yet close enough for Rachel to not have to drive a long distance for work. Claire fell in love with it the first time she saw it.

The stone house had a six-car garage, six bedrooms, formal dining room and living room with a fireplace, cathedral ceilings with matching windows to bring in the light, an entertainment room with a raised stage, and a heated pool with a sauna. The remodel involved the kitchen, a room for Rachel's office, a pottery studio for Claire, and of course, an upgraded security system that Rachel insisted on. The back of the house had to be re-landscaped, and some minor repairs to the wall and patio were necessary, but the contractor assured them all the remodeling would take no more than a few weeks. It had a magnificent view of the natural landscape from the vaulted windows and was a perfect fit for her and Rachel. The house came with twenty acres, but they also purchased an adjoining sixty. Claire didn't care how much money they spent on the property or the remodel of the house as long as she got what she wanted, except Rachel wouldn't budge about bringing the horses home. She insisted the barn would draw flies and cause a stench, even if they did hire someone to take care of it.

Olivia entered the room wiping her hands on her apron, her

peppered-gray hair tucked neatly behind her ears. Claire smiled when she saw a smudge of flour on her cheek.

"Ms. Claire, would you like some breakfast?"

"Did Rachel eat breakfast before she left for the shed?"

Olivia nodded.

Claire remembered kissing Rachel good-bye, but she'd been so engrossed in the house plans she couldn't remember what time Rachel had left.

"Breakfast, Ms. Claire?" Olivia's smile highlighted the rich-brown color of her eyes.

"Just a bagel or something. Thank you."

Olivia went back into the kitchen.

Claire had needed to go to the shed the day before to track Rachel down to show her the change in the redesign of the kitchen. Rachel looked exhausted. Claire had taken her lunch, but Rachel ate only a few bites. Never a good thing because she stopped eating when her stress level reached overload, and then the weight loss would start. Claire tried to get her to talk, but Rachel seemed preoccupied with something other than work. It concerned her. She needed to get Rachel away so she could relax, and hopefully she'd talk about whatever was bothering her. She wished Rachel would be more excited about the house so they could share the experience, but for now she'd carry the responsibility until Rachel worked through whatever weighed so heavy on her mind.

She put her finger on the redesigned kitchen wall. "Olivia, did you say you wanted the stove on the outside wall or the inside wall?"

Olivia brought her food in and freshened her coffee. She set the carafe on the table as she reviewed the plans. "It's perfect just the way you have it."

Claire reviewed the plans for a little while longer, then took her coffee and went into the kitchen and sat at the bar, watching Olivia as she skillfully unrolled freshly made noodles and laid them out on the counter to dry.

"Are you happy here, Olivia?"

"Of course, Ms. Claire. Why do you ask?"

"You aren't uncomfortable with Rachel and me, are you?"

Olivia washed and wiped her care-worn hands, probably from years of washing dishes, preparing food, and cleaning. She went to the coffeemaker, poured herself a cup of coffee, and brought it to the bar.

"Ms. Claire, you and Ms. Rachel worry too much about that. I've worked for several families over the years, and you and Ms. Rachel are wonderful to me. I love the way you two are with each other. I can see how much you love and respect one another."

"Have you noticed a change in Rachel lately?" Claire watched her closely. Olivia had a sense for Rachel and a special closeness with her. Olivia had been with them for almost two years, at their first house in Mt. Charleston, when they were married, and when Claire was shot. Olivia had been beside Rachel and helped her get through the long, difficult months of Claire's recovery.

"She looks tired, and she's working long hours."

Claire nodded. "Yes. She does look tired. She didn't eat much yesterday when I took her lunch. I think she's worried about something."

"Perhaps about the house?"

"No. I don't think that's it. I need to get her away for a while. She needs a break."

"That would be good for both of you."

Tilly's picture appeared on Claire's cell phone, and her song came on.

"Hey, Tilly. Did you know a gas range is better for cooking than an electric one?"

"Claire, I could give a shit."

"Wow! What's wrong with you?"

"What's wrong? I'll tell you what's wrong. Some sonofabitch came into my dressing room yesterday while I was at rehearsal and cut up my new gown, and on top of that, when I went out to the car, the damn passenger window was smashed in. Who the hell would do something like that?"

"I'm sorry, Tilly." Claire left the kitchen and went out and sat by the small flower garden, trying to focus her full attention on Tilly.

"I can't believe it. It's not right. If I claim it on my insurance, my rates will increase, plus I have a thousand-dollar deductible, so either way I'm screwed."

"Oh, you can afford it."

"That's not the point, Claire."

"I'm sorry. You're right." Claire stood and began to pace. "Do you think it was personal?"

"It seems like it. No one else had anything taken or damaged."

"Did you call the police?"

"Yes, of course I called the police. I filled out a bunch of forms so they could tell me they'll investigate, and then let me know in a month or two that they couldn't find out who did it."

"Wow, that's kind of negative. Surely some cameras picked up something."

"Are you kidding? What cameras? This dump is doing good to keep the electricity on while we perform."

"I'm sorry, Till."

"It's probably my fault for taking this gig in the first place. I'm just sick of it, Claire. I'm sick of the traveling and the one- or two-night shows. I need some substantial gigs."

"You sound so tired, Till."

"I am. I feel violated. Now I'm not sleeping. I keep worrying if it will happen again."

Claire stopped pacing and stared off into the roses, trying to think of some way to help. "Why don't you schedule in a vacation and come out here for a few days? It'll be good for you."

"I can't, not for a while, but thanks for the offer. I have to go. I'm due at rehearsal."

"Till, please be extra careful."

"I will."

Claire went back into the kitchen and sat at the bar, staring at her cup of coffee. Had Tilly been targeted or merely a victim of a random act of violence? If she'd been targeted, who had done it and why? Just when she'd begun to feel like life could be somewhat normal, something seemed to always come along to remind her of the vicious people in the world and that danger waited just around the corner.

CHAPTER SIXTEEN

Rachel slid the shower door open. The steam from her extra-long shower billowed out, immediately fogging the mirror. She dried and slipped into her silk pajamas and made her way to the bed. She lay still, breathing deeply and staring at the small crack in the corner of the ceiling. They'd moved into the rented house when the hospital released Claire after her surgery. It harbored too many bad memories now. They both needed a new start. Thankfully, Claire had taken charge of overseeing the remodel of the new house. She didn't have the energy or the inclination to do it, and Claire needed something fun to occupy her time. She moved her hands to the back of her head and locked her fingers together, pressing her shoulders into the mattress, scooting back and forth, trying to soothe the ache.

Claire came in, changed into her night clothes, and got into bed. Rachel put her arm around her, feeling the welcome, familiar warmth and curves of Claire next to her.

"I'm sorry I've been so preoccupied with work. Jack's taken on two new cases, and my workload has tripled because of it. Working without Steve these last few months has been hard. We all miss him. He did so much." Rachel sighed and kept her eyes on the ceiling.

Claire put her arm over her waist. "Is that what's been bothering you so much?"

Rachel couldn't bring herself to talk about Yumiko. Only the day before she'd had the sensation of being watched. No matter where she'd looked, she couldn't spot anyone, but still she couldn't shake the feeling. Could it be Yumiko or just an overly sensitive imagination? The weariness began to inch its way up into her shoulders again. "I talked with Lisa today. She and the kids went back to St. George. It sounds like they may move there."

Claire scooted closer to her. "I'm sure it's comforting being with her family."

Rachel rolled over, turned off the bedroom lamp, and yawned. "I've got the energy of a sloth."

"Tilly called today. Someone got into her dressing room and cut up one of her gowns and smashed her car window."

"Really? That's horrible. Did she call the police?"

"Yes, but she's not very hopeful they'll find out who did it."

"Does she have insurance?"

"Yes, but she's upset."

"I can understand why." As Rachel thought more about what Claire had told her, a wave of foreboding washed over her yet again. A coincidence? Could it possibly be Yumiko, or just something that happened in a big city like Cleveland? Weariness and fatigue burrowed their way in. *Is she lurking somewhere in the shadows?* She needed to stop thinking about it. She would create more stress if she mentioned her name to Claire. But she did need to pay more attention to her surroundings.

"Rachel, did you know Kathrine has been talking with Tilly a lot?"

"I figured."

"No. I mean a lot."

Rachel turned on the lamp, rolled over toward Claire, and leaned on her elbow, looking at her. "What are you telling me?"

"I don't know. I've thought about it, and yesterday when I came to the shed to see you, I saw Kathrine scrolling her calls. It had four calls from Tilly on it, and at the beginning of the week, I walked past Kathrine's cubicle and happened to look in and noticed some things on her calendar about Tilly."

"What kind of things?"

"I saw it for only a second."

"Don't give me that. I know what you see in a second. What did you see?"

Claire's eyes widened. "Her entire calendar for the month. She's going to meet Tilly in Chicago in two weeks. Her plane arrives at O'Hare at four in the afternoon, and she's staying at Pennington Plaza. Rachel, you don't think Kathrine and Tilly are, you know, doing it?"

"If they are, it's none of our business. I assume Kathrine likes her, or she wouldn't have flown to Cleveland for the New Year's Eve party."

Rachel rolled back over in the bed, fluffed her pillow, and turned out the light. She was exhausted and simply wanted to sleep.

"I think Tilly and Kathrine are going to hook up."

Rachel turned on the light again and rolled back over, looking at her. "I'm telling you, if they are, it's none of our business."

"I know. I just worry that one of them will get her heart broken. They're both very lonely and have a hard time with relationships."

"Maybe they're just getting really close and developing a good friendship." Rachel rolled over and turned off the light again, fluffing her pillow once more, waiting for Claire to say something else.

"But—"

"I'm telling you, you should stay out of Tilly's business, and for that matter, Kathrine's also. Tilly has always been very supportive of you and me, and if she and Kathrine get involved, we should support them."

"It's not like you and me. It's more like they're just hooking up because they're lonely, and one of them is going to get hurt. I've really grown fond of Kathrine, and I don't want that to happen to either of them. Tilly sounded exhausted and was genuinely upset today. Would you mind if I went with Sarah to Chicago for a couple of days to support Tilly at the club? I think she needs us."

"Is it good timing, with her meeting Kathrine there?"

"I don't know. I just think Tilly is really vulnerable right now."

"I'd rather you not, but if you do go, I want you to be extra careful."

"Why?"

Rachel grew more apprehensive. Should she tell her the real reason she didn't want her to be away from her? Was her concern about Yumiko legitimate? Her stomach knotted, and she rubbed the back of her neck. "Because it's Chicago. Are you going to fly in and meet Sarah there?"

"I don't know yet. Wouldn't it be fun if Tilly ended up with Kathrine, though? I mean, if they really did fall for each other and not just have a fling." Claire sighed deeply.

"If Tilly and Kathrine do have feelings for each other, if they can find happiness in each other for a little while, I'll be happy for them. Good night, baby. Sleep well. Love you." Rachel closed her eyes.

"If Tilly hooks up with Kathrine and doesn't tell me about it, I'm going to be so mad."

Rachel smiled. "Why?"

"*Why?* Because that will be the most significant thing Tilly's ever done. And not to share it with me and Sarah? We're her best friends." Claire moved closer to Rachel. "And I'm worried about you. Is there something you want to talk about?"

Rachel took Claire's hand and put it around her waist and held on. "I'm okay. It's just been a hard couple of months."

Should she tell Claire? Should she talk about Yumiko or just let it go? By keeping Claire in the dark about the possibility of Yumiko being around, she might be putting her in danger. But, if her imagination and instincts were wrong, she'd be upsetting Claire for no reason. She punched the pillow and closed her eyes, weary from worry.

CHAPTER SEVENTEEN

Claire pursed her lips and adjusted the earbuds. "I don't want to fly to Chicago and meet you there, Sarah. I'll fly to Cleveland, and then we can drive. We'll have more time to visit." She poured herself a cup of coffee.

"Are you nuts? Chicago is a five-hour drive from Cleveland. I'm not driving five hours when I could fly there in an hour from here. We can visit in Chicago."

Claire set the cup on the counter. "Come on, Sarah. Lighten up. Let's have some fun. It really isn't that much longer to drive. It's at least three hours to fly by the time you get to the airport, check in, go through security, and do the same thing on the return flight. And you know how Cleveland Hopkins airport is. There are always delays."

"I like fun. I just don't think fun is driving in a car for five hours when I could meet you there."

Claire laughed.

"Are you sure you want to do this? Maybe a surprise visit isn't the best idea."

"After talking with Tilly when she had the incident at the club, I think she needs us there, whether she wants to admit it or not. She seemed really upset, Sarah."

"She's dealing with it. Do you know how long Kathrine's going to be with her?"

"It looked like she'd blocked out the long weekend, so probably more than a day."

"Maybe we should call Tilly and ask her if she wants us there?"

"Honestly, I think we should just go. And if we get there and it doesn't feel right, we can hang out at the Field Museum or go shopping." Sarah was probably right. They should call first. But half the time Tilly didn't always say what she wanted, and the other half she didn't know what she wanted. And Claire needed this, maybe more than Tilly did. Life seemed so confusing and complex, and she wanted something simple and fun. What could be more fun than being with your best friends on a road trip?

"Claire, do you realize how much you've changed since the accident?"

She took a sip of her coffee. "I haven't changed. Things have just become...clearer." She laughed as Sarah let out a long, audible sigh. "I think my relationships with my family and friends should take priority in my life. Making memories is everything. You ought to try not having any."

"I can't imagine what you went through. All right. We'll drive, but I don't want to stay more than two nights in Chicago. And we're renting a car because I don't want to put that many miles on ours. And you're paying for the rental. And you're driving."

"Okay, bossy."

"What are we going to do when we see them at the hotel? Walk up and say hello?"

"We should just walk up, say hello, and invite them out to dinner. It'll be fun."

"Honestly, Claire. I don't know you anymore. But okay, if you're this bent on doing it, fine."

Claire had wanted more than that lackluster agreement, but it would have to be enough. When she ended the call, she sat on a kitchen bar stool and sipped her coffee, thinking about what Sarah had said. Had she changed that much, or was she just unwilling to hold back her feelings anymore? One thing was clear in her mind. Those she loved were important to her, and she refused to miss an opportunity to show them how much they meant to her. She wanted to make new memories and hold on to them. She'd made a good, positive decision—taking charge instead of waiting around for something to happen.

Olivia came into the kitchen. Claire wanted to ask her if she thought she'd changed, but Olivia hadn't known her that well before the accident. The only other people who could give her a fair assessment were Rachel, Tilly, and Sarah.

She called Rachel.

"Hey, babe. What are you doing?" Rachel asked.

"Am I interrupting anything?"

"I'm in between a meeting with Kathrine and Frank. What's up?"

Claire hesitated. She didn't want to sound whiny, but now she worried that she might be going over the edge. "Rachel, do you think I've changed much since the accident?"

The silence at the other end could mean one of two things. Either Rachel didn't want to answer, or she was stalling for time. Stalling wasn't good, because it took time to formulate her answer, which also meant she thought deeply about the question, which meant she *had* changed, and Rachel was trying to find a way to tell her. "It's not a test question. You won't be graded." Actually, Rachel would be, and she knew Rachel knew it.

"What's going on?"

"I just talked to Sarah, and she said I've changed since the accident. Do you think so?"

"You sure you don't want to save this conversation for when I get home and we can curl up on the couch and discuss it?"

"Just tell me. Do you think I've changed?"

"Yes. I do."

Honest. Direct. "How?"

"Well, for one thing you're much more open in expressing how you feel."

"Is that your way of saying I'm a bitch?"

Rachel laughed. "Absolutely not. It's great during sex. And now you can see better than anyone I've ever heard of, and your coordination has vastly increased. Your confidence has also increased, and you want to try new things."

Nothing negative. She took a deep breath.

"Hey, babe. Those are all good things."

"So, you don't think I'm over the edge on some things?"

"No. Not any more than you were before."

Claire cringed.

"You're as stubborn as you always were, and you still throw a fit sometimes when you don't get your own way. Do you want me to give examples?"

Claire laughed. "No. I do not."

A conversation buzzed in the background. "I've got to go. Love you," Rachel said.

"Love you back."

She did feel like she'd changed. She wanted to change, to be a better person. As hard as the injury had been to overcome, and all the struggle she went through, it had ended well. And it had done so because of Rachel. A particular memory lingered, seeming to surround and engulf her. Their first kiss at the lake in Alaska. They had bathed in the lake under the stars that filled the sky that night. She'd dried off and put on her clothes. She turned to find Rachel looking at her, almost in tears. She wrapped her arms around her and tried to get her to talk to her, but she knew before Rachel said anything. They both felt it. They were so in love, and neither of them could face it. That kiss. Warm, and soft, and wet, probing, and deep. It penetrated every part of her.

The emotion of the memory swelled. She coughed, embarrassed at how quickly the tears came. She cherished every memory once lost and now returned. She tried to rein in her emotions.

Lately, every memory of Rachel brought intense feelings, perhaps because she had experienced the loss of her memories and the void of emotion it caused. She flashed back to when she couldn't remember anything about their marriage. The frustration and anxiety, knowing she needed to remember something but couldn't recall. Sometimes Rachel would look at her, and she'd see the longing and love in her eyes but feel the emptiness and space between them. It had all changed when she recovered her memories, which brought warmth and intense emotion, and passion and yearning.

Yet Rachel seemed so distracted and tired lately. Claire took a deep breath and straightened her shoulders. Forward. The only way.

CHAPTER EIGHTEEN

Sarah kept waving to the left, looking at the map and then back at the freeway signs. "I don't care what the app says. Get in the far left-hand lane, or we'll miss the entrance to the westbound one *again*. Get over, Claire."

Claire didn't change. "The program says stay in your lane."

"Damn it. We missed it again." Sarah slapped her hand on her thigh. "Get off at the next exit and turn around *again*."

"I think someone's following us." Claire glanced in the rearview mirror. "We've gotten off twice and turned around, and every time that silver SUV back there has been two cars behind us."

"How in the hell can you tell? It's rush-hour traffic in downtown Chicago, and thanks to you, we've been on the bypass twice now." Sarah rubbed her face. "I have to pee."

"Bitch, bitch, bitch." Claire watched in the rearview again. "We have to stop and get gas. You can pee then. I'm telling you, Sarah, we're being followed."

"Well, maybe it's Kathrine and Tilly."

Claire bit her lip and gripped the steering wheel tighter. "Seriously. It's a guy with blond, curly hair in his mid-forties."

Sarah put her hands between her knees and pressed her legs together. "Sure. Hurry up and find a gas station."

Claire pulled into a mini-mart gas station and drove to the middle aisle of the gas pumps.

Sarah opened the door and quickly slid out, bending down and poking her head back in. "Do you want anything?"

Claire shook her head as she got out of the car and slipped her coat back on, shivering. She inserted her credit card and began pumping the gas, glancing into the side mirror. A silver SUV pulled in. She started to stare but forced herself to turn around and watch the car through the side mirror. The first three numbers on the license plate were the same. The same car. The same guy, wearing sunglasses. She finished pumping the gas, took the receipt, and hurried back into the car, watching as she adjusted the side mirror for a better view of the man, now looking her way.

Sarah opened the car door, and Claire jumped, letting out a half yelp.

"What is wrong with you?" Sarah laughed as she slid back into the passenger seat, closed the car door, and started opening a small bag of potato chips. Claire pulled into a parking space in front of the store and put the car in park. Sarah placed the open bag of chips on the dash and looked at her. "Are you all right? You're as white as Mr. DeAngelo."

Claire tried not to laugh. "Oh my gosh, Sarah. Don't bring up Mr. DeAngelo. We were ten years old. Stop it. This is serious."

"Well, it was pretty serious for old man DeAngelo. What was he, a hundred and four when he kicked off? It's a good thing we were cutting through his backyard that night and found him, or he'd probably still be in that rocker on his back porch."

Claire slapped her arm. "Sarah, stop. I'm not kidding. I want you to look at your lap and don't look up. Whatever you do, don't look up."

"Oh...kay." Sarah looked down.

"We're being followed, and the man is behind us and to my left, parked in a silver SUV."

Sarah started to look up, but Claire stopped her. "Don't!"

"How do you know he's following us? It could be anyone."

"I saw what he looked like and part of the license-plate number when we were driving, and I'm telling you, he's right over there." She held her hand close to her lap and pointed her finger toward her left.

Sarah put her hand to her mouth. "What are we going to do?"

Claire quickly reviewed their options. They weren't that far from where they needed to be. "We need to get to Kathrine as soon as possible."

"Should we call Rachel?"

"No, no! We're not going to use the cell phones." She'd never admit she didn't want Rachel to know anything, especially if they had a problem when she hadn't been thrilled Claire took this trip. And Rachel had drilled it into her head that you don't use your cell phone unless you're sure it's secure, and neither of theirs was.

They reviewed the directions to the hotel, making sure they wouldn't get lost again, then pulled out of the gas station and drove directly to the hotel where Tilly and Kathrine were supposed to be. Claire watched behind her as much as possible but didn't see the silver SUV.

They went to the registration desk and asked if Kathrine Henderson or Trish O'Connell had checked in. Tilly always used *Trish O'Connell* to keep the overly curious away when she stayed in hotels. She once had a fanatic fan try to climb in through the balcony.

A tall, thin man with a crop of dark hair, which stuck out like a Chia Pet, peered at her over his half glasses. Fredrick, the assistant manager, according to his name tag, looked like Vincent Schiavelli from *Ghost*. He cleared his throat and, in a singsong voice, dragging out the syllables like they were gifts from above, said, "I am sorry. We can't give out that information."

Claire stared back at him. "Okay, well, we need to check in." She gave him her credit card and information, then reached into her purse and pulled out a crisp twenty-dollar bill and handed it to him. "Has either Trish O'Connell or Kathrine Henderson checked in?" she asked again.

He promptly took the money and returned to the computer screen. "I'm sorry, ma'am. No one by either of those names has checked in yet." He wrote something on a slip of paper and handed it over. "Sorry I couldn't help you."

She glanced at the room number written on the paper and smiled wryly. "Thank you."

Claire called Kathrine's cell phone as soon they got into their room. She answered on the second ring.

"Kathrine, where are you?"

"Hey, Claire. I'm out of town. Why?"

"Would you happen to be in Chicago at the Pennington Plaza," Claire looked at the hotel number *Vincent* had given her, "in suite 802?"

Dead silence at the other end of the phone for a few seconds. "Yes. Why?"

Claire took a quick breath and nodded to Sarah, who sat on the bed. "Sarah and I are here. Can you come to our suite, room 916, right away?" What was supposed to be a fun surprise had turned into something strange, and she began to regret her decision.

"I'll be right there."

A few minutes later, hearing a knock on the door, Claire peeked through the security opening to make sure it was Kathrine. When she unbolted the door, Kathrine stepped in and touched Claire's arm, looking over at Sarah and then around the room.

"What on earth are you two doing here?" She followed Claire into the room and sat on the sofa.

Sarah came over, and she and Claire sat near her.

"It's a long story, but is Tilly with you?" Claire asked.

Kathrine looked at Claire and then at Sarah, then back to Claire, shaking her head slowly. "Don't tell me. You didn't?"

"We're so sorry. It was wrong of us. We thought it would be fun to surprise Tilly since she's been so upset about what happened, but it's not so much fun anymore," Sarah said.

Kathrine flushed pink, hopefully from embarrassment and not anger. "I guess the joke's on you two, because Tilly isn't here. Her gig got canceled, and she backed out, so I decided to come for a couple of days anyway for some me time."

Claire put her hand on Kathrine's arm. "Sarah's right, Kathrine. It wasn't one of our best ideas, and we're truly sorry if it made you uncomfortable, but we're in trouble, and I don't know what to do."

Kathrine leaned closer. "What kind of trouble? It seems to follow you. You two want to go down to the bar for a drink? I need a drink."

Claire immediately grabbed Kathrine's arm. "No. Not the bar."

Kathrine's brow arched and her eyes widened.

Sarah went to the wet bar and pulled out two small bottles of bourbon. She grabbed three glasses and carried the alcohol to the coffee table and set the glasses down, handing the bottles to Kathrine.

Kathrine opened them and divided the liquor into the glasses, then drank hers straight down and took a deep breath. "Okay. What's this about?"

"We're being followed," Claire said.

"What makes you think that?"

Claire explained what she saw.

"You got that good of a look, Claire?"

"Yes."

"Are you positive?"

"Yes. I'm sure."

"How long do you think he's been following you?"

"No clue. I noticed him when we got into downtown Chicago and got lost."

"Well, we need to confirm it."

She told them her plan and what they needed to do, then left the room.

Thirty minutes later Sarah and Claire were sitting in the restaurant, drinks and food in front of them. They were barely able to eat the meal, purposely not looking at Kathrine in a corner booth as she surveyed the room. They stayed one hour in the restaurant as instructed, managing to make small talk and trying to look natural while drinking more than eating, then went back to their room.

"Aren't you nervous, Sarah?" asked Claire.

"Yes."

"You don't look it."

"That's because of the alcohol."

Claire paced and anxiously waited for Kathrine.

Kathrine arrived thirty minutes later. "If you were being followed, you aren't now. I didn't see anyone that fit your description, and I didn't see any silver SUVs out in the parking lot with the partial license number you gave me. Are you sure you were followed?"

Claire flushed as the embarrassment spread across her face. "I'm almost positive."

"Well, unfortunately, I don't know any good reasons why you would be. I need to call Jack and Rachel, and you two need to be on the next plane out of here in the morning."

"Oh, no! You can't call Rachel. She'll have a fit. She didn't want me to do this, and I don't want her to worry and never let me out of the house again."

"Claire, I have to call one of them."

"Please, don't call Rachel."

Kathrine watched her for a few seconds. "Okay. I won't, but I need to talk with Jack right now." She called Jack, then put the phone on speaker and set it on the table in front of the sofa.

"How sure are you, Claire?" asked Jack.

"I'm almost positive we were followed, but maybe I mistook it. But…no. We got lost and turned around twice, and he was still behind us both times. That's not a coincidence. I'm begging you, please don't tell Rachel. She's had enough stress."

"Claire, I need to. If you or I kept it from her, she'd be upset. Do you want to call her, or do you want me to tell her?" asked Jack.

"Damn it. Would you mind? I just don't think I can do it right now."

"I'll do it. I'm sorry, but she needs to know." Jack ended the call.

Claire stood and paced. It was cowardly and immature not to tell Rachel. But she never liked to admit being wrong. Another thing that hadn't changed. Now she had increased Rachel's stress level. Again, she felt like she lacked control, but she shoved the sensation away.

CHAPTER NINETEEN

Rachel pressed back into her office chair. The tension crawled into her spine and settled into her neck and shoulders, digging in like a cat climbing a tree. And the headache that had started at the base of her skull the moment Jack told her what had happened to Claire began to pound like a jackhammer. She avoided eye contact, not saying anything, wanting to tell him to get the hell out of her office so she could call Claire.

"Don't be upset with her. She begged me not to tell you."

"It doesn't make me feel any better that she intended to keep it from me."

"She worried about upsetting you."

This incident struck too close to what had happened to Tilly to ignore. Were they connected? "I want Claire under security. I don't care if she gets mad or throws a fit. If they followed her, that means they've been watching her. Yumiko's a psychopath, and all of us had better get ready."

Jack raised his hand. "Stop, Rachel. For God's sake, stop just a minute. Don't you think that's a little over the top? You have absolutely no proof it's Yumiko. They were two women alone with out-of-state license plates. Someone could have targeted them for those reasons."

She moved forward in her chair and placed her hands on her desk, clasping them tightly together. "Jack, I know this woman. You have no idea what she's capable of."

"I disagree. Don't forget I've had some experience with her, and I do know how she operates."

"Operates? She doesn't *operate*, Jack. She enjoys what she does. It's her life. And I've had a big part in destroying it. Maybe it isn't her, but I'm not willing to take that chance, not when it comes to

Claire. Yumiko is too dangerous." She moved her hands to the arms of the chair and gripped until her knuckles were white. "No. You don't understand her. You think you do, but you don't. I'm telling you, don't underestimate her."

He shook his head and pushed himself out of the chair. "I do understand. Yes, it could be her, but it's only a slight probability. You're jumping the gun on this, but it's your call, and we'll back you all the way. Just think it through and act, don't react."

She swiveled her chair toward the door as he left. "You don't know her, Jack. I won't take the risk if there's even a slight chance. Yumiko is too dangerous."

Her hand trembled as she called Claire.

"Rachel, I'm so sorry. You were right. It was a bad idea." Claire sounded breathless and scared.

"I don't care about any of that now. Is Kathrine with you?"

"I know you're mad. I can tell by your tone."

"I'm not. Is Kathrine with you?"

"She's in her hotel room. She'll be back in a little while. Are you sure you aren't mad?"

"No, I'm not, but I'm a little disappointed you didn't call me right away. And I'm concerned you didn't feel you could tell me yourself."

"I just didn't want to give you any more stress, and I thought Jack telling you might help. I don't know why. It was silly, I guess."

"Don't worry about it now. We can talk about that when you're home safe. You stay in that room with the door bolted and don't open it for anyone except Kathrine. Do you understand me?"

"Yes, but we're fine."

A familiar panic swept through Rachel. Her heart raced, her palms sweat, and an anxious, overwhelming fear gripped her—the fear that something would happen to Claire, and she could do nothing to protect her. "I have to talk with Kathrine. I'll call you back in a little while."

She called Kathrine. "Do you think someone followed her?"

"I couldn't find any evidence, but that doesn't mean much in this situation. What she said about the car staying with them even when they got lost suggests it's true."

"Damn it. Please stay with them in their room tonight and make sure they get on the next flight out of there in the morning—with security."

"You want them under security? Are you sure?"

"Yes, but I don't want her or Sarah to know. Claire has no idea about Yumiko's involvement in California, and if I tell her why I want security with her, she'll get even more nervous than she already is and worry. Besides, I don't want to tell her about it over the phone."

"Rachel, are you sure about this? I mean, I understand you're concerned, but would Yumiko really do something like this? I'm sure Jack reminded you that someone else could have targeted them."

Was she overreacting? Jack made it clear he thought she was. Did Kathrine think it also? Her head pounded. "Yes, I'm sure, and make sure whoever you get is discreet."

She ended the call to Kathrine, then made the international call to Brice Chambers at MI6 London. His familiar comforting voice relieved her tension. Her shoulders relaxed, and she leaned back into the chair and crossed her legs.

"How are you and Claire? I am most happy to hear she has her memory back. How is the house coming along? Thank you for the emails. I enjoy reading about what's going on in your life."

A typical Brice beginning. First the personal connection and then they'd get to the heart of the matter. She smiled as she remembered how he had teased her. "You Americans are always in such a hurry."

And so, she followed the social protocol as long as she could stand it. After an acceptable number of pleasantries, she got down to business.

"Brice, I think Yumiko is having her people follow Claire. Does MI6 know where she is?"

Brice's silence was almost deafening.

"Brice, are you there?"

"Yes…Rachel, let me call you back in a few minutes."

She waited impatiently for him to call back on a secure line.

She answered on the first ring. "What's going on, Brice?"

"Rachel, I expected you would call." Another long pause at the other end of the phone. "We have been unofficially monitoring her whereabouts, but you must know that Jack and I both feel it's best you aren't involved."

Jack and Brice had obviously talked more than once and conspired. She felt the stab of betrayal by both. She pushed the thought out because she knew they were doing what they thought best for her. But they didn't know Yumiko like she did.

"As of right now we don't know her exact whereabouts, other than she was in Los Angeles and flew back to the Philippines. The agency is on alert. This is a delicate situation for MI6 because of the agreement she made with us."

"Why didn't you tell me MI6 let her go? That psycho is out there, free to do whatever she wants."

"I wasn't at liberty to give you that information."

"She's had people killed here in the United States. She would have killed Jack and Frank."

"I understand, and I'm sure your government is hunting her, but until the United States formally asks us for help, MI6 will not actively pursue her."

Rachel sighed, rubbing the palm of her moist hand on her thigh. They had let that nutcase back into the world again to destroy other lives. She would never say that to Brice because it had nothing to do with him. He headed MI6's covert corporate surveillance and cyber operations, not the political side that bargained with sociopaths and offered deals like they were trading stocks in the financial marketplace.

"I know how frustrating this is for you."

"I want to interview her if your agency gets her."

"That is totally inappropriate, given the circumstances you went through at her hand."

"You and Jack are wrong. I need to talk with her."

"You are much too close to the situation. No one could have gone through what you went through and feel any differently than you do, but you simply cannot be involved."

She recoiled. "You're wrong. I should be involved. I know her. I know what she's capable of doing. I know how she thinks. You are acquainted with her from the information in her file. You studied her—I survived her."

"I'm sorry you feel so strongly about this, Rachel, but I will not permit it, if it's up to me. I'm sure about this. It would do more harm to you than good if you were permitted to interview her."

There was nothing more to say.

When she finished talking with Brice, she put her elbows on the desk and her face in her hands, massaging her temples. She muddled through the maze of her emotions, trying to reason out the right course of action.

Brice and Jack didn't or couldn't see what she saw. She refused to give in, and if it *was* Yumiko, she would refuse to give up. Their collision course was set. Yumiko would keep coming after her, and she would come after Claire or Sarah or Tilly to hurt her. She would never stop. No one would be safe unless Rachel could somehow change the variables.

She went to the restroom and freshened her face, then went back to her office and called Frank.

He walked in five minutes later and sat across from her.

"I want you to talk with Jack," she said.

"Why, because he and Brice won't let you interrogate Yumiko when they finally get her?"

Rachel's mouth dropped open. "This is unbelievable."

"Hey, that's big news around here, and in answer to your question, no. I won't talk with him. I agree you shouldn't be involved."

"Did you talk with Jack about it?"

"Yes. We discussed the possible scenario after Steve's funeral. Rachel, you're too close to this situation."

"Jack and Brice are wrong, and so are you if you're going along with them. How can none of you see that? It's because of what happened that I'm the best lead we have."

"Do you really believe that, or are you just pissed off because you don't get a say in the situation?"

"You're damn right I'm pissed, because I know it's true." Rachel rubbed her hands together, trying to release the emotion rising inside her. "And when you find out I'm right, it might be too late for the people I care about. How will you feel then, knowing you grouped up and decided not to let me talk to her?" She hoped to somehow get through to them before everything went sideways. If they left her out of the investigation, she would be working blind, and everyone she loved would suffer for it. That was unacceptable.

Chapter Twenty

Yumiko checked her fraudulent but flawless passport and placed it carefully inside the zippered compartment of her leather shoulder bag. She took a black cab from the terminal to her hotel. Everything had changed since the last time she was in London. A surge of nausea passed through her. The cobra venom had done its work. The problems in her leadership had been removed, but not without a cost. It had been messy—the very thing she didn't want to happen.

She didn't give enough of the venom to Alon and the others, and they didn't die as easily or as quickly as she'd planned. Alon managed to grab his gun and fired at her. She dove for cover underneath the conference table, but not before he shot her in the arm. Agapito fired his gun and shot Alon in the head. The others died a few minutes later, moaning and gasping. She wouldn't forget the ugly scene any time soon.

She, Agapito, and Crisanto had taken the antivenom, but the recovery had been much more painful than she had expected. Blurred vision and headaches. Difficulty breathing. Muscle spasms. The gunshot wound in her arm became infected, and she had to be treated with antibiotics. For three days she couldn't move. It took weeks to fully recover, but the change in her leadership was complete, and she could now expand the operations without concern.

In the hotel bathroom, she slipped off the light-brown short wig. She carefully extracted the blue contacts and put lubricating drops in her eyes, then removed the prosthetics from her nose and cheeks, and took out the lifts in her shoes. She'd slipped into London twice this month on business, unnoticed, as usual. She'd stay one more night before she returned to the Philippines.

She walked back and forth, periodically looking out the window, not seeing the courtyard, or the roofs, or the people strolling by. She held the choko of sake tightly in her hand, her cell phone in the other. She had warned him not to be obvious. He'd called to tell her he had terminated the surveillance on Portola's wife as she had instructed.

"Did she know she was being followed?" she asked.

"Yes, she knew. She looked upset."

"Good."

The information made her smile. The prey's nest had been disturbed. She'd poked it with a stick, and now the animals were flustered. She gulped a drink of the sake, as if in tribute to her accomplishment. She wanted payback, and the more she got into Portola's life and into her head, the more she enjoyed it. She would toy with her and the others, like a cat in a nest of mice, until she was bored, and then she'd increase the stakes. She'd almost destroyed Portola's life once. She'd watch her beg like she did before, and this time she would end it.

She pictured Portola's face as she slowly took her life from her. She set the sake on the table and moved her hands gently over her arms, holding herself, sliding deeper into the fantasy. Rachel pleading, just like before. The sensual arousal thrummed between her legs.

When she was done toying with her, she would start the finale with Evans, and then Commander Brice Chambers of MI6. She would have Evans taken and then deal with Chambers. After she killed him, she would reveal her intentions to come after Portola and watch her collapse in a heap of despair and fear like she did in Manila. She had controlled her once, taken her to the depths of hell. She would have killed her if Jack Ralston and his team hadn't interrupted them. She would take her again, and this time she would not order someone else to kill her. She would do it herself.

She drained the remaining sake, then went into the bedroom and slammed the door shut. She lay on the bed, her muscles tense, the ache for release coursing through her. She turned over onto her back and unzipped her slacks and pushed them down, then reached inside her underwear and slid her fingers down, slipping easily into her warm, slick folds. She spread her legs slightly, touching, taking her firm, aching clitoris between her fingers, massaging rhythmically, feeling the surge of pleasure as the fantasy began to build.

She'd kill her slowly and touch her anywhere she wanted. And she'd be unable to do anything about it. She'd be trapped. Subdued. Completely hers.

The sexual tension increased as she titillated with her fingers, building toward a climax. She came hard and fast.

The future was ripening, like a fresh mango. And she would slice it open.

CHAPTER TWENTY-ONE

Rachel paced in her office. She glanced out into the hallway and saw Jack watching her. He'd never seen her like this. He clearly looked concerned. He had good reason. Weeks later and she still wasn't sleeping. The nightmares continued. Yumiko haunted her. Sometimes, like now, she felt like her head would explode.

He knocked softly on her open door and stepped in, the muscles in his face taut, his brows furrowed, an expression of seriousness etched on his face.

Could it be about Yumiko? Did MI6 get her? If so, why hadn't Brice called her himself? She needed to know. He had no right to keep anything from her.

"Rachel, I need to talk to you."

He reached into his pocket when he closed her door and sat across from her desk. He appeared hesitant, as if unsure what to say. Whatever he wanted to say couldn't be good. He slowly brought out a piece of paper, unfolded it, and placed it on the desk.

She sat and leaned forward, bringing the paper closer as she studied it. Her heart pounded. The trembling started in her knees. She gulped. "Where'd you get this?"

"In the mail."

She stared at the paper, a picture of her with a bull's-eye across her face with *she's going to die and there's nothing you can do about it* written underneath. She tapped it with her finger. "It's Yumiko."

He shook his head. "Now, Rachel, it may not be her. We're in security, and it could have been anyone. It's a scare tactic, meant to intimidate. Half of us here at the shed have gotten this kind of thing at least once. Kathrine has had three of them."

She stood and started pacing again. She pursed her lips as she stuffed her hands into the side pockets of her slacks. Tiny beads of sweat formed on her temple. "Why are you dragging your feet about this? I don't understand." The pulse point in her neck throbbed. "You have to calm down." He folded the picture and put it in his pocket. "I don't want you to worry about this. I just showed it to you so you'd know. You're looking for proof, and everything you see, and everything that's happened, points to Yumiko because that's what you want to believe. If you're a hammer, everything's a nail. How can I convince you otherwise? You believe it's Yumiko." He watched, as if analyzing her. "I see an emotionally drained, exhausted friend on the edge."

Rachel took a deep breath and sat back in her chair, his gaze penetrating and burning into her.

"I want you to take some time off and try to relax. You need to rest."

She looked straight into him, as deeply and as intensely as she could. "For God's sake, Jack. I *need* for you to believe me. I'm not making this up. You know me. You know how I react. I'm reasonable. I put two and two together and get four. What's holding *you* back from believing what I know to be a fact? It is Yumiko."

Jack hung his head.

What more could she say to convince him? Why didn't he see it?

"Rachel, I've been in this business a long time. Shit happens. Car windows get smashed. Vandalism happens. Crazed fans do violent things. Beautiful women alone in cars get targeted in big cities. I want to support you. I do. But this feels over the edge. I honestly think you need to get away. Given everything that you've been through in the past couple of years, anyone would react this way."

Rachel held up her hand. "Stop right there."

Jack stopped talking and stared at her, letting out a slow, forceful breath. "Okay, Rachel. What do you need from me?"

She was no longer sure what he believed about her. "I *need* you to believe I'm not fabricating what I see. You can't look at it from my perspective. You don't see what I see."

"I'm trying to, but I'm going by my logic and experience. What can I do to help you know I support you?"

"You aren't supporting me if you don't accept what I know as facts and trust me. I add up the facts and draw a conclusion, and you add up the facts and get something different."

"Okay. Let's do this. You have the resources of this office behind you, starting now. Anything you want or need, just ask. I have my doubts that it's Yumiko, but I want to support you. What can I do?"

She sighed in relief. "I'll be all right. I just need to make sure the people I care about are protected and end this once and for all."

"When are you moving into the new house?"

"A couple more weeks."

"Let us know when you're ready. We all want to help."

Changing the subject had been the best thing to do in the moment. What more could be said? She wanted to go forward, and she'd include him when he got on board. His willingness to support her and throw the company's resources behind her, even if he didn't fully believe her, spoke volumes about their friendship.

"Thanks. I appreciate it, but Claire's in charge. She has everything worked out and is itching to finally move in. She wanted new everything, so all the new furniture is already there. We were over last night, and I caught her running her fingers along the piecrust-carved wood on the back of the sofa in the living room as she passed by. She can't keep the smile off her face. Once the contractor finishes the back wall and the landscaper does the flower gardens, that's it." She leaned back into the chair. "We're ready for this change."

"That's great. You two need it."

His support meant everything to her.

Jack put his hand in his pocket. "If I'm wrong about this being Yumiko, I'd never forgive myself if something happened to you or Claire. I'm sorry if my attitude added to your stress. Let's go forward from here." He touched her shoulder as he left her office.

On the drive home she thought about Jack. He was steady, and thoughtful, and a good man. He'd also been through a lot. Steve had been his best friend, and Rachel knew he had guilt about his death.

What if Yumiko went after Jack, or Kathrine, or Frank? She had just as much reason to. The kink between her shoulder blades started to ache—the cat began crawling up the tree again. Sometimes it became too much to even think about, but more than that, she couldn't carry it alone anymore. It was time to tell Claire.

She pulled the Viper into the garage and got out slowly, not dreading the conversation, but still not quite sure how Claire would react, and not sure how much to tell her.

Claire hovered over the open door of the refrigerator, a plastic container of something in her hand. Rachel came up behind her and kissed the back of her neck.

"Ooh, that's nice." Claire turned around and kissed her. "You ready for supper?"

"Depends on what's on the menu."

"Taco Tuesday."

"But it's Thursday."

"Okay. Taco Thursday then."

They laughed.

Rachel helped set the table, and they began to eat. She waited until Claire finished her first taco. "Claire."

Claire held her glass of lemonade in midair and immediately looked at her. "Rachel?"

Rachel hesitated, still not sure how much to tell her.

"Out with it."

"Remember when we did that last case in Cleveland?"

"How could I forget? I'd had enough by the time it all fell apart in DC."

"When we went to California to get Jack and Frank, we found out the cases were connected."

Claire set her glass of lemonade on the table. "You now have my undivided attention."

"The common thread is Yumiko."

Claire's face went pale. "No. She's in prison. How could that be?"

"I know. That's what I thought, but MI6 made some type of deal with her and let her go."

Claire eyes were wide. "Rachel, no. Is that why you've been so upset?"

Rachel nodded.

Now Claire grew quiet, probably in a stupor like Rachel had been when she first found out.

"Do you think her people followed me and Sarah?"

Claire suspected immediately. She'd added it up and got the same thing Rachel did, but it was still conjecture. *No proof. No proof. No proof.* The thought bounced around in Rachel's head like a tin can kicked in an alley.

"I don't know, but it could have been. Jack seems to think it wasn't, but Yumiko could have very easily had you followed and had her people harass Tilly. At this point it's just conjecture." She couldn't bring herself to tell her about the bull's-eye flyer. She didn't know why. Maybe because she didn't have any proof. No proof of any of it. That tin can in her mind bounced against the brick wall and spun off into the alley again. How much should she tell Claire?

"Anything else happen that you want to share? You're saying one thing, but your body language is saying something different."

Rachel sat there, looking at her. Claire knew her so well. She didn't want Claire to worry about her, and she would if she told her any more. And she would influence her with what she told her. Jack could be right. It could be just the proverbial shit that happens to people in their lives or in their profession. Maybe she'd lost her perspective about Yumiko. At times throughout the day, when the thoughts came about Yumiko, she did feel like she was on the verge of becoming obsessed about her. The fact that she had no proof kept bouncing around in her head. She pushed it deeper so Claire couldn't see it. "No. I just want you to be aware. I think we're okay."

"Rachel, you're not telling me everything. What else? Something else is bothering you."

Rachel reached across the table for Claire's hand. Claire put both her hands on Rachel's.

"We're safe. If anything changes, we'll do what we have to," Rachel said.

"I know you will. I have complete trust in you. Anything I should do?"

"No. Just notice your surroundings, and let me know if anything is out of place or not quite right." She looked into Claire's eyes, hoping to convey the seriousness of her feelings. "No keeping anything from me, okay?" A tinge of guilt struck her. She was holding something back. How could she insist Claire not do the same?

Claire nodded, her gaze deepening.

Rachel would do what she had to do to keep them safe.

CHAPTER TWENTY-TWO

The weeks passed quickly. The move to the new house went smoothly, and despite Rachel's vigilance, nothing happened that indicated Yumiko was out there scheming for vengeance. She began to think paranoia had set in and she had misjudged the entire situation. Maybe Jack had been right. But she couldn't shake the feeling that Yumiko was squatting like a toad in her swamp of revenge, plotting.

Staying on high alert with no supporting evidence drained her, so she reluctantly pulled the guard at the gate. The new house had an upgraded, state-of-the-art security system, which eased her concern. She forced the thoughts of Yumiko out of her mind.

She stretched and yawned, and rolled over, watching Claire as she slept, thinking how much she wanted to wake her and make love. She looked around the bedroom, straining to see in the early dawn. The scent of fresh paint still lingered. Everything about their new house satisfied and refreshed them, like they were given a second chance, that life could go on, and things would be all right. A sense of home permeated the house.

All her life she'd struggled to get that feeling. She'd had it with Alex, but only briefly. And she'd had a big part of it with Claire, but when their house burned down on Mt. Charleston, that feeling vanished in the ashes. Even on the reservation, on her own land with Claire, something was missing. She realized it had been the sense of a permanent home for both of them. They could now call this place home for the rest of their lives.

Claire opened her eyes, her hands tucked under her chin. "You're awake awfully early, babe. Are you all right?"

Rachel sighed. "I'm just not tired right now. Go back to sleep. You need to rest." She stroked Claire's face with the back of her hand, then pushed her hair away from her eyes.

"Only if you hold me." Claire turned over and moved against her. Rachel put her arm around Claire's waist, bringing her closer, catching the scent of her coconut body wash as she kissed her shoulder, her warmth pressing against her breasts and stomach, sending a surge of want into her. Claire reached behind her and stroked Rachel's thigh, then turned and laid her leg over her.

"I've always loved making love to you in the early morning," Claire said.

Rachel touched her face. "I thought a little bit ago how I love to make love to you. I've never been able to resist you."

They kissed and began to touch, and Rachel let the feeling of security and safety and want surge through her as they entwined.

After they were satisfied, they lay together in contentment.

Rachel rolled over on her back and put her hand behind her head. Claire gently laid her hand over Rachel's waist as Rachel slowly stroked her arm.

"You're getting too thin again, Rachel. I know you're stressed, and even though you've mellowed out a little since we moved, you're obviously still worried about something."

Rachel wanted to tell her how she feared she couldn't protect her, that Yumiko might be coming for her and possibly Claire, and she wouldn't stop until it ended one way or the other. She still hadn't told her about the picture with a bull's-eye on her face. She didn't want to increase Claire's worry, but more than that, if she said it out loud, it would become real. The note tipped the scales toward Yumiko, but she still had room for doubt. She brought her hand from behind her head and placed it around Claire's shoulder, drawing her closer, trying to comfort her. But Claire read right through her effort.

Claire sat up and took Rachel's face in her hands. "What's wrong? Talk to me. You're worried. You don't have to worry about that bitch. You're smarter than she is, and you have the resources you need. I'm not afraid of her."

Claire amazed her. "How did you know I was thinking about that?"

Claire laughed. "Because I know you."

"Brice and Jack won't let me be involved, and they won't let me interview her when they catch her." As far as she knew there hadn't been any developments over the past few weeks, but they probably wouldn't tell her if there had been. It was beyond frustrating.

Claire slid next to her and put her arm over her waist again. "I think it's best."

Rachel shot her a look. "*Et tu, Brute?*"

Claire kissed her cheek and laid her head on her shoulder. "I'm just saying I think you want closure about what happened, and you aren't going to get it by talking to her. She's nuts, and no matter how rational you want the situation to be, it's not going to happen. Rachel, whatever your decision is, I'll support you, but you're too close to this whole thing to be objective, and because of what you've been through, you're extra sensitive. As far as Jack shutting you out of the decision, you'll probably have to confront him about it if you want to be involved and make your case as to why it's a good idea, when none of us think it is. I know you want to be in control, but some things you can't control." She smiled and kissed Rachel's cheek again.

Rachel kissed her face and got out of the bed. "I know, but I don't know if I want to confront him right now." She walked toward the bathroom. "And Claire, some things you either control or they control you."

"Control is an illusion."

Rachel hesitated before she closed the door. "Not in my business."

CHAPTER TWENTY-THREE

D amn it." Claire slammed the car door and stomped into the house. Olivia's eyebrows rose as Claire came into the kitchen.

"Where's Rachel?"

"She's taking a shower, Ms. Claire."

Claire went directly to the bathroom and pulled open the etched-glass shower door.

Rachel jumped. "Oh, God. You scared me. Are you are coming in?"

"Rachel, some asshole keyed my Maserati."

"Really? I'm sorry." Rachel turned the shower off, reached for the bath towel hanging on the hook beside the door, and dried off, then wrapped the towel around herself.

Claire moved aside and lifted herself onto the marble countertop between the double sinks, holding her hands out. "It's huge. Right down the center of the driver's door, from the front to the door handle. Damn it. When I find out who did it, I'm going to kick their ass."

Rachel touched her face. "Baby, you're never going to find out who did it. Where did it happen?"

"I have no idea. I went to the salon, and then to the jewelers to have our rings checked. When I got home, I got out of the car, and there it was. Damn it, Rachel. It's not right."

Rachel hugged her. "I'm so sorry. Turn it in to the insurance company."

Claire pulled back slightly. "That's not the point, Rachel. It's not right. No wonder Tilly blew up about it."

Rachel's eyes narrowed in that expression Claire knew so well.

"Rachel, don't go there. Expensive cars get keyed all the time, thousands and thousands of them. People get pissed off that they can't afford them and take it out on the paint job."

"Don't you think it's too much of a coincidence that you and Tilly have both had your cars keyed?"

"No, I don't. She lives in Cleveland, and we live in Las Vegas. Lots of people, lots of crime. And it's not a violent crime. Just a pain the ass. Let it go, babe."

"I'm just saying."

"I know, but you need to let this one go." It was a petty incident, but maybe it could be Yumiko. She killed people for a living, like a mobster. She didn't key cars. It wouldn't be worth her trouble. Would it? She felt like an idiot. She'd told Rachel to let it go, and now she needed to. This kind of crap could drive you crazy.

"What does Yumiko look like?"

"What?" Rachel acted like she'd caught her off guard.

"Yumiko. What does she look like? I should know in case she follows me or I see her hanging around."

"About five two or three, light-brown skin, dark-brown hair almost to her waist, brown eyes, high cheekbones, a little bit of a broad nose. One side of her face snarls more than the other. A small, dark mole on the left side of her face, just below the corner of her eye."

Claire smiled. "That's detailed."

"You tend to remember someone who's up close and personal, beating you with your hands tied behind your back."

Claire cringed. "I'm sure she's etched in your mind. And now, knowing she might be out there somewhere, I'm sure it's gnawing at you. But nothing's happened except these petty things, and maybe they're just things with no meaning other than bad people doing bad things."

What Yumiko had done to Rachel sent a shudder through her. Rachel had been beaten so badly Claire didn't recognize her when she first saw her on the gurney at the hospital. She pushed the memory away and looked at Rachel. She could barely see the scar on her jawline where the surgeon had rebuilt her jaw, and the scar on her cheek had nearly faded. If Yumiko was out there gunning for them, Claire needed more than the skills she had. What if she did see Yumiko? How could she protect herself? What about Rachel? What if Yumiko came after *her*? How could she protect her? She needed skills she didn't have, but she could change that.

Chapter Twenty-four

Kathrine entered Rachel's office and sat, not wanting to interrupt her, but she needed her help. At a dead end and desperate to make a decision, she needed a trusted opinion. She had debated for a week if she should ask Rachel for help, knowing how stressed she'd been, but she seemed calmer since she and Claire had moved into their new house. "Rachel, do you have a second?"

Rachel looked at her and smiled as she continued to work on her laptop. "Sure. What's up?"

"It will take a while."

"Okay." Rachel stopped working on her laptop and moved it aside. Kathrine loved that about her. When you were with her, she gave you her total attention. "How can I begin? It's so complicated, but here it is. Years ago, my twin sister was killed in a boat explosion."

Rachel frowned, and her facial muscles tensed. "I'm so sorry, Kathrine."

"Thanks. I'm telling you this because one of the men involved in it has asked me to come see him. He wasn't tried for the crime. That's another long story. Anyway, do you think I should go?"

Rachel pursed her lips. "Why does he want to see *you*?"

"He said there are some things I need to know, and he wants to tell me what happened."

"It sounds like he wants to do it for himself, more than for you. Do you think it will help you, rather than him?"

A great question. "I'm not sure, but I'm curious what he might have to say."

"Do you think it's safe?"

Kathrine smiled. "That's his problem."

Rachel laughed. "The deciding factors should be if you feel it will help you and if you're ready to hear what he might tell you."

Kathrine sighed.

"Is it far away?" asked Rachel.

"Carson, California. A few hours' drive."

"If you decide to go, would you like some company? I don't want to leave Claire alone, but we'd be happy to go along with you and wait in the car while you talk with him."

Kathrine hadn't considered that idea. It appealed to her. "Would Claire mind taking the drive?"

"Not at all. She'd probably enjoy the break. It'd be good for both of us."

"That's so kind. Yes. I'd love to have the company."

"Tilly and Sarah are coming for a visit this weekend. Why don't we do it after then?" Rachel asked.

"Sounds good. Tilly mentioned they were coming in."

Rachel looked more intently at her. "Everything okay between you two?"

Kathrine avoided eye contact. She didn't want Rachel to see that the mere mention of Tilly's name brought up a riptide of emotion, but she needed to talk to someone about it. "That's a loaded question."

Rachel grimaced. "You want to talk about it?"

"I think there's a problem, but I'm not sure. Tilly's been distant since she canceled her trip to Chicago." She clasped her hands. "I've been attracted to her for a long time, ever since I went to see her perform at the Caprice. When I found out she and Claire were best friends, I hoped I could meet her. Claire introduced us at your wedding party at Lil' Nell's. We talked and then started calling each other. Our feelings were getting stronger, at least I thought so, but all of a sudden she seemed to cool off. I want to pursue her, but Tilly's a mystery. I'm not sure now if she has feelings for me."

"I just assumed you two were together."

"No, we aren't. I mean yes, we've spent time together, but no, we haven't been *together*."

"Tilly, as far as I know, has never had any kind of deep emotional or sexual relationship with anyone. She's a complicated person. I love her, but she can be a handful at times," Rachel said.

"Don't I know it already."

They laughed.

"Do you really like her, Kathrine?"

"Yes, I do. I've been involved a couple of times, but nothing like this."

"Claire and I have loved each other from almost the first time we met, and Tilly and Sarah have both seen what we went through. Maybe Tilly is hesitant because of what she saw Claire go through. We struggled to come to terms with our feelings for each other. Me more than Claire. Sometimes it became intense, and Tilly especially seemed to be aware of it. If you really care about Tilly, may I give some advice?"

"Please do."

"Don't give up on her. Tilly doesn't love easily. She may just need some time to work through what she's feeling. I'm sure Claire and Sarah will help her."

❖

Claire watched Tilly's hands as she fidgeted. She kept moving her napkin on her lap and seemed to always be a sentence behind in the dinner conversation.

Halfway through the meal, Rachel got a call from Jack and had to leave to go back to the shed. Claire kissed her good-bye and patted her bottom as she left.

"Rachel looks stressed," Sarah said.

Claire continued to watch Rachel through the window. "She's working all the time. On top of that, she's got a lot on her mind."

A few minutes after Rachel left, Tilly stood, laid her napkin on the table, excused herself, and started to leave the table.

Sarah grabbed her arm. "Whoa, hoss. Not so fast. You were practically stoic on the plane ride here, and now you're as distracted as a cat with the plastic circle from the milk jug. What's going on?"

Tilly sighed deeply and sat back down, not making eye contact with Sarah, an unusual response. She normally had a stare-down when either Sarah or Claire confronted her. Obviously, something was going on.

"I want to be with Kathrine, but I don't think I can do it."

"Why?" Sarah asked before Claire could.

"It just seems too damn complicated."

"Tilly, all intimate relationships are complicated. Did you think you could just take Kathrine to the bedroom, pull her pants down, and have at it?" Claire asked.

"Don't be crude," Sarah said.

Claire couldn't help it. Sometimes Tilly frustrated her.

"Frankly, it scares the hell out of me," Tilly said.

"Why?" Sarah asked again.

Tilly lifted her hands. "Well, for one thing, look what Rachel and Claire went through. Remember their fight at the lake in Alaska? And all the times Claire came crying to you, Sarah. God. I thought she'd kill herself at one point."

"Hey, easy. I'm right here." Claire pushed her plate away.

"You going to sit there and tell me you didn't get your heart broken," Tilly said.

Claire had never seen Tilly this upset over someone. She looked on the verge of tears. Had she fallen for Kathrine? She wanted to be careful what she said. "Yes, I did get my heart broken. Several times. But it was worth every tear and every heartache to get where we are now."

"You can't possibly mean that. I saw the pain you went through," Tilly said.

"Yes, I do mean it. Rachel and I love each other more now because of the storms we weathered, not in spite of them."

Tilly leaned forward and put both hands on the table. "How can you say that?"

"Because that's how love grows. If I didn't have a strong love for Rachel, I would have never been able to face what we've endured the last couple of years and what we go through now. Do you think it's easy to be married to someone who has her type of job?"

"See, that's exactly what I mean. I've never felt that for anyone. No chance in hell I'm putting up with *that*. I thought I wanted to be with her, but I've changed my mind. I'm not about to live with someone who leaves at all hours, is gone for days at a time, might not come back, or has someone hunt them or make their life hell. No way."

Claire and Sarah glanced at each other.

"*Live with someone*?" asked Sarah, with a sly smile. "You've thought about *living* with Kathrine?"

Tilly picked up her spoon beside her plate and looked at it, turning it over several times. "Maybe."

Sarah laughed out loud. "Oh, Tilly, you're already in it."

Tilly tossed the spoon down. "No, I'm not. We haven't been together. We haven't even kissed yet."

Claire laughed. "*Yet?* Yeah, but obviously you've thought about it. Doesn't matter. You fell into the deep end of the girl pool, and now it's either sink or swim, baby." She spread her hands out toward the pool and laughed again.

"Bullshit. Not me."

"Oh, honey, you've got it bad," Claire said.

Sarah laughed. "Oh yeah. She's drowning for sure." Sarah slapped Claire a high-five and tossed her napkin toward Tilly.

Tilly swatted it away. "Why in the hell do you two find this so amusing?"

Sarah leaned forward. "Well, I'll tell you, Till. I've watched you sit in the cheap seats for years and go through men like they were disposable pieces of furniture, and every single time you started to get close to one of them, you made sure you gave yourself an out. You've broken hearts from Cleveland to Las Vegas, to Chicago, and back to Cleveland, and not once did you fall in love. I've hoped all our adult lives that somehow, somewhere you'd meet someone who would break open that stone-cold heart of yours. Now someone has, and it's not a guy who did it—it's a woman. At last, I can tell you, Tilly, welcome to the human race."

Sarah walked over and slipped her arm around her.

Tilly fell into her arms and moaned. "What am I going to do?"

Claire went over to Sarah and Tilly and hugged them.

Sarah stroked Tilly's hair. "Sweetheart, you're going to join the rest of us and love and get your heart broken, and live, and feel the joy of what it's like to care about someone more than yourself."

Tilly shook her head. "I honest to God don't know what love is."

"None of us know what love is until it smacks us upside the head," Sarah said.

Claire couldn't hold back any longer. "Tilly, Kathrine is a really great person. I understand your fears, but at some point, you need to let go of your fear and fall. That's why it's called *falling in love*. This feeling you have for Kathrine is the start of something wonderful. Don't smother it with fear. I know it's hard and it's scary. I know it's overwhelming because she's a woman. I get it. And on top of all of those issues, it's not easy to love someone who purposely puts their life in danger. Trust me. If you let your fears rule you, you'll rob yourself of something amazing." Claire knew Tilly needed to talk about other things, but she needed to discuss them with Kathrine, not with her and

Sarah. "I've been around Kathrine a lot, and she's worth your love. She's smart, and kind, and self-confident. She's funny, and she's really cute."

Tilly waggled her finger at her, half smiling. "So not helping. And I already know all that about her."

They laughed, and the weight of the burden of worry for Rachel, Tilly, Sarah, and even for herself began to lift. Their friendship had always carried them through the hard times, but could it sustain them through what might lie ahead? Would it be enough?

CHAPTER TWENTY-FIVE

Kathrine entered the key code to Rachel and Claire's security gate and drove her Subaru Outback down the long, winding driveway toward their house. She could see the security lights aimed toward the outside of the impressive stone house as she approached. She glanced at the touch screen. One thirty in the morning. When Tilly had called, she seemed anxious when she asked Kathrine if she could come over right away. She didn't hesitate, even though she had to get up at six tomorrow. She didn't care. She would have gone over if Tilly had asked her at three a.m. in the middle of a snowstorm.

The massive stone entranceway, bathed in soft-yellow tinted light, caused the stone to glisten and almost shimmer. She'd heard that the house, easily worth ten to twelve million dollars, had been paid for in cash. Rachel had made millions from her computer programs, but Claire had the real money. Whispers around the shed were that Claire was worth well over three hundred million with the money Derrick left her when he committed suicide in prison. Even though they had millions, Rachel and Claire always treated her as a good friend.

She turned the car off and opened the door to get out, but Tilly bounded out of the front entrance and got into the car, almost breathless.

"Thanks for coming over right away."

Kathrine shut the car door. "You're welcome. Thanks for asking. Would you like to go somewhere?"

"Like where? I don't want to be with anyone but you."

Kathrine liked the sound of that. "We could go to Sunrise Mountain."

"Can we just stay here in the car and talk?"

"Sure." She turned the car on and lowered the windows, then shut it off. A warm breeze immediately swept through the vehicle. The wind rustled through the mesquite trees, and a coyote yipped in the distance. No matter how hot the days were, the desert nights were cool and comforting. She reached down and touched the power button to move her seat.

Tilly startled.

Kathrine couldn't help but smile. "Easy. I adjusted my seat to get comfortable. If you want to adjust yours, the button's down there on your right."

Tilly reached down, adjusted the seat, and crossed her legs. "That's nice."

Silence.

Tilly stared out the window, her hands clasped in her lap.

Kathrine rested her hand on the steering wheel and watched Tilly brush the top of her pant leg and then straighten her blouse. Why did Tilly seem so anxious? She waited for her to open the conversation.

They'd talked only superficially since Tilly had canceled the Chicago trip. Had Kathrine misread her? Had she done something to offend her? They'd gotten to know each other and talked about childhood, and careers, and a thousand things that were good to share. She thought Tilly might have been ready for a more intimate relationship, but now she was confused. Why hadn't Tilly wanted to see her before now? Why hadn't she called when she got into town? She'd told Kathrine she'd be coming to town but acted like she didn't want to be with her. Maybe she just wanted to be friends but didn't want to have to spell it out. Maybe Kathrine had crossed an intimacy line that Tilly hadn't been ready for yet. Would she ever be ready? Surprisingly, Kathrine had a dry mouth, and her heart beat a little faster than normal.

More silence.

Kathrine didn't want to push her. She already felt like she'd done something or said something to offend her. Why else would she have canceled the Chicago trip and then seemed so distant on the phone? Better to keep it simple. "Did you have a good supper?"

Tilly shifted in her seat. "I'm sorry I've been so distant."

Kathrine's heartbeat slowed, and her shoulders relaxed. The bluish gray in Tilly's eyes softened. Her lips were full, and her body seemed to beckon for Kathrine to kiss her, or maybe she'd had a lot of wine tonight? Tilly was hard to read.

Kathrine turned to face her. "It's okay. I thought I'd done something to offend you."

"Absolutely not. I'm sorry you felt that way. It's me. I just can't seem to get a grip on my feelings for you."

Kathrine's mouth dropped open. Her pulse quickened. Did Tilly just say she was into her? "Um, you have feelings for me?" She wasn't wrong. She had read it correctly.

"Yes. I do."

Adrenaline rushed through Kathrine. It started in her fingertips and moved downward. She swallowed. In that moment, she recognized her feelings for Tilly went deeper than she'd realized. Much deeper. She'd been holding back because of her doubts about how Tilly felt. She wouldn't do that any longer. She slipped her arm around Tilly's shoulder and gently brought her toward her.

Tilly reached out and put her arms around Kathrine's neck.

Kathrine leaned into her and pressed her lips against Tilly's soft, full lips, slowly opening Tilly's mouth with hers, tasting the cinnamon breath mint Tilly must have used earlier. The wetness and warmth of their kiss sent a surge of sexual heat through Kathrine. They kissed deeper, lingering.

Tilly finally withdrew. "I knew your kiss would be wonderful. We need to talk." She gazed deeply into Kathrine's eyes, as if trying to find the answers to questions she hadn't asked yet.

Kathrine caressed her face. She'd glimpsed this side of Tilly before, but now she opened to her. She could ask Tilly anything, and she knew she would tell her. "What is it?"

"Are we going to be lovers?"

Kathrine tried not to smile. It wasn't that she found the question amusing. It was the intense, serious way Tilly had asked it. "Do you want to be?"

Tilly readjusted in the seat and put her hand on Kathrine's face. "Honestly, I don't know if I'm ready yet."

Kathrine kissed her again, slowly, pulling her to her, as close as the console between them would allow. She kissed her face and then her earlobe. "You know, there's no time limit on this sort of thing."

"I'm so scared."

Kathrine took her hand. "About what?"

"You. You scare me."

"I do? I don't think that's a good thing."

"I didn't say that right. I mean my feelings for you scare me."

"Talk to me about it."

Tilly slipped her hand away from hers. "Now see, that's what makes me afraid. You have this way of making me feel like I'm the most important person in the world to you, and I want to curl up inside you like you're my own personal cocoon or something." Tilly put her face in her hands.

Kathrine scooted over as much as she could and took her in her arms. "Tilly, it's okay. I love that you feel that way about me."

"Yeah, well, it scares the hell out of me."

"Why?"

"Because I've never felt this way before. I feel out of control, and needy, and like I can't get enough of you."

"You could have fooled me. I thought for sure you didn't have feelings for me after you canceled your trip to Chicago. You haven't said anything about how you felt, and you acted like you didn't want to see me while you were in town."

"I know. I'm horrible. Please forgive me. I don't have an excuse except I'm so confused."

God, this woman is complicated. "Why?"

"I can't go into it right now, but would you kiss me again? I really like it."

Kathrine suspected the deeper conflict revolved around the possibility that Tilly had never been with a woman, but if she wasn't ready to talk about it, she didn't want to push her. And they didn't need to hurry. She kissed her and then held her, running her hand along her back, feeling something hard and rigid. She traced the edges of it with her fingers. "What is that?"

"It's a back brace. I have to wear it because of an accident." Tilly relaxed in her arms and then sat back and put her hands in her lap. "You might as well know it all. As much as I don't want to admit it, I'm addicted to the pain pills. I am. And no amount of determination or willpower is going to change it. I have been since my early teens. I've lived with the back pain since I was fourteen—the day the dog ran out in front of my bike and I woke lying in the street, Claire and Sarah crying over me, and the wail of a siren ringing in my ears. I've had seven surgeries, three before I turned sixteen. Each one brought hope, but then more pain and more disappointment. Since the plane crash in Alaska with Rachel, Claire, and Sarah, and everything we went through to survive, I've had to wear the brace every day."

She slid her delicately embroidered peach-colored sweater off her shoulder and inspected the long scar on her upper arm, then showed

Kathrine. "I felt I should tell you, so you know what you're getting into."

Kathrine smiled. "My only question is where'd you get that beautiful sweater."

The tension eased. They laughed.

Tilly turned again toward her. "I mean it, Kathrine. I want you to know what you're getting into. I'm flawed." She hung her head. "Deeply flawed."

Kathrine saw the corners of Tilly's mouth turn downward, like a dark cloud hovered over her.

"Everyone has flaws, Tilly. Yours aren't any worse than anyone else's. I love that you see them and are willing to take them out and deal with them. No one's perfect, no matter how good they are."

Tilly leaned in and kissed her.

Kathrine responded and pulled her closer. They kissed longer and deeper. Time slipped by. Their breathing increased. Kathrine wanted to touch her. Who was she kidding? She wanted to rip Tilly's clothes off and caress every part of her. She was so ready she practically throbbed.

Tilly pulled back slightly and tilted her head, taking in a deep breath. "I haven't made out like this in…I've never made out like this."

Kathrine laughed and reached for her hand and held it.

Tilly looked at her watch. "Oh, God, I'm so sorry. It's almost three in the morning. I have to go inside. I know you have to get up for work in a couple of hours. I'm sorry I kept you up."

"It's quite all right. I wouldn't have missed this for anything."

Tilly smiled. "Do you want to get together for supper later tonight? Sarah and I are leaving to go back to Cleveland tomorrow."

"Yes. I can pick you up about eight. Is that good?"

"Perfect." Tilly kissed her again and then opened the car door and slid out. "Be safe going home."

Kathrine watched her until she closed the front door. Yes, Tilly had flaws, but her imperfections made her fascinating. There wouldn't be any dull moments with Tilly. She started the car and drove away, aching to hold her in her arms again.

CHAPTER TWENTY-SIX

K athrine backed the rental car out of the parking space and stopped to show the attendant the paperwork. She decided not to drive her car to Carson. Why should she give him any more information about her than he already had? What if this guy lied? Although he sounded sincere, what if he wanted to trap her or set her up? She readjusted her shoulder holster. She had weighed the possibilities and decided she would meet him, but now more than ever she was relieved she had Rachel along.

She drove to Rachel and Claire's house. They packed their overnight luggage into the trunk and started the drive to Carson, California.

"Thanks for going with me. I appreciate it."

"We're glad to. It's good to get away." Claire reached up from the back seat and took Rachel's hand.

Kathrine loved the way Rachel and Claire seemed so comfortable with her. She enjoyed their company as she drove. Claire talked about her mother and dad and growing up in Cleveland. Rachel talked about her childhood on the reservation in Arizona and how she and Claire met at Arizona State. Kathrine told them about growing up in Denver.

Finally, she told them what she had been holding back about her sister's death. "Four guys did it, but the police were never able to get enough evidence to arrest them. Two were killed in an armed robbery at a gas station near San Diego in a shootout with the sheriff's department. I called it in when I followed them and figured out what they were doing. Another one was stabbed to death in a prison in central Michigan while serving three-to-five for aggravated assault after I visited one of the other prisoners and told him what the guy had done to his little sister."

Rachel and Claire listened. Kathrine glanced through the rearview mirror to try to get a read on Claire's reaction to what she'd said, but her expression didn't change. She sat with her hands folded in her lap. Kathrine glanced over at Rachel.

"I get it," Rachel said.

"And the last one?" Claire asked.

"I let it go as much as I could after the one who was killed in prison." She gripped the steering wheel tighter. "But that's who I'm meeting now. He says he has information I need."

"I hope you don't feel guilty about what happened to the others. They deserved what they got," Claire said.

Kathrine met her gaze in the mirror and gave her a small nod.

Three hours later she pulled into a parking space near the main entrance of the South Bay motel, where she got a plain but clean room across the hall from Rachel and Claire. She closed the heavy curtains, blocking out the lights from the highway and surrounding buildings so she could rest for a few hours.

She slipped off her shoes, unholstered the Glock and set it on the nightstand beside the bed, and lay down, looking at the stained white ceiling.

The last one. It would be over by tonight. It was surreal, like she'd stared at a mountain on a six-year journey and finally reached the base.

She drifted off into a restless sleep, waking when the alarm went off. She freshened and knocked on Rachel and Claire's door. "Are you sure you two wouldn't rather stay here while I talk with him? It might take a while."

Rachel reached out and touched her hand. "We're fine waiting in the car, no matter how long it takes. We have plenty of things to occupy our time. Don't worry about us. Take as long as you need. And if you need backup, I'll be there in an instant."

Kathrine was relieved they were going, more for the moral support than a concern for her safety. She wouldn't meet with him if others were in the room. Once she knew they were alone, he would tell her everything she wanted to know, whether he wanted to or not.

She drove the twelve minutes to River Crest Road and turned left onto the narrow, dark street, parking across from the address, in between two late-model cars, one with cardboard taped over the back left window and a smashed side mirror. She turned to Rachel. "Are you sure you want to stay here?"

Rachel scanned the surroundings. Kathrine reached under the seat and pulled out a revolver. She checked the load and left the safety on, then handed it to her.

Rachel put it on the seat beside her. "We'll be fine. Go."

Kathrine waved her cell phone. "If things get uncomfortable, just drive around the block and call me." She opened the car door and slid out, leaving the car running, hearing the doors lock behind her.

Several dogs barked farther down the street. The light was on in the room facing the dilapidated front porch, but none were on in the houses next to the address. No motion lights. No porch lights. Only broken furniture piled on front porches with broken hand railings, broken swings, broken chairs—broken lives.

She knocked loudly on the wooden door with the cracked window. No response. She knocked again. This time a male voice responded. "Just a minute."

She reached in and unlatched the leather snap to her shoulder holster and shifted her weight to the right. Her mouth became dry. Her heart raced. She swallowed and kept her left hand at her waist. Could it be a trap? She scanned the neighborhood again, then her car. Rachel had moved to the driver's seat and watched her intently.

The door opened. He stood in front of her. "You're her, aren't you?" He stuttered momentarily. He turned his face, as if not wanting her to see him. She regarded him more closely. Tall—about six-one. Muscular, but thin. He had a thick mass of blond hair that hung over his forehead almost to his eyebrows. He looked even younger than she had initially thought he might be from his voice mail. She quietly walked behind him, watching to see if anyone else was in the house as he led her to the chairs in the living room.

He took a seat in a worn, brown-leather recliner and motioned for her to sit across from him on a threadbare love seat.

Kathrine glanced around the room and into the open doors once more. As far as she could tell, they were alone.

"I know you're nervous. I would be too. No one's here but me. I want to thank you for coming. I know it wasn't easy."

She sat on the edge of the seat, waiting. He wasn't what Kathrine had expected. He appeared terrified.

"I hoped you'd come sooner or later."

"What's your real name?" she asked.

"Ronald Ryan Bartolo." He reached into his back pocket and took out his wallet, opened it, pulled out what looked like his driver's license, and handed it to her. According to it, if it wasn't fake, he'd just turned twenty-three.

"You would have been around seventeen," Kathrine said. "A little young for murder, wouldn't you say?" The name Bartolo surprised her. That was who she had testified against. Was he a brother?

His bottom lip quivered. "I told 'em not to do it. I told 'em it was a bad plan, and I told 'em it would come back on 'em, but they wouldn't listen to me." Tears welled in his eyes. "I'd give anything to take it back. You got to believe me."

Kathrine sat looking at him, not quite knowing what to do. "Tell me."

He shook his head. "You pushed my brother Jimmy too far. You pushed him *too far.*" His blue eyes widened. He leaned toward her. "You backed him into a corner. He had no choice but to come after you. Either he got you to back off, or he went to prison again. He couldn't face it."

"So, it's my fault?"

He shook his head. "No! That's not what I'm saying. If you would have just let it go, but you had to push it. When Jimmy found out you were the only witness to put him at the store robbery, he wanted to scare you off, but you wouldn't let it go. Why didn't you? He lost it. He warned you three times what would happen if you testified, but you went ahead."

"I had to. The store owner was a friend of mine, and one of them shot him in the leg and crippled him for life. How was I supposed to let that go?"

"But he only drove. He didn't even have a gun. He didn't know they were going to rob that store. He thought they were going in for beer."

"That's no excuse." She leered at him, his blue eyes wet and pleading. His brother was the only one she saw in the car. The others were identified by video.

"He didn't know that woman was on the boat. None of us knew. He just wanted to scare you. That's all, just scare you so you wouldn't testify. He planted the bomb two days before. When me, Jimmy, his friend Danny, and our cousin Bobbie got to the docks, we saw you walking *away* from the boat. I swear to you we didn't know that other woman was in there." He wiped at his eyes. "And then Bobbie set it off. The boat exploded into a fireball." He put his head down and sobbed. "I deserve to die, just like the others. I swear to God we didn't know that woman was in the boat."

Kathrine straightened. "That woman was my twin sister. You sonofabitch! You took her life and mine that day. You can rot in hell with the rest of them for all I care."

Her hands started to tremble. Cassie's image flashed in front of her. She saw her smile and felt her arm around her shoulder. A thousand things they did together tumbled into her mind. Their hikes, shopping trips, parties, birthdays, graduation. Hanging out and doing nothing at all. A million ordinary, everyday things.

She suddenly became more aware of the weight of the Glock in her shoulder holster. She could fire the weapon and blow his brains out all over the chair. He deserved it. They all deserved what they got. She concentrated on the top of his head, imagining pushing the gun into his thick, blond hair, feeling the gun hit his skull. She stiffened. Her hands trembled more. Time seemed to stop. She sat in silence, digging her nails into the palm of her hand. She pulled her gun hand back slightly, trying to decide.

A barely audible voice seemed to whisper in her head. *It won't bring Cassie back.*

Her arm muscles relaxed. Her hands stopped shaking. She sat motionless for a few seconds and then lowered her hand to her side. She couldn't do it. He was too young. He'd made a horrible mistake.

He glanced into her eyes, as if hesitant to linger there too long.

She knew what he wanted and needed to go on with his life, but she wasn't ready. She couldn't give that piece of herself to him, not yet. "I can't say tonight that I forgive you. Perhaps I will be able to someday. I can see you feel remorse, and that's a good thing. I've lived with what you and the others did to my twin sister until tonight. You're going to have to live with it for the rest of your life. Maybe you can take some of that guilt and make the world a better place, one day." She stood and walked out of the house.

She got into the back seat of her car, and Rachel drove them away. She put her hands to her face and sobbed, the emotion pouring out of her like someone had opened a floodgate. She tried to stop but couldn't. She was either unable or unwilling to hold it back. She didn't know which, and she didn't care. The hate and anger and agony flowed out of her with each tear, each sob, each breath. She sobbed for Cassie and for the stolen time she'd never get with her. When the emotional storm subsided, she sat quietly, drained. She hadn't noticed Rachel pull into a park and stop.

Claire reached back from the passenger seat and laid her hand on Kathrine's knee. Kathrine reached for the tissues she offered.

"I'm sorry. I didn't think it would affect me like that."

Claire patted her knee. "You have nothing to be sorry about."

"Are you glad you did it?" Rachel asked.

Kathrine breathed deeply. "Yes. I can see now I needed it." She shrugged. "And I didn't kill him, so that's a good thing." She watched as Claire studied her, perhaps trying to decide if she was serious.

They went back to the motel and spent the night, saw some of the local sights the next day, then drove home.

Unable to sleep when they got back to Las Vegas, Kathrine finally gave up and drove to Sunrise Mountain and watched the sunrise. For the first time in six years, the weight of guilt from her twin sister's death lifted from her heart.

She reached for her cell phone to call Tilly but hesitated. She'd wake her for sure at almost four in the morning in Cleveland. She wanted to talk with her, but would she freak out if she told her what had happened to her sister and what she did about it? She didn't want to push her away. She might not be ready to handle something like that. She might not ever be ready. They hadn't talked about Kathrine's work, but she knew Tilly had concerns about it.

Casual relationships were always easier. In bed, after sex, she kept conversation to a minimum with her lovers, and she didn't explain her job or what she did. She didn't feel like she put them in any danger because of her work, but Tilly changed everything. Would being involved with her put Tilly at risk? What about Rachel and Claire, and Steve and Lisa, and what they'd been through because of the job? She sighed heavily, looking down on the Strip at dawn, the colored lights now a muted glow. The warmth of the rising sun caressed her shoulders as she sat on the hood of the car. She wanted to be with Tilly. There would always be risks. They came with the job. She pulled her iPhone out of her pocket and tapped Tilly's name.

CHAPTER TWENTY-SEVEN

"Hit with the force of the back of your hand, Claire, not your fingers. You'll break them," Kathrine said. "Make your stance wider and get your balance."

Claire punched the bag.

Kathrine aligned Claire's elbows. "Harder."

Claire hit harder and then started dancing around the bag, jabbing.

Kathrine laughed. "I take it you're ready to spar."

Claire jabbed harder.

"Okay. Go get in the ring, and no crying."

Claire laughed as she walked to the ring and climbed in. She'd told Kathrine she had managed to lose three percent of her body fat and tone her muscles over the last several weeks, determined not to gain any weight that supposedly came with settling down and being happy. Kathrine appreciated her dedication, but the jury was still out if Claire's boxing would turn out to be one of the better ideas she'd ever been involved in.

When she'd returned from her cathartic mission, she'd listened as Claire made her case for being taught in the ring. Claire had said she wanted to surprise Rachel, but Kathrine suspected Claire wanted to box to keep focused.

She knew Claire worried that Rachel would be uncomfortable about it. And Kathrine couldn't blame Rachel. Boxing and a head injury didn't seem to mix well. Frank and Kathrine had talked about training her in a crash course in self-defense, but Claire insisted she wanted to box. Kathrine hesitated at first and insisted Claire verify from her doctor that it was all right before she committed to teach her. She also asked Frank what he thought since he had had medical training in special forces. He didn't seem to have a problem with it as long as she wore the helmet.

Rachel and Claire needed some distraction. Nothing more had happened since Jack received the bull's-eye of Rachel in the mail, but they were both still on edge. Rachel told her she hadn't shared the information with Claire about the bull's-eye and asked her not to mention it to her. Kathrine could understand why. If it were her wife, she probably wouldn't have shared it either. Threatening letters frequently occurred at the shed. No sense worrying your spouse unnecessarily. The job caused enough stress.

Beth Riley, one of the special-operations agents, entered the ring and walked to Claire, holding out her gloved hands. Beth was blond and the same height as Claire but outweighed her by about ten pounds. Claire touched Beth's gloves and nodded as Beth went to her corner and Claire walked to hers.

Kathrine slipped Claire's mouthguard in, adjusted her helmet, and gave her instructions. Claire chewed on her mouthpiece, hitting her gloves together and shuffling her feet.

Kathrine inspected her stance. "Watch your shoulder. You lower that left shoulder, and it's going to be lights-out. Remember, defense for now. No offensive moves unless you defend first. Now go out there and be the tiger."

Claire slapped her gloves together and went out to the middle of the ring.

Beth came out punching.

Claire stumbled back.

"Get that arm up, and move," Kathrine said.

Rachel came into the gym and stood beside Kathrine, watching Claire.

Anyone could tell Rachel wasn't happy that Claire had stepped into the ring.

"You could have told me," Rachel said, as she watched Claire move.

"We tried to talk her into something else, but she insisted on boxing. How'd you find out?"

"Frank let it slip."

Kathrine shook her head. "Don't put me in the middle of you two."

Rachel folded her arms across her chest, continuing to watch Claire.

Kathrine saw Claire glance at Rachel, narrowly missing a right hook. "Keep your mind on what you're doing."

"She looks great. How's she moving?" Rachel asked.

"She's doing okay. A little slow on that left side, but she's doing good." Kathrine yelled to Claire, "Punch harder with your left."

"Beth knows not to hit hard on the right side of her head?" Rachel asked.

"Yes, and we put extra padding on that side of her helmet." Kathrine moved a step forward. "Time."

Claire came back to her corner, sweat pouring down her face, her cheeks flushed. Rachel grabbed the cloth and wiped her face and took out her mouthguard.

"How are you doing? You look great," Rachel said.

Claire bent over and rested her gloves on her knees. "I'm a little winded, but good." She stood and took deep breaths. "You're not mad?"

Rachel rolled her eyes and shook her head.

"Use some combinations this time," Kathrine said.

Rachel squirted water in Claire's mouth and put her mouthguard back in. "Be careful."

Kathrine smiled. "Be aggressive."

Beth met Claire in the middle of the ring and punched her in the lip. Claire backed away and glared at her.

"I'm not your momma." Beth motioned with her right glove for Claire to come after her.

Kathrine yelled again. "Be tough. Punch her. Don't let her rattle you."

Claire stepped forward but didn't keep her guard up. Beth punched her in the left cheek.

Rachel grimaced. "Did she say why she wanted to do this and not martial arts or something else?"

"Time." Kathrine motioned for Claire to come to her. "Get over here. What are you thinking?"

Claire put her hands down, hung her head, and slowly walked over to Kathrine and Rachel.

Kathrine put her hand on Claire's shoulder. "What are you doing? That was pitiful." She wiped Claire's face with the towel. "Are you going to let her walk all over you like that? Fight back. Now get in there and engage."

They watched as Claire did as she was told.

"She didn't really tell me. She obviously likes boxing more than martial arts. It's not a bad idea." Kathrine glanced at Rachel. "I think she wants to get some stronger skills in self-defense, and given the shit that's happened lately, it's not a bad idea, you know."

Claire walked back out to the middle of the ring, and Beth came at her, punching multiple times.

Rachel paced but kept quiet.

Kathrine yelled at Claire. "Keep your chin down, or you're going to get punched back to Cleveland."

Rachel paced with more fervor. "She should stop before she gets hurt."

Kathrine focused on Claire. "Oh, don't be such a wife. She'll be fine. One-two, Claire."

Claire went in, feigning left, and then slammed her right glove into Beth's face, knocking her off balance.

Kathrine punched the air. "Now!"

Claire shuffled and reset her feet, put her hips into the punch, and delivered a one-two combination, connecting perfectly. Beth went down to the canvas.

Kathrine jabbed her fist into the air. "Time."

Claire shuffled her feet again and leaned over Beth. "Who's your momma now?" She strutted back to her corner, punching her gloves together.

Kathrine went to Beth and pulled her up by the glove, then took Beth's mouthguard out, taking off one of her gloves. "You all right?"

"I'm good." Beth reached for her mouthguard in Kathrine's hand.

Kathrine leaned close. "You took a dive, didn't you? She didn't hit you that hard."

Beth smiled and left the ring as Kathrine walked back to Claire and Rachel.

"Now that's more like it, Claire. You're done for the day. Go shower, and make sure you talk with Beth to let her know everything's okay between the two of you."

She took off Claire's gloves and then removed her mouthguard. Claire left to shower.

Kathrine turned to Rachel. "At least she'll know how to do something if she gets into a difficult situation."

"I just don't want her to get hurt. She's still so vulnerable on the right side of her head. It's a bad idea to let her come into the ring. I know we talked about some self-defense, but I don't want her doing this anymore. She'll have to choose something else. One good hit to her head and she could be in the hospital." She folded her arms tightly across her chest. "Or lose some memories. Or forget me again."

"Her doctor approved, and she's well protected."

Rachel shifted her weight and jammed her hands into her pockets. Her jaw muscles flexed.

"If you feel that strongly about it, we won't do it anymore, but I think it's still a good idea to let her work out with us. We'll just make sure she doesn't spar anymore. Don't worry about her. Beth barely boxed with her, and she wouldn't have hit her very hard."

"No more boxing, Kathrine. It's too much of a risk." Rachel walked off.

CHAPTER TWENTY-EIGHT

Rachel stopped undressing and sat on the bed, trying to get her head around what Claire was saying.

"You had no right to tell Kathrine you didn't want me to box."

"I don't want you to get hurt, Claire. It's not a smart thing to do. What if you had gotten hit on the side of the head?"

"I had a helmet on, with padding, and the doctors said it was okay as long as I'm careful."

Rachel needed to make her point. "You feel you have the right to tell me when you think I'm doing something too dangerous. Why can't I tell you not to box?"

Claire sighed and rubbed her forehead. "Okay. I see your point, but what we do is between you and me, not anyone else. You had no right to tell Kathrine not to let me box."

Rachel took her hand. "I'm sorry. I was wrong to do it."

"I want to ride motorcycles."

"What?"

"I want to ride motorcycles, off-road bikes."

Rachel let go of her hand. "Are you nuts? What is wrong with you, Claire?"

"Nothing's *wrong* with me. I just want to do some physical things. You ride off-road motorcycles, so why can't I? I rode in college, and you said I did great."

"Absolutely not. Choose something else."

Claire threw the covers off and got out of the bed, spun around, and glared at her. "What is wrong with you? *You* are such a control freak."

"Don't you have enough to do with your pottery business and working out at the shed?"

"No. It's not enough. I need something more to do."

"Not motorcycles, Claire, please." Rachel watched her pace.

"Rachel, you have to quit trying to control me. I don't understand why you're so against off-road motorcycles."

"I'm not trying to control you, just keep you safe. I've ridden off-road bikes since I was twelve years old. It's different than learning to ride again at your age."

"I've ridden before. I'm not a doll. You don't have to worry that I'll break."

"But why push it? Can't you find something less dangerous? It's not like you."

"Well, I've changed."

"Well, that's kind of obvious."

Claire crossed her arms. "When you think about me being in danger, does it make your stomach churn? Do you get a headache? Do you feel anxious, like you're going to explode?"

"Yes."

"So now you know how I feel every damn time you walk out that door to go to that job."

Rachel's mouth dropped open. "That's what this has all been about, isn't it?"

Claire stared at her. Her face tensed. Her eyes narrowed.

"Who's trying to control whom?" Rachel got off the bed. "I've tried to do what you wanted, Claire. I've turned down some of the jobs at work because you were afraid and didn't want me to do them. What do you want now? For me to give it up completely. You're the one who wants to control everything. That's selfish, Claire, and it's not fair. My work is important to me, and you knew what it would involve when I started working with Jack."

"I'm not selfish. Don't call me selfish. Not after what I've been through with you."

Rachel moved to her, already regretting her phrasing. "I've been through a lot with you too."

"That wasn't my fault, Rachel."

"What I went through wasn't my fault either."

"Yes, it was. If you hadn't gone to London with Brice Chambers and worked with MI6, none of that would have happened to you."

"You're saying that being caught and tortured by Yumiko was my doing? What happened to me happened because of the program Justin stole. It's not my fault he stole it from me."

Claire's cheeks turned red. "Because of you, we almost died in that plane crash."

Their conversation turned from bad to worse, and neither of them could stop the emotional landslide barreling down on them.

The words tumbled out before Rachel could stop them. "Well, *you* led Derrick on, and that's why he tried to shoot me, but the shot ricocheted and got you instead."

Claire gasped and slapped her.

The stinging burn spread through Rachel's cheek. Her eyes began to water. For a split second, she wanted to slap Claire back. She did the only thing she could do. She walked out of the bedroom and slammed the door behind her.

She paced the living room and then went into one of the guest bedrooms, throwing herself onto the bed. She turned over, fluffed the pillow, and stared at the wall. She hadn't brushed her teeth or taken a shower, but no chance in hell she would go back into their bedroom to get her toothbrush. She punched the pillow again. She wanted her own pillow. She heard a noise in the hallway and stared at the closed door, hoping Claire would come in, but the door stayed shut. She sighed.

An hour went by. She stripped and lay back in the bed in her silk chemise and underwear. The clock on the nightstand guarded against her sleep. One twenty a.m. She turned onto her back and stared at the ceiling. One forty a.m. She needed to take a hot shower and relax, but she wanted to go into the master shower, not a guest bathroom. One forty-five a.m. Should she go to Claire and grovel? No. It wasn't her fault. Yes. She'd said some harsh things, and she didn't mean it about Derrick, but Claire had it coming. She always apologized. Claire slapped *her*. Tilly got it right. Claire was a spoiled brat. Even in college she acted like a spoiled brat. One fifty-six a.m. Motorcycles? She wouldn't be able to ride a motorcycle. It had been too long. She'd get killed. God, she was such a pain in the ass sometimes.

She threw the covers off and went into the guest bathroom. She tucked her hair under a shower cap, stepped into the shower, and let the hot water run down her aching neck and shoulders. She stared at the bathroom tile. They'd been through so much together, from heartbreak to horror, and everything in between. They'd get through this, but maybe Claire wasn't strong enough to handle her being an agent. Being with Claire could be putting her life in danger, again. Her fears were justified. Look where they were right now. She couldn't bear the thought of letting Claire go for any reason. How could she live without her?

She got out of the shower, dried herself, and wiped the steam from the mirror with the towel. She wrapped another towel around herself, then held her left hand up and inspected her wedding ring in the mirror. She loved Claire, but was love enough?

She opened the bathroom door and walked into the bedroom. And there stood Claire, eyes red from crying and wearing that sexy turquoise negligée.

She ran to Rachel and threw her arms around her, holding her. "I'm so sorry, Rachel. I'm an ass. I don't know what happened."

Rachel wrapped her arms around her and buried her face in her neck. "No. I'm wrong. I'm sorry. I didn't mean what I said, Claire. I just said it to hurt you. I mean…I meant it about the motorcycle but not about Derrick."

"I know. I didn't mean it about the plane crash or any of it. I'm so sorry I slapped you. I'll never do it again. I swear." She kissed Rachel's cheek and then her mouth. She stroked her hair. "I'm so sorry." She pulled Rachel onto the bed with her. "Never, never again. I don't want to fight with you. I hate it. I feel so out of control."

"I do too. I think it's from everything we're going through. My emotions are bottled up inside, and someone is shaking the bottle, and I'm going to explode from the pressure."

"Rachel, we can't go on like this. Things need to change. We need some significant stress release, but for now, I know what we both need." She slipped Rachel's towel off.

Rachel hungrily took Claire's nightgown off her and began to kiss her neck, touching her breasts, aching, starving. Whatever the problems were between them, they'd always come back together.

Chapter Twenty-nine

When Rachel got home the following day, she felt like she'd been dragging a hundred-pound weight. Her knees hurt, her back ached, and her head pounded. She couldn't wait to take a hot shower. She put the key fob on the hook in the kitchen and took two ibuprofen. A package about the size of a toaster was on the counter, with a note from Olivia taped to it. Rachel removed the note and read it.

This package arrived for you by messenger around seven as I was leaving to go home. Didn't have time to call you. Sorry. Olivia.

Rachel placed the note on the counter and picked up the box. The address was handwritten, but the return address was a computer-generated post-office number in San Francisco. She inspected the package closely. What could it be? It didn't weigh much. She hadn't ordered anything. She took it with her to the bedroom, shaking it as she walked to see if she could hear anything. She set it on the nightstand and lay on the bed beside Claire. She yawned and nestled onto her pillows, too tired to open it right now.

Claire slipped a bookmark into the book she held and laid it beside her on the bed. "Hey, you. You look beat."

"I am."

"What's in the package?"

"I have no idea. I don't remember ordering anything. Olivia said it came this evening."

"Really. I didn't notice. I ate early, worked in the studio on a special piece, and came in and took a shower and started reading. You going to open it?"

"I'm too tired." Rachel rolled over toward her and yawned. "You do it. I have no idea what it is. It can't be that important."

Claire opened the box and peered in. "That's an odd purchase." She reached in and brought out a brown leather strap and showed it to Rachel.

Rachel looked at it and jumped out of bed, practically tripping over herself.

Claire looked baffled. "Rachel, what's wrong?"

"Put that back in the box." Rachel staggered into the bathroom, slammed the door behind her, and vomited. Her hands shook so hard she could barely wet a washcloth to wipe her face. She splashed the water over her face. Images of Yumiko violently beating her with the brown leather strap flashed into her mind. She rushed to the toilet and threw up again.

Claire knocked on the bathroom door. "Rachel, are you all right?"

Rachel put her hand toward the door. "Give me a minute. I'll be fine." She didn't want Claire to see her like this—trembling, weak, feeling like she would vomit her insides out at any moment. A sense of darkness and dread hung over her. She had to shake it off, get away from it somehow.

The door started to open.

"Don't come in. I'll be out in a minute." She tried to get herself under control, but her hands continued to shake, and the tight knot in the pit of her stomach burned and ripped through her.

She looked at her ashen face in the mirror.

Claire knocked on the door again. "Rachel, what's going on?"

"Give me a minute. I'll be right out." She brushed her teeth, washed her face again, and emerged from the bathroom.

Claire sat on the edge of the bed, her face tense, and immediately stood and went to her. "Seriously, you are not all right. You look awful."

"I'm okay. Just too many long days."

"Bullshit." Claire walked to the bed, stuffed the leather strap back into the open box, and shoved it at her. "What does it mean?"

Rachel inspected the box and wrapping, carefully looking, searching for anything unusual, but Yumiko wouldn't make that kind of mistake. She threw the box on the floor.

"Rachel, what's going on?"

Rachel raised her hand. "I need to make some phone calls. I'll be back in a little while."

She phoned Olivia as she walked toward her office. "Who delivered the package?"

"A man."

"What did he look like? Anything out of the ordinary?"

"He was about five six or seven, thin, black hair, dressed in brown shorts and a tan shirt. He looked like a delivery man. I noticed he had a name above his shirt pocket, but I didn't pay any attention to it."

"Did he leave after he delivered it?"

"Yes, Ms. Rachel. Everything was fine."

After she finished talking with Olivia, she pulled out the gun in the desk drawer, checked the load, and took the safety off. She went through the house and checked all the security alarms, then stepped outside and called Jack while she surveyed the property around the house. "Are you in town?"

"No. I'm in Flagstaff, but I'm taking an early flight tomorrow morning and should be in the office by ten. Why?"

"We need to talk. I want someone visibly out here on the property tonight."

"What's going on?"

If she asked, Jack would fly back immediately, but she couldn't bring herself to do it. She needed time to process and talk with Claire. If they were safe, she could wait to talk with him. "We'll talk in the morning." She scanned the darkness, feeling like she was being watched. She palmed the gun tighter.

"I'll send someone out immediately. You want one or two guards?"

"Two. I'm outside, and I'll wait out here until they get here."

"Do you want me to fly back?"

"No. I want to wait." He couldn't get there for hours, and the guards would be there in less than thirty minutes.

Yumiko had tipped her hand. Intentional or not, it didn't matter. Rachel no longer had any doubt. The leather strap was a personal message. Now she clearly saw it. Each incident had been a subtle message. She almost felt relieved. No more guessing. No wondering if it might be her. But how long would Yumiko play this game? What would she do to increase the stakes? Would she try to wear her down like she did when she tortured her? Would she personally come after her or send her people to do her dirty work?

"Okay. Let me know if you want or need anything. Are you sure you're all right? I can get back quickly."

She barely heard what he said. She couldn't concentrate on anything but Yumiko. "I'll be okay as soon as security gets here. We'll talk in the morning."

Relief washed over her when she recognized the security vehicle as it turned off the main road to their long driveway. She gave them the key to Claire's studio so they could use the bathroom facilities and told them a credible threat existed and to be extra vigilant. She dead-bolted the doors when she came into the house, rechecked the alarm system, and went into the bedroom.

Claire sat up in the bed, her stare fixed on her.

"Just so you know, we have two guards outside."

"What happened?"

Rachel couldn't tell her everything, at least not until she had the answers to the questions she knew she'd ask. But Claire needed to know enough to be safe.

"I don't want you to leave the house tomorrow. I'll be home after I talk to Jack. Then we can talk." She sat down on the bed beside her. "I think it's Yumiko." Her stomach writhed when she said her name out loud.

"Because of the leather strap?"

Understanding passed between them. Rachel didn't have to explain it. "I want to be sure. I know you have questions, but I don't have the answers yet."

Claire wrapped her arms around her. Rachel felt the immediate comfort.

"You're trembling." Claire kissed the side of her face. "She knew you'd react like that. That's why she sent it. That bitch. She's toying with you, Rachel."

Rachel held on to her. "Yes, she is, but we're safe for now. I want to talk with Jack. He'll be back in the office later tomorrow morning." She leaned back to look Claire in the eye. "This means she's watching us, babe. You can't take this lightly, okay?"

The reality of the situation set in, sending a wave of pressure into her chest. The sensation surprised her. A part of her had hoped Jack was right, that her reasoning was distorted, dysfunctional, caused from a residual mental scar because of what Yumiko had done to her. But Yumiko was coming after her. It couldn't be clearer if she'd left a voice mail telling her so. How would she deal with it? How would she protect Claire? And what about Sarah? Tilly? Her heart skipped a beat. They were all in danger.

She held Claire through the night as she slept, but Rachel couldn't sleep. Every noise, every creak made her pulse race. By dawn, exhausted and on edge, she used a long, hot shower to wash away some of the cobwebs, though it did nothing for the tension.

Later in the morning, Claire reached down and got a forkful of omelet, holding it to Rachel's mouth. "Eat something before you go."

Rachel took the bite and touched Claire's cheek. "Remember. Don't go anywhere until I get back."

Claire nodded. "I'm glued to the house. Don't worry about me."

Rachel kissed her, then said good-bye to her and Olivia as she walked out the door with the package. It felt like a bomb ready to explode.

Jack quickly walked into her office and sat heavily in the chair. "What's up?"

She reached into the open package, pulled out the leather strap, and tossed it onto the desk. "I got this delivered last night."

Jack's face tensed. She didn't have to explain it to him either. He leaned back in his chair. "I don't know what to say, Rachel. I'm sorry. You were right. I didn't put it together as quickly as I should have. You need a plan."

Her hands began to tremble. She knew better than anyone what the leather strap meant. She'd have to fight with everything she had to survive. None of them were ready. And to not set in motion some type of protection and plan would leave her and Claire vulnerable.

"I traced it back to a PO box in San Francisco, but it led nowhere. The guy who owns it is some self-employed salesman who said he didn't know anything about it. Jack, I need your help. I can't do this by myself."

Jack leaned in and put his hands on her desk. "You don't have to. You have all of our help. Tell me what you think."

"Yumiko blames me for the Philippines and for the US exposure. She had her people follow Claire. She sent you the threatening note. Tilly's gown and car were damaged. Claire's car was keyed. And now this." She picked up the strap and threw it into the trash. "She sent it to our house, Jack. Our *new* house. I want different pass codes for the security system, and I want everything changed. I want two guards at the house at all times. I want the best, most experienced security you can get for Claire, me, Tilly, and Sarah. We're going to need it."

Jack's concerned expression intensified. "You got it."

"Tilly's more at risk than Sarah because she's in so many places by herself. We need to get security on her and Sarah immediately. Can you have Kathrine handle security for Tilly?"

"Yes, but it might be better if we used someone else. Kathrine's involved with Tilly, and it's always better to have an outside person provide that kind of protection. You that sure she'll go after Tilly?"

Rachel nodded. "She'll start from the outside and work her way in."

"Yumiko's smart. She'll expect a guard after sending you that." Jack pointed to the leather strap in the trash can. He walked over and dug it out. "We may need this as evidence. I'll keep it in my office."

"Just as long as I don't have to see it. She or her people could have gotten into the house while the contractor worked on it. Who knows what they did?" The possibility of Yumiko or her people being in their house made her shudder. She could have just as easily been killed in her sleep. Or Claire.

"You know, Rachel, sometimes it's better to let the enemy in and feed them what you want them to know. If she put any kind of listening devices inside the house, it'd be better if you left them where they are. We'll do a full sweep of the house and find anything placed there. It'll only be audio because visual is too hard to hide. If anything's there, we could investigate and find out who put it in, but if we do that, it may tip off Yumiko. Better to not show our hand until we get some information and benefit from it. We'll use her snoop against her."

Rachel smiled. She liked the plan. Her heartbeat slowed. She knew what Yumiko was truly capable of, and from now on, until it was over, she had to make sure she and Claire were ready. "I'll call Tilly and Sarah and talk with them, let them know to be extra careful, but it's best if we don't let them know we have security on them. They'd worry, especially Tilly. She'll make a big deal about it. And Ricky might throw a fit."

"I agree. I'll send Kathrine to get it started. She won't do direct security, but she can coordinate it and get the reports." Jack tucked the box under his arm and stood. He tapped her desk with his index finger. "All right. Let's do this, but I want you to know, it may be a waiting game. To get her to play the game we want, you need to maintain the appearance of your normal life. She'll expect you to respond in some way about the leather strap, but we want her to be confident and underestimate you."

"It'll be her mistake when she does." Rachel sat back in the chair after Jack left, wanting to feel relief, but Yumiko was out there, scheming.

She gazed out the window, trying to get her mind to settle. She picked up the phone and called Claire. "We need to go to the reservation and get ourselves together. What do you think?"

"Absolutely."

Rachel's shoulders relaxed. What would happen if she under-estimated Yumiko? She and Claire weren't the only pieces in this deadly game Yumiko wanted to play. Tilly and Sarah were also at risk. None of them were prepared, not like they needed to be. How could they get ready? How much time did they have? She and Claire would go to the reservation, and she'd work things through, away from the listening devices Yumiko could have placed in their home. Rachel's cousins Ilesh and Joseph would help them. She had something Yumiko would never have—people who loved her and who had her back, no matter what.

CHAPTER THIRTY

Kathrine exited the plane and stepped over the connection to the attached walkway like a drunken sailor trying to maneuver on the deck of a rolling ship. One of the pilots, saying good-bye to the disembarking passengers, caught her when she staggered. "Sorry," she said, flashing him a smile.

The Ohio humidity struck her full force. Her hair went limp, and she imagined she'd lost every curl she'd put in with the curling iron that morning. She followed the other passengers toward baggage claim, then saw Tilly wave and smile at the bottom of the escalators. Tilly hugged her and slipped her arm in the crook of Kathrine's elbow as she walked her to the baggage turntable.

"I'm so glad you're here, even if it's for only a couple of days. Will you get to spend some time with me, or will you be busy working the entire time?"

Kathrine had told her she was coming to Cleveland on assignment but didn't tell her it was to assess her security vulnerabilities and to meet with the bodyguards Jack had hired for her and Sarah. Tilly didn't press her. She patted Tilly's arm. "We'll make time."

"No hotel. Sarah insists you stay at her house. I gave up my apartment and have a permanent room at her house, so you can stay in one of the guest rooms next to me."

Kathrine tasted a dash of disappointment in Tilly's words. She'd hoped to take their relationship to the next level, but obviously Tilly wasn't ready yet. She told herself it was probably best since their time together would be limited. But still, the words left a bitter aftertaste.

Tilly clung to her arm, not letting her go until Kathrine reached for her luggage on the turntable and dragged it off. "I'm parked on Level Three."

Kathrine gripped the armrest on the car door as Tilly drove onto the interstate, weaving in and out of traffic, honking at drivers who apparently didn't get over soon enough to suit her. Did she drive that way because she didn't know any better or didn't care? She couldn't figure it out and hoped they'd get to Sarah's before they had an accident. Relief washed over her when Tilly finally pulled into Sarah and Ricky's driveway. She released the door support and rubbed her hand, trying to get the circulation back. "Who taught you how to drive?"

Tilly laughed. "Would you believe I taught myself?"

"No surprise there."

Kathrine surveyed the two-story brick house in an upscale neighborhood, surrounded by beautiful trees and shrubs. It would be easy to watch the house and see anyone who approached from any direction.

Sarah greeted them at the door and hugged Kathrine.

As they sat at the kitchen table, drinking coffee and visiting, Kathrine tried to focus, but she couldn't take her eyes off Tilly. Now that they were physically together again, the attraction seemed stronger than the last time they were together in Las Vegas.

Sarah glanced at her several times and smiled.

Her cell phone went off. Samantha Dupont, Tilly's bodyguard, called to report in. Kathrine excused herself and went into the living room, where Tilly and Sarah couldn't hear the conversation.

She ended the call and walked back into the kitchen. "I have to go out for a while."

"Everything all right?" Tilly asked.

"I just need to take care of some business."

Tilly looked disappointed and nodded. "Hurry back."

Kathrine walked out the front door and slipped into Samantha's car. Samantha was a perfect fit for Tilly—the same height and unremarkable in her appearance, which meant she would blend in well in a crowd. They discussed the specific details of her assignment. Samantha assured her she would coordinate with Sarah's security.

"You're lead for this assignment. I want your people to stay back. Rachel and Jack want Tilly and Sarah covered, but not overtly. Make sure none of them suspect. Remember, Tilly's somewhat well-known here in Cleveland, so she's going to have people around her."

The meeting took longer than Kathrine had expected. By the time Samantha drove her to the house, the streetlights were on.

Tilly met her at the door and led her into the living room. Kathrine settled on the sofa, and Tilly poured herself and Kathrine a drink, handing it to her when she sat down beside her.

"Where's Sarah?"

"She and Ricky went out. I think to the country club."

Kathrine took her hand. "I'm sorry I had to leave." She felt the reassuring pressure as Tilly squeezed.

"It's okay. I know we're limited in time while you're here. Can we go out tomorrow, or do you have business?"

"Actually, business is taken care of, and I have all day and night tomorrow."

Tilly's eyes danced. "That's wonderful. I planned the day for us just in case, and tomorrow night, you, Sarah, and Ricky will come to the club. I'll do my set, and then we can go out. Do you like country music?"

Before Kathrine could answer Tilly added, "I love country music."

Kathrine laughed. "Yes. I like it."

Tilly set her glass down and then took Kathrine's out of her hand and set it beside hers on the end table. "I'm so glad you're here." She leaned closer, slid her hand over Kathrine's waist, and kissed her.

Kathrine wrapped her arms around her and pulled her next to her, returning her kiss. "I've missed you, Tilly."

"I've missed you. More than I thought I would." Tilly kissed her again.

Kathrine held her. The urge to be near her was overwhelming.

The next day the sun finally broke through the clouds in the afternoon, but a damp chill hung in the air. Kathrine drew Tilly's borrowed jacket tighter around her shoulders as they sat on the wooden bench. "I'm used to Las Vegas weather."

"I know. Ohio can be a shock." Tilly looked at the sky filled with white, billowing clouds. "I like Las Vegas, but I love the season changes here in Ohio. I wish we had more sunny days, but it has its charms."

Kathrine watched several covered, black, boxy-looking horse-drawn buggies pass, mixing with the line of cars when the traffic light changed to green. She closed her eyes and listened to the rhythmic *clip-clop* of the horses' hooves as they trotted gracefully by. It was all so strange, yet beautiful. The men had long beards and wore black, wide-brimmed hats. Their black suits didn't have collars or lapels. Each time a buggy passed, she tried to get a better look.

"They're called mutza suits. They're usually black, but sometimes the men wear lighter colors. Their trousers don't have cuffs, and they wear suspenders. The men with beards are married."

A buggy turned into the parking lot of the local hardware store, and a family clamored out. The woman and two young girls were wearing simple, long, dark dresses and white tie bonnets. Kathrine reached for her cell phone to take a picture.

Tilly slowly pulled her hand down. "They don't like their picture taken."

Kathrine put her phone back in her pants pocket. "Why?"

"It's a privacy thing and has something to do with their religion."

Kathrine nodded and continued to watch. "What's the name of this city again?"

"Middlefield."

"I feel like I've stepped back in time. It's quite relaxing."

Tilly smiled. "I hoped you'd enjoy it."

Kathrine patted her thigh. "I do, very much. I'm glad we came here, but *I'm* driving back to Sarah's and to the airport tomorrow."

Tilly glanced at her and smiled. "You don't like the way I drive?"

Kathrine ate the last bite of sandwich and finished her bottle of water. She crumpled the wrapper and put it and the empty plastic bottle into the paper bag and tossed it into the trash can a few feet from the bench. "I value my life and yours. That's all I'll say."

Tilly playfully slapped her arm. "Come on. I want to show you some of the Amish furniture and craft stores before we go."

The day and evening went by too quickly. Kathrine said good night to Sarah and Ricky as they left the club after Tilly finished her last song. Tilly made her way through the crowd to join her at their table. Several people came over to the table and complimented Tilly.

When there was a lull, Tilly leaned over to Kathrine. "Let's get out of here and go somewhere. I know a great bar." She hailed a taxi and took her to Evie J's. The doorman waved them through as Tilly grabbed Kathrine's hand and pulled her past the crowd waiting to get in.

"Come on. You'll love it," she told Kathrine.

The large area with tables and a dance floor was packed, with barely enough room to get through the press of people. Tilly waved and greeted people as she dragged Kathrine through the maze of bodies to a door and then through a dim hallway and up a flight of stairs.

The sound of the country band's music bounced off the walls.

When they reached the top step, Tilly let go of Kathrine's hand and hugged a man she called Henry. She turned and introduced Kathrine. Henry reached out and gently shook her hand. "I've heard so much about you, Kathrine. Welcome. I do need to ask, are you carrying a concealed weapon?"

"Is that a problem?" Kathrine asked.

"No. Not at all. I just need to know."

Kathrine nodded, and he motioned for them to go into the room.

The music from the band was at a controlled volume and easy on the ears. The room was dimly lit, with about two dozen round tables, some with four armed cushioned chairs, others with two, and several comfortable-looking booths at the far side. About half the tables were occupied. Several security guards stood along the wall near the entrance, their posture relaxed. People in this room were either rich, powerful, or well known.

Most of the front tables near the large picture window with a view of the band and dance floor below were filled. The bar was at the opposite end of the room. A woman about their age with braided red hair came over and greeted them, telling Tilly how much she missed hearing her sing. Tilly spoke to her and then pointed. They were led to a booth in a darker area of the room, where Tilly slid into the small, cushioned booth, and Kathrine scooted in across from her.

Kathrine ordered a sidecar, and Tilly asked for a brandy.

"I wanted to come here because we'll be left alone. You can relax. Henry and the staff will make sure we're not bothered."

"This is a nice place. Do you sing here?"

Tilly nodded. "The band that's playing tonight just cut a record in Nashville. I think they're going to be big if they can keep themselves together. So many of the bands that are good and would make it break up before they can get any momentum going."

The waitress brought their drinks. Kathrine reached for her credit card, but Tilly put out her hand and stopped her. "No. Drinks for us are on the house. I work here about ten weeks out of the year and bring in a lot of business. The owner treats me well."

Kathrine thanked the waitress and tipped her a twenty-dollar bill.

The waitress smiled, thanked her, and left.

Tilly remained quiet. Was she tired or uncomfortable now that they were alone without any distractions? She cleared her throat and straightened her shoulders. "Kathrine, I'm really glad you were able to be with me. It's helped me so much to be with you. I've thought a lot about our talk in the car in Las Vegas and what you told me when you called me that morning after you got back from Carson. I'm so sorry about your sister." Tilly took Kathrine's hand and held it. "I hope you don't regret telling me about what you did and how you felt."

"No. Not at all. It helped me to share it with you."

"Are you feeling better about everything?"

"Yes, I am. It's been difficult to let it all go, but I think I'm doing pretty well."

Tilly let go of her hand. "I'm glad."

They stayed there in the booth, talking, sharing their thoughts and feelings about the day. Tilly glanced at her watch several times.

"Tilly, would you like to leave?"

"No. Definitely not."

"Then why do you keep looking at your watch?"

Tilly touched her half-empty glass and looked at the table. "Because the time's going by too quickly, and in just a few hours you'll be leaving. I don't want you to." She gazed into Kathrine's eyes. "Can we go now? I want you to come to my room and be with me. I want to be alone with you."

Kathrine smiled.

Tilly slid out of the booth. "Let's go."

Tilly paid the cab driver, and they quietly entered the house and went to her room. She closed and locked the bedroom door and turned toward Kathrine. "I want you with me." Tilly moved against her, pressing into her. "I need you next to me. Please, Kathrine, just lie with me until it's time for you to go." Tilly's eyes were moist, and when she reached for Kathrine's hand, she was trembling.

Kathrine kissed her. Deep and open. Tilly was vulnerable and would surrender if she pursued her. But she didn't.

No more words passed between them. But in the quiet morning stillness, as the earth was beginning to wake, Kathrine watched as Tilly took off her back brace and slipped her blouse on again, then kicked off her shoes and lay on the bed and waited for her.

Kathrine set the alarm on her cell phone and laid it on the nightstand. She took off her holster and gun and placed them beside her cell phone. She slipped her shoes off and lay next to her. Tilly turned and scooted against her, pressing into her. Kathrine held her, feeling her warmth, her beauty, her need.

Kathrine hungered for Tilly's touch, but more than that, she yearned to be near her. She stroked Tilly's hair and caressed her arm, cradling her as close as she could.

Tilly clasped her hand and held on.

They would have no sex. But they had the tender beginnings of love, and they were together. And that was more than enough for now.

CHAPTER THIRTY-ONE

Rachel bent closer to Ash's neck, catching the scent of hay and wood, and today she swore he smelled like chocolate. She wrapped her legs tighter around him and gave him his head, pushing him as fast as he could run.

Claire stayed close behind on the mare.

The Arizona dust kicked up from Ash's thundering hooves, and the wind caught his mane and swirled gently against Rachel's face. In that moment of sheer joy, she began to feel the stress ebb out of her. The blues of the sky, the white, billowing clouds, the sun-faded bronze, beige, and rust colors of the mountain range in front of them, the yellow-greens and sage on the sweeping hills all became more vivid as the smells and feel of the environment swept over her. It was good they were back on the reservation and their land. It was a balm to them both. They desperately needed its safety and comfort, and Rachel needed to be with family. Her aching soul needed relief from the constant tension of Yumiko's sick game. Jack would be sweeping for devices and surveillance on the house while they were gone, which partially put her mind at ease.

Ash's breathing became labored. She slowed him to a walk as Claire reined Łichíí, the chestnut mare's coat glistening with sweat. Łichíí reared slightly, shaking her head.

Claire laughed. "She's full of vinegar. She almost caught him." She patted Ash's rump, damp from sweat, as he breathed heavily. "Łichíí wants to go, but Ash has gotten fat and out of shape."

Rachel reached down and stroked Ash's neck. "He's just had too much of the good life. He'll be in great shape by the time we get back." She wiped her sweaty hand on the leg of her jeans.

"Look." Claire pointed in front of her toward the mountain as they turned. "There it is." She pushed her heels into the mare and took off.

Rachel called after her. "You'll have to walk her out if you run her much more before we get there."

Claire slowed her horse and walked back to Rachel. "Isn't this exciting? I can't remember all of it, but I know it was wonderful." She looked toward the mountains. "Everything looks so clear."

Rachel took her hand as they walked their horses, watching the sun begin to sink over the far side of Gouyen Mountain. She surveyed the mountain range. "She's fierce today."

"What do you mean?"

She let go of Claire's hand and pointed toward the mountains. "The sunset is spreading out over her ridges. See the deep colors of gold, pale green, and azure blue? Galmoreachee, the warrior woman of the mountain, is fierce—ready for battle."

Claire smiled.

"She'll protect us while we're here this week," Rachel said. When they crested the hill, she saw their teepee off in the distance.

"Rachel, look. There it is." Claire reached over and touched Rachel's shoulder. "We're home."

Rachel smiled. *Home indeed.* She loved that Claire loved it as much as she did. Before her injury and her memory loss, Claire had talked every day about the teepee and their honeymoon, but then she lost the memories. Now Claire could remember bits and pieces, and feelings. Rachel was eager to get her back to the teepee, make new memories, build Claire's confidence, strengthen their relationship, and, most of all, prepare her to face Yumiko if it was needed.

They settled in, got the horses fed and bedded for the night, and then built a fire and ate. The hot coals cast a warm glow onto Claire's skin, the moonlight reflecting off her soft features. Rachel leaned on her elbow, watching her slowly stir the fire with a stick.

Claire gathered the small woolen blanket around herself and lay next to her. "The time here always goes so fast. This is just as wonderful as I remember, except a little cooler."

"If you're cold, we can go back inside the teepee." Rachel reached for her, bringing her closer.

"I want to stay out here as long as we can. I love being naked with you under the stars." She looked into the night and shivered.

Rachel laughed and stood, reaching for her. "Come on. We can stay naked in the warmth of the teepee."

She led Claire back to it, feeling the comfort from the small fire as they entered and closed the flap. She lay on the soft fur of the rug and reached out for her. Claire opened her blanket and lay on her, covering them. Rachel responded. Her nipples hardened, and heat thrummed and radiated between her legs as Claire, naked, engulfed her, pressed into her, warm flesh molding to hers. Claire raised and repositioned, straddling her.

Rachel slipped one hand behind her head and lay watching Claire as she slowly rocked against her in the soft light of the fire—the dance of her eyes, the rise and fall of her firm, full breasts as she breathed. She watched her for a long time.

"You're so quiet, Rachel."

"I'm enjoying the view."

Claire smiled. Her hair had grown almost shoulder length. Flashes of light from the fire sparkled in her vivid green eyes. Her soft full lips parted. Rachel looked into her eyes, then moved her hand, running it through her hair, touching her lips, her cheek, and then she cupped one of her breasts, feeling the nipple harden as she caressed it. Claire's smile broadened, and she leaned down and kissed her, moving her hot, wet center slowly over her, the night calls surrounding them.

Rachel moved her hand and skimmed Claire's thigh, then gently raked her fingers through her triangle of thick, amber hair, catching the faint familiar scent of Claire's sex. Everything intensified. The colors. Claire's scent. The feel of her as she rubbed against her.

Claire took one of Rachel's nipples into her mouth and sucked.

Pleasure surged through Rachel. Her breath caught. Her heart pounded. She throbbed for more of Claire's touch.

Claire locked eyes with her, pressing more firmly against her, sliding slowly over her. "You want it bad now, don't you." It wasn't a question, more like a declaration, like Claire revealed a secret only she knew, found hidden deep inside Rachel.

Rachel's need and urge to join with her, to feel her, to taste her, penetrated every cell. It coursed through her blood and in her heartbeat. And when her lungs filled with air, she moaned, unable to stop the words of her native language as they flowed out of her in a low, almost hushed murmur. She dipped her fingers into Claire, feeling her way into her as Claire opened to her.

Claire breathed deeply, slowly, and continued to move rhythmically against her, whispering back, "I don't understand a word you're saying, but oh, how it turns me on."

When they were both fully satisfied, Claire collapsed into her arms.

"This is how love is supposed to be, Rachel."

Rachel held her, moving her hand slowly down her back, circling with her fingers, slipping her hand over her.

"I love it when you touch me. When you run your hands over me, everything just melts away," Claire said.

"You do the same thing to me. Sometimes, when I couldn't be with you, while I waited and hoped you'd get your memory back about us..." Rachel stopped, the pain too intense.

Claire glanced at her. "Did you ever masturbate?"

Rachel laughed. "A couple of times I almost did, but no. I waited. How about you?"

Claire looked into her eyes. "I did. That night we got back from Seattle, after we had Derrick's will read. Remember? I came to your room and kissed you, and you refused to have sex with me because I couldn't remember us?"

Rachel smiled. "Yes. That was one of the nights I almost did it, and then the night you showed up at the hotel room in Cleveland when we told you we were going to let you use my program to help us." Rachel laughed.

Claire's laughter filled the teepee. "I wanted to go to bed with you, and you said we couldn't because I couldn't remember. I was so ready that night. I was an overly ripe melon."

Rachel laughed again.

"That night I got drunk, and when I got back to Sarah's, I just barely touched myself, and man, that did it. I came hard and fast."

"Was it good?"

Claire hit her gently on the arm. "No. I was too desperate. It's not funny, Rachel. I don't want to ever need you like that again and not have you with me."

Rachel rolled over and lay on top of her. "Never again, Claire. We'll never be apart for so long that you can't wait."

The night drifted into early morning as they lay in each other's arms and talked.

"Rachel, I'm scared." Claire's voice softened and floated on the predawn light.

Rachel studied her face. "About what?"

"I don't want you in the security business anymore. It's too dangerous."

Rachel had known the subject would come up again sooner or later, especially since Steve's death. She could see the concern on Claire's face every time she left for the shed. Each time she went, she saw the increasing anxious dread in Claire's eyes. "Claire, I don't want you to worry, and I don't want you to be stressed about it."

"But I do worry, and I'm stressed, and the situation isn't going to change unless you change jobs. Why do you even have to work? We both have more money than we know what to do with, and our bank accounts are growing every year. Why the hell do you need to be doing this?"

Rachel knew it would come to this. She expected it. Claire had inherited money. It was drawn to her like metal to a magnet, but Rachel was at the opposite end—poor, half-blooded white trash, living on the government dole at the worst end of the reservation, and then foster care. She knew what it was to not only have nothing, but to feel like nothing.

"Claire, I know you don't remember, but we've had this conversation many times."

Claire sat and wrapped the blanket around herself, pulling the other one over Rachel. "Then tell me, Rachel. Tell me why? Why do you do this kind of job when you don't need to?"

Rachel also sat, covering herself more completely with her blanket, reaching for Claire's beautiful face.

"Because I have skills that can help save lives. I love what I do, Claire. I know what it is to be helpless. I can help people. It makes me feel good about the path I walk in this life."

Claire took her hand and held it. "And when I worked with you, using my increased vision and your computer program to help the team, I felt good about it, but it was just too dangerous, and when I walked away, I walked away for you and for me."

Rachel squeezed her hand. "Claire, you did not walk away for me. You walked away for you because you wanted to."

"Okay. I'll be honest. You're right. I did it for me, but I begged you to come with me. Something is going to happen to you if you don't stop this. I feel it. I've always felt it. Look what you've already been through."

Claire's hands began to tremble. Things were in play that she couldn't comprehend right now. Danger already bit at their heels, like a vicious dog held at bay, snarling to attack.

"Please, Rachel, stop this before it's too late. I couldn't endure it. Not again." Claire put her hands to her face.

Rachel watched her for a moment and then reached for her and held her, trying to comfort her. She didn't want to say it. She didn't want to give it up, but she knew Claire needed it.

"All right. Let's try a compromise. I won't go in the field on any more cases, and I'll just stay at the shed. I want to do this for you, and I'll do my best. But, Claire, you need to understand if someone's life is put in jeopardy because of this compromise between us, I will break it to save a life."

Claire threw her arms around her. "Thank you. I know how much you want to work there, and I know how much the work means to you, but thank you."

"Do you understand it's a conditional compromise?"

Claire nodded.

Rachel watched her as the relief washed over her face. She gently guided her onto the soft fur of their bed and wrapped the blankets around them, engulfing them in warmth. She stroked Claire's hair. "It's going to be okay. Somehow it'll be okay."

She knew Claire had a hard time with her emotions, and it wasn't just Rachel's job and what she did. It was Yumiko. They both felt the pressure. Would Claire feel better about Rachel's work once the threat of Yumiko was resolved?

She should not have made a compromise she knew she couldn't keep. She shouldn't have said it. The idea of a lifetime of desk duty made her chest hurt, but if that's what it took to make Claire happy, then so be it. She had to at least try to do it for Claire.

❖

Claire looked toward the horizon and shaded her eyes, focusing more clearly on Itza-chu, Rachel's cousin Ilesh's beautiful paint horse. She watched as Ilesh bent forward and patted his neck. She called out to Rachel. "He's here."

Rachel put down the leather tool and scanned the area where Claire looked. "I don't see anything."

Claire pointed. "There by that mesquite tree on the right, just past where the rocks jut out."

She laughed as Rachel strained to see.

"I can barely make out a horse kind of blur. How can you see that far?"

Claire put her arm around Rachel's waist as she watched the tall, handsome Native American man ride closer, his long, dark-brown hair blowing gently in the wind. She was awestruck. "He looks like something from a Charles Marion Russell painting. He is a sight to behold." She waved, and Ilesh raised his hand in greeting.

He dismounted, the sun reflecting off his hair, his hazel eyes shining. He walked to Claire and gathered her in his arms, lifting her. "And here you are safe and well." He swung her around and put her down, then reached for Rachel, surrounding her with his long, muscular arms. "My joy is full to see you both, Moon Shadow."

He and Rachel spoke in their native tongue.

Claire listened intently, trying to recognize any of the words. She couldn't understand, but his meaning was clear—he was happy to see his cousin and her.

He turned to look at her once more, slipping his arm around her waist, looking at her from head to toe, putting his other hand on his hip.

"Well, now, look at you." He touched her face, then moved his hand behind her ear, gently tracing her scar. "We will celebrate tonight, give thanks, and ask for your continued protection. Moon Shadow, did you see her in the mountain?"

Rachel nodded. "Yes. Claire and I saw her when we rode in."

Claire looked to the mountain range, remembering what Rachel had told her about the warrior woman.

They built the fire, set their blankets down, and Ilesh presented them with the items he had brought. Gourmet coffee and expensive wine for Claire. A curious turquoise figurine for Rachel. He gently slipped the figurine into Rachel's hand.

"It is time for you to have it," he said.

Rachel showed her the figurine of a Native American woman.

"That's so beautiful." Claire inspected it more closely. The wood looked almost petrified. Embedded in the carved dress were delicate ornamental pieces of turquoise and gold.

"It's been in our family for over four hundred years," Ilesh said.

Claire and Ilesh drank the wine as they talked and laughed. When the bottle was empty, Ilesh became serious. "You two are very precious to me." He looked at Rachel. "The gathering is set for tomorrow evening."

Rachel reached over and slipped her arm through his. "I'll be ready."

"What are you two talking about?" Claire asked.

Ilesh looked intently at the mountains and then at her and Rachel. He put his arm around Rachel and brought her close, then smiled at Claire. "Rachel will explain when it's time."

The night passed quickly as they lay under the stars, talking of their times together, his and Rachel's childhood, and his hopes for them.

In the morning, he prepared Itza-chu. When he readied himself to leave, he held Claire in his arms for a long time. He kissed her forehead and then turned to Rachel and held her as she embraced him. He reached into the leather bag on his shoulder and placed a beautiful beaded, turquoise-and-gold necklace over Rachel's head. He touched it gently as it lay around her neck. "Remember," he said.

Claire saw something unspoken pass between them. "Why are you two so serious?"

He smiled again at her. "Be patient, dear Claire."

He mounted Itza-chu, raised his hand to them, turned, and rode away. Rachel wrapped her arms around Claire's waist as Claire leaned against her, watching Ilesh until the morning sun obscured their view.

Claire remembered her and Rachel's conversation from the previous early morning and felt a tinge of guilt. Had she asked Rachel to do something she couldn't do? Would not working in the field and being in on the action at the shed change her? She knew what Rachel was getting into when she went to work with Jack. She couldn't remember everything they had talked about, but she had agreed to it. Rachel's involvement at the shed had probably saved her mental health.

Claire could barely function by the time Jack and the team brought Rachel home from the Philippines. Did she have a right to insist Rachel give up something she loved because she was afraid of losing her? Was it as selfish as it seemed? The peace of their environment surrounded her. She wished they could stay here, in comfort and safety, until it was all over. Why couldn't Jack and Brice and the rest of the team take care of Yumiko and leave them the hell alone?

CHAPTER THIRTY-TWO

Rachel looked beyond the canyon walls, shading her eyes against the afternoon sun, watching a red-tailed hawk swoop down for its prey, the captive's screeching plea echoing off the sandstone walls. Ash jerked his head, as if he disapproved of the menu arrangements. Rachel laughed and patted his neck. "All God's creatures have to eat, buddy."

She and Claire continued to maneuver through the twisting natural path of the canyon. When they dismounted for a break, Claire immediately left her horse and moved closer to the canyon wall. She bent down and moved slowly along its base.

"Claire, what are you doing?"

"I'm looking."

"For what?"

Claire put her hands on her knees and continued her activity. "I don't know. Maybe fossils. I read last month in one of the geology journals that canyons are formed by all kinds of geological activity like flooding, plate tectonics, and other awesome stuff. Sometimes fossils are trapped in the canyon walls from the original geological forces."

Rachel found it fascinating that Claire knew those details. She seemed to absorb everything she read now. She would have viewed the canyon before and seen only colors for her pottery. She watched as Claire continued to search. Then she took out her cell phone and read the text from Jack again, confirming he had found listening devices in the house.

"Come over here and sit with me."

Claire stood and brushed the dust and dirt off her hands, then walked back to Rachel. They sat in the shade of the canyon wall.

Rachel smiled as she watched Claire brush more dirt off the back of her hand. "Later on, this evening, I need to go away for a while.

I need to be with some of my family. I can't explain just yet. You're going to have to accept that you can't know for now. I will eventually explain, but for the time being, you have to trust me."

She stroked Claire's hand. She needed to help her understand the concerns and apprehension she had, but if she told her Yumiko's people had bugged the house and had access to what they said, Claire's anxiety level might skyrocket. And she couldn't blame her. Her skin crawled at the thought, but the audio was going to stay in the house for now. She had weighed the consequences of each side of the coin and decided she had to tell Claire everything, especially about the listening devices so she wouldn't give anything away. She had no idea how she would take the news, so she eased into it.

"Jack and I talked about what happened in Chicago." She watched as Claire studied her face.

"I'm so sorry, Rachel. You were right. I knew you were upset about what we did."

Rachel let go of her hand. "Claire, like I told you before, I'm not upset about what you did, but I want you to know I've had you under tighter security."

Claire shook her head and diverted her eyes.

Rachel put her hand on her shoulder. "I mean it, Claire. You have to trust me."

"But why more security? Aren't the guards already at the house enough?"

"I'm sure you were followed, and I trust your instincts. You're going to have to trust me. Tilly and Sarah will also be under security."

Claire frowned and shook her head again. She took Rachel's hand. "I knew if you thought about what happened and everything else, you'd go off the deep end about it."

Rachel looked into her eyes. "What did I just say, Claire?"

"That I need to trust you."

"It's Yumiko."

Claire took both of Rachel's hands and held them, shaking her head vigorously. "You don't know that. She could have sent that leather strap just to toy with you. That's all. To mess with your head."

"Yumiko was behind the scam. She went after Jack and Frank. Her people followed you and Sarah. She probably had Tilly's gown ruined and car keyed, and your car keyed."

Claire looked around, as if trying to give herself more time. She'd put the facts together and reach the same conclusion.

"What are we going to do? Can't we just stay here on the reservation and let Jack and Brice handle it? Why do we have to go back? I don't want you involved."

Rachel cupped Claire's face in both of her hands again and turned her head, looking into her eyes. "Listen to me. Yumiko seems to always have the upper hand partly because people constantly underestimate her. I *know* her. I know what she's capable of, and I will not allow myself to underestimate her." She stroked Claire's arm. "I can't let Jack and Brice do this without me. We need to work together to take her down. It's going to require all of us."

Claire picked up a pebble and tossed it, staring off into the distance. "How long do we have to go through this?"

Rachel pursed her lips. "I have no idea. We're just going to have to dig in and see it to the end."

Claire's shoulders seemed to relax. She nodded slowly and took a long breath. "Okay."

"There's something else."

Claire turned toward her. "What?"

Rachel took her hand again. "Jack and the team found some listening devices at the house."

"You mean at our old house? The one we rented?"

Rachel shifted. "No. Our new one."

Claire's face turned red, and she jumped up. "That bitch! That fucking bitch. I'll kill her myself."

Rachel hadn't expected rage. She'd been ready for panic. She stood. "Now, Claire. Calm down."

"I swear to God, I'll kill her. Who the hell does she think she is?" She kicked the dirt. The dust swirled around her knees. "Seriously, who does she think she is?"

Rachel raised her finger. "One more thing."

Claire froze in place.

"This is a good thing."

"Huh. I'm sure," Claire said, putting her hands on her hips.

"Jack left the devices active. We're going to use them against her."

Claire threw her head back and made a noise. Rachel hoped it was a laugh, but she couldn't tell.

"You mean we're actually going to do something to her for a change?"

"That's right. We're going to take some control of the situation." Rachel hugged her. "I don't want you to worry about me. I promise you we know what we're doing. We need to leave for my cousin Joseph's soon. I want you to stay with Elaina while I go with Joseph, Ilesh, and other members of the family. I'll be back later in the night."

"Is everything all right?"

"Yes. It will be…eventually."

Claire never ceased to surprise her. Would she be okay with what Rachel wanted to do?

❖

Claire tossed her head back and laughed as she tickled the baby's round, soft belly. The baby reached out and grabbed her hair and pulled it toward his mouth. "No, no. You don't want that." She laughed again as she untangled her hair from his delicate little fingers and put him against her shoulder. She rubbed his back, nestling her face against his. "He's so beautiful."

Elaina smiled. "You seem to have found a soul mate. He never warms up so quickly to others."

After the evening meal was finished and the dishes were done, Claire went for a walk. No other members of the tribe were near Joseph and Elaina's home. Claire followed the rutted pathway for about a mile, noticing smoke in the distance and hearing the faint, unrecognized sounds of people talking as their voices carried on the wind. An uneasiness swept over her, a feeling as if she had invaded a place she shouldn't be, as if she would see or hear things not meant for her eyes and ears. She turned abruptly and walked back toward the house.

She helped get the children ready for bed, then read to Elaina and Joseph's older daughter, tucking her in while Elaina took care of the baby and their almost-three-year-old son. Claire went out on the porch and watched the earth settle into the night. Elaina joined her but was unusually quiet.

"Is everything all right, Elaina?"

"It's very kind of you to notice. I'm worried about one of our young women. Her name is Ileonna. Her mother and father have passed, and she lives with one of her father's cousins. She has gotten into some trouble recently, and I'm not sure how to help her."

"Can I do anything?"

"Thank you, that's very sweet, but I'm afraid she must deal with the consequences of her choices."

"What happened?"

"She fell in love and left the reservation to be with him. Now we have heard he beats her and has gotten in trouble with the police in Phoenix. She's pregnant, and if she refuses to return to the reservation, we can do little to help her. Ilesh visited her, but she won't return."

"That's a hard situation."

"Yes, and to make matters worse, her relative has now refused to take her in if she does come back because he feels she'll be a bad influence on his family."

They continued to discuss the situation, and then Claire went out by the trailer she and Rachel would be sleeping in and made a small fire as she waited for Rachel. As the night passed, she got blankets from the trailer and lay near the fire, listening to the night sounds, enjoying the warmth of the fire and the comfort of her surroundings.

The more she thought, the more she worried about Rachel. Yumiko was devious and cunning, and a psychopath. There was no rational way to deal with her. It put Rachel at a disadvantage, not physically, but certainly emotionally.

The more she thought about the leather strap, the angrier she grew. What kind of sick monster would do something like that? The expression on Rachel's face when she realized what was in the box haunted Claire. She wished at that moment Jack and Frank, or Brice Chambers, would kill Yumiko. Walk up to her, put a gun to her chest, and fire before she could do anything more to Rachel.

She tossed a stick onto the coals.

She needed to remain calm and try to encourage Rachel to let Jack and the others handle this canker. How could she keep Rachel out of this mess? She lay on the blanket and tried to sleep, but the troubling thoughts continued. Finally, the weariness got the best of her, and she drifted off into a half sleep.

She woke when Rachel lay down beside her, smelling of campfire smoke, sage, and other herbs. Claire reached for her.

Rachel wrapped her arm around her waist and moved next to her. "Do you want to go into the trailer?"

Claire put her hand on Rachel's and moved closer. "No. Let's sleep out here tonight. I don't want to leave tomorrow to go back home."

Rachel's lips brushed against Claire's neck, her warm breath causing a thrill.

"I'm glad you don't want to go because I'd like you to spend time with Ilesh for a couple of days. I've asked him to help you with some skills."

Claire smiled and patted her hand. "Really. I get to be trained by Ilesh? That's fabulous."

She'd been disappointed when she'd given in to Rachel's request that she not box anymore, even though Rachel was right. Why take a chance? Working out her frustration and fear when she boxed eased the stress. It kept her mind focused. She needed the physical release. They compromised, and she agreed to take body combat instead, exercise that used boxing moves without any contact. She'd already approached Beth to help her regain her skills on a motorcycle, although that too probably qualified as foolish. If she fell off and hit her head, it could be game over. But anything she wanted to do seemed a risk, so damn if she would let fear of injury run her life.

Ilesh was skilled at many things and well respected within the tribe. Her excitement grew when she thought about what she could learn from him. What would he teach her? Where would they go? Would she be able to do what he asked of her? She smiled when she thought of Rachel. Rachel knew she would like it. She snuggled in, safe and content in Rachel's arms under the full moon.

CHAPTER THIRTY-THREE

Ilesh stirred the fire with a stick, moving the newly added small pieces of wood. A momentary flame shot up as he poked the red-hot coals.

Claire sat close to the fire and stared into them. The rich, deep colors of red, orange, and amber, the warmth, the crackle of the burning wood, and the quiet caused an almost hypnotic feeling. Once her skill with the bow had returned, Ilesh announced she was ready to go into the mountains. She didn't know what they would do, but Rachel's words rang in her ears. "Remember that everything Ilesh says and everything he does is for a reason."

Ilesh drew up his knees and poked the coals again with the stick. "Most people hurry to get things done, but it's important to be a part of what you do, and that takes time. When you climb the mountain, be a part of the environment. Feel your surroundings. What was the lowest point in your survival in Alaska?"

Claire searched through her memories, separating the hazy recollections of the plane crash and all they'd gone through. Some were clearer than others, some out of sequence, but she had no trouble remembering the worst of it. "When we were in the cave and Tilly and Sarah had gone for help. Rachel's condition worsened, and I couldn't do anything to help her."

"What made it your lowest point?"

She wrapped her arms around her knees, trying to focus, trying to clarify her thoughts. The memories surfaced, strong and vivid. "I felt so helpless. I'd done everything I could think of, but her fever and infection still raged. We were at the end of our fight to live. After all we'd been through and all we'd survived, she was dying." She glanced out into the darkness, away from Ilesh, hiding her face so he couldn't see what she knew was written on it. Shame and failure. "She lay there dying, and I couldn't do anything but hold her in my arms and beg her not to leave me." A ragged chill swept through her.

Ilesh smiled, his face almost amber from the reflection of the fire. "Dear Claire, it is not what we can't do, but what we *can* do that matters the most."

She sat by the fire and continued to talk, surprised at how open she had become with him. She'd always loved Ilesh, from the first time he came to visit her and Rachel at the teepee, during the week of their honeymoon. He had a strong bond with Rachel and now also with her. As the evening passed, she talked about her feelings for Rachel and her concerns. She found herself wrapping her arms tighter around her knees as she spoke of Yumiko.

"This Yumiko gets her power from others' fears. Moon Shadow knows what she's doing. She is a true shadow dancer."

"Shadow dancer?"

"Yes. One who watches over and protects others, often without them even knowing it. She moves with the flow of energies, dances with them, so she can make the world a better place and care for the people around her."

Claire picked up a small pebble and tossed it into the darkness. "A shadow dancer indeed." It was a perfect description. She leaned back on her elbows, looking into the night sky, filled with an endless array of stars upon stars.

"Do not worry, dear Claire. Moon Shadow will conquer her enemies. She has all she needs."

"How do you know? Yumiko devastated Rachel once. She could do it again."

"I know Moon Shadow, and if you search deeply, you will know also. She will subdue her enemies."

"How can you be so sure?"

His gaze pierced deep into her soul. "Because darkness cannot tolerate the least degree of light, and Moon Shadow is filled with light."

Claire slipped into her sleeping bag, pondering what Ilesh had said. Had Rachel told Ilesh what Yumiko did to her? Did he know what she was like? Did it come down to trust? Claire trusted Rachel with her very soul, but Yumiko had devastated Rachel. Could she do it again? Ilesh seemed confident in Rachel, and Claire wanted to believe Rachel could triumph also, but Yumiko was no ordinary enemy.

Claire's eyes were heavy and filled with the need for sleep. She immersed herself in the comfort of the night's beauty as she slipped into a deep slumber.

She woke startled, hearing a voice. Her eyes quickly adjusted to the immense darkness. Ilesh was standing over her.

"Up, dear Claire. It is time to train."

She rubbed her face and yawned. "But it's the middle of the night."

"Yes, and your enemies are cowards and have no honor. They will come at you in the dark. Therefore, you must train in the dark to be ready."

Ilesh began to gather his things. Claire followed his lead, thinking they were preparing to leave, but suddenly he grabbed her from behind and threw her onto the hard, rough, uneven ground. She let out an uncontrolled yelp as the air escaped from her lungs when she hit the surface. She lay there, stunned, trying to catch her breath, her right shoulder aching from the impact.

Ilesh bent toward her and rested his hands on his thighs. "What will you do, Claire?"

She rolled and started to push herself up, still confused and angry, trying to comprehend why he would do such a thing.

Ilesh raised one hand. "No! Stay still. Look at your surroundings. Where is your enemy? How many? Where can you go for safety? How will you defend yourself?"

Claire's acute vision helped her see him and her surroundings clearly. A grouping of large boulders just behind him. A knife near her sleeping bag to her right. A large rock inches from her reach.

"That's right. You are not defenseless." He reached down and helped her. "You have exceptional vision and skill with a bow, but your mind and body will become your greatest weapons."

All through the darkness of night he taught her to move, defend, attack. By the time the sun rose over the mountaintop and began to warm the crisp morning air, exhaustion had set in, and she could barely move. She sat quietly by the fire and ate breakfast.

"You will rest for a time, and then we will continue."

She groaned but said nothing.

That night she lay in the sleeping bag, looking at the sky, wondering what Rachel was doing. The full moon was clear, its form distinct. She could see the shadows of the craters in the upper left portion at the ten o'clock position. The canopy of stars spread out in a never-ending array. She pulled the sleeping bag tighter around herself and closed her eyes, wanting to turn over on her side, but too tired and too sore to move. "I need a hot soak."

"You *need* to go to sleep. Your body needs rest. Tomorrow you will climb all the way to the top of the mountain to get what you need. I will place items throughout the day for you to find. The purpose is not just to hone your hunting skills, but to listen and watch. Be mindful of the sounds and your surroundings. The prize is not in gathering the items. The prize is in learning what they will teach you. Open your eyes and heart and learn. Do you remember the mark of the rattlesnake I taught you on your honeymoon and how to take its life?"

She stiffened and her heart rate increased. "Yes, but I don't want to see any snakes."

Ilesh smiled. "You must conquer your fear. The rattlesnake is in the mountain. Be respectful. I'll use his rattle to help you find your way." He pulled out a red cloth. "And this is your mark. You will find three of them. Bring each one back with you."

"How will I know your sound from a real rattlesnake?"

"You know the rattlesnake well enough to tell the difference. He gives warning signs of danger."

Sometimes Claire's mind went into overload trying to figure out the hidden meaning of what Ilesh said. Was he comparing Yumiko to a rattlesnake? The more she thought about it, the more she realized Yumiko had given warning signs.

"Remember, there are many ways to kill a rattlesnake," he said.

In the morning, she slowly ate her breakfast. Every muscle in her body protested with each small movement. Even her fingers ached as she gripped the spoon and held the bowl.

Ilesh smiled as he watched her. "When you return to Moon Shadow, she will rub your body with warm oil, and you will enjoy her touch. Yes?"

Claire laughed. "Yes, very much." She put her hand over her mouth and yawned.

"We will ride to the mountain as soon as we finish eating."

She moaned, unable to imagine pulling herself up on her horse or climbing the mountain.

Ilesh laughed as he began to cover the small fire with dirt.

She cracked her neck and stretched, trying to loosen her muscles. She placed the saddle blanket over the mare and swung the saddle onto the horse's back, then reached under its belly and grabbed the leather cinch-strap. She adjusted the strap into the rings and tightened the saddle, watching Ilesh as he talked to Itza-chu.

"You and Rachel are always talking to your horses. Why is that?"

Ilesh stroked the paint's neck. "Because the horse is a friend, and we treat them as a friend. It would be rude not to speak to a good friend."

Claire patted Łichíí's soft warm neck, grabbed the reins, and swung into the saddle, her muscles continuing to ache with each movement. She wished she had the insight and connection that Ilesh and Rachel had to the environment and the creatures around them. She wanted to be more sensitive, to understand and appreciate all of it, but she hadn't been brought up in their special culture and doubted she'd ever really understand on the level they did. She gazed out at the Arizona landscape, taking in the vivid colors, the different shades of tan, reddish brown, the green of the high mountains and the sandstone of the plateaus, the contours of the pebbles and boulders, the textures of the brush trees near their campsite. The greens of the trees and brush were so different than in Ohio—a more blueish sage color. The air seemed purer, lighter, easier to breathe. She inhaled deeply and closed her eyes, trying to smell the differing scents of the earth, the dirt, sand, the shrub brush, but she could feel only the wind and the sun as they caressed her face and arms. She slipped her other boot into the stirrup, and as they left, she heard the comforting sound of the give and take of the leather saddle, the horses as they breathed, and the sounds of the gentle clip and clop of their hooves as they walked.

As she rode, quiet and at peace, a poem came to her mind, the author's name long ago forgotten. "Nature's Gifts." A simple poem, yet it had filled her with wonder when she read it for the first time as a sixth grader. It was the first thing she'd ever enjoyed memorizing. She hadn't thought of it in years and strained to remember, trying to recite the words in her mind.

> *Did you not see the purple flowers, nestled in the meadow clear?*
> *Did you not see the circling hawk or the running white-tailed deer?*
> *Did you not hear the babbling brook as it traveled on its way?*
> *Did you not hear the whippoorwill as it called to you today?*

*Did you not smell the luscious pine, or the fragrance of fallen
   leaves?*
*Did you not smell the apple's scent as it danced upon the
   breeze?*
*Did you not partake of Nature's gifts as you hurried on your
   way?*
*Did you not partake of the wondrous things she offered you
   today?*

She smiled as she stroked Łichíí's neck, pleased that she had
remembered the poem. It still brought a sense of wonder, but its
meaning seemed much deeper now, more personal. Was that what Ilesh
and Rachel felt? Were those gifts in the poem a part of their everyday
life growing up? Was Rachel full of light because she allowed those
gifts in?

She dismounted at the base of the mountain and stretched, trying
to work out the twinges of soreness in her back and legs. She rubbed
her shoulder as Ilesh pointed to the side of the mountain.

"Remember, go all the way to the top of the mountain to the grove
of pine and follow the east ridge. Bring back the sassafras bark, a
handful of pine nuts, and the rattle from the rattlesnake."

Claire nodded as though she received such vague and odd
instructions all the time. She handed her horse's reins to him. Did he
expect her to take on a rattlesnake? Surely not. She checked the pouch,
the width of her hand, and retied it around her waist, repositioned the
quiver and bow around her shoulder and under her arm, and made sure
the knife was secure in its sheath on her left side. She placed the leather
water pouch over her neck and shoulder.

She began to climb the mountain, maneuvering around the large
boulders, careful not to slip on the loose gravel and underbrush. She
ached for rest, but she continued, climbing, listening, watching. The
scent of pine filled the air as she moved higher. She rested on a level
spot of fractured rock, scouting her surroundings carefully. Over to her
right, in the dusty pathway, she saw the distinct track a diamondback
rattlesnake makes as it slithers. Her heart rate increased. She drank
from the water pouch, then climbed more, digging her boots into the
graveled dry earth to keep a secure footing.

Out of breath, her lungs aching and leg muscles straining, she
finally reached the crest of the mountain. She sat and watched, listening,
the aroma of pine now heavy in the air. When she caught her breath,

she searched the grove of pine and found the pine nuts, placing them carefully in the cloth pouch. She moved east, along the crest of the mountain, walking for about an hour before she saw the sassafras trees in the distance. Rachel had showed her how to dig up the root and make the sassafras tea in Alaska. She maneuvered carefully through the aspen trees, winding around the boulders and patches of tall grass. She easily reached a cluster of sassafras trees and took her knife, dug around a root, pulled it out, and cut it from the small tree. She cleaned her prize the best she could, then cut a small piece off the root, washed it with water, and chewed it as she sat, surveying the area, placing the remaining portion of the root in her pouch. The taste, similar to that of root beer, filled her mouth as she chewed slowly, her saliva mixing with the root.

She startled when she heard the faint distinct sound of the distant rattle, off to her left. She quickly stood and drew her bow, placing an arrow, ready to release. She moved slowly, quietly, watching, focusing on the twigs, dead grass, and debris but not seeing what she needed to. She scanned the tree line more closely as she crouched and stilled herself, looking once again to her left. Then she saw it. She focused, aimed, and released, impaling the red cloth into the bark of the aspen tree with the arrow. She moved quietly to the tree, removed the arrow and cloth, and placed the cloth in her pouch, the arrow back into the quiver.

She moved deeper into the woods, hearing the sound of the rattle again, about a hundred yards away. She followed the sound, watching as she reloaded an arrow. Ilesh was out there, somewhere, imitating the sound of the snake's rattle. She crept up, spying the cloth. She turned ninety degrees and released, hitting the cloth dead center hanging on the outcropped limb of an aspen tree, its golden leaves quivering. She retrieved the arrow and cloth, placing the second cloth in her pouch. The third cloth should have the snake's rattle attached.

She once again watched and listened, moving through the now-rocky terrain. When she came around a boulder, she heard the rattle and loaded the bowstring with the arrow, ready to draw back into position as the sound became louder. She scanned the area, seeing every detail. Then she saw it, but it wasn't a cloth with a rattle in it. It was a two-to-three-foot live rattlesnake, raised, ready to strike—the sound of its rattle warning her of the danger. She saw the red cloth beyond the snake. She carefully stepped back, making her way over the pebbles and rocks, her heartbeat in her throat. She removed the arrow from the bow and slowly put it into the quiver, carefully easing the bow over her shoulder. She drew her knife. She knew exactly how to take the snake's life, thanks to the other times she'd spent on the reservation. The sunlight bounced off its glistening skin, illuminating its colors and patterns, its black eyes.

In that moment she made her decision. She would back away instead of standing her ground. She controlled her breathing, feeling her heartbeat decrease as she slowly retreated, not taking her eyes off the snake. Unwilling to take the life of the snake or risk her own, she would face Ilesh without the last prize. She climbed down the mountain and met him as he sat by the campfire.

She handed him the pouch. "I didn't expect a live rattlesnake. Just a rattle."

He studied her. "You must be prepared and not assume."

"I won't kill for sport." She sat by the fire and placed a ladle full of cooked beans and a piece of flat bread on her tin plate.

"What *will* you kill for?"

His question pierced her, sending a disturbing, ragged chill radiating through her, settling in her heart. Could she ever kill another human being? She shuddered and shook her head slowly, pondering the question. "I don't know."

"Will you take a life to save a life?"

She studied him, sure of one thing. She would give her life for Rachel if necessary. But could she take someone else's life to save her? She shuddered.

"Dear Claire, I fear you will find out soon enough. The mark of a true human being is not in the killing, but what is in the heart before and after the kill. What did you learn from the rattlesnake?"

Claire sat quietly, eating, pondering, amazed at how his few words brought so much emotion to her. She could have discussed his simple questions for days. "I learned that he was protecting himself. He didn't attack just because he could."

Ilesh took a portion of the food and began to eat. "The moment you hunt, you become the hunted."

Claire stopped eating. "I don't understand."

"When the hunter hunts, he is focused only on the hunt, capturing his prey." He tore a portion of the bread. "The prey is free to do anything, go anywhere, but the hunter must always follow the prey." He dipped the bread into the beans. "You must become the hunter if you are hunted. Set your strategy so that *you* become the hunter. Once you do, you are the victor and no longer the prey. Lead where you want the hunter to go, and he will follow because he thinks about nothing but capturing his prey. Why the pine nuts and sassafras root?"

She set the empty plate beside her and wiped her mouth. "The pine nuts to assure the climb, and the sassafras to remind me of the fruits of my labors."

Ilesh patted her knee. "Yes. Now make us some sassafras tea."

Was all this preparing her to face Yumiko?

CHAPTER THIRTY-FOUR

Rachel used the time while Claire went with Ilesh to focus on her concerns about Yumiko. One thing was clear. She couldn't afford to wait for Yumiko to come after her. She had to somehow lure her in and turn the odds in her favor. Using the listening devices in her home was a start, but they needed a solid plan.

She straddled Claire, positioning over her thighs, pouring the warm, soothing oil over her nude back, rubbing her muscles gently but firmly, the night sounds surrounding the teepee, the small fire warming them as she continued to massage.

"Oh, Rachel, that's heaven." Claire continued to moan and groan.

Rachel laughed. "He worked you pretty hard?"

Claire moaned again. "Unbelievably hard, but I learned so much. He's a wonderful teacher."

When Rachel finished the massage, she rinsed Claire with warm water and then dried her. She removed the blanket from underneath her and laid it near the edge of the teepee and covered Claire with a dry, warm blanket. She took off her own clothes, lifted the blanket, and lay naked beside her, continuing to caress Claire. Claire turned toward her and kissed her.

"Rachel, when you went with your family the other evening, what did you talk about?"

Was Claire ready to discuss it? Did she understand more fully what they were up against? "We talked about the hunter and the hunted, and the attributes of the rattlesnake."

Claire smiled. "Yumiko will give us signs, won't she?"

"Yes. She'll reveal herself before she strikes. It's in her nature. We just have to figure out what her signs are. She's toying with me right now, but she's already given us some signs too."

"Have you figured out how you're going to deal with her?"

"I don't think we should wait for her. We should do exactly what Ilesh taught you. Turn the tables on her so she becomes the hunted. We have a lot of ways to do it, but the best way is to lure her into our space and then spring a trap. She's confident she can mentally devastate me again. Maybe she still can. She's an expert at preying on weakness. That leather strap rattled me, and I won't deny it. But my biggest fear has always been that she would hurt you or someone I care about, like Tilly or Sarah. She wants to see me in pain. It's what gets her off." Rachel remembered the look on Yumiko's face when she stood in front of her, holding the metal bar, telling her how she would give her morphine to stop the pain if she would divulge the codes. "It's about pain and power for her. We need to use what we know about her nature to get her into a contained environment so she can't run."

"That's a great idea, but how?" Claire asked.

Rachel kissed her neck and ran her hand over her waist. "How would you like to go on a cruise?"

"Really, or do you mean a fake cruise?"

"A real one. We could take Sarah and Ricky, and Tilly so we know where they are. And we could set a time and place to lure Yumiko in. She won't be able to resist an opportunity to have all of us together. We'd have security on one of the islands we stop at and make sure we can take her. I worried that I was obsessed about her, but she's the one who's obsessed with me. Let's use that weakness to our advantage. I'm pretty sure she'd fall for it."

"Let's go to the Bahamas. Lots of the cruise ships own private islands down there."

Rachel could tell Claire bought into the idea.

"Once we trap her, we can spend the rest of the cruise celebrating," Claire said.

Rachel laughed, appreciating Claire's optimism.

"How do we lure her in?" Claire leaned forward, totally focused, muscles tensed.

"Don't tense. The massage is supposed to help you relax."

Claire took a deep breath.

"The listening devices are in our bedroom, the living room, and kitchen."

Claire made a fist. "Sonofabitch."

"Easy, tiger. Let's use them to set her up. We'll work with Jack and the team on a script."

"Rachel, if the devices are going to stay active, how are we ever going to live a normal life or even have any privacy until this is over?"

"We have to use them until the cruise. Then it'll be too late for her, and we can get rid of them. And if something does go wrong and she gets away, she'll know we set her up, and we can get rid of them anyway."

"How long to get the plan ready and do it?"

"Four to six weeks at the most."

"I get sick to my stomach when I think of her listening to us. I don't think I can do it."

"It's just for a little while. We'll make some recordings and turn them on in the bedroom and sleep in one of the guest rooms until this is over. We can have Olivia play some throughout the day. Yumiko will never know the difference."

Claire sighed. "I suppose so. Why don't we make a recording of us talking about what an asshole she is? I'd like that."

Rachel laughed.

"I want to make love, but I'm exhausted."

"We have time to make love later. You need to rest." She drew Claire close and held her, hearing her relaxed, even breathing within a few minutes. She kissed her shoulder and watched as she slept, safe in her arms. Could she keep her safe? Would setting a trap for Yumiko put Claire and the others in more danger? No matter what they did, Yumiko would come for her. Better that she controlled the time and place. This time she would be ready for her.

CHAPTER THIRTY-FIVE

Yumiko sat cross-legged on the white brocade sofa in the London hotel room, a rocks glass of sixty-seven-year-old Macallan in her hand. She skimmed the blueprints of Rachel and Claire's house spread out across her lap. She swung her leg slowly and sipped the delicious whiskey.

She held the drink and scrutinized it against the light. "It's dry and has a licorice aftertaste." She smiled and took another sip. "It's good. How much did I pay for it?"

Agapito poured more of the Macallan into her rocks glass and then stepped away. "Seventy-two thousand."

"Worth it. Is everything arranged for their cruise?" she asked, still focused on the plans.

"Yes."

"My boat?"

"It will be on the starboard side of the dock."

"Where will the scuba gear be if I need it?"

"Just off the dock on the starboard side of the pier. You must remember to exit the port side of the boat. The gear will be attached to the second pylon from the end, on the dock's starboard side."

"And the jet scooter?"

"It will be sunk on the opposite side of the pier. Put on the scuba gear first, then swim to the scooter. We'll be waiting for you offshore. The dive compass will be set and will be attached to the drive bar on the scooter."

"And the helicopter in case I need it?"

"It will be standing by on one of the barrier islands."

"Flight time to get to me?"

"It should not take more than seven minutes. Surface when ready. Activate the homing device. They will pick you up."

"Then it is indeed time to celebrate." She breathed deeply, drank more alcohol, and continued to look at the house plan. "I like the master bedroom, but the stove should not be on that side of the kitchen wall." She folded the plan and handed it to Agapito. He and Yumiko's bodyguard stepped silently out of the hotel suite as a tall, fair-skinned woman with brown eyes and long, dark-brown hair stepped gingerly in. She wore a short, tight, low-cut, form-fitting black dress, showing every curve, hinting at the full breasts nestled within. Her red stiletto heels matched her purse.

She was just the way Yumiko wanted her. She wiped the corners of her wet mouth, trying not to stare as the surge of sexual heat intensified between her legs. She motioned for her to sit beside her on the sofa. The woman carefully laid the purse on the coffee table and sat close, running her long, delicate fingers over Yumiko's silk-covered thigh.

Yumiko slapped her hand away. "You will not touch me until I give you permission."

The woman smiled demurely and lifted her long, shapely leg, crossing it in an exaggerated fashion, like a leaf falling in slow motion on a summer breeze.

Yumiko swallowed and made a fist, feeling the momentary quickening of her heartbeat and the spasm of sex-craved need deep in her core. It had been months since she'd been with a woman.

"My name is Isabella."

The fantasy immediately shattered.

Yumiko wanted to slap her—hard. She flashed a penetrating glare at the woman to let her know who was in charge. "I don't care what your name is." She stood and walked to the window, the mixture of muted colors of green, white, and red from the lights below in the street mingled as they reflected back through the glass, casting misshapen shadows across her arms. She swiped at the shadows, as if to brush them away, then folded her arms tightly across her chest.

She had Portola right where she wanted her. As a matter of fact, she had Portola, her wife, and her friends right where she wanted them. A cruise. It couldn't have been more perfect. She could take all of them if she desired. Line them up and kill them. All of them except Portola. She'd save her for last. She could take her like she did before. She could drug her and transport her to Manila or wherever appealed to her. Take her time with her. Portola was right where she wanted her to be, and hearing her reaction when she'd received the leather belt had been priceless. She craved to taste that fear again.

Isabella half whispered.

Yumiko turned toward her. "What?"

"I said, would you like a drink?"

"The Macallan. Two fingers. On the rocks."

Isabella walked to the wet bar.

Yumiko watched her closely, her hand motions, the way her legs moved, the sway of her hips, each motion titillating and igniting her. Isabella was very good at what she did, and if nothing more, Yumiko appreciated her skill.

She brought Yumiko's drink and handed it to her, a slight smile crossing her face as she slowly sipped her own.

Yumiko took the drink and set it on the coffee table, studying her, feeling the want growing, the pressure building, the need for release beginning to pulsate. She pressed her legs slightly together as her breath quickened. "Undress, slowly."

Isabella took a step back. "You get down to it, don't you?"

"I didn't pay for that mouth to talk."

CHAPTER THIRTY-SIX

Tilly slid her foot over the decking and swayed back and forth as if in a half-dance. "I don't care what anyone says, I can feel the ship rocking. My suitcase will roll to the gangplank if I let it go."

Rachel and Claire continued to pull their suitcases toward the designated drop-off area. Sarah, Ricky, Tilly, and Kathrine followed close behind.

"Let's go to the pool deck and have a drink," Tilly said.

"And so it begins," Rachel said.

After several drinks they were informed their rooms were ready, and they went their separate ways as the ship set sail. Rachel leaned over the side of the railing of their balcony suite and watched the dolphins jump as they swam alongside the cruise ship. No turning back now. She tried to settle her mind and focus on the moment, but the uncertainty of their future loomed over her.

Claire nudged her shoulder. "Those dolphins have the right idea."

Rachel nodded and squeezed her fingers around the railing. Two dolphins did a three-sixty in the air.

"When do you think it will happen?"

Rachel took a deep breath and let it out slowly. "I expect her to make her move sometime tomorrow night while we're at the island party. Tomorrow is her only opportunity. Everything is set up to force her there. We hinted as clearly as we could without giving it away completely."

Claire turned and faced her. "I'm glad Jack's going to rip out the listening devices at the house while we're gone. I can't stand the thought of them being in there any longer than necessary. Are you worried?"

Rachel nodded. "Something could always go wrong."

"Relax. All she has to do is show up on that island, and we have her. It's the only time we're getting off the ship, and she's not going to come on board this ship to get us."

"I know. She'll most likely have her people try to take one of you at the island party later tomorrow night." Rachel ground her hands over the railing. Her stomach churned.

"Why are you so sure she'll try to go after one of us and not you?"

"Because she's not ready for me yet." Rachel pointed to the dolphins. "She's still playing. It's all a game to her."

"Do you have your gun?"

Rachel nodded. "And so do Kathrine, David, and Beth."

"What's got you so addled then? It's a good plan. If she or her thugs get anywhere near us, they're going to get what they deserve."

Rachel leaned against the rail. Claire was naive and didn't understand how quickly something could go wrong.

Rachel had put every one of them in danger. The thought caused her heart to ache. She gripped the railing, trying to release the nervous energy, reminding herself that she either had to go after Yumiko or wait for her to come after them. Better this way, but still the risks were…She forced herself to let go of the thoughts and sighed heavily.

Kathrine, David, and Beth were on the cruise to help guard them. Jack and Frank weren't there because Yumiko might recognize them, but there would be ample security on the island. It *was* a good plan, but Yumiko was smart, and the game they were about to play had a lot of moving pieces. Yumiko would give up her people in a heartbeat to save her own skin, just like she did in Manila, and in Los Angeles. If she got away, would it cause her to be more determined to hurt Rachel or those around her? They were poking a wounded animal and had better make damn sure she couldn't get up and come after them. "We have one chance. If she slips away, it will make things much worse."

"Do you think we should go through with it?"

Rachel released the rail and rubbed her hands together, nodding slowly. "We need to try. I'm sick of it, Claire. I'm sick of the stress and the constant worry that she'll hurt you, or Tilly, or Sarah. I can't stand it another second. The peace I had on the reservation, and being with you there, makes this almost unbearable."

Claire slipped her arm around her waist. "In a way, you've been dealing with her since Manila. You're right. We need to finish this as soon as possible."

"I'm worried about Tilly and Sarah. I think you were right. We should have told them and Ricky what we were doing," Rachel said.

Rachel, Claire, Kathrine, and Jack had argued about telling them. Claire said they should be told, but Jack, Kathrine, and Rachel disagreed. Jack said Yumiko's people could be watching them when they boarded the ship, and they might act differently if they knew and give the whole thing away. Claire finally agreed, and they decided not to let them know until the day they left the ship for the island.

Tilly believed Kathrine had come on the cruise to be with her. Jack made the contacts on the island and set the trap. They were using that particular island stop because of the increased number of security guards available. It was more difficult to get off the island, and it wasn't as big as the others. If they'd miscalculated and Yumiko chose one of the others, they had contingency plans in place, but none were as good as plan A.

Claire kissed Rachel's cheek. "Tilly's going to be a piping hot mess when she finds out Kathrine's her bodyguard and not her date for the cruise."

"I hope she gets over it."

"She's going to throw a fit. You watch," Claire said.

Another thing for Rachel to feel guilty about. "Can't Kathrine be both?"

"Not in Tilly's eyes. She's already insecure about her feelings for Kathrine as it is."

"Well, they'll just have to work it out. Better that than Tilly being hurt."

"I get why we're doing it, but I'm just saying Tilly's going to take it hard." Claire watched as the dolphins swam off. "I don't know if it's the sea air, being on the cruise ship, or knowing we have the night to ourselves before we tell the others and spring the trap on Yumiko, but all I want is to be with you."

Rachel moved behind Claire, put her arms around her waist, and tried to relax. She watched the pink, blue, and coral of the sunset spread over the ocean.

Claire slid her hands over Rachel's and leaned back against her. "I don't want to ever leave this spot. It's so beautiful, and warm. We have tonight. I don't want to think about anything else."

Rachel tried to settle her mind and focus on Claire. She was right. They did need to push everything out and be together, even if they had only a few hours. She began to unzip the back of Claire's sundress as she kissed her shoulders. The touch of her skin sent chills into her breasts and down her spine. "I want to see you," she whispered.

Claire let her dress fall to the floor as Rachel led her to the bed. She unbuttoned Rachel's blouse and peeled it off her shoulders, undid her bra, and slid the rest of her clothes off. She leaned near and whispered, "I wish you could see the expression on your face right now. It's so beautiful."

"It's because I'm looking at you." Rachel took the rest of Claire's clothes off and tossed them on the floor.

"What have you done to me, Rachel? I can't think of anything but loving you."

"It's good for us to have a diversion."

"It's a great diversion."

When they were both satisfied, they lay naked together on the bed, Claire's leg draped over Rachel's thigh.

Claire kissed her. "I don't know about you, but I think we should have taken a cruise long ago."

"I'm afraid this isn't going to be much of a vacation."

"Well, we have tonight."

The morning sun beat down through the spaces in the tan-and-red striped canopies shading the round tables on the sun deck. Tilly sat beside Kathrine.

Rachel adjusted the straps of her pale-blue camisole, making sure the scars on her back were well covered, and then adjusted her shorts, making sure the scars on the back of her thighs didn't show.

"You're good, babe," Claire said.

Sarah and Ricky drank their coffee, watching the swimmers in the pool.

Rachel made sure everyone had eaten before she told them. She cleared her throat. What if Yumiko didn't show on the island and nothing happened? They'd be upset for nothing. Maybe she shouldn't tell them. But, if Yumiko *was* there, they needed to know what was going on and be extra careful. She crossed her legs and tried not to appear too nervous.

Claire must have picked up on her indecision because she leaned in and whispered, "Go ahead."

Rachel cleared her throat again. "I need to tell you something."

She nodded toward David and Beth, who came over from the other side of the pool and stood by the table. "This is David Hampton and Beth Riley."

Ricky stood and shook hands with them. Sarah shook hands too, and Tilly waved at them from where she relaxed in the sun.

No one spoke for a few seconds.

Tilly watched Kathrine as if she thought she was being rude by not greeting them. Kathrine rubbed her brow.

Rachel folded her hands. "These are your bodyguards."

Ricky stiffened, Sarah tensed, and Tilly looked as if she didn't comprehend a word Rachel said.

"What do you mean, *bodyguards?*" Ricky asked.

Rachel motioned for David and Beth to sit. She explained everything—what Yumiko had done, her concerns about them being harmed, how they had been watched over, how they had set a trap for Yumiko, and why it would be safer for all of them to be together.

Ricky, Sarah, and Tilly acted like someone had thrown cold water in their faces.

"Sarah's not leaving this ship," Ricky said. "And if I'd known what you planned, I would have never permitted her to come on this trip. It's just asinine, Rachel. What were you thinking? How could you put our lives in danger like that?" Ricky got up from the table, pulling Sarah with him.

David stood and placed his hand on Ricky's shoulder. "Please sit, sir."

David's tone told him it wasn't a request.

Ricky sat, his expression like thunder, as Sarah followed his lead.

Beth spoke. "If Rachel hadn't acted to protect you, you might have already been harmed. Her actions have kept you safe. We're here to protect you until this is over. An entire security team is discreetly placed on the island just to watch over you."

Ricky glared at Rachel. "It's still a risk. I'm not deliberately endangering my wife. If she doesn't leave the ship, she won't be in any danger. And for that matter, how in the hell can you guarantee that Yumiko's people haven't already boarded the ship as passengers and aren't waiting to kill one or all of us, now that you've stuffed us into a nice little package for them?"

Rachel shoved her plate across the table and stood. "I'll tell you how I know. Jack and the team vetted every single passenger on this ship, and the crew." She waved her hand. "This entire ship is practically on lockdown, and no one knows it but us. If you and Sarah," she looked at Tilly, "and Tilly want to stay on the ship, then stay on the damn ship. I get it, you're scared. But if we were spread out all over the place at home, I couldn't protect you at all. And yeah, maybe I should have told you before you agreed to come, and that's on me. Do what you want to. Call a helicopter and have them come get you. Hell, I'll pay for it. But just remember, the moment you leave this ship and you're out of your bodyguards' sight, you're putting your life in Yumiko's hands." Rachel left, unable to get away fast enough.

She unlocked her stateroom and slammed the door behind her, throwing the keycard across the room. She paced. Did they think she hadn't thought it through? Did Ricky think she'd deliberately put them in danger without some kind of protection? Did Sarah? They had no idea how bad things were. She pulled the locked gun case out of her luggage and opened it with the key from her purse. She checked the safety and loaded the gun. She'd had enough of all of it. She'd go to the island, find Yumiko, and shoot her. No one would blame her. She was sick of Yumiko's games. All it got her was heartbreak and stress. Screw her game—she was done.

CHAPTER THIRTY-SEVEN

Kathrine glared at the others after Rachel left. "You don't have any idea what Rachel's been through these last few months. She's kept it from you to protect you and keep you from worrying so you could have some semblance of a normal life. Who do you think paid for your security?"

"Her life is anything but normal," Ricky said.

Claire's cheeks turned pink. "What's that supposed to mean?"

"It means every time we're with Rachel, some type of critical, life-threatening event occurs. The plane crash, Alaska, Justin, Yumiko. And you. You can't seem to stay out of trouble either."

"That's enough," Sarah said.

"Who else here knows anyone who's been shot in the head?" Ricky asked. "Excuse me. Anyone except those of you who work with Rachel."

"Well, it's never boring," Tilly said, halfway smiling.

So much tension stretched around the table they could have bounced on it like a trampoline.

"It's either do this or sit around and wait for Yumiko to pick us off one by one," Claire said. "You saw how easily she got to us before. Sarah, you must see it. Yumiko had us followed. She was behind trashing Tilly's dress and car, and she had her people key my car, or maybe she did it herself. It doesn't matter who did it. She's harassed Rachel. She knows where we live, and she sure as hell knows where you live. The point is, she's coming after us whether we do something or not. And it's not Rachel's fault. Yumiko's nuts."

"Rachel's got a shitty job, and this is happening because she works there," Ricky said.

David started to say something, but Kathrine motioned for him not to speak. The others needed to talk it out.

"I'll be the first one to say I don't particularly like what Rachel does for a living, but it's the work she's chosen. She and the rest of the people she works with save lives. And the price isn't cheap." Claire looked at Kathrine, Beth, and David. "How many of you have been shot?"

Kathrine wanted to acknowledge that she had but changed her mind. Beth and David had been shot, but neither one of them responded, either. Getting shot, coming out of it alive, and not being permanently handicapped made it like a badge of honor, something to brag about when they got drunk at Lil' Nell's. After an hour or two, usually one of the guys wanted to show their scars. And it was entertaining when the women matched them. So far Rachel and Jack were the reigning champions. And as far as Kathrine was concerned, they could remain in those positions.

"You people need to find a new line of work," Ricky said, clearly taking their silence for confirmation.

"You're missing the point," Claire said. "They chose this *line of work* because they care. They care about you and me, and anyone else who's in trouble. I know you care about Sarah, and you don't want her to be in danger, but that train has already left the station. Yumiko won't stop until we do something about her. Rachel knows it, I know it, and they know it." Claire pointed to Kathrine and the others.

"And Rachel wants to use us as bait," Ricky said.

"In a manner of speaking, that's true," Claire said. "But, if you look at it from a different angle, we're already targets. Rachel's just marketing the product."

"Clever, but nope, not buying it. Sarah and I are not leaving the ship."

Claire frowned. "Suit yourself. Tilly, how about you?"

"Hell. I'm up for a party. She ripped up my good gown and trashed my car. Maybe I'll get a chance to bitch-slap her."

Kathrine laughed.

The color drained from Tilly's face as she looked at Kathrine. "Oh, shit."

Claire and the others looked at Tilly.

Kathrine put her head down. She knew Tilly had finally put two and two together.

"You're my bodyguard? *That's* why you came on the cruise with me?" Tilly scooted her chair out and stood. "Excuse me." She left the table.

Kathrine stood. "I need to go talk with her."

"Go," Claire said. "I'm going to talk with Rachel."

"See what I mean," Ricky said. "Drama."

Sarah elbowed him. "Stop it. You made your point."

Kathrine left them arguing by the pool. She stood outside Tilly's door. Should she use the keycard or knock? Either way, she was sure of Tilly's initial response. She decided the best way to begin the negotiations was to follow her dad's advice. "When dealing with a firecracker, always use caution!" She knocked.

"Go away," Tilly yelled. "Or better yet, stand outside my door all day and guard me."

Kathrine sighed heavily and hung her head. She had a headache, and her shoulders and neck were stiff. This was not going to be easy. She knocked again. "Please, Tilly, open the door."

"You have a keycard. Use it."

Kathrine slipped the keycard into the slot and opened the door. Tilly sat on the sofa, legs crossed, a rocks glass of probably whiskey in her hand. She watched her enter the room but didn't say a word.

"It's not what you think." Why did she feel like she had to explain herself? "Yes, I'm here to be your bodyguard, but I'm also here in this room because I want to be with you. I slept on the couch last night because I know you aren't ready yet. Don't let this be a wedge between us."

Tilly took a long drink from the glass, then set it on the end table. She wiped the corners of her mouth with her fingertips, then blew out a breath and looked over at her. "Ricky's right. You have a shitty job. I bet you hate having to be my bodyguard. Look at it this way. You're getting paid to be with me. Has it been that way all along?"

"No. Of course not. It's not like that, Tilly. Rachel and I thought it would be better for you this way. Yes, I'm getting paid to be your bodyguard, but only on this trip. Rachel paid someone else in Cleveland to watch over you without you knowing."

"Why didn't she tell me?"

"I'd be guessing. You'll have to ask her that question." Kathrine knew, but she wasn't going to tell her.

Tilly picked up the drink and drained the glass.

"You should go easy on that stuff."

"Why? I'm on vacation, remember? I'm here to have fun. It's a cruise. Let's party." Tilly put her hand to her mouth. "Oh, that's right. You're the bodyguard. You can't party. You're on duty." Kathrine touched her arm. "Tilly, don't." Tilly jerked her arm away and stood. "I believe I'll have another." She walked to the wet bar and poured herself a whiskey. On the rocks. She drank a third of it before she got back to the sofa. She plopped down and kicked off her sandals, slid her feet under her, and sipped more, looking straight into Kathrine's eyes, as if daring her to say anything.

Her eyes were deeper blue today, but with a hint of fire—maybe from the reflection of the whiskey or the morning sun shining through the sliding-glass door that opened to the balcony. Kathrine stopped herself from leaning over and kissing her. She was so hot when she was angry. What was behind her anger? Insecurity? Lack of self-confidence? She was so complex. "Do you really want to bitch-slap Yumiko?"

Tilly threw her head back and laughed. "That's what you got from all of it?"

"You know, Tilly, I understand why Ricky said what he did. I understand why he doesn't want Sarah to leave the ship, and I get why Sarah didn't speak up or protest. You're the one who surprised me. You could stay on the ship, and every one of us would understand and not judge you for it, but you didn't hesitate to say you'd go to the island. Why? Why put yourself at risk when you don't have to?"

"Isn't that what you do?"

"I'm a trained professional. I'm an expert marksman. I can hunt someone down and, if I had to, kill them with my bare hands. But you? Why?"

Tilly set the glass on the end table and ran her hand over her dress, smoothing out the wrinkles. "Because I know Rachel. And I know what she's been through. She saved my life in Alaska. She saved all of us. She's watched over us from the moment Yumiko started her shit. She'd give her life for me. All she's asking is that I go to the party on the island, surrounded by the best bodyguards in the world, have a little fun, be careful, and return to the ship, hopefully in the same condition as when I left. I don't think that's too much to ask of her friends. Ricky's wrong, but I get why he's doing it. And you're right. No one thinks less of him or Sarah, and no one has the right to judge them."

Kathrine found herself engulfed in her emotions. "Tilly, I'm sorry I didn't tell you before. Please, don't let this be a wedge between us. I'm your bodyguard because Rachel cares so much about you, and I'm your bodyguard because I care about you. Jack wanted to use Beth instead of me because we don't normally pair someone who has an emotional attachment. But Rachel insisted because she knew I wouldn't be able to focus on anyone else but you anyway." Kathrine reached for her hand.

Tilly clasped it and didn't let go. A very good sign.

"We have some things we need to talk about, but not right now," Tilly said. "Not with everything going on. When this is over. But... okay. I accept what you're saying, and I'm glad you're watching over me."

Kathrine wanted to kiss her but didn't because it was a toss-up if Tilly would kiss her back or slap her. What did Tilly want to talk about? Were they ending before they began? Could the nature of her job be too much for Tilly to deal with?

Chapter Thirty-eight

The island breeze moved the curtains in the room. The muscles in Yumiko's back tensed. Her neck stiffened, and her head throbbed. Something about the plan didn't feel right, and she didn't like it, but she couldn't determine what was so unsettling. Maybe the fact that she put all this effort into getting Evans instead of Portola. "Go through it again."

Agapito reviewed his notes. "You will stay on the boat with Venancio at the dock. Antonio and Louis will enter the island as food distributors from Harbour Island. They will take the crate and leave it behind the medical building. Antonio will pay the band leader to assure he calls Evans to the stage to sing. When she enters the backstage area, they will disable whoever is with her, *if* someone is with her, and then Louis will inject the drug. It should take effect in a few seconds. They will put her in the wheelchair behind the stage entrance, wheel her to the medical facility, eliminate whoever is in there, put Evans in the crate, and fill the top with the fruit. They will carry the crate back to the boat, show their papers to the guards, board the boat, and you will all leave the dock. We will meet you at the far side of Inagua Island. If it's a clean escape, the yacht will be there. If not, the helicopter will be waiting to transport."

"What about communication and visual?"

"Both Antonio and Louis will be wired for sound. The telescope will be mounted on the captain's bridge disguised as an underwater sonar device. You will have a clear view of the tables, stage, behind the stage, and the route to the medical facility, and of course down to the dock."

"And if there are problems?"

Agapito lowered the notes. "You must decide to leave the boat before Antonio and Louis reach the dock. Once you have made the decision, you must be sure you are seen on the boat, then slip over the port side and swim to the pier. Remember, the scuba gear is at the second pylon from the end, starboard side."

"What if I can't find it?"

"You'll find it. Follow the pylon down until you touch it. The underwater scooter is on the other side of the pier. You'll find it."

"When do I set off the detonator?"

"When you see the indicator light on your wrist flash, press the button. The boat will explode within five seconds. You will be well out of range when it happens. Continue following the set course and surface when the indicator flashes again. We will be right above you."

"And if not?"

"Continue to the coordinates set in the indicator. Detach the light from the underwater scooter and turn it on when you surface. The helicopter will hover until you are spotted."

Agapito observed her as if waiting for another question.

She didn't ask it.

He answered anyway. "Most likely Venancio will be the only one on board when the boat explodes."

Yumiko shrugged. It was the price that had to be paid for it to look like she was there when the boat exploded. Someone had to be driving the boat. She was relieved after reviewing the plan, but one more thing needed to be clarified. "If the crate doesn't make it on board, I want them to open fire on it." She stretched her neck and heard it crack. "I need a massage before we leave."

Agapito bowed slightly and left the room.

Chapter Thirty-nine

Rachel heard the door unlock and watched Claire sweep through the room, then jump on the sofa beside her. She set the glass of ice water on the end table.

"Well, did you get it out of your system, or do you still need to let off some steam?" Claire asked.

"I need to do something physical, big-time!"

"Let's go to the pool."

Rachel shook her head. "Too many people."

"I know the very thing." Claire picked up the in-house phone. "Do you have any court times right now? Great. We'll be right there." Claire stood and pulled Rachel up. "Come on. Let's change."

"Where to?"

"Racquetball, babe, and we're not keeping score, so you can hit the frigging ball as hard as you want."

After Rachel managed to get the physical release she needed from racquetball, they showered and went to the sundeck. Claire folded her towel and placed it behind her head, then sipped her drink. Some type of coconut-spiced-rum concoction she said tasted way too sweet, although not so sweet she didn't have a second one. She lay in her lounge chair close to Rachel, looking out at the people in the pool. She set what little bit was left of the drink beside her on the deck.

"I'm definitely feeling the coconut." She laughed out loud. "I think I had one too many of those rum thingies. Rachel, are you all right? You seem a little fidgety. Try to relax. We have hours before we leave for the island."

"You're relaxed enough for both of us." Rachel couldn't get the morning's discussion out of her head. Should she be asking Tilly to do this? She readjusted her sunglasses.

Kathrine and Tilly were up to their shoulders in the water, talking. Rachel wondered what they were discussing. She was sure it wasn't anything romantic. Claire had told her what happened after she left the table.

"I hope they can get together after this is over. They probably should have some alcoholic refreshment." Claire laughed.

"You know what I think?"

Claire put her hand over her eyes, blocking the sun, and looked at her. "What, baby?"

"I think they need a game of strip poker." Rachel smiled, hoping to mask her fear and anxiety. She didn't want to ruin these last few hours for Claire. If things went sideways, it might be their last.

Claire laughed. "You know, I think you're right. A couple of drinks and a game of strip poker, and they'll be on their way. Rachel, have you ever wanted any other woman?"

Rachel pondered her question. In the time they'd been together, Claire had never asked her that. "Why would you ask?"

"I don't know. Just wondering."

"Claire, I know this sounds trite, but it's always been you I've wanted or fantasized about. I never had an interest in other women. I mean, I find some women very beautiful and attractive, but I don't have a sexual interest in them. I think it's because I fell in love with you almost the moment I saw you. How about you?"

Claire made a noise with her lips and then licked them. "Wow! Um, I had a crush on my seventh-grade music teacher, Ms. Mason. She was so hot, but other than her, it's always been you and only you."

Rachel tried to let herself relax, but the minutes were slipping away too quickly. Were they ready? The security was in place, and they'd had another tense group discussion after Claire and Rachel had returned to the pool.

Claire and Tilly were told they were not to go anywhere on the island without their bodyguards, including to the bathroom. Tilly threw a fit about it, but Kathrine managed to settle her. Ricky and Sarah were still adamant that they were staying on the ship, although Sarah looked apologetic. Rachel knew Yumiko and her people wouldn't be able to get on the ship. Security had been checked and rechecked. The cruise ship's chief security officer readily cooperated with the team. Rachel paid a good deal of money to make sure the cruise line cooperated with what they needed, but it was worth it to have the peace of mind.

Yumiko would come after her at some point. It was just a matter of time, and Rachel, not Yumiko, would have the advantage if she chose the place and time. But they'd get only one chance. Did they plan it well enough? She remembered what Steve had told her the night they left to get Jack and Frank. "No plan ever goes perfectly."

"Rachel, did you hear me?" Tilly asked, standing by her with a beach towel wrapped around herself.

"No. Sorry."

"I said what time do we have to leave for the island?"

Rachel picked up her iPhone. "Three more hours." She glanced at Tilly and then Claire. Claire held her hand.

"Let's meet in our stateroom in an hour to go over the plan one more time," Rachel said.

Tilly nodded.

"You and Kathrine work things out?" Claire asked.

"Kind of. I get why she didn't mention the bodyguard thing, but I'm still not totally happy about it."

Claire let go of Rachel's hand. "Have you talked to Sarah or Ricky since this morning?"

Tilly shaded her eyes with her hand. "I stopped by their stateroom on the way here. Ricky's still pissed. I doubt we'll see them until the end of the trip. Ricky can be a real ass sometimes."

"Maybe I should go talk with them," Claire said.

"I think Rachel should be the one, but not until after tonight. They need some space," Tilly said.

Rachel noticed Kathrine keeping her distance but close enough that she could reach Tilly in a few seconds if she had to. She had a tense expression. This entire situation had everyone on edge.

"We're going back to the room to change. See you in about an hour." Tilly waved as she walked away.

Rachel watched them leave. She shifted in the lounge chair and let out an audible sigh before she could stop herself. She couldn't get the heavy feeling out of her heart. Ricky had every right to be angry. Tilly should have been angry but wasn't. She should have told them before the cruise. Ricky was right. Claire's hand brushed over her arm.

"We should go back to our room, babe. It's time."

The words echoed in Rachel's ears. *It's time. No plan ever goes perfectly.*

The evening sun's reflection cast a glistening shimmer over the ocean. Rachel walked back into the room, closing the sliding door. Tilly, Claire, David, Beth, and Kathrine were seated around the table.

"All right. It's time to get serious," Kathrine said. "No more alcohol for you two for the rest of the night."

Claire nodded, and Tilly slid her glass toward Kathrine.

"You're just jealous because you can't have any," Tilly said. "Because you're workin'." She left the table and put the glass on the wet bar.

"Where are you allowed to go on the island, Tilly?" Rachel asked.

Tilly turned around and smiled. "Anywhere I want."

Everyone looked at her.

"Just kidding. I stay in the table area, and I can't go to the bathroom without permission and an escort. That's so disgusting. Can I dance if someone asks me?"

Kathrine glanced at her. Rachel couldn't help but smile. Tilly was really giving it to Kathrine.

"Yes, you can dance, but remember who's taking you home," Kathrine said.

Tilly laughed. "I thought maybe I'd have to make them show an ID or something."

"All the cruise guests will be wearing one of these." Rachel held a yellow fluorescent wristband. "But ours are a little different."

David reached into the cloth bag on the floor beside him and pulled out a bundle of wristbands, separated six, and put the rest in the bag. He picked one and motioned for Tilly to hold out her wrist.

"Which arm?" she asked.

"Either," David said.

Tilly lifted her left wrist, and David snapped the band in place.

"These bands are larger for a reason," Rachel said. "They're trackers, and they have an alarm. The button is here." She pointed to the raised area on the band. "You have to push it once to activate the alarm. It makes a shrill, loud, irritating sound, like a home fire alarm."

"I hate that sound," Claire said.

Rachel put Claire's wristband on her. "If for any reason you get separated from us, or you're in trouble, push the button. Don't worry about the noise. We want it loud so we can find you. One more thing. The band starts flashing when you push the button. I'll be tracking all of them on my iPhone."

A few seconds later Claire's wristband went off. She jumped and started yelling, "What do I do? What do I do?"

Rachel couldn't believe it. She reached over and pushed it twice, shutting it off. She, David, and Kathrine reached into their pockets and pulled out a five-dollar bill and laid the money in front of Beth. She picked the money up and thanked everyone.

"You didn't just do that," Claire said.

Everyone laughed.

"I can't believe it was you. I thought for sure it'd be Tilly. Once again, don't press the button unless you get separated or you're in trouble," Rachel said.

The rest of the team put on their wristbands.

David, Beth, and Kathrine checked their weapons and slipped them into the holsters at the middle of their back. A rush of adrenaline surged through Rachel. They were ready. All they had to do now was go to the island, act like they were having a good time, and wait for Yumiko or her men to show themselves and make their move. Her legs were rubber. She began to feel sick to her stomach. What if Claire or Tilly got hurt? The walls began closing in on her. The next thing she knew, David and Beth were standing over her.

Kathrine knelt beside her chair. "Put your head down and take deep breaths."

Claire knelt on the other side of her. Rachel reached for Claire but shook so hard she almost couldn't close her hand around Claire's.

Claire put her other hand around Rachel's and held it tight between hers. "We can do this, Rachel. Tilly and I will be fine."

But what if they weren't fine? What if Yumiko outsmarted all of them again?

CHAPTER FORTY

Yumiko adjusted the telescope. Portola sat at the middle table with her wife, Evans, and two other women. They were talking. People were dancing. The multicolored lights around the dance floor cast enough reflective light that she had to keep adjusting the telescope to get a clear view.

A tall man with thick brown hair, on stage with the band, said something to the crowd and then pointed toward Evans. A spotlight fell on her. Portola had a surprised expression. Evans stood, and the man motioned for her to come to the stage, pointing to his right. Evans walked slowly toward the right of the stage, a tall woman with lighter brown hair following close behind her. Several men also moved closer toward her.

Yumiko immediately scanned the crowd.

Louis spoke into his microphone. "She's coming toward us, but a woman and several men are also moving toward her. They look like security."

"Send in the diversion," Yumiko ordered.

Seconds later, three scantily clad women gathered by the stage entranceway, blocking the men's entrance as Tilly and the woman passed. They started a conversation with the men. "Go," Yumiko said.

She readjusted the telescope in time to see Antonio knock the tall woman in the back of the head with his gun. She went down hard. Louis injected Evans in the left arm. She fought him but only for a few seconds. They slid her into the wheelchair and quickly made their way toward the medical station. She watched them open the door and enter. A flash of light caught her eye by the stage entranceway. She moved the telescope back. The tall woman was up and moving. Something on her wrist flashed. Suddenly a swarm of security guards and Portola, her wife, and another woman were running toward the backstage area. A man and woman pointed toward the medical building.

It was a trap! She heard gunshots, then screaming. Louis and Antonio came running out of the medical building without the crate or Evans. She swung the telescope back toward the front of the medical building. Portola's group and others were closing in. More gunshots. She looked toward the docks. Security guards were gathering.

"Start the engines. Now, Venancio."

Venancio did as she ordered. The engine roared to life. Yumiko quickly made her way down the steps to the main deck and went toward the stern, making sure the guards at the end of the dock could see her. She then unhooked the spring lines to the dock and moved inward and out of sight. She could hear the engine idling. She ripped her sundress off and adjusted the wet suit over her arms and legs as she made her way to the port side of the boat. "Leave now."

"But Louis and Antonio aren't on board yet."

"Go now."

The boat jerked as the engine shifted into forward gear. No time. She had to get off the boat. She slid over the side, gasping as the dark, cold water engulfed her.

The boat sped out to sea, its wake pushing her into the pier, slamming her head against a barnacled pylon. Warm blood ran down her face as she touched the gash in her forehead. She was dizzy and confused. Scuba gear. She had to get to the scuba gear. She took three deep breaths and then dove toward the second pylon, feeling her way along the rough, jagged mass. The darkness consumed her. She had to slow her heartbeat to conserve oxygen. She groped at the pylon, feeling her way down, until she finally gripped the scuba tank with the regulator and mask, and the other items attached to it. She had to go up for air. She unfastened the gear and pulled it with her as she made her way to the surface. She came up under the pier, gasping for air. A white light was flashing on her wrist. She tried to clear her head. The indicator light for the detonator. How long had it been on? She pushed it.

An explosion sounded in the distance. She spun, searching, barely able to see the burst of yellow, orange, and white light. She hid behind the pier and put on the fins and mask, then the buoyancy-control vest and tank. She cleared the regulator as she watched for movement. No one seemed to be above her on the pier. No voices yelling, only the rhythmic slapping of the waves against the dock and pier. She adjusted the mask once more and slipped the regulator into her mouth. She treaded water as she checked her position. The underwater scooter was supposed to be on the far side of the pier, right below her. She went underwater, pointing the light downward, and slowly made her way to the scooter with little difficulty. She found the dive compass, recalculated it, and started the scooter. All she had to do now was hang on and let the scooter maneuver automatically to take her to the rendezvous point. Everything was as Agapito said it would be.

Her head throbbed, but she could do nothing about it yet. The face mask fit just below the wound. How badly was she bleeding? The cold would slow the blood flow, but what about sharks? They could detect a drop of blood a quarter mile away. She needed to get out of the water as soon as possible.

Portola had tried to trap her. She'd set her up! They must have found the listening devices in the house. The rage began to build. Her muscles recoiled. Her breathing increased. She became aware after a few seconds and purposely slowed her breaths, relaxing her grip on the bars of the scooter. A trap!

She couldn't get the thought out of her head. She should've seen it sooner. All those security guards had nagged at her. But now they'd think she was dead, and she could move more easily.

Evans had been a misdirect. She wouldn't try to go after her again. It'd be too difficult and a waste of time. Going after her wouldn't get her who she wanted. She'd wanted to wound Portola and throw her off her game, but that had been a mistake. Time for blood. Chambers would be next.

Agapito was right. She needed to stay out of sight. He had prepared the apartment in San Francisco. She would go there and carefully plan, and then she'd fly to London. Her contact within MI6 would give her the information she needed about Chambers's schedule. And after she dealt with him, it would be time to go after Portola. She would be more careful this time. She wouldn't make any mistakes. Portola had set her up, but soon her time would come.

Chapter Forty-one

R achel rushed into the medical building, Claire right behind her. It was a bloody mess. A male and female, dressed in white clothing, were lying near the entranceway, their head and clothes covered in blood. It looked like the man had been shot three times. Tilly lay on the floor near the back entrance, eyes shut, not moving, a wheelchair tipped over beside her. Rachel held her breath. Her heart beat so hard she felt like her chest would explode. She ran toward Tilly, looking for blood, trying to see her breathing. Claire tried to push her way toward her.

Kathrine, kneeling beside Tilly, checked the pulse in her neck and touched her arms. She moved her, obviously looking for blood or gunshot wounds. "She's alive. I don't see any wounds. I think they drugged her."

Rachel dropped next to Tilly and put her hand on her shoulder. "Tilly, wake up."

"I don't know how much or what they gave her," Kathrine said. "This looks like a needle mark here on her upper arm."

"She'll probably be out for at least an hour or so. That's Yumiko's style." Rachel took Tilly's hand and strained to see out the rear door toward the dock. Guards were standing over what looked like two men on the ground. At the dock, a group of guards had gathered with David and Beth, pointing out to sea. She didn't know what happened. She didn't care. Tilly wasn't bleeding, she was breathing, and she and Claire were safe. That's all that mattered right now.

At first, they had all been surprised that the band leader had called Tilly to the stage. Kathrine refused to let her go, but the band leader kept calling Tilly, insisting. When Tilly left for the stage, Kathrine followed close behind with a small group of island guards, who met them by the stage, and then Rachel's iPhone went off, alerting her Kathrine's alarm had been activated.

The moment Kathrine's alarm sounded, Rachel, Claire, David, and Beth rushed behind the stage. Kathrine was sitting in the sand, and Tilly was nowhere to be found. Then they heard screaming. By that time, a flood of security had surrounded them. A man and woman yelled and pointed toward the white building about fifty yards from the stage.

David and Beth had drawn their weapons and pushed Rachel and Claire behind them as two of the island guards helped Kathrine up. She had a large bump on the back of her head, about the size of a golf ball. Kathrine drew her weapon and ordered the island guards to surround Rachel and Claire. "Rachel, stay here with Claire."

Rachel started to protest, but Kathrine insisted. "We have this."

Kathrine followed David and Beth as they raced to the white building. Shots rang out. Rachel tried to break away from the guards, but they held on to her. Suddenly what sounded like a distant explosion came from the ocean.

When she and Claire were finally permitted to enter the building, Tilly lay on the floor, and Kathrine was kneeling over her, checking her.

Medical staff pushed their way through the small crowd and demanded that Kathrine, Rachel, and Claire move away from Tilly. As they began to assess Tilly, Rachel left and went to the dock.

David motioned her to him. She passed the small group of guards. Two darker-skinned men, dressed in service uniforms, were lying on the ground, blood on their clothes. Rachel could tell by their faces they were dead.

Beth touched Rachel's arm when she got to the dock and stood beside them. "Is Tilly all right?"

Rachel folded her arms across her chest. "I think so. They may have drugged her. The medical staff are with her. What happened?"

David pointed toward the white building. "Beth and I got there first. A man and woman had been shot and were lying near the doorway. There were two men." He pointed to the men on the ground near the back of the white building. "One was pushing Tilly in the wheelchair, then turned and fired at me. I shot him. He shoved the wheelchair, and both the men made a break for the back door. Beth shot twice, hitting the man I shot, and then the second guy. They both went down. I saw

Yumiko in the back of the boat just before it pulled away from the dock at full speed."

Rachel rubbed her arms, hanging on every word David said.

"We ran back inside, and by that time Kathrine was beside Tilly. I thought I heard an explosion and ran out of the building. I saw a burst of color out on the ocean about where the boat may have been."

"Are you saying Yumiko's boat exploded?" Rachel could hardly get the words out.

David nodded. "Yeah. That's what we think. Shore patrol is organizing a search now. They won't be able to find much in the darkness, but they're going to try."

Rachel looked out beyond the dock toward the open sea, straining to see any remains of the explosion, but saw only darkness and a night full of stars. The news was almost too much to comprehend. Relief swept over her. She wanted to jump up and down, raise her fists in triumph. Could it be true?

"We'll wrap up here. You go back and be with the others," Beth said.

Rachel walked to the white building. The bodies had been removed. Tilly lay on a bed in an exam room, several IVs running. Claire stood to one side of her, Kathrine on the other.

"How's she doing?" Rachel asked.

Claire brushed Tilly's hair away from her face. "Vitals are good. She's starting to come out of it. They gave her some type of stimulant to bring her out quicker."

Tilly moaned.

Claire kept her hand on her head, continuing to stroke her hair. "Tilly, wake up."

Rachel moved beside Claire.

Tilly moaned again and opened her eyes. "I'm thirsty. What happened?" Her eyes widened. She thrashed and struggled to get up.

Claire placed her hand on her shoulder and forced her down. "Easy, Tilly."

Tilly moved her gaze from Claire, to Rachel, and then to Kathrine. "You saved me." She grabbed Kathrine's hand. "You saved me." She started crying.

Kathrine clasped her hand in hers. "It's all right, Tilly. We all saved you."

Claire handed her a tissue.

Tilly dabbed her eyes. "Did you get her, Rachel?"

"I think she was killed in a boat explosion."

Kathrine and Claire looked at Rachel. Claire put her arm around Rachel's waist. "Are they sure?"

Rachel nodded. "We'll know more when they search the area where they think the boat exploded." She struggled to comprehend the implications of what she'd just said. Yumiko might be dead. She pulled Claire to her and wrapped her arms around her. Could it be over? A flood of relief swept through her, but then exhaustion hit, and her energy gushed out like a shark had bitten a hole in her life raft. Her legs wobbled, and she lost her ability to think clearly. She slipped her arms from around Claire and slid into a chair beside the bed. Could Yumiko be dead? Could it finally be over?

CHAPTER FORTY-TWO

K athrine gazed at the clear night sky full of stars and a full moon. The warm, light breeze swirled as the band played. It was a perfect night to be on a cruise. They had two more nights on the ship before they got back to port.

Tilly, Rachel, and Claire didn't want to leave the ship, but for some reason, when Ricky was told what happened, he celebrated by dragging Sarah away to go jet-skiing and party on the beach. Rachel insisted they have double guards. David secured island guards for them and remained on the island with them, while everyone else stayed on board.

Kathrine finished her lemonade just as the waiter brought another round of drinks in anticipation of the band's final song.

Rachel leaned over to Kathrine. "Are you going to be all right tonight? Is Tilly still giving you a hard time?"

"She's softened since we saved her life, but I'm still on the couch." Kathrine couldn't stop from laughing. "Maybe I'll get lucky tonight."

"She's a handful," Rachel said.

"Don't I know it."

Rachel laughed as she sipped her ginger ale.

Tilly and Claire toasted each other and drank more.

Tilly left to use the restroom, and when she sat back down at the table and reached for her drink, her hand trembled slightly. She drank most of her mojito and ordered another.

"Are you all right?" Kathrine asked.

Tilly nodded and took another sip of her drink. "It's been a hell of a couple of days."

Rachel leaned toward Kathrine. "I know she can hold her liquor, but she's pushing it."

"I'll take her back to the stateroom. Don't worry about her."

"You sure you don't need any help?"

Kathrine shook her head. "She'll be all right." She stood and placed her hand on Tilly's shoulder. "You ready to go, Tilly?"

Tilly looked at everyone at the table and then slowly stood.

Kathrine walked her to their stateroom and slipped the keycard into the slot. She heard Tilly sigh when she opened the door and followed her inside.

Once they were in the room and the door shut, Tilly started fidgeting with her hands.

Kathrine watched her and then moved closer to her. "Are you sure you're all right?"

Tilly's pupils were dilated from the alcohol, her breathing quickened, and she shifted her weight from side to side. Kathrine brushed Tilly's hair away from her face. "Would you like to sit and talk?"

Tilly's face relaxed. "Yes, please. That would be great."

Kathrine took her hand and led her over to the sofa and sat, pulling her gently down beside her. "What's going on?"

Tilly swallowed. "I want to be with you."

"Tilly, I hope you don't think you owe me something because I'm your bodyguard. I was doing my job, and I failed."

Tilly touched her face. "You didn't fail. I made the mistake, and you almost got killed because of me." Her eyes moistened.

"Don't look at it that way. I should've never let you go to that stage."

"You tried to stop me, but I went anyway. I'm sorry."

"You have nothing to be sorry about." Kathrine put her arms around her.

"I feel like I'm on the verge of tears all the time. I can't seem to get my emotions under control."

"You went through a traumatic experience. It's normal."

"I didn't though. All of you did. I missed it because they drugged me."

Kathrine laughed. "Tilly, you were drugged and almost killed. It's traumatic any way you look at it."

"I keep thinking about you. I've wanted to be with you almost from the first time I met you, but I don't know if I'm ready."

"There's no pressure. If you're not ready for this, I'll sleep here on the couch. It's very comfortable. We don't have to do anything. You're absolutely under no obligation to me in any way." She let go of her and touched her hand.

Tilly's shoulders relaxed, and she smiled softly. She shifted and started to pick at a loose thread on the skirt of her flowered sundress. Her behavior confirmed Kathrine's suspicions about why she was nervous.

Kathrine moved slightly away from her and gazed into her eyes. "We haven't talked about this, and we probably should have way before now. Have you ever been with a woman?"

Tilly put her hands to her face and blushed as she lowered her head. "No. I'm so sorry, Kathrine. I feel totally inadequate. I've never felt like this before. I've wanted to touch women before, but it just never went that far. But each time you and I have kissed, it's made me want to be with you more."

Kathrine took Tilly's hand from her face and held it. "Tilly, don't be embarrassed. I'm honored that you feel that way about me. I just assumed you've been with other women."

"Why?"

Kathrine shrugged. "You're in show business and have access to so many beautiful people. I thought you'd have had anyone you wanted, and I guess because you seem so comfortable around me when we've kissed. You're gorgeous. Who wouldn't want you?"

"Men are around me a lot, but not women, at least not anyone I've found interesting enough to go to bed with." Tilly squeezed her hand. "Until you. You're the first woman I've ever really wanted to be with. Are you disappointed?"

Kathrine moved her hand to Tilly's waist and then down her thigh, touching her bare knee as she leaned in. "Are you serious? I couldn't be more flattered. You really are quite beautiful. I've wanted to be with you since the first time I saw you at the Caprice." She brushed her lips against hers and then kissed her. Fleeting thoughts of their early morning at Sarah's before she left to go back to Las Vegas raced through her mind. Her desire began to build, but she held herself back. Tonight wasn't about her. No matter how badly she wanted Tilly's touch, she needed to focus on Tilly's needs. "It's okay if you're nervous, but honestly, you have nothing to be nervous about."

"Oh, yes, I do."

"What?"

"That I won't be good at this. I think that's why I backed out of our trip to Chicago. I know I come across like I'm a hard-ass, but it's all an act. I feel like I'm watching one of those damn horror movies. You know, the one where you know what's going to happen, but it still scares the hell out of you."

Kathrine leaned back slightly, trying to get a read on her. Obviously, Tilly was more nervous than she realized if she compared what they were about to do to a horror movie.

"I'm sorry. That wasn't the best analogy."

"We really should have talked about this sooner. It's my fault. I should have brought it up," Kathrine said.

"No. It's *my* fault. I should have come out and told you I haven't been with a woman." Tilly locked her fingers together. "But I was afraid you wouldn't want to be with me then. It's just that it's a little overwhelming. I guess it's the performer in me. I want to be good at this for you, and I haven't practiced. Sex hasn't been that exciting for me in the past. At least until you."

That admission appealed to Kathrine. Tilly was adorable when she unbottled her emotions and feelings. "Don't be nervous. I'm glad you haven't practiced. Trust me. I'm not going to grade you." She scooted closer and placed her hand on Tilly's shoulder. "The fact that you're so nervous is extremely seductive. Are you worried about your back because you don't have your back brace on?"

"Yes. That's another game changer. I'm sure you don't want to go to bed with a…a liability."

"You're not a liability. You're definitely an asset." Kathrine gently wrapped her arms around her, pressing into her. She kissed her deeply again, probing, tasting the liquor and the sweetness of Tilly's mouth.

"You kiss so good," Tilly whispered.

She kissed Tilly's neck, sliding down, feeling her pulse beating against her lips. She began to unbutton Tilly's sundress.

Tilly's respirations quickened.

She stood and reached for Tilly, walking her to the bed as they kicked off their shoes.

She continued to unbutton Tilly's dress, letting it fall to the floor. She pulled the silk slip over Tilly's head and then peeled the pasties off her nipples and tossed them. She cupped her hand on one of Tilly's hard, erect nipples, rubbing gently.

Tilly moved against her and slid her arms around her neck. "I love your touch. It's so tender and soft."

Kathrine kissed her again as she caressed her breasts.

Tilly's fingers trembled trying to unbutton Kathrine's blouse. She finally got her blouse off, then unbuttoned and unzipped Kathrine's slacks and slid them down.

Kathrine's want built with each touch of Tilly's fingers.

Tilly unfastened her bra, moaning as Kathrine stepped out of her slacks and moved into her, their nipples rubbing against each other, growing harder with each touch.

Kathrine's breath caught, and the tingling want surged through her.

Tilly reached behind Kathrine and slid her hands inside her underwear. "Sonofabitch, I knew you had a fine ass."

Kathrine laughed.

Tilly wrapped her arms around Kathrine's neck again, pressing more firmly into her, their lips meeting. "This feels so good."

Kathrine moved her hands around to Tilly's well-muscled back, then slid her lace panties over the curve of her hips. "You have a fine ass yourself." She bent and stripped Tilly's panties over her thighs, seeing again the wide, rough scar halfway down her thigh. She'd noticed it when they were swimming but hadn't said anything. She kissed it. "Is that from the plane crash in Alaska?"

"Yes."

"I thought so." She pulled Tilly's panties down farther and guided her to step out of them, her sex scent rising, igniting Kathrine's want even more. She tossed the panties on the floor, then slipped her own off and threw them, not knowing or caring where they landed. She pressed her thigh between Tilly's legs and into her center, feeling the nest of thick hair and the warmth of her swollen mound. She adjusted and pressed harder, working her thigh into Tilly's wet, hot folds, sliding easily against her.

Tilly held her closer. "That's embarrassing. I think it's obvious I'm really into you."

"It's incredibly sexy."

They kissed longer, deeper.

Tilly moaned, making Kathrine want her more, feeling the lust and ache in her nipples, sending waves of sexual tension into her already throbbing body.

"Tilly, I can't wait any longer to touch you."

She started to lay her on the bed.

"I have to be careful how I lie."

Kathrine took a hard erect nipple into her mouth and sucked, caressing the other with her fingertips.

Tilly moaned and pulled her into her.

Kathrine withdrew, so full of desire she could barely focus. She had to think of Tilly, or Tilly wouldn't enjoy it as much. "Show me what works for you."

Tilly lay down slowly and scooted over on the bed, patting the bed beside her. "I'm okay once I'm in bed. Just no sudden moves."

"I promise, no sudden moves." Kathrine lay next to her.

Tilly pulled Kathrine to her and slipped a breast into her mouth and sucked gently, then the other.

Kathrine could feel her breasts expand, her wet center aching for release. She ran her fingers through Tilly's hair as Tilly continued to caress with her hot mouth. Her tongue moved perfectly across the tip of Kathrine's aching nipples. She pressed her thighs together, trying to hold back. She had to stop her. It wouldn't be right if she came first. She lifted Tilly from her breast, feeling the reluctant release of her mouth.

"Are you sure you've never been with a woman?"

Tilly laughed. "It must be a natural thing. Who would have thought?"

Kathrine smiled, feeling the excitement of Tilly's experience. "Would it be better for you on top or on the bottom?"

"What?" Tilly eyes widened as she ran her hand down the curve of Kathrine's hip. "I get a choice?"

Kathrine was a little caught off guard. "Yes. Of course you get a choice."

Tilly's cheeks were flushed, and her lips were full and ripe. She kissed her again.

"I've never had a choice before." Tilly's breath caught as she spoke.

Kathrine forced in a deep breath. "Never?"

"No. Mm, Kathrine. I'm throbbing all over."

Kathrine kissed her neck. "I promise it's all about you tonight. I think you might feel more comfortable on your back, but whatever you want we can do."

Tilly pulled her gently over on to her and whispered, "Kathrine, I'm so sorry, but I don't know. I—"

Kathrine leaned on her elbows, watching her. "I don't want you to worry. We can take our time. I want you to enjoy it."

"But I'm not sure what to do, and I want to please you."

Tilly was no pillow princess. "Tilly, trust me, you're doing fabulous. Let me show you, and then you do whatever you feel comfortable doing. Whatever you want to do is good for me, but talk to me. I want to please you, and you have to let me know what you want and like."

Tilly held her closer. "I've never had anyone say that to me." Kathrine kissed her and then moved down her neck, licking and kissing, feeling her own desire to be touched so powerful she had to force it back. "I can't wait to please you."

She slid down and took one of Tilly's full, hard nipples into her mouth and massaged her other nipple with her fingers, engulfing its feel and taste. She lingered, not wanting to stop, enjoying one and then the other. She moved slightly to Tilly's side and gently spread her legs with her hand, touching her thighs, her own clit pulsing at the feel of Tilly's response. She slowly slid her fingers down into Tilly's wet, swollen folds and gently explored.

Tilly moved against her hand, spreading her legs.

Kathrine pressed the heel of her hand onto Tilly's firm clitoris. Each time she thrust her fingers, Tilly arched. She slid her fingers deeper, feeling her hot, wet sex surround her until she couldn't wait any longer to taste her. She slid down, spread her legs wider, and opened her glistening, swollen flesh. She took her engorged clit into her mouth, surrounding it, sucking, massaging in a slow circle.

Tilly groaned, slowly moving her hips, placing her hands on Kathrine's shoulders as she lifted slightly. "That feels so incredible, but I can't move my hips very far."

Kathrine went into her, thrusting with her tongue several times, feeling Tilly throbbing for her to go deeper. She withdrew slowly.

"Hand me that pillow."

Tilly slid the pillow to her, and Kathrine positioned it under Tilly's hips.

She hungrily slid back into her again, thrusting her tongue deeper, rubbing and squeezing her muscled ass as Tilly began to slowly move with her.

"Kathrine...your touch is so..." She groaned.

Kathrine could feel Tilly reaching for her climax. She withdrew, then slid her fingers into her as she moved, taking her swollen clitoris into her mouth once more, gently sucking, loving, devouring. Tilly let out long groans as her breathing caught and she pushed into Kathrine's mouth.

She increased her thrusts and went deeper, moving to Tilly's need, feeling her begin her pulsating contractions, helping her ride the waves of her climax as far and as long as she could. She continued until Tilly completely relaxed, and then she lingered, helping her enjoy the afterglow, not hurrying to leave her. Tilly continued to moan and slowly moved her hips. Kathrine finally withdrew from her and carefully slid onto her, licking and kissing her stomach and then covering her breasts, feeling Tilly's heart still beating rapidly.

Tilly wrapped her arms around her.

Kathrine slid farther on to her and held her, stroking her hair.

"I've never in my life had anyone ever love me like that. It was so incredible." She sighed as Kathrine held her. "I want to love you like that, but I can't lie on my stomach. Will you let me love you on top?"

Kathrine couldn't stop her smile. "Yes, of course, if you're comfortable with it."

"Yes. I want to do it. I can't wait. I've imagined what it would be like to taste you and be inside you."

Kathrine slipped a pillow under Tilly's head. "This will help you not strain as much."

"I want to explore every part of you."

And she did.

After hours of lovemaking, they lay together, listening to the ocean and the cries of seagulls outside the open balcony door.

Kathrine rolled over and kissed her. "You're so quiet, Tilly. Are you all right?"

Tilly moved her hands gently over Kathrine's back, then touched her ass again and smiled. "Yes. Oh, yes! You're a wonderful teacher."

Kathrine laughed. "I don't feel like I taught you much. How's your back? I didn't hurt you, did I?"

Tilly rolled slightly, moving closer to her, gazing at her as if studying her. Kathrine could see the contentment in her eyes.

"Kathrine, I've never, ever in my life been loved like that. You are…I can't find the words for it."

Kathrine touched her face. "Tilly, I want you to know I've never enjoyed myself more. You are a wonderful lover."

Tilly fell asleep in Kathrine's arms.

Kathrine kissed her head as she slept. Tilly seemed relaxed now, content. It had been difficult for her, and now that they'd been together, Kathrine could see how afraid Tilly had been. It wasn't easy for her to put her fears aside and take what she wanted. In her own way, Tilly had been very brave. The more she discovered about Tilly, the more fascinated she became. She was getting in deep, and she knew it.

It had been a wonderful night. As Kathrine started to drift off, thoughts of Yumiko slipped in at the edge of sleep. Had Yumiko's death been too perfect? She opened her eyes again, reviewing the events.

Rachel didn't talk about what had happened, but obviously she suspected Yumiko had faked her own death. It was written on her face and the way she couldn't seem to relax. It was probably why she and Claire didn't want to leave the ship or why she'd insisted Ricky and Sarah have double guards. Rachel hadn't mentioned it in conversation. Kathrine knew her well enough to realize she probably wasn't ready to discuss it with the team, and she wanted her loved ones to relax as much as they could for the rest of the trip. The subject remained unspoken, but they were all still cautious.

Yumiko faking her death seemed a real possibility. When Jack heard about the explosion, he immediately wanted to know if they had found her body or pieces of it. They hadn't. Just a male, which added to their suspicions. It was the nature of their business to be suspicious.

None of them could let their guard down, at least until they found proof of Yumiko's death.

CHAPTER FORTY-THREE

Rachel watched through her sunglasses as Tilly stomped toward them, carrying something in her hand. She tapped Claire's arm to get her attention and pointed to Tilly.

"Oh, crap. Now what?" Claire turned over and sat up, nudging Sarah, who was half asleep in a lounge chair.

Rachel pulled her sunglasses down and glanced over the top of them at Tilly. "That doesn't look good."

Tilly slapped the side of her thigh and glowered at them. "I need to talk to Rachel right now."

Ricky, Sarah, and Claire looked over at Rachel.

Rachel almost laughed out loud, thinking Tilly was going to stomp her foot and throw a hissy fit any second. "What's going on?"

"What kind of games are you people playing?"

"What are you talking about?"

"You know exactly what I'm talking about, Rachel." Tilly held out passports and an identification badge. "I found these in Kathrine's suitcase this morning. I got up to pee and was curious about what she lugged around. And look what I found. I don't even know who she is. What the hell? *Three* different passports and names, and an ID badge for a company she doesn't work for? I knew this would happen."

"What *would happen*?" Claire asked.

"That I'd get bitch-slapped by reality. That she was too good to be true."

Rachel couldn't see the humor anymore. She reached out with her towel and covered the items, taking them from her.

Tilly threw one hand on her hip and pointed at the towel. "What in the hell is going on? Do you know anything about those?"

Kathrine came through the entryway and walked to the group. Rachel stood and grabbed Tilly by the arm. "Come on. We're going to my room."

Claire stood and called after them, "I'm coming too."

Rachel most definitely didn't want Claire to go, but she didn't know how to justify stopping her.

Sarah and Ricky started to get up, but Rachel put her hand out and shook her head, then motioned for Kathrine to follow them.

"See, Sarah, more drama, more intrigue," Ricky said.

"Shut the hell up and sit down. You've already caused enough tension on this trip," Tilly said.

"Easy, Tilly," Sarah said.

"Sorry, Sarah." Tilly flashed a glare at Ricky. "But I'm not sorry to you."

Rachel hid her smile as they walked to their room. She handed Kathrine her passports and ID when they got inside. "That's the problem with being intimate with someone, Tilly. You learn their deepest, darkest secrets."

Tilly glared at Kathrine. "Why do you have those fake passports?"

Kathrine frowned. "Interesting to know you were going through my things. I thought we were building trust."

"So did I, until I find out you're some kind of…I don't know…a spy or something. Is Kathrine your real name, or is it Katrina or Natasha?"

"Stop it. Of course Kathrine's my real name." She put her hand to her chin and rubbed it gently. "Hm, maybe it's not. Maybe some foreign government abducted me, and I was brainwashed. Pick one of the passports, and we can start over."

"Now you're making fun of me."

"I always carry them."

"Just because you're in security doesn't mean you carry fake passports," Tilly said.

"That's true," Kathrine said. "But I need them." She didn't elaborate or say anything more.

"You're being evasive," Tilly said.

Kathrine started to move toward her. "Tilly, I can't tell you very much. I'm sorry."

"Tilly, Kathrine isn't deliberately trying not to tell you. She's under a legal obligation. She *can't* tell you," Rachel said.

Kathrine mouthed *thank you* to Rachel.

"Why do you have that ID with a badge that has ADC on it? I thought you worked for Jack's agency at the shed. What the hell does ADC mean anyway?"

Kathrine scrubbed her face and looked at her and then Rachel. Rachel gave her a look that said *be careful.* Rachel knew she was on very thin ice with Claire. Not only could she not talk about Kathrine, but more importantly, she hadn't told Claire she was also in the ADC, or that she had been since the team got back from Los Angeles. She wanted to tell Claire, but with everything that had happened, and knowing how Claire felt about her job, she didn't dare.

Kathrine sighed deeply. "Sorry, Rachel."

"Screw it." Rachel nodded reluctantly. "Sit, Tilly."

They all took a seat around the table. Claire was silent, her expression neutral. It probably wouldn't stay that way for long.

Kathrine opened her ID and handed it to Tilly. "I'm an agent of the American Defense Council."

"What's that?" Tilly asked.

"I work for an agency that does work the FBI and CIA can't do because of legal restrictions. It's always classified, and it's always covert."

"I thought the CIA could do whatever the hell they wanted to."

Kathrine continued to look serious. "That's just in the movies."

"I still don't understand. I thought you worked for Jack."

When Kathrine looked at her, Rachel wished they had mental telepathy.

"I do work for Jack, but some of us within Jack's organization also work for the ADC. We do private work, but we're also contracted under the ADC to do special assignments, like when Jack's task force went after Rachel when she was taken. Some things have to happen off the books."

"Why the passports?"

Kathrine shook her head slowly. "I can't talk about it, Tilly."

Tilly glanced over at Rachel. "Are you a part of this secret shit?"

A bolt of panic shot through Rachel. She didn't dare look at Claire. She didn't know what to do. It finally dawned on her that she didn't have to answer Tilly either, so she just sat there, glued to the chair. Tilly looked at Claire. Claire looked at Rachel. And suddenly Rachel felt like she had a huge, flashing, red sign over her head that read *Yes, Claire. I lied to you.* She almost thought she heard Claire's trust gush out of the room. What was she going to do?

"Tilly, the less you know, the safer you'll be. That's the rules," Kathrine said.

"You aren't going to tell me very much, are you?"

Kathrine took her hand. "I promise, I'll always tell you as much as I can, but I just won't be able to tell you some things."

Claire diverted her eyes away from Rachel, after she'd been staring at her for what seemed like what was left of their lifetime together. Rachel tried to hold in a groan.

"Tilly, I know you feel like you don't know anything," Claire said. "Believe me, I understand. But you've been told a lot already, and Kathrine has trusted you with very confidential information. You need to guard that trust and information."

Rachel sank deeper into the pit of it's-my-own-fault. She'd promised Claire nothing would ever be between them, and now something had wedged there again. She was totally disgusted with herself. But how could she tell her this, knowing how much Claire didn't want her involved in it and how she worried for her safety?

Kathrine stood. "Come on, Tilly. Let's go back to our room and talk about it. I'll let you play with my passports, and you can tie me up?"

Tilly slapped her arm. Kathrine opened the door, and they left.

Rachel lay on the bed, relieved they were gone. "That was unpleasant." Liar. Keeper of secrets from her wife. The shame was so thick in her throat she coughed.

Claire lay beside her and kissed her. "I thought you and Kathrine handled it really well."

Rachel didn't want her to be nice to her. She didn't deserve it. She was a horrible spouse.

Claire lifted the top Rachel had on over her bathing suit and then slipped the straps of her bathing suit off her shoulders. She bent down and kissed her. "You smell like coconut." She kissed her again.

How could she tell her? It would ruin everything.

"Rachel, why do you love me so much?"

Claire's green eyes pierced her soul. The waves of guilt began to rise, towering over her. The tsunami crashed down on her, and she collapsed under the pressure and weight, drowning in it. "Claire, I have to tell you something."

Claire got off the bed and went to Rachel's suitcase, raised the lid, and reached in, rummaging through the contents. She walked back and tossed Rachel's ADC identification onto the bed beside her.

Rachel lay there, mortified. She spit out the words all spouses have spewed from the beginning of time when they find themselves in deep shit. "I can explain."

Claire sat on the bed. "Rachel, I'm your wife, and we've been best friends since college. Do you really think I don't know you? I told you. I get you. I'm sorry I put such pressure on you that you felt you couldn't tell me. Like I said to Tilly, there are things you can't share with me, things I won't know, and I get that. I don't like it, but I get it. The only thing I've ever been worried about is your safety. That's why I asked you to do desk work. After you left the other morning, Ricky said you had a shitty job, and that's why things happened to you. I defended all of you, but I've thought a lot about what he said. I think he's right about you having a shitty job, but I realize he's wrong about why these things have happened to you, and I've been wrong too.

"This all started because you invented a computer program that Justin stole and sold to Yumiko. It had nothing to do with the job you have now. If anything, the job you have now saved our lives. The shit that happened to me happened because Derrick was obsessed and ended up a nut-case. It didn't have anything to do with your job. What I'm saying is, yes, you have a shitty job, and it's dangerous, but that's not always the reason bad things happen.

"I told Ricky it was the job you chose." Claire touched her face. "And you and Kathrine, and Jack, and all of them at the shed are very good at what you do. We all saw that again on the island. I wish I could not worry about you when you're working outside the office, but I do, and I wish you wouldn't do it, but you do. I know you love your job. I know you're torn because you love me and know how I feel about it. We need to work this out right here, right now."

Rachel kept looking at her, dumbfounded, searching her eyes, scanning her beautiful face. "I'm so sorry, Claire. I wanted to tell you. I did. I swear. It tore me up inside."

"I know it did. I was so angry when I found that ID. I felt like you'd betrayed me, but then I realized I was the one who put so much pressure on you that you felt you couldn't tell me. I don't want you to ever feel like that again. I hate what you do, Rachel. I hate it. I know it's selfish of me. Do you remember when we were at the hospital in

Alaska, and I told you about what happened when I thought you were dying in the cave?"

Rachel nodded and cleared her throat. "Yes. You said if I died, you were going to take your own life."

"I felt that way because I couldn't imagine my life without you in it, and I still can't. But what I've realized is that you chose this work because of who you are, and I need to accept your decision. Your job is a part of you, just like my pottery is part of me. We could have just as easily died in that plane crash, or fighting our way out of the Alaska wilderness, or been killed by Justin, or certainly by Derrick. It didn't have anything to do with your job. Some days, though, I'm still back there in that cave with that dying woman I love." Tears dripped down Claire's cheeks. "I don't want us to be in that cave anymore. Life is for living, and I want you to have a rich, full life and do what you love. I'm sorry for my selfishness."

Rachel wiped the tears from Claire's face and then her own. "I'll do my best to stay at the office and out of the field." She smiled and kissed her. "How did you find out?"

Claire laughed. "Really? You think you're the only investigator in the family? Besides, there's no way every lead agent at the shed is in the ADC except you."

She swung her legs onto the bed, crawled to Rachel, and hovered over her. "Why do you love me so much?"

Rachel put her hands on Claire's waist and brushed her lips against hers. "Because when I look at you, I see such love reflected back."

"I love you so much, Rachel. We still have some things to work out, but let's not let anything get between us. It's you and me first, and everyone and everything else second, no matter what."

Rachel remembered Steve and Lisa and what Steve had told her about how they didn't let anything get between them. She kissed her again, lingering. "Claire, I love you. I feel so overwhelmed when I think that you love me."

"I feel exactly the same way about you. What do you love the most about me?"

Rachel studied her face, her lips, the way the corners of her mouth curved upward, seemingly always ready for a smile, or a fight. The sparkle in her eyes. Her perfectly shaped eyebrows, the blush in her cheeks. She kissed her as she rolled her over, stalling, giving herself a moment to gain control. If she spoke her name at that moment, every thought, every word would gush out in a blubbering stream of incoherence. She fought her tears and stroked Claire's face, feeling her beneath her. "I love the person you are, Claire. The first time I saw you, I thought you were the sexiest person I'd ever laid my eyes on, and when we met and I got to know you, I discovered the most loving, beautiful soul I've ever known. I love everything about you."

Claire kissed her. "Rachel, sometimes when we're like this, I feel like you're inside me, and I don't know where I end and you begin."

Rachel couldn't speak. The words wouldn't come out of her mouth. Claire was the gravity that held her world together. She didn't remember the cave, but she vividly remembered Claire crying over her bed in the hospital. She'd done the same thing when Claire had been shot. They'd been through so much together.

She touched Claire's face with the back of her hand, and then with her index finger she lightly traced the faint scar on her temple. As if she had fast-forwarded on a screen in a place in time that stood still, the experiences they had shared over the years flashed in Rachel's mind. She could see each one vividly and in exquisite detail, and she was certain she and Claire would be there for each other. Always. No matter what happened. Rachel knew in that moment they'd crossed over to higher ground. Their bond was set, etched and chiseled from the solid granite of their love, heartache, pain, suffering, sacrifice, and experiences they shared. No outside force could break it.

Clouds passed over the sun, and the light in the room turned to a gray hue, casting a dark shadow directly over Claire. In that instant a foreboding washed over Rachel, and their moment was ripped from her.

"Claire, I think Yumiko is still alive."

CHAPTER FORTY-FOUR

It had been weeks with no sign of Yumiko, but Rachel couldn't shake the feeling she was out there somewhere. She had talked with the team at the shed, and everyone agreed she had somehow escaped. They found no evidence of her death. She could be lying low for some reason, maybe hoping Rachel would be complacent and let her guard down, or maybe she hadn't worked out a plan of attack yet. Or perhaps Yumiko had let go of her thoughts of revenge for Rachel. That, however, was unlikely.

Whatever the situation, Rachel didn't buy her death. After they got home from the cruise, she insisted Jack assure Claire that the listening devices were no longer in the house. Then she increased the security guards, one stationed at the main gate and two on the grounds of the estate day and night.

To assure Olivia's safety, Claire had talked her into moving into the finished apartment over the garage, since her grandson, who lived with her, had left when he started college at USC. She and Claire had adjusted well to the guards. Olivia made extra cookies every week for them, and Claire sent home some of her specialty pieces of pottery to their wives.

Tilly had a personal bodyguard—not Kathrine, but hired by Jack and paid for by Rachel. Kathrine and Tilly had decided not to push the limits of their developing relationship. Tilly hadn't said a word against having her own bodyguard. Clearly her near-kidnapping still made her skittish.

Kathrine went on an ADC assignment to London.

A security guard discreetly watched Ricky and Sarah's house because Ricky had insisted Rachel overreacted. Claire had told Sarah, "Better to overreact than find you dead."

Rachel didn't know how long it would go on, but for now they were doing the best they could.

Claire came into Rachel's home office, holding a laptop, and sat on the leather sofa. Rachel swiveled her chair around to face her. "What's up?"

"I was going over the calendar, and can you believe we have only a few months until our anniversary?"

"It's gone by quick."

"I thought we could have a big party since neither one of us was able to celebrate last year. I couldn't remember, and you spent it alone." Claire frowned. "Sorry about that."

Rachel smiled. "It's not your fault you couldn't remember. That's a really good idea, but maybe we should wait a little longer to plan it."

Claire's shoulders drooped as she slumped back into the sofa.

Rachel didn't have to say it. They both knew it was because of the uncertainty of Yumiko.

"I feel like our lives are still on hold because of her. Can't you somehow find out for sure if she's still alive? If she is, she'll be living somewhere, and a leopard doesn't change its spots."

"That's clever. You're right. If Yumiko is still alive, she must be living somewhere. And she's probably doing the same things she always did, just a little more covertly."

Two days later Rachel was sitting in her office at work, hunting through all the information about Yumiko, when she got an overseas call from Kathrine.

"Guess who I went out to dinner with last night?"

"Um, Brice Chambers?"

"Wow. You're good."

"Not really. He's the only one I know in London. How are you doing?"

"Good. I'll be back in the office later this week. He told me to say hello and to tell you he started digging into Yumiko's finances on his own time."

Rachel's curiosity level immediately soared. If Brice was looking into Yumiko's finances, he must feel she was still alive. "Has he found anything?"

"I don't know. I didn't ask and he didn't say. I'm having dinner at his house with him and his wife tomorrow before I leave for Heathrow."

"Give him my best, and tell him I said to be extra careful."

After Rachel hung up, she sat drumming her pen on the desk. She picked up the secure phone and then set it back down. She continued to drum the pen, then finally picked up the phone again and called Brice.

"Rachel, what a pleasant surprise. How are you and Claire?"

"We're both well, thank you. How's your family?"

"Very well. My wife and I are leaving for Eygalières in a couple of weeks. We were invited to stay with some friends. Can't wait to go. Should be great fun. Out in the country and all that."

Rachel smiled. She'd never heard Brice this excited. "It sounds wonderful."

"You and Claire should come visit, and we will take you to some of the more fun spots in Southern France."

Rachel was taken aback. In the time she had known Brice, they talked only about their work and Yumiko. It would be exciting to take a trip and not have to constantly look over her shoulder. What would it be like? She realized at that moment she'd been living a life she didn't want to live any longer. She was sick of looking over her shoulder, Yumiko lurking in the background, dead or alive. She now became sure of what she wanted to ask him.

"Brice, Kathrine told me she had dinner with you."

"Yes. Lovely woman. I am so impressed with how she handles herself."

"She told me you're doing some research on your own regarding a mutual interest." Rachel didn't want to say her name. She didn't know why, and she had no desire to try to figure it out.

After a break in the conversation, it sounded like he'd clicked through to a secure line. Brice finally spoke. "Yes. That's correct."

"Have you found anything yet?"

"I just recently started, but I did locate a couple of things. First of all, a number of bodies were discovered in a river, all of them formerly known associates of our friend. Either she cleaned house, or her group got hit. I'm betting on the former. Also, it's not much, I'm afraid, but could be something. I found an old credit-card number of the company. It hadn't been used in a year, but now, it's active again. Three purchases at a clothier in San Francisco, of all places."

Rachel felt a chill, and the hairs on the back of her neck stood up. "Do you have the name of the clothier?"

"J.W. Steiner Clothier, LLC." He gave her the address and phone number.

"Do you have the dates of purchase and a list of the items?" She could hear him shuffle papers as her excitement grew. Her heart beat so hard it almost jumped out of her chest. She couldn't keep her hands still. The seconds were dragging into minutes.

"Yes, it looks like six blouses on one date and slacks on another, but I can't tell how many." He told her the dates the items were purchased. "The other purchases are for a handbag and undergarments." He gave the dates of those purchases. "Was that information helpful?"

"Yes. Very much. Thank you." Rachel couldn't wait for Kathrine to get back.

When Kathrine walked into Rachel's office after her return from London, Rachel wanted to hug her. "I think we have a lead on Yumiko's whereabouts."

Kathrine sat in a chair. "Brice mentioned that you two talked. Spill."

She told Kathrine what she knew. "It means some travel and looking through video files at a clothier store. And if she cleaned house, she's going to be upping her game and moving product again. We just have to figure out who her contacts are, and I bet at least one of them will be in San Francisco."

Kathrine raised her hand. "You're not going."

"What?"

"No way you're going, for a couple of reasons. Mainly, if it is her, she could spot you. Also, if it's her and she spots you, we'll blow our element of surprise. If she's alive, that means she's plotting. If she's plotting, we might be able to find out what she's up to before she catches on to us. If she sees you, that dog ain't gonna hunt."

"Okay. I get it. But who should go investigate? She may have seen you on the island, and Beth, and David. She already knows who Frank and Jack are. Nobody's left."

"Yes. I know someone." Kathrine reached into her pants pocket, pulled out her iPhone, and punched in a number. "Hi. Can you take a day to go to San Francisco and get some information for me?" Kathrine nodded at Rachel. "Great. I'll email the information to you in a little while...Perfect. Send me the bill." She ended the call.

"I'll pay any costs," Rachel said.

Her mind raced. If Yumiko was alive, this might be the way to prove it, and they might be able to find her. Maybe they could finally end this nightmare.

CHAPTER FORTY-FIVE

When the CD of the security videos from the store finally arrived by priority mail, Rachel was so excited her hands shook when she slipped it into her computer. "Let's hope your friend got something good."

Kathrine leaned over the back of Rachel's chair and watched as the video appeared. "Do we know what we're looking for?"

"Bring that chair over here and sit beside me."

Kathrine did as she asked.

Rachel handed her the information Brice had emailed her—a list of specific dates with items of clothing written in columns under the dates. "We need to find someone who's buying those items. Obviously, we're watching for Yumiko specifically, but she might have had someone shop for her." She motioned toward the paper. "Tell me the dates and items that were bought."

Kathrine scanned the paper. "On the fifteenth, six blouses. On the twenty-second, undergarments and a purse. Holy shit. Sixty-five hundred dollars for a purse? Fendi? On the twenty-ninth, slacks."

"What kind of undergarments? How many?"

Kathrine reviewed the paper. "Doesn't say."

"How about how many slacks?"

"Doesn't say. Should we call Brice and see if he has more information?"

Rachel sighed heavily. "No. It's all he had, or he would have sent it. All right. Let's start with the fifteenth. Six blouses."

They began to review the video, watching every person in the store who came to the counter, what they purchased, and what they looked like. Rachel stopped the video after two hours and rubbed her face. "How could that store possibly be that busy? This is going to take forever."

One hundred and fourteen women made purchases that day. No women bought more than three blouses. Seventeen of the women were Yumiko's size and skin tone and had the same hair color.

Kathrine tapped the computer screen. "Looking at their physical attributes is a waste of time. If I were Yumiko and trying to play dead, I wouldn't dream of walking into a store without some type of disguise."

Rachel scrubbed her face. "You're right. It's the items we need to focus on. Let's run through it again."

They reviewed the video the entire day and found nothing. Rachel called Claire to tell her she would be late.

"Olivia made you enchiladas. I'll wrap one and bring it to you."

"Enchiladas? Sweet. Kathrine's with me. Can you bring two?" Rachel glanced over at Kathrine and smiled when she gave a thumbs-up. "Is any apple pie left?"

Claire laughed. "Yes. I'll bring you both a piece."

Forty-five minutes later Claire came into Rachel's office and placed the food on the small conference table. They sat and ate.

"You didn't drive here by yourself, did you?" Rachel asked Claire.

"No. Matt's with me. He's at the front desk."

"What were you doing today?" Rachel tried to maintain some level of politeness, when all she really wanted was to get back to the footage.

"Beth gave me another motorcycle lesson."

Rachel rolled her eyes and dug into her food.

"Stop. We agreed. So, what are you working on?"

"We got the CD with the videos back from Kathrine's friend, and we're going over it one date at a time," Rachel said.

"Anything so far?"

Kathrine shook her head. "A big, fat zero." She wiped a smudge of sour cream from the side of her lip. "None of the women purchased more than three blouses at a time on the date that six were bought."

"What makes you think it's a woman?"

Rachel and Kathrine looked at each other, pushed their chairs out at the same time, and ran to the computer. Rachel sat and turned the computer on and brought up the video. Kathrine sat in her chair as Claire leaned over Rachel's chair and watched.

"Skip all the women. We already know none of them bought enough blouses," Kathrine said.

Rachel scanned and then slowed the video as each male appeared.

"There," Claire said, pointing at the screen. "Two forty-five p.m. The man standing behind the woman with the outfit in her hands. He's got a lot of clothes."

Rachel zoomed in on the man when he reached the counter. They leaned into the screen to get a better look.

"It's a pair of jeans. Damn it," Kathrine said.

"Wait for it," Claire said.

The man put the jeans on the counter and then what looked like women's blouses. He took out a credit card and paid for the jeans, then took out another card and paid for the blouses.

"Hot damn," Kathrine yelled.

He had a slight build and dark-brown hair.

"He could be our guy," Rachel said. "He looks Filipino or Asian."

Claire patted her arm. "All you have is a guy buying blouses. Can't you run his credit cards?"

"Brice has already checked the card that was used. It's Yumiko's old company card, with the company address in the Philippines. We'll run the cards he used," Kathrine said.

Claire shrugged. "I still say all you have is a guy buying blouses."

"Well, just watch us work our magic," Kathrine said.

Rachel opened the next video and began to scan. Claire stretched a half hour later. "Anyone else but you two in the building?"

Rachel didn't take her eyes off the computer screen as she continued to review the video. "I think Jack and Frank are still here."

"Jack left two hours ago," Kathrine said.

"I'm going to see if Frank's still here," Claire said. She kissed the top of Rachel's head.

Rachel waved but didn't take her eyes off the screen. She and Kathrine continued to search the videos.

Hours later, Rachel rubbed her neck. "What are we looking for again?"

Kathrine yawned and reviewed the printout. "Uh, slacks, but we don't know how many. It's plural, so more than one pair."

Rachel stopped the video toward the end. The time-marker on the video read 8:16 p.m. "There he is."

Kathrine leaned near and inspected the screen. "Yep. It's him."

She pinched the bridge of her nose and yawned again. "I've got to get some sleep. We'll start again tomorrow."

"Tomorrow's Saturday. Why don't you come over to our house about ten, and we'll pick up where we left off?"

Kathrine nodded and patted her shoulder. "Good night."

Rachel looked around the room. "Where's Claire?

Kathrine laughed as she twirled her key fob on her finger. "She left a long time ago."

Rachel yawned, shut off her computer, and walked out with Kathrine.

She was exhausted, and the oncoming car lights seemed extra bright as they passed. The night sky cleared, and the stars multiplied as she headed out of the city. She waved to the guard at the gate as she drove down the long driveway, then turned right and into the garage.

The moment her head hit the pillow, she fell asleep beside Claire, who didn't stir.

When she woke, full sun was shining in through the window. She smelled the heavenly scent of Olivia's homemade cinnamon rolls and bacon. She showered and dressed in sport shorts and a T-shirt, then made her way to the kitchen. Claire sat at the bar talking with Olivia and drinking coffee.

"Good morning, sleepyhead." Claire kissed her and slid a glass of cranberry juice in front of her.

Rachel mumbled a greeting and rubbed her eyes. "I feel like I've been on a bender."

Claire laughed. "How late was it when you two finally stopped?"

Rachel yawned and took a sip of the juice. "I got home around one thirty."

"Did you find anything?"

Rachel yawned again. "I think he's our guy."

"Olivia and I are going to the grocery store. We'll be back in a couple of hours. Matt's driving us."

"Who's Matt?"

Claire put her arm around Rachel's shoulder. "One of the security guards. You told me I had to have one with me when I leave the house. Steve and Juan are on the grounds today, Garrett is at the gate, and Matt is driving me and Olivia."

"Who came with you last night to the shed?"

"Remember? I told you. Matt."

"You're seeing an awful lot of him. Do I need to be worried?"

Claire laughed and kissed her. "How are you holding up?"

Rachel stood and put her arms around her and kissed her. "I'm okay. How are you doing?"

"Okay."

Rachel looked at the stove clock. "Kathrine's coming over in a little while. We're going to start back on the videos."

Claire patted Rachel's behind, picked up her purse, and she and Olivia went out the door to the garage. "Save me a cinnamon roll."

Rachel feasted on a bacon-and-tomato sandwich and a cinnamon roll, then went into her office, turned on the computer, and waited for Kathrine.

Four hours later she leaned back in her office chair and put her hands behind her head and stretched. "He's definitely our guy. He bought the blouses, slacks, underwear, and the handbag. He's not buying all those items for himself."

Kathrine lay on the leather sofa, tossing the small pillow into the air and catching it. "Correct. So, the question is, who's he buying them for?"

"No. That's not the question. Is Yumiko alive? That's the question that matters to me."

"Don't you want to know who he is?"

Rachel blew out a breath and rubbed her thighs. She stood and bent over and stretched, touching the floor. "Not really. Not unless he leads us to Yumiko."

Kathrine threw the pillow up and then swatted it, landing it perfectly on the opposite end of the sofa. "We should send his picture to Brice and see if he can get a match in the system."

"That's a great idea." Rachel walked back to the computer, made a copy of his picture, and sent it to Brice's email with a quick note. "Done. What now?"

"Now we analyze the crap out of the video."

Rachel leaned back in the chair. "Okay. Where do you want to start?"

"Dates of purchase? Is there a pattern? Time of purchase? Is there any significance? Obviously, that's relevant. Why him? If the purchases are for Yumiko, why use him? Like I said, who is he? Once we confirm he's connected to Yumiko in some way, we can search the surrounding video cameras in the blocks near the store to see if we can track him or find any sign of Yumiko. It's a long shot, and it's going to take days, but we shouldn't leave anything to chance."

Rachel watched Kathrine as she rubbed her temples. How important was the man to this puzzle they were trying to put together? Could Yumiko be in San Francisco? If so, what was she doing there? Plotting? California was next door to Nevada. Why hide in the United States? Why San Francisco? Something felt familiar. If she was alive, why didn't she choose somewhere else to hide?

CHAPTER FORTY-SIX

On Sunday morning Rachel received an email from Brice informing her the picture she'd sent wasn't good enough to make an identification. The thought of going through all the videos again to find a better picture made her cringe, but she inserted the CD and began the search.

Claire came in later with a sandwich and drink and set them on the end table beside the sofa. "You have to eat. It's been hours since you took a break. Come over here. What are you doing?"

Rachel got up from the desk and sat on the sofa beside her. "I can't find a better picture of that guy to send Brice. The one I sent wasn't good enough."

"I'll look while you eat." Claire sat in Rachel's chair. "Does Brice want a full profile?"

"Yes, but his facial features have to be clear."

Rachel ate the delicious veggie sandwich and drank the juice. "What did Olivia put in this?"

Claire held her finger in the air. "Rachel, did you see this when you isolated this guy's footage?"

Rachel put the napkin down on the empty plate and walked behind her chair, bending over Claire. "See what?"

"This guy is talking. Look."

Rachel watched him on the footage. Now that Claire had pointed it out, the man did look like he was talking to someone.

"He does it throughout the store, so it can't be someone next to him. How do you zoom in?"

Claire got out of the chair to let Rachel sit. Rachel zoomed the footage and watched as the man moved throughout the store. "You're right. He is talking. Good catch."

"Freeze it," Claire said.

Rachel paused the video.

"Go back a couple of frames."

Rachel moved the video frame by frame.

"There. Stop."

"What are we looking at?" Rachel asked.

"There, in his right ear. It's an earpiece."

Rachel leaned in closer to the screen. "Maybe it is."

"Trust me, it is."

Rachel stood and kissed her hard on the lips. "You and that great eyesight are a piece of work." She kissed her again. She picked up her cell phone and made a call.

"Who are you calling? It's Sunday."

"Jack. He needs to get me someone who reads lips."

Monday morning Rachel, Kathrine, Jack, and Jack's friend Sally Richards went into the conference room. Rachel connected her computer to the wall screen and keyed in the surveillance video of the man who bought the items. It was hard to contain her excitement as she made the keystrokes. Claire had seen something significant. "Is that good for you, Sally?"

"Yes. That's perfect. You'll have to play it at a normal speed for me to read his lips. Go ahead. I'm ready."

Rachel started the video.

Sally was fixated on the screen. Her eyes narrowed, and then she raised a brow. She pursed her lips and shook her head. "Play that part back again, please."

Rachel replayed the part Sally requested.

Sally once again watched carefully, but this time she put her fingers to her lips and pinched her lower lip, then rubbed her chin. She licked her lips. "Okay. You can stop it."

Rachel watched her, sitting on the edge of her seat to hear what she would say.

"I'm sorry. I can't read it."

Rachel's heart sank as she slumped back into her chair.

"Why?" asked Jack.

"Because it's not English."

Immediately Rachel had a feeling she knew what it was. "It's Tagalog," she said, sitting stiff, unable to contain her excitement.

"I have a contact at the university. I'll see if someone there lip-reads Tagalog." Sally turned away to make her call.

The hours slipped by and still no response from the university. The language department had promised they would find someone who read and spoke Tagalog, but they didn't know of anyone who could read lips. Rachel wasn't worried at this point. She just needed to confirm the man in the video spoke Tagalog. It would be a bonus if the interpreter could decipher any words. Finally, at five thirty, she got the call. A teaching assistant would be at the shed the next morning around nine.

She was glad but disappointed. Another day wasted.

She and Claire were at the office by eight the next morning. The rest of the team filtered in, and a little before nine, Jack, Kathrine, Frank, and Beth were gathered with Rachel and Claire in the conference room. They all wanted to know.

A tall, dark-haired, tanned young man from the university walked in at 9:10. He had the sweetest facial expression. It was like his eyes danced and his smile said, "I'm so glad to meet you." He introduced himself as Jacob McCormack and shook hands with everyone in the room, telling Rachel how much he enjoyed the opportunity to help.

And she knew he meant it. "Jacob, it's good to meet you."

She keyed the video onto the wall screen once again.

"Whenever you're ready," he said.

She played the first segment as he watched carefully, moving his lips silently. "Play that segment once again, please." He smiled halfway through the segment.

Rachel paused the video when the segment ended.

No one spoke. All eyes were on Jacob.

He turned and looked at Rachel. "You were correct. It's Tagalog. He's asking about the colors red, green, and yellow. He's uncomfortable about the time change and said something about the temperature or climate. I couldn't quite make it out. Would you like me to try to do more?"

Rachel wanted to hug him and pinch his cheek for some reason. He seemed like a beam of sunshine in the room. When she glanced around the room, everyone watched her.

Jack came over and hugged her. "You were right, Rachel. She's still alive."

Everyone seemed to want to move close to her. It made her feel comforted and protected.

"We'll get her," said Jack. "Jacob, how did you do that?"

Jacob smiled. "My mother and father are deaf. I served my mission in the Philippines in the Baguio Mission, where I taught and helped deaf members of my church. Would you like me to continue, Rachel?"

Rachel nodded. "Yes. Whatever you can tell us will help."

Kathrine hugged Rachel before she sat back down. "We'll get her this time."

Rachel noticed Claire hadn't moved. Her expression turned rigid, like her face was made of stone. Rachel asked something of the group she'd never asked before. "Would you all excuse us for a few minutes?"

Everyone left the room without questions or comments. Rachel pushed the button at the head of the table, and the window glass went opaque, blocking them from view. She walked over to Claire and sat beside her, taking her hand. Claire's hand felt cold and clammy, and she trembled. The news had hit her hard, harder than Rachel thought it would. Her heart ached for her. She wished she could take the sting away. They knew the truth now, but the truth didn't make them free. It covered them like a shroud, suffocating them.

Rachel moved closer and wrapped her arms around her. Claire seemed to relax against her shoulder. She reached down and held Claire's hand again. "It's going to be all right. I promise you."

Claire straightened, squeezing her hand. "I told you before, Rachel, you can't make that promise. Go straight at her with everything the team has." She put her arms around her, as if wrapping her soul around her. "Annihilate her," she said firmly, then stood to leave the room.

Rachel wished Yumiko had died on that boat, but she hadn't. She understood Yumiko too well. Now she knew the truth, and because of it she also realized one of them had to die. It was the only way to end this. And Claire knew it also. Rachel could see it in her eyes.

"Claire, wait." Rachel slipped her arm in hers and walked her out to the car. Garrett opened the door for Claire to get into her Maserati.

"You're too upset to drive," Rachel said.

Claire nodded and got in the passenger side. Garrett slipped into the driver's seat, a big smile on his face. He tapped the pad, and the car jumped to life. Rachel motioned for him to roll Claire's window down. She leaned close to Claire. "I won't be too late tonight. You relax and try not to worry."

Claire patted Rachel's arm. "I'll be okay. I just need to process this now that it's been confirmed." She sighed and bit her lower lip.

Rachel grew more concerned about her as she watched Garrett drive her away. She went back inside to talk with Jack.

"I've been thinking about San Francisco and why it feels so familiar. I've asked myself a thousand times why I felt that way, and then it hit me. The box with the leather strap was postmarked San Francisco. It must have some significance for Yumiko. And the clothier. Why there? Why that store? I want to drive her to me, Jack, and I have an idea."

From that very moment they began working on a plan to force Yumiko to her. She and Jack agreed it was the best way to deal with her. They could have spent an endless amount of time and resources chasing her, but this way worked better. Once again, they would need bait, and this time only she could satisfy Yumiko's lust.

The late-afternoon sun streamed in through the window in Jack's office. He sat in his chair, studying the flyer Rachel had given him, rubbing his temple in little circles. He handed the flyer back to her, his lips tight, eyes narrowed. "Are you absolutely sure you want to do this?"

She nodded.

"This is really going to piss her off."

"I hope so."

Jack breathed deeply and let it out in an exaggerated exhale. "Okay. Let the games begin."

She smiled and went to Kathrine's office, handing her the flyer. Kathrine scanned it and sent it to her friend with a request to post it in the vacant windows and areas near the J.W. Steiner Clothier.

Kathrine looked at the flyer again. "Man, this is good stuff."

Rachel got home later than she wanted. Claire was in the TV room watching a movie. She seemed more relaxed, calmer than she had been when she left the shed that morning. Rachel curled up next to her. "Feeling better?"

"Yes." Claire reached for the glass of red wine on the stand beside her.

"How much have you had?"

"Not enough." Claire took a drink of the wine.

It wasn't good when she got this quiet. She was brooding, smoldering, like a campfire from the night before. Rachel turned off the TV. "Talk to me."

Claire set the glass of wine on the stand and turned to her. She took Rachel's hand. "More than anything I want this to be over, and I know it's going to come down to you and her. Don't you dare let her get the best of you."

Rachel held her hand. "What do you mean?"

"You belong to me, not her. Don't lose your focus. Don't turn this into an obsession like she's done. I want us to be as normal as possible while this is going on. This is not our life. It's just a small part of it, a side road. If you have to back away and let Jack or Brice take the lead, then you've got to promise me you will."

Rachel slipped her arm around her waist. "I promise I'll keep my perspective. Claire, I feel like I've been preparing for this situation from the moment Yumiko's people took me. Everything I've gone through has helped me get ready. We're not alone in this."

What more could she say? Claire understood what it would take to end it. And without telling her, Claire knew what she had in mind. She saw the apprehension and concern in Claire's eyes. She held her hand, rubbing her thumb over the back of it. If Rachel could prevent it somehow, she would, but Yumiko intended to come after her, and they had no choice but to get ready and deal with her.

CHAPTER FORTY-SEVEN

No other videos they gathered from the surrounding areas near the store with the dates of purchase had shown any sign of Yumiko or the man who bought the clothing. They were gambling that Yumiko didn't live too far from the clothier. The flyer would cause a reaction. Rachel hoped it would affect Yumiko the way the leather belt had affected her.

She stood with her arms folded across her chest, the warm afternoon breeze blowing through the open garage door as the delivery truck left.

"When did you buy them?" Rachel asked, surprised at what Claire was telling her.

"The day after we had the big fight about me boxing. It just took a while for delivery. How do you like them?" Claire waved her hand toward the new red and gold Ducati Enduro motorcycles, one with black grip handlebars, and the other with gold.

"They're great, but I still can't believe you did this. Are you sure you're ready to take them out?"

"Yes. Beth has taught me well. Which one do you want?"

"I get to pick?"

Claire laughed. "Yes. Whichever one you want."

"The gold one." Even though she was nervous about Claire riding, she did know she had skills. And she had confidence, both in Beth's training and in Claire's abilities. Claire desperately needed the distraction. Rachel tried to downplay her excitement about the bikes, but Claire saw it.

Matt and Garrett walked over to the garage to look at the bikes, clearly in awe. Rachel couldn't help but feel a little proud of Claire.

They rode the motorcycles around the property and surrounding area, under the watchful eyes of all the security guards.

"You ready to race?" Claire gunned her bike throttle.

"Are you sure you want to do this, Claire? Maybe we should wait a few days until you get some more experience."

"I'm fine. Are you...chicken?"

Rachel laughed. "Oh, now you've done it."

"Okay, past the hill, and the finish line will be the pile of rocks on the property line with the cacti on the far end. The first one to cross the finish line wins," Claire said.

"What are the rules?"

"Rules? There are no rules. Whoever crosses the finish line first wins."

They rode the motorcycles over to the agreed-upon starting point and rechecked their helmets.

"I'll start us off," Claire said. "One, two—"

"Wait. What if—"

"Three. Go." Claire gunned the throttle and took off, leaving Rachel staring at the south end of Claire's northbound motorcycle.

"Hey, wait!" Rachel took off and passed Claire within a minute, settling into a comfortable lead as she continued to push the Ducati, squeezing her thighs tighter around the bike, clenching the handlebar grips. She could see the finish line, the two cacti and pile of rocks straight ahead. She just had to pass the last hill, and she would beat her. She opened the throttle as far as it would go and flew by it, smiling smugly because the last time she checked, Claire was at least fifty yards behind her.

A large red-and-gold object suddenly appeared in her peripheral vision and passed level with her shoulder on her left. She turned her head momentarily. "No way. No way. That's not possible."

"Pussy," Claire yelled as she came over the hill and landed in front and to her left, speeding to the finish line, besting her by what felt like minutes but was only a few seconds.

Rachel watched as Claire eased off the throttle and waited for her to catch her. They both brought the motorcycles to a stop and took off their helmets. Rachel bent over and shook her hair. "How did you do that?"

"I just saw the hill, calculated I could get ahead of you without crashing into you, and took the jump." Claire threw her head back and laughed. "Rachel, you didn't really think you could beat me, did you?"

Rachel shook her head in disbelief. "No way you should have beat me. I had you by at least a few seconds."

Claire held out her hands and shrugged. "All's fair, baby. Maybe next time."

"Claire, you shouldn't be that coordinated on a motorcycle this soon."

Claire shrugged again. "It was like I never stopped riding. Beth's a really good teacher, and I love riding."

Rachel shook her head. "That's unbelievable."

They rode back to the garage, where Rachel saw Garrett hand Matt some money. "I hope he chokes on it." She scoffed as they walked into the house.

Claire tapped the edge of the round glass table with her fingertips, then stood and walked over to her yellow rose bushes, touching the delicate petals, the fragrant scent filling the air. The afternoon sun lingered over the patio, as if not wanting to leave.

Kathrine waved to Claire when she emerged from the back entrance of the kitchen.

Claire waved and motioned for her to join her at the table.

"What's going on?" Kathrine slid gracefully into a white wicker chair.

"I'm worried Rachel is in way over her head about Yumiko, and we need to help her. Her plan may not work."

"She's involved emotionally, but that's understandable, given everything that's happened."

"Don't sugarcoat it. I know you're worried about her too."

Kathrine nodded. "Yes, I am, but it's a solid plan."

"We have to do something."

"What do you have in mind?" Kathrine asked.

"First, if Jack or Brice captures Yumiko, Rachel will eventually want to see her. You have to convince her not to go."

"I think she *should* see Yumiko. She needs to resolve this." Kathrine leaned back in the chair. "I'll tell you what I'll do. If she does go to see her when she's captured, I'll go with her."

"Do you really think she needs to?"

"After what she's been through? Yes. She needs to settle it in her mind and put it behind her, so she can move on."

"Yumiko will just mess with her head," Claire said.

"I thought that also, but now I think Rachel is ready to face her. Besides, Yumiko will be in chains if she's captured, in an enclosed environment, and Rachel will have the advantage mentally and physically."

Claire bit her lower lip, unsure if she should mention something. Just the thought of it caused her stomach to churn. "What if one of the agencies gets her before Jack and Rachel do, and somehow she bargains her way out again? She'll come back here for Rachel or try to hunt her down. Again. It'll never end."

Kathrine folded her arms across her chest. "You have to face the probability that's exactly what Yumiko will do. Rachel knows it. That's why she and Jack have tried to make sure this all ends with Yumiko permanently behind bars here in the United States, and not some other country.

"Rachel doesn't want to give Yumiko any opportunity to get to her or you before *she's* ready. Yumiko is desperate. She won't waste her time on Sarah or Tilly, not after her last plan failed. We verified that the man purchased the items. Rachel sent the man's photo to Brice, and he connected him to Yumiko. Brice searched through the data base and found the man with a woman. They ran a facial analysis and stripped away Yumiko's disguise. He sent their picture to all the other agencies. It's plastered in every airport, train station, and bus terminal. I'm sure Yumiko got wind of it and knows her cover is blown. I'm sure she's seen the flyer Rachel had posted around San Francisco, and she knows Rachel sent it. Yumiko's not stupid, and neither are the people she has around her.

"I know it's hard for you, and for Rachel, to drag this out. But the longer it goes on, the more desperate Yumiko becomes. Rachel plans to force her to go right where she wants her. All Yumiko can see now is getting to Rachel. I'm sure her obsession has grown stronger. That's why I think Rachel's plan is good. It preys on Yumiko's obsession. She's going to lure her in because of it."

Claire thought of Ilesh and what he had taught her about the hunted turning into the hunter.

In the quiet of the rose garden, among the beautiful flowers, Claire and Kathrine formulated a backup plan in case Rachel's went horribly wrong. It would keep Claire sane, help her hang on when the thoughts of Yumiko harming Rachel were unbearable. It also gave her some small sense of control in the chaos headed their way.

Kathrine stood to leave after they finished.

"Are you sure our part of this plan will work?" Claire asked.

"Well, no plan is a hundred-percent foolproof, but yes, it's solid. As solid as we can make it. Something could always go wrong, but we're prepared."

"Maybe we should just get Rachel the hell out of here."

"That won't solve anything. You know better than anyone what she's like. She won't go, and if we don't get Yumiko, she'll keep coming after her. This is the way to help her."

Claire ran her hand through her hair and gazed at the clear, blue sky. "I couldn't live with myself if something happens to Rachel because of what we're going to do. Are you sure we shouldn't tell her?"

"I'm sure. If she knows, she might act differently, and that would be a bad thing. Remember that was her rationale for not telling Ricky, Sarah, and Tilly on the ship. Her plan is solid, and so is ours. We've done the best we can. That's all we can do. Now don't get all wobbly on me. Woman up."

"I don't like Rachel putting herself in harm's way."

"She'll go after Yumiko no matter what we do. We're just going to make sure our plan backs up hers. Besides, you're a big part of her plan anyway."

Claire's stomach muscles tightened. "I wish I knew if this was absolutely the best way to handle it. Tell me again which medal you won?"

"It *is* the best way. Silver medal. Summer Olympics. United Kingdom. Pistol at twenty-five meters. Execute the plan. No hesitation. No regret."

Claire stayed out in the garden after Kathrine left. Their plan would work. It had to. Rachel's life depended on it.

CHAPTER FORTY-EIGHT

The evening sun beat down on the back of Yumiko's neck as she made her way through the crowded sidewalk. The press of people bumping into her fueled the rage as it seeped in, first in her hands, then into her chest. She wanted to reach into her shoulder bag and pull out her gun, hold it in the air, and rapid-fire. That would clear the sidewalk. The scent of fish, clams, and baked bread wafted through the air, but even that couldn't help her mood. She was stuck here, confined, trapped. Trolley cars on the Powell-Mason route clanged as people rushed off and on as one stopped. *Idiots.*

She entered the tan-brick, three-story apartment building and pressed the elevator button to see if it worked today. It didn't. She cursed and climbed the stairs to her third-floor apartment. She could easily afford something better, but for now she needed to remain inconspicuous. She walked through the darkened living room, not talking to the two guards standing near the kitchen. She was sick of seeing them. She took out her mouthpiece, grabbed the wig off her head, and tossed them onto the counter. She was sick of the disguises too. She was sick of it all.

She went to the wet bar and poured alcohol into the glass, lifting it to her lips and gulping. She set the empty glass by the decanter and wiped her mouth with the back of her hand, then reached for her cell phone.

"I don't want your excuses, Agapito. Don't tell me it can't be done." She dug her shoes into the carpet as she listened, then squeezed the phone tighter and pushed it against her ear. "I will not stay here another month. Everything is almost set in London. I want to go home."

"You can't come back, not yet. It's too risky," Agapito said. "I am taking care of everything. You have nothing to be concerned about. I'll send Crisanto."

"Crisanto doesn't know his ass from a hole in the ground. You were supposed to take care of it, not him."

"I can't be there with you. No place is safe since MI6 got hold of my picture with you next to me at the airport in your disguise."

"Danito has advised me to get home as soon as possible and handle things myself," Yumiko said.

"That's easy for him to say. MI6, CIA, and Interpol have all made you their top priority. No country is safe for you right now." Agapito raised his voice. "And all you can think about is getting even with Brice Chambers and Portola."

"Don't you raise your voice to me, you little shit. I made you who you are. I gave you the power you have, and I can take it away from you."

Silence at the other end of the call.

Yumiko gripped the edge of the counter. "Now you listen to me. You have Crisanto bring the plans for the layout of Chambers's apartment building to me, and the aerial shots of Portola's, and I want all the street maps to all three airports. And as far as the business is concerned, no negotiations are to be made unless they're with me personally. Our three top partners know I'm not dead and will wait, and everyone else can get in line."

She disconnected before he could say anything more.

She poured the last of the whiskey from the bottle into the rocks glass, picked it up, and walked into her bedroom. She sat on the bed, kicked her shoes off, and reached into the nightstand, pulling out the flyer. She didn't have to read it. She had it memorized. She gulped more whiskey and set the glass on the nightstand. She held the flyer with both hands, then traced the words at the bottom with her finger. She didn't like the picture of her that Portola had used, but she had placed the bull's-eye perfectly over her face. Her fingers trembled as she traced the words again.

I know you're alive.
Come and get me, you crazy bitch.

Agapito had brought the flyer to her when he had gone to the clothier. He said it had been displayed in several of the buildings near the store. She saw a glint of amusement in his eyes when he showed it to her. She had thrown a half bottle of whiskey across the room and ordered him and her two guards out of the apartment. She couldn't sleep for two nights. Portola had sent the information about Agapito to Brice Chambers. She was sure of it. They'd conspired, and now she couldn't go anywhere. Agapito had told her that pictures of him, and her in her disguise, were posted in every airport from the Philippines to London. And she had to assume they were posted in major international airports in the United States. She had to rearrange her plan in order to get to London and then to Las Vegas. Who did Portola think she was?

When Crisanto arrived the following week, she didn't greet him. He gave her the items and the cash, credit cards, and the paperwork to Brice Chambers's apartment building and Portola's estate. She ripped the plans out of his hand and told him to leave her alone. She studied them for days, barely able to sleep. She kept the information of Portola's estate and the street maps beside her on the bed.

She opened the box containing the new facial prosthetics and wigs Crisanto had brought her. She didn't care what she looked like, as long as it got her through airport security and customs. She set the picture of what she was supposed to look like beside the lighted makeup mirror as she applied the disguise. It took hours, but by the time she finished, even she didn't recognize herself. She looked like a fifty-year-old, gray-haired woman without any distinguishing facial features. The photographer arrived that evening, set up the background, and took several pictures. She had her new passport the next day.

She grew anxious to be on her way. Every day she waited increased the risk of being recognized and captured. Her plans were set. Everything was in place. First London and then Las Vegas. Would the disguise and passport be good enough? She would make no mistakes. Not this time. This time she would kill her.

CHAPTER FORTY-NINE

Jack abruptly entered Rachel's office and sat across from her. "I'm going to London tomorrow." He tapped her desk, announcing the news like he was already on his way.

Rachel almost jumped out of her chair. "Do they have Yumiko?"

"Brice called me. They think they have her general location in London, and they're closing in. I'm flying over there to question her personally."

She closed the laptop. "I want to go with you."

"No."

"If anyone has a right to interrogate her, it's me."

"That's true, but the answer is still no. You're not going." His blue eyes were fixed on her face, as if he was daring her to question his decision. She took the challenge.

"I want to go."

He continued to watch her, doing that thing he always did. Evaluating. "Rachel, you're not up to this. Stay here. Brice and I will handle it. You will have a chance to talk with her, but not for a while."

Immediately insulted, she recoiled. "What makes you think she won't outsmart you again?"

Jack's jaw muscles tightened. "You're not going."

"That is total bull crap, and you know it." Heat rushed to her cheeks, and her eyes burned. She grabbed the pen on the desk for something to hold on to. Her heart began to pound. Her temples throbbed. She swallowed, trying to force the bile back as it inched its way up. Her knuckles ached from gripping the pen.

He stood. "It should be obvious to you that you're in no condition to go to London. I want you to stay here and relax, focus on Claire and your job. Besides. This is not an absolute. They may not get her. If they don't, our plan is in place, and I'm sure it will be enough to bring her here. Brice and I will take care of this. I'll call you as soon as I have any news. If you have any problems, Frank's in charge." He started to leave her office.

"This is nothing but bullshit, Jack, and you know it." The sound of her voice echoed out against the hallway wall and bounced back into her office.

He rolled his neck. "See you after my trip."

She stared at his back as he walked out. She wanted to follow him, make him understand her need to go, to see Yumiko in chains—why she had to make sure she was subdued and could never hurt her or Claire.

The pen snapped. Black ink seeped between her fingers. She quickly stood and grabbed a tissue, swiping at the ink, making a bigger mess on her hands. She kicked the chair away from the desk and stomped out of her office to the bathroom.

She turned the water on, lowered her hands into the sink, and lathered them with soap. She scrubbed as hard as she could, rubbing, trying to get the ink stain off, but the more she scrubbed, the more it remained. She rubbed faster and harder, looking at herself in the mirror. She stopped and gripped the sink as she lowered her head, watching her arms as they trembled. When did her life become so out of control? She took a deep breath, trying to stop the hesitation in her breathing.

Kathrine came through the door and stepped behind her.

Rachel watched her through the mirror.

"Jack's right, Rachel. You know it. I know it, and so does everyone else." She put a steady hand on Rachel's shoulder. "You can't carry this alone. Let us help you."

Rachel returned to her office and tried to calm herself. She wasn't alone in this. Jack and the others were doing what they thought best because they cared about her. But she alone had to decide what was best for her.

The day stretched into evening. She went home and told Claire the news. She sat on the living room sofa, watching Claire pace, bite her lip, and rub her hands together.

"Do you think MI6 will get her?" Claire's pace quickened. She walked to the window, pulling the drape to the side.

"I don't know. I hope so. Claire, you're upset. Calm down. It's a good thing if they get her. We won't have to do anything."

"But what if they make a trade with her again and let her go?"

"They won't do that. Too much has changed. The CIA, MI6, and

Interpol are all salivating to capture her. They all suspect she's alive, and she's burned her bridges with them. No one will let her go now." Rachel moved to her and put her arms around her.

Claire buried her head in her shoulder. "God, is this never going to be over for us? How much more?"

Rachel stood beside her, staring out the window as the two heavily armed guards passed each other, their semiautomatic weapons drawn as they walked the perimeter.

Claire reached out her trembling hand and touched Rachel's arm. "I'm sorry, Rachel. The reality of this has set in, and I'm scared. I thought I could handle it, but now that it's happening, I'm not so sure. She'll come here if she eludes them. I don't want you to get hurt. I don't want any of us to get hurt."

"I know." Rachel breathed deeply and continued to look out the window.

"What is it, Rachel?"

"If MI6 has spotted her in London, she wanted them to. I know her, Claire. I don't know what she's planning, but she's up to something. We can make this work if she gets away from them again. She'll be coming here. She thinks she has us, but she's wrong. We'll lead her right where we want her to go."

Claire put her hand to Rachel's face. "You really believe that, don't you?"

"Yes, baby. I do. The moment she comes after us, she'll become the prey, and we will not hesitate or regret a thing."

Claire gazed into her eyes as if searching for something. Reassurance? Understanding? Safety? Rachel saw a flicker of hope.

"We'll become the hunters?" Claire pleaded for the answer.

Rachel drew her close, feeling Claire relax in her arms. "Yes. We *will* become the hunters."

CHAPTER FIFTY

Yumiko had slipped into London, unwilling to leave the final moves of the game to anyone else. But the clock was ticking, and MI6 would find her soon. She had to get in and out as fast as possible. She paced and held the phone close to her ear, hanging on every word. She'd been waiting hours for the call.

"Chambers has left MI6 Cyber Operations and is on his way home." The deep male voice with the British accent disconnected.

She attached the silencer to the handgun and slipped in the full clip. She placed the small black tool in her overcoat pocket, her fingers grazing the note she would leave for Portola somewhere near Chambers's body—a last greeting before the end.

Nothing else mattered now but working her way to Portola. Agapito had double-crossed her. All the while he had fed her information, he and Crisanto had been making plans to take over. But she'd deal with them later. She had resources they knew nothing about.

The driver dropped her off at the corner of High Street and Brighton. Her footsteps fell almost silent on the cobblestone as she walked the two blocks down Brighton Street in the thick fog, then made a left on Hanover. The night air's chill seeped into her bones. Her muscles stiffened. She swung her arms and fought the throbbing, dull ache moving up the back of her neck. She reached into the deep pocket of the black hooded raincoat and fondled the note. She'd have Portola soon. A momentary surge of exhilaration passed through her.

The lights in the second-story flat danced in the darkened alleyway, casting shadowy images against the worn brick walls, passing over her like ghosts over a grave. She continued to watch the movement in the window. Two. His wife. What was two instead of one? Nothing more. Better for his wife this way. She'd do it quickly.

The lights went out.

She waited an hour, then moved to the security door and opened it with the key. She climbed the stairs to the hallway, unlocked the window, and maneuvered out onto the ledge. She clung to the facing as she inched her way to the drawing-room window. If the maintenance worker she'd bribed hadn't done what he was paid to do, she wouldn't be able to go any farther. She held her breath and engaged the tool, disarming the security system, then slowly raised the window, watching and listening as she climbed inside. She took the gun with the silencer out of her coat pocket, pausing momentarily to get her bearings, then moved quietly across the carpeted floor. She stopped near the open bedroom door, hearing a faint creak on the wooden floor. One of them was awake and moving. She stepped forward and aimed in front of her just as she saw him standing at the side of the bed, his back to her. She didn't hesitate. Two shots. Chambers collapsed, falling facedown on the bed, then sliding onto the floor. The female moved and reached for him, her mouth open, ready to scream. Yumiko fired three more times before she could make a sound. The top part of her head splintered, spraying brain matter onto the headboard and wall.

She went in and checked for a pulse in his neck, then fired one last time into the side of his head.

She took the white piece of paper with the handwritten note to Portola, kissed it, and placed it gently on the nightstand by the bed. She looked at Chambers's bloody body once more, then left through the front door, relocking it with a key she found on the entryway table. She didn't care how soon they found them. By the time they did, she would be on her way to *her.*

CHAPTER FIFTY-ONE

Rachel gripped the arms of the chair. The color drained out of her hands, and a deep, bone-chilling numbness swept through her, like someone had opened the window and the room temperature had suddenly dropped to below zero. Frank and Kathrine sat watching her as they listened on the speaker phone.

"Rachel?"

She tried to focus, but it was as if her mind had put up a wall and wouldn't accept what Jack had just told her. She braced herself for wave after wave of reality as it pounded against her. It finally overwhelmed her, and the wall of resistance came crashing down.

Yumiko had shot them like they were nothing, merely obstacles in her way. She'd shot Brice for no other reason than because she wanted to. And his wife? Why? Because she had been there with him? How could she protect herself and Claire against someone like that?

She shuddered and forced herself to regain control. She wasn't a civilian. She was a trained professional. And she'd damn well better get ready for the firestorm that was about to descend upon her.

Frank touched her arm, bringing her back from her stupor of thought. She cleared her throat. "I'm here, Jack. When did it happen?"

"About seven hours ago. Rachel, there's more. I'm sending a picture of the note she left for you. She signed it *yours truly,* and, from the position of the saliva on the envelope, it looks like she kissed it."

Rachel clenched her fists, her breath catching, every muscle tensing.

"She's settling business. Get everything ready. I think she's coming back there," Jack said.

"Unbelievable," Kathrine said.

"Oh, believe it," Frank said.

"I could stay here and eventually find out if she left for the US, but it's a waste of time. She's obviously able to move under the radar. And like you said, she wanted MI6 to know she was in London. She's toying with us."

Rachel leaned forward, slowly running her hand over the smooth surface of her desktop. She looked straight ahead as she spoke. "I know she's coming here, Jack. I have no doubt."

"I'm glad we went through with your plan. Everything's in place. I'm leaving on the next flight." Jack ended the call.

She stared out the window, wanting to scream, rage, or run. It was one thing to deal with Yumiko coming after her, but why Brice, and his wife? Yumiko was a heartless animal. Rachel had no doubt now what she intended. Kathrine and Frank stood, looking at her. "Everyone clear on what to do?"

They both nodded and left the room.

She called Claire, her hands shaking. "Where are you?"

"What's wrong?"

"Where are you?"

"I'm in the studio, working on a piece. You sound awful."

"Who's at the house?"

"Olivia is here, and I think the gardener is out back, plus the security guards, of course. Rachel, what's wrong?"

"I'll be home as soon as I can. Don't leave the house. Do *not* leave the house under any circumstances."

"Rachel, what is it?"

"I'll tell you when I get there." Rachel printed out the note Jack had sent.

I'll be there soon.
I can't wait to see you bleed.
Yours, truly.

Rachel immediately left for home. She showed Claire the copy of the note and told her what had happened. She held her as Claire cried, and then Claire broke away and ranted. She assured her their plan was solid, and they would get Yumiko. It didn't help.

Days passed and still no sign of Yumiko.

Rachel watched two security guards as they walked down the path toward Claire's studio. Two more made their way in the opposite direction.

"How many more days do you think?" Claire asked.

Rachel pursed her lips. She placed the pool balls into the rack and slid it into position on the pool table, then pushed the balls tightly against the rack with her fingers. She lifted the rack away, forming a perfect triangle. She motioned for Claire to break. "Time's running out. She'll put as much stress on us as possible and hope the strain will cause us to make a mistake."

Claire chalked her stick. "With all the agencies after her, she'll have to do it fairly quickly. Do you think she'll go after Tilly or Sarah?"

Rachel stepped away from the pool table. "No. She doesn't have time to risk it. She'll focus on us. She knows I'll be here with you. The flyer we posted sent an invitation, and she won't be able to resist. Here is the only place she can get to us. We're not leaving the house, and time isn't on her side. She's aware we'll have security here, but she won't care."

"Do you think Ricky will ever forgive us for insisting he and Sarah have all the security?"

"I don't really care anymore. They're safe. Yumiko can't get them, and that's the thing that matters. We'll have to deal with it when this is over. How do you feel about it?"

Claire shrugged. "Like you do."

That feeling of doubt crept in again, causing Rachel's heart to race, like being on the precipice of panic, yet knowing she wouldn't go over the edge. She felt anxious and afraid, yet also confident and eager. The mixture confused her.

Kathrine had told her it was PSR, prebattle stress release. "All soldiers get it in some degree or another before combat. It's the body's way of dealing with the stress. The unknown causes the anxiety and fear, and your training and preparation trigger the confidence and anticipation."

The waiting took its toll. She slept little, and the weight loss started again. Claire had dark circles under her eyes, and besides being grouchy, she paced most of the time.

Rachel saw Claire's hands tremble when she positioned for the break.

"It's a waiting game, and I'm sick of waiting." Claire struck the pool stick onto the cue ball. The ball collided with the rack, and the eight ball rolled across the table, hitting the edge of the corner pocket, almost going in.

Rachel took the cue stick out of Claire's hand and moved beside her. She kissed her, putting her hand around her waist. "We're ready, Claire. This isn't about me anymore. It's about Brice and his wife, and every life Yumiko has destroyed."

They were all counting on Yumiko coming to Las Vegas. Everything depended on her making the first move. Did they plan this right? Had they done absolutely everything to protect themselves?

CHAPTER FIFTY-TWO

The team and their wives and friends, and some of the other employees from the shed sat around Rachel and Claire's recreation room, drinks in hand, the evening sun filtering through the windows. Bluesy music played softly in the background. Olivia had made hors d'oeuvres and kept their glasses filled with whatever they wanted. This would be their last gathering until it was over. Claire felt the tension yet also a certain sense of comfort being together.

She took Rachel's pale hand and saw the worry in her eyes. "We needed this."

Rachel smiled and nodded, then lowered her head, not holding Claire's gaze.

Claire touched her chin. "Hey. I'm the one who's supposed to be down about all of this. Not you. Not my rock." She saw Rachel's vulnerability. What she and Kathrine had planned was the right thing to do. No matter what happened, she needed to stay strong and focused for Rachel.

A slow song with an easy beat began to play. Jack, Frank, David, and Beth's boyfriend were playing pool. Some of the women were sitting in small groups laughing and talking.

Kathrine came over and sat beside her and Rachel at the game table. "It's good to be together. Thanks for this." She raised her glass to them.

"It's our pleasure to have all of you here," Claire said.

"I better mingle," Rachel said and excused herself.

Claire watched her walk away. "This is weighing heavy on her mind most of the time. I hope it's over soon."

Kathrine also watched Rachel. "It will be. Since Brice's death, the agencies are throwing everything they have into finding Yumiko. She won't be able to hold out much longer."

Claire turned toward her. "In all of this, I haven't asked how things are with you and Tilly. I know you haven't seen each other in a while."

Kathrine slowly traced the edge of her glass with her finger. "Okay. At least I think it is. It's hard to tell with all this crap going on."

Claire put her elbow on the table and propped her chin on her hand as she studied her, feeling the effects of the first whiskey and the bourbon sidecar sneak up on her. "That doesn't sound too inspiring."

Kathrine frowned. "I know you're best friends so…"

"Hey, Kathrine. We're more like sisters. I know her pretty well, and I can guess what's wrong."

Kathrine leaned back in the cushioned chair and folded her arms in her lap. "Okay. Tell me."

It didn't take a genius to figure it out. Claire glanced over at Rachel, who was visiting with Frank and a few of the employees from the shed. "Let me guess. Tilly likes the relationship you have. She thinks things are great, but you want something more. You've tried to discuss it with her on several occasions, but she changes the subject and avoids it like you asked her to go with you to cut fish at the market."

Kathrine smiled and moved closer to the table as she sipped her drink. "Go on."

"That's classic Tilly. She'll run over you until you show her that she can't."

"Why is she like that?"

Claire glanced over at Rachel again. "Because of her insecurities. She and her mother don't have the best relationship. Her parents stay together because they're too codependent to separate and get a divorce. Tilly has problems with intimate relationships, and her line of work caters to the temporary, to being in the excitement of the moment, and then it fades."

Kathrine sat quietly, not moving.

"I'm telling you, Kathrine, if you want to have any kind of a long-term relationship with Tilly, you better stand up to her and tell her how you need it to be. Otherwise, she'll slide along, until one day you'll get sick of it and leave." Claire saw the concern on Kathrine's face. "She has very strong feelings for you. If she didn't, she'd be long gone by now, but getting her to admit she does is most of the battle."

Was this the right time for a serious conversation? The others were far enough away that Claire didn't think she and Kathrine would be heard. "Will you describe what happened when you and the team went in to get Rachel in Manila?"

"Hasn't Rachel ever told you?" Kathrine glanced at the others in the room.

"What she could remember, but I want to hear the other side of it."

"She was pretty out of it by the time we reached her." Kathrine took another sip of the brandy as Olivia brought Claire a drink. "There's not much to tell. By the time we got there, the beatings were over. We entered the room, and Yumiko threw her hands in the air and started yelling not to shoot her. It's called a distraction technique, meant to give her people enough time to draw down on us. Jack and I both turned at the same time when her men came through a back room. We fired while Frank kept Yumiko pinned against the wall. Once we took down her men, I guarded Yumiko, and Jack and Frank went into the back room to get Rachel. At that point I didn't know if she was dead or alive. Jack carried her from the back room, her face beat to a pulp, her knee the size of a grapefruit, and her clothes covered in blood. I didn't see how she could have survived."

Claire winced and looked at her drink.

"Rachel started to come out of it as we were leaving and insisted Jack seat her at the computer so she could undo whatever the hell Yumiko had made her do." Kathrine brought her glass to her lips and took a sip, then set it down and looked into Claire's eyes. "The bravest damn thing I've ever seen."

Claire saw Rachel walking toward them. "I think I know the rest." She pulled the chair out so Rachel could sit beside her.

Rachel sat and slipped her arm on Claire's chair. "How are you two doing?"

Claire smiled. "We're great. How are you?"

Rachel nodded and half smiled.

Claire reached for her hand.

"Thank you for doing this for us. We all needed to be together," Kathrine said.

"It was important to do this, don't you think, Rachel?" Claire asked.

"Yes. We're all under a lot of stress." Rachel looked away.

Claire studied her, more concerned for her than ever.

❖

Another day passed.

Rachel was weary of the waiting. She went into the bathroom, turned on the shower, and stepped into the steamy enclosure, placing her hands on the tiled wall. She shut her eyes as the hot water washed over her, the soothing ripples of relief cascading over her shoulders and back, muscles relaxing as the tension slowly began to ebb away.

She opened her eyes. They were ready for Yumiko, but perhaps they were showing a little too much protection. If she wanted any control of the situation, she would have to force Yumiko's hand and let her be the one to make the mistakes. Yumiko wasn't stupid, and she'd have to be stupid to come onto the property right now with all the guards. She stared into the tile, deep in thought, until the color faded, and the grout lines disappeared, and then she knew exactly what she was going to do.

She closed her eyes again and lowered her head. She would force her into their plan by opening the gate and letting her come in.

The glass shower door opened. Claire stepped in naked. She reached behind Rachel and turned on the other shower head at the opposite side of the wall. As the steam rose quickly, engulfing them, Claire maneuvered and wedged her way in between Rachel and the wall, pressing herself into her breasts. Rachel slid her arm around her waist as she stepped back to give her room. Claire's presence sent surging ripples of pleasure and want into her.

Claire pulled Rachel to her, weaving her fingers into her wet hair. Rachel gently moved her against the tiled wall, running her hands over the curve of her breasts as she moved down, taking a nipple into her mouth, feeling it rise and swell. She massaged Claire's other nipple between her fingertips, the hot water merging with the sexual heat as it washed over her. The water ran down Rachel's face, dripping into her mouth as she kissed the side of Claire's neck. Claire lifted her leg and wrapped it around her thigh.

"You do know we're using this as a diversion," Rachel said.

Claire laughed. "Yes, but it's a diversion with benefits." Claire kissed her, moving into her, leading her where only they could go.

They lay in bed, satisfied, naked, entwined. Confidence washed over Rachel. She explained what she wanted to do.

"We'll pull most of the guards off and open the property. Yumiko can't hold out much longer. When her people tell her what we did, she'll think we've created a weakness and that we're over-confident or careless. That's when she'll pounce on us."

"Do you think it will work?" Claire asked.

"I don't see how she can hide out much longer. She's most likely drooling at a chance to enter the property and kill me and get the hell out of Dodge. Word is that someone else has taken over her business, and that her absence and the reorganization she did have allowed the new person to slide into the main leadership position with no problem."

They reviewed the plan once more. "You'll see them long before she and her people enter the side road and the alarms trip. Remember, you must stay ahead of them. Once they start after you, you have to move fast."

"What if Yumiko comes into the house?"

"She won't. From what Jack told me, she gave up immediately when they entered the building in Quezon City to get me. She's a coward. Once she senses she's not going to get what she wants, she'll make a run for it. She won't like it, but she'll realize she doesn't have a choice."

"What if she brings too many people for the team to handle?"

"It's a calculated risk, but she wants this up close and personal. Jack and I both feel she won't have more than four or five with her."

"What will happen to her people when they follow us?"

Rachel turned to her. "You need to be clear about this. We can't turn back once it starts. Kathrine and David will take care of them."

Claire blinked and swallowed. "You mean *take care of them* as in buried in the desert like the mobsters did?"

"I mean *take care of them* as in we'll never have to worry about them again. Remember. You need two identical outfits."

Chapter Fifty-three

A ll but two security guards left last night." Claire adjusted the wireless earbuds and yanked open the refrigerator door, bending over and staring at the food, choosing nothing.

"Good. That will draw Yumiko in. Are you ready?" Kathrine asked.

"What if we guess the wrong airport? Some of the team will be out of position."

"Quit worrying. We've done the best we can. You and I will stick with Rachel no matter where she goes."

Claire squinted and reached for the Gaviscon, gulping a swig, the cold liquid slipping down her throat and easing the aching burn ripping through her stomach. She wiped the smear of the thick liquid at the corners of her mouth with her fingers, then rubbed her midriff, putting her elbow on the kitchen bar and leaning in. "Rachel's too close to the situation to see all the danger. Her perspective is clouded. We all know there's much more to it. No matter how much we plan or how much you and I alter our own plan to protect Rachel, Yumiko will always be an unknown." She shuddered and took another swig of the mint-tasting liquid. The course was set. Whatever was going to happen was already in motion.

Jack had told them there would always be risks, and he had pounded that reality into Claire's and Rachel's heads again and again.

"I'm betting on Yumiko's obsession for Rachel," Kathrine said. "We have to give Yumiko enough room to reveal her intentions. Expect her to do anything and be prepared for it, because she'll be prepared. She's focused on one thing and one thing only—getting Rachel. That's her weakness, and that's what we'll exploit. See you in a few hours."

Claire disconnected and set her earbuds on the kitchen bar. Expect her to do the unexpected and be prepared. How were they supposed to do that? Between all of them, they had done everything they could to get ready and anticipate, but they would still miss something. Some unknown, unexpected thing could go wrong or wouldn't happen the way they planned. If Claire had learned anything over the last two years, it was that no matter how much you planned, some type of screwup would always take place. That's why she and Kathrine had made their own plan. Yumiko and Rachel were so focused on each other that the only element of surprise would be the wild card—her.

Which of the three airports would Yumiko run to? That was the critical unknown. They could make an educated guess, but if they were incorrect, Kathrine wouldn't be where she needed to be to help Rachel. They had discussed it among the group ad nauseam. Rachel finally decided it would be North Las Vegas. "McCarren is too busy, and private-jet takeoff could be delayed too long."

They eliminated Henderson because of tight security.

Wherever Rachel went, she and Kathrine would go. Rachel's plan had Kathrine with David at the explosion site, but Rachel didn't know Beth had taken Kathrine's place so Kathrine could go to the airport and wait.

Everyone at the shed agreed. If Yumiko somehow got away, the entire team would regroup and hunt her down. No matter where she went. No matter how much it cost. No matter how long it took. And Claire wouldn't hesitate to join the hunt.

She had accepted what would happen. Someone was going to die—but it wasn't going to be Rachel.

Time seemed to hang in the air.

She cringed as she watched Rachel and Kathrine load explosives into a container and slip it into an SUV. It would be better to take Rachel away, force her to leave, but she would never go, not until this ended, and she would never have any peace until it did. Yumiko squatted inside Rachel now, like a cancer eating away at her, cell by cell, hour by hour, day after day. Rachel showed the effects. Her face was drawn, her eyes were dull, her skin pale. Even her long, beautiful chestnut-colored hair had lost its luster. She'd lost more weight, so much that she was now almost a shadow of what she had been two months earlier, or even a month ago.

Claire hated Yumiko for what she'd done to Rachel. She loathed her. Her stomach churned. Yumiko had done this. Deep inside she felt a satisfaction that Yumiko would finally get what she deserved. And then it will be over, and things would get back to normal. She half laughed under her breath. No such thing as normal existed around here. They had never experienced a normal. Normal seemed overrated.

Rachel lifted a semiautomatic weapon and placed it on top of the container.

Claire's thoughts drifted off again. What if she had to face the ultimate decision to take a life for a life? Could she do it? She would never be able to answer that question until she faced the situation. No matter what happened, it would be over one way or the other. Rachel couldn't go on like this, and neither could she. It had to end.

She walked behind Rachel and wrapped her arms around her waist, feeling her now-pronounced hip bones and ribs, and whispered in her ear. "Have you eaten today?"

Rachel turned and held Claire's face in her hands, avoiding her question. "It's going to be all right. It's a solid strategy."

Claire nodded. What would Rachel do if she knew what she and Kathrine had planned? Rachel would never agree to it. That's why they'd kept it to themselves. Plans within plans. Secrets within secrets.

The evening dragged on. It pressed in on her, the silence hanging in the air like a thick fog. Even the animals were quiet, as if sensing what was going to happen.

And then the call came to Jack. A friend of his. Someone had rented a helicopter from his service for a lot of cash. Tonight. A night flight with an odd pickup point, about a mile from Rachel's property. His friend didn't know the destination. He said the caller wouldn't say, just that someone had hired the helicopter for the entire night.

The team had an emergency on-line meeting. The information threw a monkey wrench into their entire plan. With a helicopter, Yumiko could fly into any surrounding airport, including Phoenix. Nerves were on edge. The team couldn't possibly cover an area that large. Frank and Kathrine argued about what Yumiko might do. Jack finally broke it up.

He calmed the group and modified their basic plan. "She'll stick to an airport near Las Vegas. She doesn't want to be in the air that long. No, she's not flying far. She's using the helicopter to make a fast get-away, not an extended flight somewhere else. And now we can be waiting for her at the pickup location too, just in case we miss her at the house."

The night descended, stretching out its thick darkness, spreading out over the desert like a never-ending black cloak of anxiety and dread.

Claire remembered what Ilesh had told her. "Your enemies are cowards and will come in the night."

She watched with Matt from their elevated position in the attic. She brought the binoculars down and held them in one hand, looking at her left hand. She trembled, but she had no knots in her stomach, and her heart didn't race. She was ready.

She blinked, adjusting the microchip contact in her eye, then peered through the binoculars once again and scanned, searching, hoping she wouldn't see her, but deep inside she knew she would. She reminded herself that no matter who else died, Rachel would live. The thought brought her the comfort she needed.

She saw the reflection of the full moon on the lead vehicle's windshield, then the puffs of dust as the tires dug into the terrain. They were here.

Matt whispered, "Yumiko will probably be in the second vehicle, not the lead. She'll make her people go in first, as a shield."

Claire strained to see all she could through the binoculars. She listened as Matt pressed the button and spoke quietly into the radio to the team.

"Three men in the lead vehicle. She's in the second vehicle, passenger seat, not driving. Confirmed, second vehicle, passenger seat."

Claire laid the binoculars down and climbed out of the attic.

She heard the alarm as the lead vehicle tripped the perimeter marker.

The report of the guard's rifle shot told her Yumiko's vehicle had been hit.

"Claire, go now." Rachel grabbed the handgun, checked the load, took the safety off, and went out through the kitchen door.

Time to divide the vehicles.

Claire adjusted her Kevlar vest and ran through the living room. Bullets crashed through one of the cathedral windows, hitting the oak-wood doorframe on Claire's right. Another whizzed past her right ear, landing in the new custom-made Burrow Nomad sofa.

"Damn them. That's going to be expensive to fix. Move faster," she shouted to herself.

She ran out the back door of the kitchen and into her studio, jumping onto the Ducati in one motion. She positioned her foot, started the motorcycle, and launched out the open doorway.

More shots rang out, hitting the left handlebar and one of the side mirrors, just missing her hand. She weaved and zigzagged, racing toward the point where the terrain dipped just before the hill. The beams of the headlights and search light from the vehicle behind her cut thick lines of jagged sporadic light through the darkness and onto her as it bounced and swerved. The faster she went, the more the vehicle's lights lost her in the darkness. The night sky filled with a blanket of stars, and the dim light cascading down from the full moon illuminated enough of the terrain for her to see every rut and rise. At the precise moment she reached the curve of the ravine, she turned her headlight off. Beth came flying out of the depression on Rachel's motorcycle, timing it like a runner passing a baton, headlight on, full throttle, dressed in the same clothes and helmet as Claire.

Claire sat still and silent, low in the ravine, in the darkness. The black Hummer passed, never slowing, the men in the vehicle shooting at Beth, maneuvering to keep her in their sights.

And now the hunters became the hunted.

As soon as the vehicle passed, she turned the motorcycle, looking back toward Beth, watching her slow her motorcycle for them to catch her, leading them right where she, David, and José wanted them to go—to the explosion point, where David waited to set off the charge when the Hummer arrived.

Claire raced back toward the house. A few moments later, she propped the motorcycle on its stand and bent down as she quickly moved toward the helicopter.

Rachel waited in the front passenger seat. Claire stepped into the helicopter, careful to make sure Rachel didn't see the earpiece to her program in her ear.

Rachel looked back at her. "She ditched the car like Jack suspected she would and was picked up by a different helicopter, not the one we thought she'd use. She never made it into the house. Jack identified the jet she's using. She's headed for the North Vegas airport. Jack's posing as a maintenance worker, stalling the jet's takeoff." Rachel immediately put her hand out toward Claire. "And no, you're not going. You stay in the helicopter like we planned when we touch down at the airport."

"Oh, hell if I'm staying and you're going without me."

"Please don't argue with me this time, Claire."

Claire leaned back in the seat, knowing full well what she was going to do. Could Kathrine see Rachel, and what she was saying? Everything they'd planned came down to the next few minutes. Did they plan well enough and smart enough?

CHAPTER FIFTY-FOUR

Rachel scanned the airfield as the helicopter landed on the tarmac. Frank ran to her as soon as she got out and cleared the rotor blades.

"She's over there at the main hub, near the construction site. I think she's pissed as hell that they can't take off yet. Jack had to duck out when she got here. He was afraid she might recognize him, but he has it under control. The jet isn't leaving the ground any time soon. We'll have to be careful. She'll have some sort of backup plan."

They immediately made their way toward the hub, detouring around the cement forms, piles of sand, heavy equipment, and a few night workers. Caution lights and signs were flashing. One full side of the north section of the second floor of the building was unfinished, with large cement blocks, sheet metal, and other construction materials piled near the edge.

"I bet she didn't plan on all the construction." Frank smiled.

"I'm sure she did." Rachel quickly scanned the area, searching, wanting to see her, yet dreading it. Her heart pounded. She had to calm down. She spotted her. Her breath caught. She pointed a trembling finger past the main entrance to the terminal. "There she is."

Yumiko stood in the lit foyer, looking at something out the window.

Rachel started toward her, but Frank grabbed her arm. "Wait. She probably has some type of weapon."

Rachel opened her suit coat and showed Frank the handgun in the holster at her side.

He checked his own gun. "I'll cover the far side of the building in case she tries to make a run for it." He looked at her again.

She touched his arm. "I'll be fine."

"You be extra careful, and don't take any chances. I'll be on the other side. Stay in touch."

She took a quick, deep breath. The rocks in her stomach turned into boulders, her mouth so dry she almost choked when she swallowed. This was the moment. The one she had dreaded. The one she anticipated. She wanted it to be over, but *over* meant one of them was probably going to die.

"I'll be fine," she said again, trying to convince herself more than him. She slipped her badge on the front waist of her slacks and adjusted her earphone. "Can you hear me?"

Frank nodded and also touched his earphone. "You watch yourself."

He moved quickly away, and she lost him in the shadows.

She searched the entranceway. Yumiko had disappeared. She half ran toward the hub. Could she have gotten away that quickly?

The *swish* of the automatic glass doors vibrated in her ears as she entered the main lobby. She stopped to get her bearings, immediately spotting Yumiko at the far side of the building, headed for the new addition to the terminal. Was she making a run for it? "Frank?" She spoke his name again. No response. She readjusted the earphone. "Frank, do you hear me?" Silence, not even a crackling noise. She punched his code into the cell phone but couldn't get a response. Communication was somehow being jammed. She unholstered her gun and held it behind her, moving past the few people sitting in black leather chairs by the large picture window. She touched Frank's code again. *No service.* She slipped the cell phone into her pants pocket and moved through the corridor where she had spotted Yumiko. The corridor made a sharp detoured turn to the left, leading toward the dimly lit side of the building in the heavy construction, full of shadows and dark areas. She hesitated. Would Yumiko lure her there, or was she just running?

She made her way to the exit, looking out through the glass door, searching the perimeter. More construction. If Yumiko escaped through that exit, Frank and Jack had it covered. They had anticipated her. They wouldn't let her get away. Rachel continued to peer out, rolling her shoulders, squeezing the handle of the gun. Where could she be? Then it dawned on her. She *was* leading her into a trap. She was still in the building.

She brought the gun into firing position and moved toward the dimly lit corridor, stopping at each opening, her adrenaline surging at each shadow. She continued to work her way down the corridor in the opposite direction of the main hub, toward the heavy areas of construction. It was impossible to hear any subtle noises of movement because of the sporadic noise of the engines as the planes took off and landed, and the distant *beep...beep...beep* of the construction vehicles. She climbed the stairs to the unfinished second floor, stutter-stepping her way through the murky darkness as it grew thicker, obscuring more of her vision. Yumiko was there. She could feel it.

The construction sounds faded. The warm wind coming into the open building blew against her face and arms. The torn plastic sheeting on the partially constructed walls crackled and popped as it whipped back and forth. She made her way forward, barely able to discern the shapes and forms of what looked like ladders, plastic chairs, tables, and stacks of concrete blocks.

She heard a gunshot, instantaneously feeling the burning fire and sharp pain rip through the calf of her left leg. She turned, trying to catch herself from falling. She managed to get three random shots off in the general direction of where she thought the shot came from before she went down hard, hitting the side of her head on something metal. The gun flew out of her hand. She lunged forward to try to get it, her fingertips grazing the handle as it slid under a pile of construction debris.

For a moment everything seemed distorted, like seeing sunshine through thunderclouds after a storm subsided. Her ears were ringing. Her head pounded. The pain in her calf surged into her knee. She reached to touch it, to stop the pain, to get some relief, but the moment she touched her calf, more pain and burning bolted through her leg. She forced two long breaths through her nose and pressed on the side of her head, feeling a huge lump, and stinging when she reached the gash. A stupid mistake. Stupid! How could she make that kind of rookie error? Where was Frank? Why wasn't he responding?

Yumiko yelled out. "Don't worry. I won't kill you yet. I wouldn't count on your friends any time soon. I blocked your cell-phone and radio communication." She laughed.

Rachel knew that laugh so well. She wanted to vomit at the hideous sound of it, but she'd had enough of being afraid. She wasn't going to give up, not this time. No more. She fought her fear. She fought with everything she had left. Her leg began to spasm. She grabbed at the gun again but only managed to push it farther away from her. "Sonofabitch.

You've got to be kidding me." She reached wider, inching, stretching her fingers along the cement flooring, trying to feel her way to the gun, trying to control her breathing to manage the pain.

Another shot rang out, hitting the pile of construction debris, barely missing her arm. She recoiled, groping for the table near her. She pushed it over and crouched behind it, dangerously close to the edge of the open building. More surging pain pulsed through her leg. She gripped the edge of the table, trying not to pass out.

"Do you really think I didn't anticipate you would set a trap for me? You are predictable. *I* led *you* here. You have done exactly what I thought you would do. I know my jet's been detained. You don't think I haven't planned another way out of here? I've waited a long time to have you again."

Rachel's stomach knotted. Yumiko taunted her, like she did before, trying to break her down. She had to get the advantage somehow. If this was the end, she wouldn't give her the satisfaction of breaking her, not again.

"You'll never have me. I see you still haven't gotten help with your delusions."

Yumiko slithered out from behind a pillar. "I only regret I couldn't kill your bitch in front of you first."

Rachel flinched like she'd been stabbed with a knife. She pulled herself along the length of the table, desperate to find the handgun, or something she could use as a weapon. More lightning bolts of pain shot into her leg. She could feel the blood oozing out and smelled the salt and metallic scent of it as it trickled over her ankle and dripped down the side of her foot. Now she knew what it felt like to be a hunted, wounded animal.

"You won't live to lay a hand on her, you crazy bitch." She could barely make out what looked like an electric hand drill on the floor to her left. She unplugged the cord from the power strip, positioned on one knee, and swung the cord of the drill in a circle to get some momentum. When she felt the centrifugal pressure against her hand, she flung the cord as hard as she could, aiming the drill toward Yumiko's voice. She heard the impact when it hit.

Yumiko spit out words Rachel didn't understand, probably Tagalog.

"Aww, did that hurt?" She frantically searched for more cover, hearing Yumiko struggle.

"Did you lose your handgun, Rachel? I still have mine. Maybe seven or eight more rounds. Why don't you give up like you did before? Don't prolong it. Why do you always fight it so hard?" Yumiko fired a shot, and then another, striking the end of the table and hitting the cement blocks beside Rachel.

Rachel dove to the side, around the edge of the table, near what she thought was a bandsaw table and metal ladders. She cried out from the pain.

Yumiko laughed again. "Now who's hurting?"

"Why don't you come over here a little closer, psycho? This nail gun will do the job nicely." She was bluffing, since she saw nothing more around her that she could use as a weapon.

Lights from a landing plane flooded into the open room, almost blinding her. Ripped plastic sheeting, half covering the partially built outside wall, whipped and slapped in a gust of wind. She could see Yumiko standing to the right, holding the gun out and protecting her eyes from the plane's invasive lights.

She saw a shadow move to the far side of Yumiko. *Frank.*

Encouraged by his presence and knowing she needed to give him time, she chided Yumiko as she wedged behind the bandsaw table. "Things haven't gone the way you thought. Poor psycho."

Yumiko fired another shot.

Sparks flew near Rachel's thigh when the bullet ricocheted off the metal leg of the table.

Yumiko moved near the edge of the open wall, the plastic sheeting continuing to flap in the wind. Rachel could see her clearly now, her face contorted with a half smile smeared across it. But it looked more like a dog's angry snarl. She limped. Rachel had hit a home run with the drill.

Yumiko aimed. "I almost don't want it to end."

The shadow came out of the darkness. Not Frank. Rachel couldn't believe it. "No…No!"

"Bitch, that's my wife you're shooting at."

Yumiko spun around.

Claire raised her left leg and kicked the gun out of Yumiko's hand and moved into her, hitting her with her fist on the left side of her jaw, then an uppercut to her chin.

Yumiko staggered backward.

Claire kicked her with a roundhouse to the stomach, sending her to the floor.

Another light from an approaching plane flooded the area. Yumiko lunged for the handgun just inches away. She grabbed it and rolled toward Claire.

Rachel screamed, "Get down."

Yumiko aimed the gun at Claire.

A shot rang out.

Chapter Fifty-five

Rachel couldn't breathe.

The intensity and recoil of what she expected to see sucked the air out of her lungs, consumed her, plunged her into a gnarled black abyss. If Claire died, nothing mattered. If Rachel lived or died, if the world exploded into nothing but ash and rubble, if the universe collapsed in on itself—she had no reason for any of it to exist now.

Uncontrolled rage spewed out of her. She gripped the top of the table and pulled herself up. She'd kill Yumiko with her bare hands. She didn't care if she had a gun. She'd wrap her fingers around her scrawny neck and squeeze as hard as she could until the life drained out of her. And she'd enjoy it. She was happy to do it. She couldn't wait to do it. She stepped forward but couldn't move her leg and collapsed onto the floor. She rocked back and forth, gnashing her teeth. "I'm going to kill you." She rolled and started to drag herself toward Yumiko.

"Rachel, stop! Look at me. I'm all right."

Rachel froze. She tried to see the image, but confusion engulfed her. *Claire? She's alive?*

Claire stood rigid, her eyes fixed on Yumiko, who was now leaning against a table, holding her right hand to her chest, her gun on the floor.

Kathrine stepped out from behind a pillar, her Glock pointed at Yumiko. She motioned toward the weapon on the floor. "Kick it to me. Now!"

Claire ran over to Rachel, wrapped her arms around her, and helped her stand. Rachel clung to her. Every sense in her body awakened, heightened, lifting her higher and higher. She didn't care about the pain. Claire was alive!

Light from a taxiing plane on the tarmac washed over them.

Claire stared at Rachel, her mouth open, clearly terrified.

Rachel tried to reassure her. "I'm all right."

"No. You are not *all right*. You're covered in blood."

Rachel repositioned her arm around Claire's shoulder for support and turned. She wasn't about to let Yumiko out of her sight until she was in cuffs or dead.

Yumiko held her bloody right hand, missing part of her first two fingers. Rachel understood then where the gunshot she'd heard had come from.

"I *said* kick it over," Kathrine shouted.

Yumiko barely tapped the gun with the side of her foot as she glanced at Rachel with a smirk.

"Oh, that's cute. I'd just as soon shoot your foot off." Kathrine moved toward her, never taking her eyes off her. "What? Nothing clever to say now. No witty repartee?"

Yumiko straightened. She fixed her gaze on Kathrine.

For the first time Rachel saw what looked like fear in Yumiko's eyes.

"How did you make that shot?" Rachel asked.

Claire smiled and pointed to the microchip contact in her left eye and the miniature earbud in her ear. "You're not the only one who can operate your program. It's the little things that matter."

Kathrine held her wrist computer toward Yumiko, showing the images Claire saw. "Now you're going to an American prison so you can feel a needle in your arm."

"No. Not hardly. I have information your government needs. Badly. And they will give me whatever I want for it."

Kathrine kicked the gun across the floor as she maneuvered closer to Yumiko. She grabbed the back of her collar, but Yumiko kicked into her stomach. When Kathrine bent over, Yumiko tried to knee her chin. Kathrine blocked her knee and delivered a solid pistol-whip to the left side of Yumiko's face. Yumiko fell back against one of the tables and grabbed a crowbar, swinging it toward Kathrine's face.

Claire yelled out a warning.

Kathrine leaned back like she was doing the limbo, avoiding Yumiko's swing, then straightened and delivered a blow to Yumiko's shoulder. Yumiko staggered back on to the edge of the open flooring of the building, grabbing for the cement pillar with her bloody fingers.

Kathrine took a step toward her. "Go back to hell where you came from." She raised her leg again and kicked her in the stomach, sending Yumiko flying out beyond the open flooring, screaming into the darkness. A bone-crushing thud echoed back up to them when the screaming abruptly stopped.

Claire helped Rachel move toward Kathrine just as another plane's descending lights flashed into the building. Rachel looked down and saw Yumiko impaled on the steel pylons below. She grimaced and turned, holding onto Claire.

Kathrine came over to the other side of Rachel and stood beside her.

Claire moved to look down at Yumiko's body, but Rachel put her hand out and blocked her view.

"You don't want to see that, Claire. It's an image you'll never get out of your head."

Rachel was unable to sift through her feelings. It was over. She wanted to feel relief, but she didn't. Instead, a deep weariness, guilt, resentment, confusion consumed her. Why? She stood, leaning on Claire, trying to understand what she felt. She began to tremble. The sharp, pulsating pain in her calf radiated up into her knee, then into her chest, and continued upward to her head. Her strength waned, and she started to collapse. Kathrine grabbed her as Claire slid her arm tighter around her waist.

She realized in that moment why she felt the way she did. Yumiko was dead—but so were Jacob, Brice, his wife, and Steve. Lisa's life would never be the same. How many other lives had Yumiko destroyed? She stared down at her bloody, lifeless body and burned with rage. "Fuck you!"

Chapter Fifty-six

Kathrine set her brown leather duffel bag on the kitchen table and leaned on the counter, watching Tilly.

Tilly pressed her finger four times against the button on the coffeemaker, sweeping her hand through her morning hair, which stuck out on the side.

Adorable. "It'll work just as well without pressing it so hard."

Tilly jerked her head toward her, squinting her blue eyes.

Kathrine half smiled, more to herself than at Tilly. "You can pout all you want, but I still have to leave. I told you I'll be back in four days."

Tilly didn't take her eyes off her, still not speaking.

"All right, enough. It's time we had that talk." Kathrine moved toward her and put her hand on her shoulder. "We both know you're in love with me."

"I am not."

"Yes, you are."

"I am not. I just like you a lot."

Kathrine laughed and wrapped her arms around her. "It would be a lot easier if you just admitted it. Then we can move on."

Tilly stood silent.

"I promise your secret's safe with me." Kathrine kissed her neck. "Tilly, it's okay. I can handle it. It's okay if you tell me."

"You're so damn smug." Tilly slid her hands to Kathrine's shoulders and wrapped her arms around her neck.

Kathrine searched her eyes, trying to break down the walls. She could get lost in those eyes, but she held back, not willing to make the commitment until Tilly said the words.

"I'm scared."

"I know you are, but it's all right." Kathrine kissed her. "I'm here. I'm not going anywhere."

"You promise."

"Yes. I promise." Kathrine waited, hoping Tilly would say the words. She had told Tilly she loved her, but Tilly needed to say it. She needed to open her heart and trust her with it. For once in Tilly's life, *she* had to take the leap.

Tilly buried her face in Kathrine's neck. "Kathrine."

Finally. "Yes?"

"Do you want French Roast or Black Silk?"

"Oh my God, Tilly. Are you serious?"

Tilly stepped back. "Why do I have to say it? You know how I feel."

Kathrine also stepped back. If Tilly couldn't do this, the relationship reached a standstill. "No, Tilly. I don't know how you feel. I don't know how you feel because you won't tell me."

"Why don't we talk about it when you get back?"

Kathrine didn't know what to say. She searched Tilly's face, trying to figure her out. She didn't want to push her, but what could be so hard about admitting how she felt? Why was it so hard for her to say the words? She knew Tilly loved her, but did Tilly know it? She moved around Tilly and put her hand on the duffel bag. "I'll call you when I get to the hotel."

"Hey. You don't have to leave for another hour yet. Where are you going?"

She turned toward her. "I'll call you later tonight."

Tilly grabbed her arm. "Don't go."

"Why?"

"I don't want you to go."

"Why?"

"Because I don't want you to go, that's why."

"That's not good enough. Why?"

"Because…damn it."

At least some type of reaction. "Tilly, do you think I'm with you just because of the sex?"

Tilly remained silent.

Kathrine gripped the handle of the bag tighter. The sound of the leather crackled, filling the silence. Why wouldn't she tell her she loved her? Could it be insecurity? Did she really think Kathrine wanted to be with her only for the sex? In that moment Kathrine ached to tell her how wonderful she was. How she loved the way she got mad and cussed like a sailor, or the way she fought the world for something she believed in. Or her quirky sense of humor, or her laugh, or when she tried not to cry about something because she was afraid she'd appear vulnerable. Or especially those not-too-often moments when she let her guard down, and the real Tilly came shining through, like a bright ray of sunshine. God, she was beautiful. And complex. And all the things she wanted. And some of the things she didn't want. But that was Tilly.

Tilly reached out toward the bag and slipped her hand on top of hers. "Don't go. Not yet. Please?"

Kathrine released her hand from the bag and slipped it around Tilly's waist, gently bringing her closer. "I wouldn't go at all, but I'm the lead agent on this case."

Tilly wrapped her arms around her and held on.

Kathrine kissed the side of her head. "It's okay, Tilly. You don't have to say it."

Tilly released her and stepped back. "No, it's not okay. Yes, I do have to say it. I owe us that much." Tilly took a deep breath and looked straight into her. "Sarah was right. All my life I've gone through relationships like an outsider looking in, always holding back. I think it was out of fear of being hurt, or maybe from a fear of caring for someone who might not care back, or that I'd be in a relationship alone. But to be honest, I don't think I've ever met anyone who interested me enough to take a risk with my heart. Until you. When you aren't with me, nothing feels quite right. The sun's not as bright, colors aren't as clear. Even the coffee doesn't smell as good." She smiled. "I don't know what love is. All I know is I don't want to wake without you next to me. I don't want to go to a performance unless I know you'll be waiting for me when the music stops. You're the first thing I think of in the morning and the last thing I think of at night. Nothing's as good if I can't share it with you. If that's what love is, then I'm in love with you."

Kathrine moved to her and kissed her. "That sounds like love to me."

"Then I'll be damned—I'm in love!"

Kathrine held her tightly and breathed a little easier. That morning on Sunrise Mountain, when she'd told Tilly about her trip to see the man who'd been involved in killing her sister, she still searched for answers. Tilly had asked her the one question she needed to hear. "Why did you go to see him?" Kathrine had pondered her question, and now she finally had the answer. She went to say good-bye to her sister and let go of the past. Life was precious, and she was ready to move on. And now, with Tilly at her side, she'd do just that.

Rachel sat on the blanket, a short distance from the teepee, rubbing the scar on the calf of her leg, seeing the deep blues of the sky. The beginnings of fall danced on the breeze. The scents of pine and sage lingered in the air, and the rich smell of the earth grew denser. She'd seen a few of the migrating hummingbirds and warblers, their yellow, orange, and olive colors dotting the landscape. She slowly surveyed her surroundings once more, taking in all that they offered her. She limped to the teepee, opened the flap, and tied it to the side with the leather straps.

She entered but stopped midstep, captivated. The bright light of the early afternoon sun flooded in and embraced Claire, bathing her in light. Renegade strands of Claire's hair sparkled as they lifted on the soft current of air. Her skin glowed. The gentle rhythmic rise and fall of her breasts as she breathed seemed to emanate peace and tranquility. She was lying on her side, one hand tucked under her chin. Rachel maneuvered over beside her, moving Claire's hair away from her face, catching the scent of her coconut-and-almond shampoo and the vanilla body wash she'd used the night before when they'd bathed in the stream. A few strands of Claire's hair brushed across Rachel's cheek as she watched her, bemused in the stillness before she woke her, stealing a sliver of time to take in her beauty, to hold it, to treasure it, to appreciate it. She hesitated, not wanting to speak, not wanting to interrupt the peace of her slumber, but when she woke, they'd be together to share the day. Their time. Their life.

"Claire, we have to get ready to go."

Claire slowly opened her eyes. She stroked Rachel's face with the back of her hand, as if she were touching velvet. Rachel took her hand and kissed it.

"It's too early." Claire moaned and stretched, reaching out for her. "Can't we stay here a few more days?"

Rachel smiled and kissed her. "I wish we could, but we have to get back. We've been gone three weeks. You do realize it's early afternoon?"

Claire laughed. "I'm sorry, but I was exhausted. You wore me out last night." She stretched again. "I feel so alive, so full. It's you who fills me. Your love surrounds me and lifts me. I can't get enough of you." She brought Rachel closer and kissed her, moving her hand over her back and then wrapping her arms around her. "You feel so good to touch and hold."

Rachel ran her fingers over Claire's full lips. "Could you be any more beautiful? Come on. Up. We need to be at Joseph's long before dark. We'll stay the night there and then drive home in the morning."

Claire dressed while Rachel finished their packing. She'd be sad to go too. It'd been the perfect place to recover from her wounds, both physical and mental. But it was time to return to the life they were building.

She no longer felt rage. Now, in its place, was a sense of gratitude for life, an appreciation for the love of those around her. Yes, she harbored a deep sadness for the loss of those who were no longer with her, but also a joy for having had them in her life, if only for a few brief moments.

Claire swung the saddle onto the red, purple, and yellow blanket on Łichíí's back and then tightened the cinch. The late-afternoon sun shone down on the hills when they reached the stream to water the horses. Claire slipped off her boots and waded in the cool water.

"How's your leg today, Rachel?"

"It's good. Just a little soreness now when I put my full weight on it."

Claire put her boots back on and stood by Łichíí, slowly stroking her neck.

Rachel watched her. "Are you all right?"

"I still don't know if I could have killed Yumiko if it came down to it." She mounted Łichíí.

Rachel swung onto Ash and tuned him toward Claire. "It's not important anymore. You don't have to worry about it ever again."

Claire sighed. "I know. I'm just glad I never had to make a choice like that. I only know I wouldn't have been able to let her hurt you."

Rachel took her hand. "I'm glad you didn't have to make that choice."

She needed to leave it in the past. The time here on the reservation with Claire had cleansed them both, and she wouldn't bring it up—ever again.

Elaina greeted them, but not in her usual way. Tension tightened her face, and sadness dimmed her eyes.

They dismounted and went into the house.

What's wrong?" Rachel asked.

"Joseph is with Ileonna. There has been some trouble."

"Ileonna? The young woman you told me about?" asked Claire.

Elaina nodded.

Rachel moved to Elaina. "What is it?"

"She left the reservation and fell in with a bad man." Elaina shook her head slowly.

Rachel glanced at Claire.

"He beat her, and then when he got her pregnant, he beat her more. He was killed three days ago in a gas-station robbery in Phoenix. Ileonna went to Ilesh, and he helped her get back to the reservation. Now she is in labor and having trouble."

Claire nodded. "I'm sure it's very difficult for her."

A few minutes later Elaina looked out the kitchen window. "There's Joseph."

Rachel moved to the window. The dust swirled around his truck as it came toward the house, and when he got out of the truck, the light revealed his dark and solemn face. He reached back into the truck, bringing out a wrapped bundle in his arms. They met him at the front door. He handed the sleeping infant to Elaina.

"Ileonna did not live," said Joseph. "There is no family now to take care of the infant."

Elaina lifted the top of the ragged blanket and peered in. Claire moved to her and peeked at the sleeping baby. She reached out for Elaina to put the baby into her arms.

Claire drew the infant close and kissed her delicate cheek. "She's so beautiful."

Joseph's eyes were downcast as he moved slowly into the house.

Rachel forced back her tears, remembering her childhood, her past, her family, and how the People had gathered around her mother through the years of their trials. But this little one had no such welcome.

Claire cuddled the infant as she held her in her arms.

Rachel moved over to Claire to look more closely at the infant and saw the mass of dark-brown hair, her delicate long fingers, and her long eyelashes as black as coal. She felt an instant bond, strong and as real as anything she'd ever known. She touched the infant's face with the back of her finger as Claire cradled her closer.

Elaina took the baby from Claire and sat on the couch. She began to wet nurse, holding the infant to her breast as she began to suckle.

Claire and Rachel made the evening meal and watched over

Joseph and Elaina's two older children while Elaina cared for the infant and their baby boy.

When the children and the babies were asleep, Rachel and the others gathered outside by the fire. Joseph stirred the fire with a stick and sat quietly, staring at the mountains. Rachel saw the weight of the situation in his eyes, the responsibility heavy on his shoulders.

"I will take the infant to the clinic in the morning. They will hopefully find a place for her," he said.

Little was spoken the rest of the evening. When Joseph and Elaina went inside, Rachel and Claire stayed out by the fire.

Rachel watched as Claire gazed at the moon and then toward the mountains. The stars and moon cast a muted light through the clouds, creating ambling shadows over the landscape.

"They're called Shadow Dancers," Rachel said.

"What?"

"The shadows. The tradition is that the Warrior Woman of Gouyen Mountain sent them to protect us. When we see them, changes are coming our way." Rachel slipped her arm around her.

"I love that thought." Claire moved closer.

Rachel went to the trailer and brought back woolen blankets, spreading them out near the fire so they could lie down. They lay on the blankets in each other's arms, the soft glow of the small fire casting dancing shadows around them. "A strong spirit is with us tonight."

"Rachel?"

"I know, Claire."

"Are we ready for this responsibility?"

"I don't think any parents feel they're ready for the responsibility."

"I want to name her Rachel Elizabeth, after you and my middle name."

"But she'll keep her mother's last name as part of her heritage, and together we'll choose her tribal name when it's time," Rachel said.

Claire kissed her and breathed out her name. "Come to me."

The fire warmed them. The night sounds drifted into a serenade, calling them to rest in peace and safety. Rachel drew Claire closer, immersing herself in her beauty, her strength. She was complete, fused and intwined with her, their love as solid as the mountains around them.

The future was theirs, and they'd cherish every moment.

About the Author

Suzie Clarke is a native of Northeast Ohio and has a medical and business background. Before her life as a writer, she specialized in public health, working with women in all aspects of their lives. When not writing, she can be found spending time with her family, backpacking, or out on the golf course.

Books Available From Bold Strokes Books

Always by Kris Bryant. When a pushy American private investigator shows up demanding to meet the woman in Camila's artwork, instead of introducing her to her great-grandmother, Camila decides to lead her on a wild goose chase all over Italy. (978-1-63679-027-5)

Exes and O's by Joy Argento. Ali and Madison really only have one thing in common. The girl who broke their heart may be the only one who can put it back together. (978-1-63679-017-6)

Paris Rules by Jaime Maddox. Carly Becker has been searching for the perfect woman all her life, but no one ever seems to be just right until Paige Waterford checks all her boxes, except the most important one—she's married. (978-1-63679-077-0)

Shadow Dancers by Suzie Clarke. In this third and final book in the Moon Shadow series, Rachel must find a way to become the hunter and not the hunted, and this time she will meet Ehsee Yumiko head-on. (978-1-63555-829-6)

The Kiss by C.A. Popovich. When her wife refuses their divorce and begins to stalk her, threatening her life, Kate realizes to protect her new love, Leslie, she has to let her go, even if it breaks her heart. (978-1-63679-079-4)

The Wedding Setup by Charlotte Greene. When Ryann, a big-time New York executive, goes to Colorado to help out with her best friend's wedding, she never expects to fall for the maid of honor. (978-1-63679-033-6)

Velocity by Gun Brooke. Holly and Claire work toward an uncertain future preparing for an alien space mission, and only one thing is certain—they will have to risk their lives, and their hearts, to discover the truth. (978-1-63555-983-5)

Wildflower Words by Sam Ledel. Lida Jones treks west with her father in search of a better life on the rapidly developing American frontier, but finds home when she meets Hazel Thompson. (978-1-63679-055-8)

A Fairer Tomorrow by Kathleen Knowles. For Maddie Weeks and Gerry Stern, the Second World War brought them together, but the end of the war might rip them apart. (978-1-63555-874-6)

Changing Majors by Ana Hartnett Reichardt. Beyond a love, beyond a coming-out, Bailey Sullivan discovers what lies beyond the shame and self-doubt imposed on her by traditional Southern ideals. (978-1-63679-081-7)

Highland Whirl by Anna Larner. Opposites attract in the Scottish Highlands, when feisty Alice Campbell falls for city girl about town Roxanne Barns. (978-1-63555-892-0)

Holiday Hearts by Diana Day-Admire and Lyn Cole. Opposites attract during Christmastime chaos in Kansas City. (978-1-63679-128-9)

Humbug by Amanda Radley. With the corporate Christmas party in jeopardy, CEO Rosalind Caldwell hires Christmas Girl Ellie Pearce as her personal assistant. The only problem is, Ellie isn't a PA, has never planned a party, and develops a ridiculous crush on her totally intimidating new boss. (978-1-63555-965-1)

On the Rocks by Georgia Beers. Schoolteacher Vanessa Martini makes no apologies for her dating checklist, and newly single mom Grace Chapman ticks all Vanessa's Do Not Date boxes. Of course, they're never going to fall in love. (978-1-63555-989-7)

Song of Serenity by Brey Willows. Arguing with the Muse of music and justice is complicated, falling in love with her even more so. (978-1-63679-015-2)

The Christmas Proposal by Lisa Moreau. Stranded together in a Christmas village on a snowy mountain, Grace and Bridget face their past and question their dreams for the future. (978-1-63555-648-3)

The Infinite Summer by Morgan Lee Miller. While spending the summer with her dad in a small beach town, Remi Brenner falls for Harper Hebert and accidentally finds herself tangled up in an intense restaurant rivalry between her famous stepmom and her first love. (978-1-63555-969-9)

Wisdom by Jesse J. Thoma. When Sophia and Reggie are chosen for the governor's new community design team and tasked with tackling substance abuse and mental health issues, battle lines are drawn even as sparks fly. (978-1-63555-886-9)

A Convenient Arrangement by Aurora Rey and Jaime Clevenger. Cuffing season has come for lesbians, and for Jess Archer and Cody Dawson, their convenient arrangement becomes anything but. (978-1-63555-818-0)

An Alaskan Wedding by Nance Sparks. The last thing either Andrea or Riley expects is to bump into the one who broke her heart fifteen years ago, but when they meet at the welcome party, their feelings come rushing back. (978-1-63679-053-4)

Beulah Lodge by Cathy Dunnell. It's 1874, and newly betrothed Ruth Mallowes is set on marriage and life as a missionary...until she falls in love with the housemaid at Beulah Lodge. (978-1-63679-007-7)

Gia's Gems by Toni Logan. When Lindsey Speyer discovers that popular travel columnist Gia Williams is a complete fake and threatens to expose her, blackmail has never been so sexy. (978-1-63555-917-0)

Holiday Wishes & Mistletoe Kisses by M. Ullrich. Four holidays, four couples, four chances to make their wishes come true. (978-1-63555-760-2)

Love By Proxy by Dena Blake. Tess has a secret crush on her best friend, Sophie, so the last thing she wants is to help Sophie fall in love with someone else, but how can she stand in the way of her happiness? (978-1-63555-973-6)

Marry Me by Melissa Brayden. Allison Hale attempts to plan the wedding of the century to a man who could save her family's business, if only she wasn't falling for her wedding planner, Megan Kinkaid. (978-1-63555-932-3)

Pathway to Love by Radclyffe. Courtney Valentine is looking for a woman exactly like Ben—smart, sexy, and not in the market for anything serious. All she has to do is convince Ben that sex-without-strings is the perfect pathway to pleasure. (978-1-63679-110-4)